THE
ISLAND
ESCAPE

Jess Ryder is the bestselling author of nine psychological thrillers. Her novel *The Ex-Wife* was recently adapted into a Paramount+ TV series to the acclaim of critics and viewers alike and her thrillers have been read by countless readers. She lives with her partner in London and has four grown-up children.

PRAISE FOR JESS RYDER:

'The perfect holiday read' Kia Abdullah

'A great read' Catherine Cooper

'You won't be able to put it down' *Business Post*

'Gripping' *Sunday Times Style*

'Full of surprises' *Sun*

'Kept me up late into the early hours' Ali Lowe

Also by Jess Ryder

The Villa

THE
ISLAND
ESCAPE

JESS RYDER

PENGUIN BOOKS

PENGUIN BOOKS

UK | USA | Canada | Ireland | Australia
India | New Zealand | South Africa

Penguin Books is part of the Penguin Random House group of companies
whose addresses can be found at global.penguinrandomhouse.com

Penguin Random House UK,
One Embassy Gardens, 8 Viaduct Gardens, London SW11 7BW

penguin.co.uk
global.penguinrandomhouse.com

First published 2025
001

Typeset in 10.4/15pt Palatino LT Pro by Jouve (UK), Milton Keynes
Printed and bound in Great Britain by Clays Ltd, Elcograf S.p.A.

The authorised representative in the EEA is Penguin Random House Ireland,
Morrison Chambers, 32 Nassau Street, Dublin D02 YH68

A CIP catalogue record for this book is available from the British Library

ISBN: 978–1–804–94688–6

Penguin Random House is committed to a sustainable
future for our business, our readers and our planet.
This book is made from Forest Stewardship
Council® certified paper.

For Harry and Cathy

Prologue: August 1985

ESTELLE

He held out his hand to steady her as she stepped into the rowing boat. She sat facing the shore and he took the bench opposite, looking out to sea. They gave each other a nervous smile. His face was obscured by the brim of his leather Stetson, which was tipped over his eyes against the glare of the morning sun. He was wearing the usual short-sleeved shirt and jeans, but it was the hat that identified him beyond question. Niko was seldom seen without it.

There was a swell coming from the ferry, which was idling further out in the bay, being too large and unwieldly to dock in the tiny port. The rowing boat bobbed about as they sat waiting for the other passengers to board. She yawned, and he caught it, covering his mouth with his hand. They'd been up all night and were exhausted, sickened by the horror of what they'd done. The sound of gunshot still rang in her ears. When she closed her eyes, she could see the blood.

The ferry klaxon blasted, as if to say time was up. A small boy unwound the rope from its bollard and threw it to the old fisherman, who picked up his oars and started to row, cutting easily through the water, putting distance between them and the shore.

Estelle saw a young man running along the quayside

towards them, frantically waving his arms. It was Andreas, Niko's brother. He stumbled onto the beach and started screaming in the direction of the rowing boat.

'Don't react, don't turn round,' she said. 'Don't look at him, whatever you do.' He buried his head in his lap. 'It's okay. We're too far away. He can't stop us now.'

The boat drew along the starboard side of the ferry, where a rope ladder dangled from an open door. He climbed up first, a small bag swinging from his shoulder. Not much luggage for the rest of his life, Estelle reflected, as she hefted her rucksack onto her back and followed him into the gloomy interior.

The lower deck was hot and stuffy. It smelt of stale sweat and there was nowhere to sit. 'I need fresh air,' she said, but he didn't budge. 'Come up top with me. Please.'

He frowned. 'Is that a good idea?'

'We need to say a proper goodbye.'

They climbed the spiral steps to the top deck and stood against the railings. He put one arm around her shoulders and clasped the crown of his Stetson with the other.

'We did it,' she said, leaning into him.

'Yes. So far, so good. But we're not out of the woods yet.' His bent his head and whispered in her ear. 'We can never speak about what happened, never tell anyone, no matter how much we love or trust them. We have to take this secret to our graves.'

'I know,' she replied.

'We could spend the rest of our lives in prison for what we did. Promise me you'll never tell.'

'I promise.'

'Good.' He took a breath. 'This is the plan. I'll get off at Paros. We'll say goodbye and never see each other again. I'll only contact you in an emergency. Other than that, you won't hear from me. Is that clear?'

'Yes. Of course.'

He went back inside in search of coffee, but she stayed on deck, unable to drag herself away. Her gaze swept across the scene that had become so familiar to her – the tavernas clustered around the square, the travel bureau, the bakery that sold the most delicious pastries, the kiosk where she'd bought postcards to send home. It was still early and not everything was open yet. But soon the port would be bustling again, from about 10 a.m. until four the following morning. She loved the place so much. But all those wonderful memories were ruined now, indelibly stained with tragedy. How strange that just a few seconds could change a life forever.

The ferry reversed at an angle, then lumbered round until it faced the open sea again. She ran to the aft deck to catch a final glimpse of the island. As they pulled away, the white flat-roofed buildings grew smaller, and the tiny people looked stiff and unmoving, like a child's playset. She couldn't make out Andreas anymore, but no doubt he was still there. Fuming.

They passed the point, turning north towards the next island stop on the long journey to Athens. The view became more generalised – a parched, barren hillside, a sandy beach, some treacherous-looking rocks, a white church with a blue dome.

For the first time in what felt like days, she took a deep

3

breath. She'd been in emergency mode, her body refusing to let her brain think while she'd had so many things to do. But now she was safe, the terrible events of the last few hours suddenly rushed at her. She leaned over the railings and vomited with a loud, raw groan. The contents of her gut splashed yellow against the side, a strand of spittle hanging from her chin like a wet cobweb. She found a tissue in her bag and wiped around her mouth, apologising to the woman standing next to her.

They'd made their escape, but she felt no relief, only sadness. Tears gathered behind her eyes, clouding her vision. She blinked several times, then took her final glimpse of the island, knowing that she could never come back. Not now. Not after what she'd done.

Chapter One: Now

JUNO

I lift my suitcases off the luggage racks and join the queue to disembark. Many passengers are already assembled by the doors, rucksacks hoisted onto their backs, luggage at their sides. Others are getting into their cars or onto motorbikes. There's an impatience in the air, as if we're responding to an emergency, rather than about to start a holiday. We're ready. Poised for action.

The ferry blasts a warning that it's about to dock, makes a circle, then grinds noisily into reverse. The door opens like the yawning mouth of a whale, its jaw clattering onto the quayside. Daylight bursts into the space, and the vehicles immediately drive out. There's a thundering of suitcase wheels as the foot passengers surge forward. Propelled by the weight of my luggage, I almost run down the ramp.

I stop to print these first images on my memory, to breathe in the island air. This is it. Inios. I've been dreaming about this moment for weeks. It still feels unreal, as if I've stepped into a picture book – sailboats tinkling in the harbour, the sparkling sea, whitewashed buildings perched on the hillside, the cloudless blue sky . . . It's even more beautiful than I'd imagined.

The port is small but extremely busy. There are people

everywhere, newly arrived or about to depart, ready to meet and greet or to say goodbye. Dragging my suitcases behind me, I pass along the line of taxi drivers and travel reps holding up signs. I see my name scrawled on a piece of paper.

'Hi,' I say to the young woman, smartly dressed in a shirt and pencil skirt. 'I'm Juno Curnell.'

'Ah! Excellent!' She beams at me. 'My name is Athena. Pleased to meet you. Welcome to Inios. Did you have a good journey?'

'Yes, thanks.'

'Excellent.' Clearly, it's her favourite word. 'Have you been here before?'

'No, never. Actually, this is my first time in Greece.'

'You will fall in love with the island, I promise. Please. This way.'

She insists on taking one of my suitcases and I follow her to the car park. I get into a cool minibus with tinted windows, and we drive away from the port.

'Inios is twenty-two kilometres from north to south and ten kilometres east to west, but the landscape is mountainous,' she explains, as we climb a steep, winding hill. 'There is only one village – Chora. It has everything you need. To get to the main beaches you can take a bus or taxi. Or you can hire a car. There's a path from the port to Chora if you prefer to walk.' She gestures to her right. 'But there are three hundred and twenty-five steps!'

The hotel is small and modern, built on flat ground at the base of the original hilltop village. There's a tiny swimming pool, where a handful of guests are sunbathing. Athena takes me to the reception, where a woman – who seems to be her mother – checks me in.

'You are with us for only seven nights?' she queries, noticing the large amount of luggage I've brought with me.

'Yes,' I reply, although in truth I haven't a clue how long I'll be in Greece. As a UK citizen, I'm allowed to stay for up to ninety days, which would take me to the end of the season. Unfortunately, my savings won't last that long. Maybe my courage won't either. I've never done anything like this before – by myself, *for* myself. Although I'm excited, I'm also scared. What if I don't like what I find?

Athena helps me take my luggage up some steep steps to my room. There's no lift and the facilities seem basic, although new and clean. She hands me the keys and shows me how the air-con works, then announces that she'll leave me to settle in.

As soon as she goes, I throw open the balcony doors and step out into the sunshine, staring at the higgledy-piggledy rooftops and the blue-domed churches of the village beyond. I breathe a loud sigh of relief.

This time yesterday I was in the UK, in the grey sub-urbs of London, walking around the house with a note in my hand, wondering where best to leave it. Luke isn't the most observant of husbands – I'm always teasing him that he never notices when I've had my hair cut or am wearing a new dress – so I wanted to make sure he found it as soon as possible. Leaving the note on the kitchen table felt like too much of a cliché, and there's no mantelpiece in our modern, boxy living room. If I'd left it on his pillow, I'd feared he might not have seen it until he'd gone to bed. In the end, I put the note in an envelope and left it on the windowsill by the front door, where he puts his keys.

I'm sorry. I feel awful about leaving without telling you, but I was frightened you'd try to stop me. I still love you, but the situation is killing me. We can't go on like this. All we're doing is making each other miserable.

I'm not saying it's definitely over between us, just that I need some space and time to sort myself out. I'm sure you'll want to take some time to think too.

I'm going to Inios – you'll know why. It's something I have to do. I have so many questions that need answering. I can't wait any longer. Please don't call, or follow me, or try to make me come back. I don't want a row over the phone. I promise I'll get in touch as soon as I feel up to it. Please try to understand.

Take care. Love you, xx

I knew Luke would be upset and want to talk despite my pleas to be left alone. He started calling me shortly after 7 p.m. which is when he normally arrives home from work. I didn't pick up. He rang and texted so many times during the evening I had to turn off my phone.

By then, my flight had already landed in Santorini. The ferry to Inios didn't leave until the following morning, so I'd booked into a hotel for the night. I sat in my room, debating whether to open the little bottle of wine that was beckoning to me from the minibar. I hadn't drunk any alcohol since

New Year, part of a resolution to get super healthy and turn my body into a temple. Luke had said he would do Dry January with me in case the alcohol was affecting his sperm quality. We made it through the month together, then he lapsed into old habits – a cold beer when he came in, a glass of wine with our evening meal, two or three pints if we went to a pub. I carried on with Dry February, then March, April, May, June . . . Not that it helped.

Luke had been the first to talk about having kids. He wanted at least two, he said, ideally three. He comes from a large family. His parents are still together, and he's close to his brothers and sisters. He has always felt entirely positive about fatherhood. In contrast, I'm the only child of a single mum, who left me with my grandparents when I was eleven so that she could travel the world. We don't have a normal mother–daughter relationship. I've never even called her 'Mum' – she only let me call her Estelle. I rarely see her, and we go for months without contact. I wasn't sure what I thought about motherhood, but I loved Luke, and I wanted to please him. By then, we'd been married for five years – it was time.

But the months went by, and we didn't conceive. We tried not to panic or get too stressed about it. We paid more attention to my ovulation cycle and made sure we had sex at the right times. We read pregnancy blogs and scoured websites looking for tips. After we'd made love, I'd lie with my legs up for half an hour, even though I'd read it was an old wives' tale and wouldn't make any difference. We tried everything, but it didn't work.

Meanwhile, couples we knew started to get pregnant. I

was constantly being invited to baby showers and gender reveals. My girlfriends swapped grisly tales of childbirth and then swapped buggies and highchairs. Every month it seemed to be another little darling's birthday party. That was how we socialised together – standing around in a park with a paper cup of warm wine, snacking on leftover caterpillar cake, debating the pros and cons of baby-led weaning. I had nothing to contribute to the conversation. It was unbearable. I felt like a freak.

After two years of trying and failing, Luke and I went to the GP who referred both of us for tests. The fertility clinic said there was no medical reason why it wasn't happening and suggested it might be due to anxiety and stress. It didn't help. If anything, it made things worse. I retreated into myself, made excuses not to make love. Luke became frustrated with me, and we argued over the stupidest of things. I became depressed and started to question our relationship.

Then I found the letters, and everything changed.

I sit on the bed and take the large brown envelope out of my bag. I press it to my cheek, inhaling the faint scent of my grandmother's perfume, imagining that she's by my side. She died three months ago, and I still can't quite believe she's not with us anymore.

After Gran's funeral, Estelle ran back to her home in Portugal, claiming she was too upset to sort out her mother's belongings. The job fell to me. At the time, I was aggrieved to be landed with all the work, but now I'm grateful to Gran for never throwing anything away. If I hadn't found this envelope, I'd still be in the dark, believing my mother's lies.

Estelle always maintained that my father was an Italian

waiter with whom she'd had a drunken one-night stand. As I grew up, I wondered endlessly about the stranger who'd given me my Mediterranean features. All of my friends knew their fathers, even if they no longer lived with the family. If nothing else, they knew their names. I didn't even have that. On my birth certificate, my father is described as 'unknown'.

The letters – a small collection of airmails and postcards – told a different tale. They'd been written by my mother to her parents from this island over two summers, 1984 and 1985. I sat on Gran's bedroom floor, reading until my legs went numb, checking the date of the postmarks, counting the years and months on my fingers. There was no doubt about it – Estelle wasn't even in England when I was conceived. She was in Greece, in love with a man by the name of Niko. He *had* to be my father.

I called her and demanded an explanation. She was clearly shocked that she'd been found out, but refused to talk about her time in Inios, or her relationship with Niko. I begged her to give me his surname, but she claimed she couldn't remember it. I didn't believe her. She persisted with the Italian waiter story, but there was a false note in her voice. She almost sounded panicky. Why was she lying to me?

I took a DNA test and sure enough, I was 50 per cent Greek. When I confronted Estelle again, she ended the conversation and refused to answer any further calls. I realised that if I wanted to know the truth, I would have to go to Inios and look for him in person. Luke was against the idea. He said I didn't have enough information about him, that Niko could be dead or have emigrated to Australia. Even

11

if I managed to find him, he probably wouldn't remember Estelle. He might deny that he was my father and reject me. It would be a wild goose chase, would cause me a lot of pain and cost us a lot of money, which would be far better spent on a course of IVF treatment.

That was the final straw. How could I think about having a child when I didn't even know who I was? I felt like our relationship had reached an impasse. Finding my father became my obsession. Luke was increasingly exasperated with me, and it led to lots of rows. But I couldn't give up my dream. If he wouldn't support me, I would go on my own. I started to make plans in secret. I negotiated some unpaid leave from the recruitment company I was working for and booked a one-way flight to Greece.

And here I am. When my friends find out what I've done, they'll probably think I'm having a midlife crisis, although I'm not forty yet. But my motivation is positive, not negative. I'm running *towards* my life, not away from it. I'm determined to find my Greek family, and nobody is going to stop me from discovering the truth.

Chapter Two: July 1984

ESTELLE

Dear Mum and Dad,

Arrived safely in Athens last night. The hostel was fine, just a bit noisy. Didn't sleep much. Today, I'm making my way to Piraeus which is the main port. My ferry leaves at seven this evening and takes twelve hours! I hope I don't get seasick! Don't worry about me travelling alone. Lots of people seem to be doing it and it's quite safe. I'm sure I'll make friends. Will try to phone soon, but it might be difficult so don't get in a panic if you don't hear from me for a bit!

I hope you are both well and the weather in England is not too bad. It's <u>very</u> hot here.

Lots of love,
Estelle xx

Chapter Three: Now

JUNO

It's lunchtime, but I'm too nervous to eat anything. I want to explore. I go back to reception and ask Athena for a map of the island, which she scrawls over in red pen, circling the best beaches and sightseeing spots. I pretend to be taking it all in, but I'm only really interested in one place – Sunset Bar, where Niko used to work in his father's business. I ask Athena if she knows where it is.

'Sunset Bar . . . No, sorry. I've never heard of it.'

'It was around in the eighties. People used to go there to watch the sunset. They played classical music . . . ?' Her face is blank. 'Sorry. You're far too young to remember.'

'One moment, please.' Athena disappears into the back office for a few moments, returning with her mother, Maria.

'You ask about Sunset Bar?' she says. 'That closed about fifteen years ago.'

My heart sinks. 'I see . . . That explains why it wasn't coming up on social media.'

'Why do you want to know?' she asks, a slight note of suspicion in her voice.

'Oh, no particular reason. My mum went there when she was young, that's all. I promised I'd check it out.'

'Your mother wouldn't recognise it. It's Club Inios Sunset

14

now – a very different place.' Maria arches her eyebrows and laughs ironically. 'It used to be for hippies but only the rich can go there these days . . .'

'I don't suppose you remember the name of the family that used to own it?' I ask hopefully. 'The father's name was Yannis.' *My paternal grandfather,* I add silently.

'Yes, Yannis Zimiris, he died a long time ago.'

My breath hitches. Zimiris. At last, I have the family surname.

She purses her lips. 'The Zimirises are a very powerful family. They own most of the island.'

'Mamá! That's not true,' admonishes Athena.

'Not yet, but it is their plan,' she retorts. 'They would own all of it if they could – every last grain of sand!' She goes back into the office, muttering to herself in Greek. Athena rolls her eyes in irritation. I seem to have inadvertently touched a nerve. I'd love to ask more questions but decide I should probably be discreet. If Niko is the head of the family now, he and Maria could be enemies . . .

'Thanks. That's really helpful,' I say instead. 'Can you show me Club Inios Sunset on the map, please?'

Athena obliges with another red circle and tells me it's a half-hour walk away.

Thinking I might need my swimming stuff, I go back to the room. I pack a small bag and apply sunscreen, then leave the hotel with the map in my hand. There are very few roads on the entire island, so it's almost impossible to get lost. Unfortunately, there are no pavements beyond the village; the road is full of sharp bends and although there isn't much traffic, walking is dangerous.

15

It's almost unbearably hot. The road is dusty and there's hardly any shade to walk in, but the views from up here are extraordinary – the hillside dotted with whitewashed houses, endless blue sea, and utterly clear skies.

It's a relief to reach the sign for Club Inios Sunset, pointing to the right down a steep slope. I follow the unmade track, which is just wide enough for a vehicle. There are olive trees and various spiky shrubs on either side, alive with buzzing insects. I round a bend and find a car park. At the far end, I can see a modern flat-roofed building with a canopied entrance. A large sign over the door welcomes me.

Inside, it's cool and airy. Everything is styled in calming neutrals and organic textiles. There isn't a trace of the traditional white and blue colour scheme that you see everywhere else on the island. A mirrored bar dominates the space. The tables in the restaurant area are laid with white linen. Lunch service is just beginning. People are drinking cocktails while studying the menu. They are properly clothed – no bikinis or bare male chests here. I feel a little out of place in my creased dress and flip-flops and walk quickly through to the sun terrace.

The club has been constructed on several levels, everything connected by paved paths, their edges whitewashed in the traditional island style. Pampas grass sways gently in the breeze. There are beautifully landscaped gardens, and an amphitheatre lower down. I follow the path to my left which leads to a swimming pool, decorated with glittering mosaics, and surrounded by enormous square sunbeds shaded by cream canvas sails. A sign directs me to the beach, which is at the bottom of some stone steps. There are more sunbeds and parasols on the sand and a boat is moored at a small jetty. A couple are sitting on the edge of it, dangling their feet in the crystal-clear water.

I screw up my eyes and try to take myself back in time, whisking away the contemporary luxury and restoring the grubby old hippy bar that Estelle describes in her letters. But the place looks so incredibly different, it defies the power of my imagination.

'Good afternoon. Can I help you?' asks a young man. He has an Eastern European accent. 'Do you have a day pass?'

'Um . . . no. Sorry. Do I need one?'

He nods. 'We have one sunbed left, over there,' he says, pointing to the corner.

'Right . . . Thanks.' If I want to keep looking around, I don't have much choice. He brings me a large fluffy beach towel and adjusts the sail on the sunbed to give me more shade. Then he fetches a card machine from the pool bar.

I'd like to know the cost of the day pass, but I'm too embarrassed to ask. I hand over my credit card and try not to wince when I see the receipt. At fifty euros – just for the use of the sunbed and swimming pool – I won't be able to come here again, so I'll have to make the most of it.

I use the changing room to get into my bikini and take a shower before lowering myself into the pool. I manage a few lengths of breaststroke, then lie on my back with my eyes closed, slowly circling my hands to keep myself afloat.

It's so strange to be in the very spot where my parents met, just over forty years ago. What if Niko is the club owner? He could be sitting on the terrace right now, eating his lunch. I could have already walked past him.

I feel a sudden impulse to get out of the water and search for him, but I have no idea what he looks like. There were no photos among the stash of airmails and postcards. All I have to go on is my own face, but I doubt that will help much. Everyone says I look like my mother, although I have olive skin and dark wavy hair, whereas she's fair and freckly. Her hair used to be blonde, but now it's grey. The last time I saw her she'd added a pink streak and a nose stud to complete the aged hippy look. But my father is a blank page.

The club towel is soft and luxurious. I dry myself, then lay it on the sunbed. I'm just about to lie down when a young woman in her early twenties with long blonde hair scraped back into a ponytail and wearing a lot of make-up approaches me.

'Hi,' she says. 'I'm Millie, the club's beauty therapist. Are there any treatments I can offer you today?' She's English, with a slight London accent.

'No, thanks.'

'Are you sure? Massage? Pedicure?' She glances down at my unpainted toenails.

'I'd love to, but . . .'

'I can offer you a discount for your introductory treatment. Full body massage for the price of a head and shoulder. Only thirty euros,' she adds, temptingly.

Thirty euros on top of the fifty I've just forked out . . . It's a lot of money, but it would give me an opportunity to find out more about the Zimiris family.

'Do you do the massage out here?' I ask.

'No! In the hut. Sorry, in the "Wellbeing Cabana". You won't regret it. I'm good.'

'Okay, why not?'

The extravagantly named Wellbeing Cabana is a small, dark hut with a thatched roof. It reeks of scented massage oils which only just mask an underlying smell of sweat. Millie asks me to lie down on the therapy table and put my face into the hole. She washes her hands, then runs them over my back.

'Wow, you're so tense,' she remarks, starting to work her way up my spine. 'You're rock solid here.'

Millie wasn't boasting. She *is* good. I let her work her magic on my stiff muscles, trying not to groan too much with pleasure.

'How's the pressure for you?' she asks. 'Only you're so knotted I've really got to dig in.'

'Dig away. It's fantastic,' I murmur.

'I haven't seen you before. Just arrived?'

'Yes. This morning. I'm Juno, by the way.'

'Nice. Who are you with?'

'Nobody. I'm on my own.'

'Oh, okay. That's brave. Do you normally travel alone?'

'Not always. Sometimes,' I lie. 'Whenever I need a bit of time to myself.'

'How long are you staying?'

'Not sure. I'd like to stay the whole summer. It depends . . .' I tail off, not wanting to reveal too much.

'On what?'

'Um . . . you know . . . how long the money lasts . . . I might get a job . . .'

'There are heaps of vacancies,' Millie continues, kneading my skin as if it's a lump of dough. 'It's the accommodation that's the problem. Most of the rooms where summer workers used to stay have been turned into Airbnbs. The situation's got so bad some bars and restaurants haven't been able to open this season.'

'Really? I didn't know that.'

I try to lose myself in the massage. Emotions that I've been keeping locked away start to break free and rise to the surface. Before I know it, I start to cry. A fat tear drops through the hole in the table and onto the floor.

'Sorry, can I have a tissue, please?'

Millie whips one out of the box and passes it to me. I lift my head and wipe my nose, apologising.

'No need. It happens a lot. Massage releases stuff you've been holding on to . . . Are you okay?'

'Yes, fine.' I sniff.

'Do you want me to carry on?'

'Yes, please!'

She continues in silence, applying more oil and gently massaging my legs. I stop crying and try to calm down. This isn't supposed to be a therapy session. I'm here to find my dad.

'So, what's it like working here?' I ask.

'Fine.'

'It's a family business, isn't it?'

She laughs. 'All businesses in Greece are family businesses.'

'The owners are the Zimiris family, right?'

'Yup.'

'And, er . . . what's the name of the boss?'

'That would be Andreas.'

'Andreas?' A shiver runs down my spine. From Estelle's letters, I know that Andreas is Niko's brother.

'How old is he?'

She pauses. 'Dunno. In his sixties, I guess. His children, Christakis and Despina, run the place day-to-day.'

I'm desperate to find out if she knows Niko, but I hold back. I mustn't go in all guns blazing. I decide to change tack.

'Have you worked here long?'

'Just since the start of the season,' Millie replies. 'This is my third summer in Inios. The last two were holidays; this is my first actual job here. I mainly do hair and beauty for the weddings, but if there isn't one on, I offer treatments to day guests. Like you. Turn over, please.' I heave myself onto my back.

'This is also a wedding venue then?'

'Yeah. They don't do them all the time, just a few here and there. It's very exclusive.' She scoops my hair off my neck and holds my head until it falls heavily into her hands. 'Try to relax your shoulders a bit . . . That's better.' She starts to massage my scalp. 'Actually, there's a job going here if you fancy it. Wedding coordinator.'

'Oh, really? How come?'

'The woman who was doing it left suddenly. They're mad keen to find someone else,' Millie continues. 'I think they'd bite your hand off. I don't mean to be rude, but you're a bit more mature, know what I mean?'

The only wedding I've ever organised is my own. I've been in recruitment for years, but I *did* work for an events company in my twenties. It was mainly shifting chairs and ushering, but I could probably blag it . . .

As Millie drags her fingers through my hair, the idea takes root. Being the wedding coordinator would put me right at the heart of the family. Hopefully, I'd get to meet Niko. It sounds like he doesn't work here, but maybe he runs another venue elsewhere on the island. I could get to know the family naturally without feeling any pressure. It's a little risky, I suppose, because I'd be deceiving them, but it would be for a good cause . . .

I lift my head. 'Does the job come with free accommodation?'

'Oh, yes. A nice little flat in the centre of Chora. You'd have to share with me, but I'm out most nights, so you'd hardly know I was there.'

'I'm very quiet. I wouldn't bother you.'

'It'd be nice to have another English girl around. You should go for it. It's a great job. We get the odd Bridezilla, but mostly it's fine.' She finishes my head massage, wiping the oil off her hands with a paper towel. 'There! You're done.'

I sit up slowly, feeling all soft and woozy, like my bones have mulched. 'Wow . . . That was amazing. Thanks so much.'

'You're welcome. Members of staff get a fifty per cent discount too!'

I laugh. 'I haven't got the job yet.'

'No, but you will.'

I feel rejuvenated, not just from the massage but from the thought of working here. Fate has opened a door for me – I *have* to walk through it.

'How do I apply?' I ask.

'Just talk to Christakis. He's the manager. Come on, I'll take you to him.'

Millie leads me back to the main building, where a good-looking guy in his late twenties is sitting at the back of the bar, working on his laptop. He has black wavy hair just like mine.

'Christakis,' Millie begins, 'this is Juno. She's interested in the wedding coordinator job.'

My cousin looks up at me and smiles.

Chapter Four: July 1984

ESTELLE

Estelle finished the remains of the ham roll she'd bought in Piraeus before boarding the ferry yesterday afternoon. Crumbs tumbled into her lap, and she carelessly brushed them onto the floor. It had been an arduous trip, hot and stuffy inside, windy and chaotic up on deck. She was relieved to be getting off at the next stop.

Her original destination had been Santorini, but she'd met some English backpackers last night who'd warned her that the island was really expensive. They were heading for Inios, which was less developed and therefore cheaper, and also had better beaches, the sand golden instead of volcanic black. Apparently, Inios was *the* place to go if you were on a budget and liked to party. That just about summed her situation up. Angela, one of the backpackers who was about her age and also travelling alone, had insisted Estelle join her. It'd felt nice to be wanted for a change.

She wasn't supposed to be here on her own, but her boyfriend, Simon, had pulled out at the last moment – not just of the trip, but their relationship. They'd been an item since Freshers' Week last September. He was in the year above, studying Ancient History. Having an older boyfriend had made settling into life at Manchester University a lot easier.

Eager to escape her all-girls hall of residence, she had spent most of the time hanging out with Simon and his mates, who shared a huge tumbledown Victorian villa a bus ride away from campus. It had been his idea to go island-hopping in Greece, visiting some ruins along the way – an aspect of the holiday that Estelle had never been keen on. When he'd dumped her – in cowardly fashion on the very last day of term – she'd been devastated.

Friends had rallied around. She'd had several offers to join them on all-girl trips to the Costa del Sol, but as everything had already been booked, it had been too difficult to tag along. And it wasn't just her summer that had been wrecked. She'd been supposed to move in with Simon for her second year, but now she would have to find somewhere else. If travelling alone worked out, she might choose to live alone too, she thought. At least there would be no arguments about fridge space or whose turn it was to clean the bathroom. But it would be more expensive than sharing, and not as much fun . . .

A host of negative thoughts swirled through her head: the humiliation of having been rejected, the need to find somewhere to live, her less than impressive marks in the end-of-year exams, whether doing an English degree was right for her, whether she should quit university altogether and get a job . . . She glanced around at her fellow travellers – a mix of Greeks and foreign tourists. There was a sick feeling in her stomach, partly due to hunger, but also anxiety. She'd never been on holiday by herself before.

She could easily have cancelled, but that would have let Simon win. More importantly, she needed some time away to reflect on her own life. Her parents were very unhappy about the trip, warning her of the dangers of being a single woman and making her promise to keep in touch with letters, postcards and a weekly telephone call.

'Don't worry about me,' she'd said, although she was probably more worried than they were.

Hopefully, everything would turn out fine. She wasn't the only lone traveller and she'd already met some nice people who'd been island-hopping before and knew the ropes. At least she wouldn't have to tramp around boring ruins in the searing heat. She could lie on the beach all day and spend the evenings in bars and discos. Maybe she'd even meet someone. She wasn't looking to start a new relationship but was definitely up for a holiday romance.

'Estelle!' She looked up to see her new friend stepping over luggage and prone bodies as she made her way across deck. Angela was pretty, with a mop of permed blonde hair, and was simply dressed in cut-off jeans and a white T-shirt. 'There you are!' she cried. 'I've been looking for you everywhere. Thought maybe you'd got off at Paros.'

'No. I've been trying to get some sleep.' Estelle looked at her watch. It was quarter to six in the morning. No wonder she felt groggy.

'We're nearly there. Are you ready? You have to be quick. The ferry doesn't dock. You have to climb down a rope ladder into a rowing boat. It's a bit tricky but they'll help you. Come on, this way.'

Estelle got to her feet and swung her rucksack over her shoulders, fastening the belt across her tummy to keep it in place. She followed Angela through a side door to some spiral steps leading to the lower deck. People were already queuing to disembark. The lads she'd met last night were there – Paul and Tony, two mates who came from Barking in Essex, and who claimed to be 'barking mad', and a Northern hippy chap called Rob whom they'd picked up on their travels. All three were yawning loudly, their eyes red and watery from drinking and playing cards all night.

The ferry had come to a halt and the queue was moving forward. 'Inios, here we come!' shouted Rob as he broke into deafening song. 'No, nay, never! No, nay, never, no more!'

Estelle climbed gingerly down the rope ladder. A Greek man with a wizened brown face and gaps between his teeth was waiting with arms outstretched. He helped her into the rowing boat. There were only ten passengers disembarking that morning, all but two of them tourists – or 'travellers' as they would no doubt prefer to be called. Estelle shuffled along the bench to make room for Angela. When everyone was seated, and some large cardboard boxes and drums of cooking oil had been unloaded, the boat made its gentle way to a small gravel beach.

The port was smaller than Estelle had been expecting – not much more than a couple of tavernas, a few shops and a travel agency – but it was full of life. Men and young boys stood in a row, holding up handwritten posters offering rooms to rent.

'Take your pick,' said Angela. They chose an elderly man who welcomed them in Greek. After a few exchanges using sign language, he beckoned the girls to follow him up a steep narrow track.

'Hah! The notorious donkey path,' said Angela, hitching her rucksack frame above her hips. 'Last summer we did this trek twice a bloody day. Going down's okay, up is a killer. People have accidents all the time, especially when they're drunk, but you can't avoid it, it's the only way to get to Chora. That's where all the action is at night.'

The sun had only just risen, but it was shining right into their faces. Estelle's armpits sweated beneath her T-shirt. The straps of her rucksack rubbed against her shoulders, leaving livid red marks.

The old chap was surprisingly sprightly. He cheerfully ignored the sleeping bodies that were lying under the trees next to the path. They looked as if they'd simply collapsed on the spot, empty bottles strewn by their sides. They were as still as corpses and looked strangely comic.

'See what I mean? Some people never make it back to where they're staying,' Angela said, chuckling.

A few minutes later, they left the track and were led through a grove of olive trees to a small whitewashed farmhouse. The man went inside for a few moments, then re-emerged with his wife, a woman in her seventies or eighties, wearing a patterned cotton dress with a scarf tied around her head. She greeted them very enthusiastically in Greek and showed them their accommodation, a tiny squat outbuilding in the corner of the yard. A few goats were wandering about, the bells around their necks tinkling.

The room was only just big enough for two narrow metal bedframes with thin, sagging mattresses and lumpy pillows. There was no bathroom, but they had use of the toilet attached to the farmhouse. A hose was attached to an outside tap. Estelle's vision of having a hot shower instantly evaporated. But at least the place looked clean.

'*Efcharistó! Efcharistó!*' they repeated, as if they'd just been shown a palace.

'We're going to get to know each other well over the next few weeks,' Angela remarked once they were left alone to unpack – not that there was anywhere to store anything.

'Yes, we are!' agreed Estelle. Although she'd tried to persuade herself that she would enjoy travelling alone, she was grateful to have some company. Everything was so different here. Exciting, yet overwhelming.

They took off their heavy rucksacks, relieved to be free of them at last. Estelle unfurled her brand-new sleeping bag and laid it on one of the beds. The room was warm and airless. There was a small grilled window but no shutters or curtains. They would need to burn mosquito coils at night, she thought.

'I don't know about you, but I can't wait to go down to the beach,' said Angela, stuffing a towel and a bright yellow bikini into a tote bag. 'Wanna come?'

'Of course. Which one?'

'The easiest to get to and most popular is Kalapos. It's on the other side of the village, about half an hour's walk from here.'

'Sounds great,' replied Estelle, grabbing her stuff.

On the way, they passed a shop selling groceries and tobacco. There was a carousel of postcards outside. She needed one for her parents, to let them know she'd arrived safely.

'Is that where we're going?' she asked Angela, pointing

to a view of a wide sandy bay with only a couple of build-ings dotted about.

'Yup! Although it'll be a lot more crowded than that,' she replied. 'Come on! I want to get in the sea.'

Estelle quickly bought a few postcards and stamps, then followed Angela down the stony track. Her spirits soared into the bright blue sky. She'd found a beautiful island, had somewhere to stay, and had already made new friends. Everything was going to be alright.

drives us the few hundred yards to a car park next to a large white church, its dome the colour of the sky.

'This is as close as he can get to our place,' Millie says. 'The village streets are too narrow for cars. Here, let me help.' She grabs one of the suitcases.

'Be here tomorrow. Eight o'clock, okay?' Vasilis tells me. 'Don't be late.'

Chora is picture-postcard beautiful: sparkling white houses, blue doors and shutters, window boxes spilling over with pink and purple flowers. Millie points out her favourite haunts as she rattles my case over the cobbled pavement. She leads me through a small square, home to just one taverna. Apparently, it's a popular meeting place for locals and holidaymakers alike. I take careful note.

'There's a larger square further up,' she says. 'That's where most of the action takes place at night.'

We continue through narrow, twisted streets, passing elegant boutiques and sophisticated restaurants, jewellers and art shops as well as small scruffy bars and bakeries selling pastries and slices of pizza. It's very quiet, with hardly any visitors around.

'Inios is a party island,' she explains as we pass the black studded doors of a nightclub. 'People spend the day sleeping off their hangovers or relaxing on the beach, then come back in the evening. It starts to heat up around ten. Quietens down at about four in the morning.'

'Four in the morning?' I echo.

'Yeah, not so great if you've got to work the next day. You get used to the noise. Promise.'

The streets – now more like alleyways – form a circular

maze that climbs upward to the top of the hill, on which sits another beautiful white church. It's even more tranquil here, more residential. Washing hangs out of upstairs windows; skinny cats peep out from shady corners. I feel myself getting ever more lost, ever more enchanted.

She stops outside a blue gate and pulls back the bolt. 'Here we are. Your home for the summer. I'm afraid it's a bit of a tip.'

We climb some stone steps and Millie opens a door, also painted blue. We enter a small kitchen, with an electric hot plate sitting on a wooden counter, a sink unit with cupboards beneath, a slim table pushed against the wall, and two dining chairs. Shelves display a few items of crockery and a couple of cooking pans. It's sparse, to say the least, and looks unused.

'I thought you said the place was a tip,' I say. 'It's spotless.'

'That's because I never cook. Wait until you see the bedroom.' She drags my case up a narrow open staircase, and I follow. 'The toilet's separate,' she says pointing to a door on the small landing. Next to it is another door, which she pushes open with her shoulder.

Like downstairs, the room is simply furnished with blue-painted shutters at the window. Everything is white, from the rough walls to the beamed ceiling, woven with rushes. There are two single beds, which almost touch each other due to the lack of space. One of them is unmade and several items of clothing lie draped across it. A paperback novel sits on the side table next to a dirty wine glass, its bottom stained red.

'Er . . . sorry . . . Is this the only bedroom?' I say, puzzled.

'Yeah. I did say we'd have to share.'

'I thought you meant the apartment, not . . .' I tail off.

'No.' She pulls an apologetic face. 'Sorry.'

I survey the furniture – a small white wardrobe, artfully chipped and dented, two bedside cabinets and a single chest of drawers. Behind a gauzy curtain that sections off the end of the bedroom, there's a shower unit and a washbasin. Feminine toiletries and sun protection items already take up every inch of shelf space.

My resolve weakens for a moment. I'm too old to be sharing with a stranger, especially someone as young and untidy as Millie. What am I doing?

'There's nowhere to put my stuff,' I mutter.

'I'll make room for you. It's my bad. After Lana left, I spread out.' She immediately opens the top drawer of the chest and gathers its contents into her arms.

'Lana? Was she the previous wedding coordinator?'

'Yup.' Coloured lingerie and several bikinis fall onto the bed like confetti. 'Will one drawer be enough for you?'

'Um . . . yes, I guess. Why did she leave?'

Millie pulls a face. 'I promised Christakis I wouldn't talk about it.'

'Why not?'

'It's complicated.' She opens the wardrobe and starts removing dresses and shirts. 'I'll give you some hangers.'

'What happened?' I press, intrigued. 'Did something go wrong?'

'You bet.' She laughs grimly.

'What did Lana do? Was she sacked?'

'Yup. And booted off the island. Nobody's heard from

her since. But you didn't hear it from me, okay? Now, no more questions or you'll get me into trouble.' She throws the empty hangers onto the bed. 'Here you go. There's a roof terrace too, it's a great chill-out space. I'll show you around, introduce you to some people. We'll have a laugh . . . Just one thing. Do you snore?'

I'm about to reply that my husband never complains, then stop myself. 'I don't think so. Do you?'

'Only when I'm waved.' She grins. 'Which is quite often, to be fair.'

I pick up the hangers. 'Thanks. We'll just have to make the best of it, I suppose.'

I place one of my suitcases on the bed and unzip it. I've brought so much stuff – I've no idea where it's all going to go.

'Right. I'm going to take a quick shower, then I'm meeting some friends for a night out. Want to come?' She starts undressing, then disappears behind the curtain. 'Shower's a bit temperamental, by the way.' She turns it on, and the pipes groan loudly.

'Um . . . that's really kind of you,' I shout over the sound of the water. 'But I think I should stay in tonight. It's all been a bit of a whirlwind.'

'Up to you!' she shouts back. After a few minutes, Millie turns off the shower, emerging from behind the curtain wearing a towel. I busy myself with the unpacking, trying not to look at her while she's getting dressed.

'So . . . fill me in on what I need to know,' I say. 'What are the Zimirises like to work for?'

After a tell-tale pause, she says, 'Fine. As long as you stay on the right side of them. They're one of the most important families on the island, if not *the* most important. They have plenty of friends, but they have their enemies too.'

'I think the owner of the hotel I was staying in is one of them.'

'It's mostly jealousy. They're rich and successful, while a lot of other businesses here are struggling . . . Andreas has fingers in lots of pies so he's not around much. His wife died a few years ago. Christakis is the manager, even though he's several years younger than Despina. She's stuck in the office while he swans about – she does the accounts and stuff. Miserable old bag.'

'How old is old?'

'I don't know. Forty maybe?'

I think ruefully about my age as I hang up a few dresses and jeans, then stuff my underwear into the top drawer.

'Make sure you pronounce her name correctly,' Millie carries on. 'It's *Des*pina, not Des*peena* – she hates people getting it wrong . . . Think "*des*perate" – which she probably is. I mean, she's not married or anything.'

'Maybe she doesn't want to be.'

She shrugs. 'Who knows? Andreas has two other sons, but they live in Athens. They're lawyers or doctors or something, can't remember. Vasilis is related to them in some distant way. The rest of the staff is either local or from places like Ukraine and Armenia. They keep to themselves.' She puts on a skimpy red mini-dress. 'And last, but by no means least, there's you and me, the wedding brigade.'

'And that's everyone, is it?' I persist. 'I mean, from the family. There's nobody else that works there – from the older generation, perhaps?' She glances at me curiously. 'Just out of interest.'

'Well, there's Phaedra. She's in her sixties – not sure how she fits in. I think she's a cousin or maybe an aunt? I don't have much to do with her. She used to run the kitchen, but this year Andreas brought Michalis over from Athens to modernise the menu and she's been relegated to chopping tomatoes. Michalis is horrible to her, but he's an amazing chef, so nobody cares.'

'Poor Phaedra,' I murmur.

Millie reapplies her make-up then brushes her hair vigorously, tying it into a French twist and popping in a large tortoiseshell comb. 'Right. I'm going to grab something to eat then head down to the Outta Sight. Sure you don't want to come?'

'The Outta Sight?' I repeat, my ears pricking. It's a place Estelle mentions in her letters. 'Is that still going?'

'I hope so! It was open last night.' Millie laughs.

'Hasn't it been around since the eighties? It's a cafeteria, right? With a campsite.'

'Not anymore!' Millie replies. 'I don't know about the history, but it's a really cool beach club now. Huge! They have, like, the best DJs. The music's banging, everyone dances, the swimming pool's standing room only – it's a totally crazy vibe. It's just as good as Ibiza. You can't come to Inios and not do the Outta Sight.'

At thirty-nine I feel like I might be a bit old for clubbing, but I nod enthusiastically. 'Sounds amazing. But I'm quite tired. And Vasilis is picking me up at eight o'clock tomorrow. It's my first day: I need to be fresh.'

'You've got to make the most of your free time, Juno. You won't get much of it.'

'I know. Thanks for the offer but I think I'll stay in.'

'No worries.' She pauses. 'Hope you don't mind me asking, but – why are you here? Is it just for a holiday or is there some other reason?'

'Just a holiday,' I reply firmly.

'It's just that when I was massaging you, I noticed there was a white mark around your wedding finger, where a ring used to be . . .'

My cheeks redden. 'My husband and I are on a break.'

'I guessed as much. That's why you were crying earlier. Look, I don't want to intrude, but if I can help in any way . . .'

'Thanks, but I'd rather not talk about it.'

'Fair enough. We all have our secrets.' She smiles at me warmly. 'The wi-fi code is on the noticeboard downstairs. Oh, and the supermarket is open until about eleven if you want anything.'

'Thanks.'

'Right then, I'll leave you to settle in.' She sweeps out, leaving a waft of perfume in her wake.

I sit on the bed for a few moments, trying to catch my breath. Then I take my phone and go down to the kitchen to find the wi-fi code. I've got to switch my phone back on – I can't put the moment off any longer.

As soon as it wakes up, it bleeps incessantly, telling me I've seven voicemails and thirteen WhatsApp messages. I listen to the voicemails first, all from Luke. The first two sound calm. He says he's very concerned about me and is worried about my mental health. The next three are more demanding, insisting that I let him know exactly where I am and that we talk immediately. The last two are angry and sound like he's drunk. 'What the fuck are you playing at Juno?' he shouts. 'You can't treat me like this. Come home!'

There's almost no point in reading his WhatsApp messages – they'll be just the same. I check to see who else might have contacted me and see to my astonishment that I have a message from Estelle. She's been avoiding me for weeks. It can't be a coincidence.

Nervously, I open it and read. The message is formal, as if she's writing me a letter.

Dear Juno, Luke called to say you'd left him and gone to Inios to find your father. I'm begging you to give up your search and come home now. Don't tell anyone that you're Niko's daughter. Do not contact his family. They must NOT find out who you are. I wish I could explain more but I can't. It's not safe there. Leave the island as soon as you can.

Chapter Six: July 1984

ESTELLE

Dear Mum and Dad,

Arrived safely in Inios, a small but pretty island in the Cyclades. Things are going well and I'm feeling much better in myself. I think I'm finally over Simon!! I've made friends with a nice girl called Angela. I met her on the ferry – she's also travelling alone. She has been to Inios before and knows it well, which is very useful. Also met two painter-decorators from Barking called Tony and Paul, and a hippy student called Rob who's from Leeds. Everyone is really friendly – we all look out for each other.

Angela and I are sharing a room just outside the one and only village on the island with an elderly Greek couple called Yiorgos and Sofia. They are so sweet – keep giving us free stuff like olives and watermelon. Our room is in the garden, there's an outside loo, no bathroom. I miss having hot showers! It's very basic but they only charge us 400 drachmas (less than 2 quid!) a night each so I'm not complaining! Everything is very cheap here, so my money is lasting well.

41

Off to the Outta Sight now – a bar/cafeteria place right on the beach, with a campsite behind it. Everyone hangs out there. You meet people from all over the world and everyone is so nice.

Lots of love, Estelle xx

Chapter Seven: Now

JUNO

I stare at the selection of wine in the supermarket, trying to decide what to buy. I haven't drunk alcohol in so long I don't know what I want. White? Red? Some kind of spirit? In her letters, Estelle always went on about retsina and ouzo. They sell both here, but maybe I should go easy to begin with. I definitely want to drink *something* this evening. I'm still in shock after reading Estelle's message.

I buy a reasonably expensive bottle from a local vineyard, plus things for dinner. Back in the apartment, I find a glass and a corkscrew and take the wine up to the terrace. I sit on one of the small rattan sofas, pausing for a moment to look out across the rooftops.

Questions revolve in my head. Why mustn't I look for Niko? Why mustn't I tell my Greek family who I am? What did Estelle mean when she said I wasn't safe? There's no point in my phoning her – she won't explain, and it'll only turn into an argument.

It's early evening now, but still sunny. I shield my eyes as I take in the view – the curved roof of a church directly in front, its white crucifix stark against the sky, a tumble of buildings on the brown, parched hillside, two spindly windmills on the horizon. There's not a glimpse of sea.

If I was on holiday with Luke, we would have relaxed here together after a long day on the beach. But I'm not going to think about Luke. Nor am I going to call, despite his pleadings. I was feeling guilty about not talking to him, but now I'm angry. He shouldn't have contacted Estelle and told her where I was.

I take a long indignant drink of wine, almost draining my glass. The taste is sharp and the alcohol shoots through my veins like a drug. Wow . . . I'm not used to this feeling. Better slow down.

The sky starts to darken. I stay on the roof terrace, the breeze playing gently across my bare arms – sipping my drink, shelling pistachios, and contemplating the last twenty-four hours. So much has happened in such a short space of time. I made it to Inios, went to Niko's old place of work, got myself a job, moved into this flat, met my first Greek relative, Christakis. I'm not stopping now, despite Estelle's warnings. She lost her right to tell me what to do many years ago.

My mother was only twenty-one when I was born. She was a single 'hippy-chick' who'd crashed out of university, with no job, and no support – financial or moral – from my father. She dragged me around Europe in search of an alternative lifestyle and a place to belong. Summers were spent camping on beaches or staying in abandoned villages in the Spanish or Portuguese mountains without running water or electricity. In the winter, we'd return to the UK and find shelter in various squats, or with friends until we'd outstayed our welcome. She tried to home-school me, but it never lasted for more than a few weeks at a time.

I learned to sleep in corners and on hard surfaces while Estelle and her companions drank, talked and smoked weed into the early hours. Men appeared in her bed, then disappeared just as suddenly a few weeks later. Life was chaotic; we never had any money or sense of security. I loved her because she was my mum, but I wasn't sure she loved me because I was her daughter, which made me feel very insecure.

When I was eleven, my grandparents stepped in and took charge of me. It was hard at first, but soon I was loving every minute of my new routines, thriving at school, making new friends. I drew closer to my grandparents and further from Estelle, whom I saw increasingly less often. By the time I left school and went to university, our relationship had all but evaporated.

Even though my grandparents gave me a wonderful life, I still felt unwanted. In my twenties, I found it difficult to hold down relationships – running away because I feared being abandoned again. It wasn't until I met Luke that I believed I could be loved. He reassured me that I didn't do anything wrong as a child and it wasn't my fault that Estelle gave me up. She *had* loved me, but for some reason neither she nor my grandparents would ever explain, she'd been unable to look after me. Sometimes, I'm able to accept my difficult childhood, but at other times I feel angry with her.

After I found the letters, I became convinced that whatever happened on this island all those years ago changed my mother's life. But if she refuses to share it with me, I've no chance of understanding, let alone forgiving her. My father remains my only hope. I want to hear his side of the story. But first, I have to find him.

I go to bed early, but I feel so churned up it's impossible to sleep. Scared of being bitten to death by mosquitoes, I shut the windows and turn on the air-con. It's ancient and makes such a terrible noise I have to turn it off again. The room soon becomes intolerably hot so I've no choice but to open the shutters and take my chances.

Down below in the village, the partying reaches its height. Loud music blares out, clashing sounds coming from different bars and clubs. I can hear constant whooping and shouting from tourists, sometimes even screaming. I pull the sheet over my head and press the pillow to my ears, but it makes no difference. My mind is racing with everything that's happened and I can't get comfortable.

Millie finally comes in at just before 4 a.m. She crashes around the bedroom, swearing and apologising. I turn the light on and explain that I'm not asleep anyway, so she might as well see what's she's doing.

'Soz,' she says. 'Oh, wow, you missed a great night.'

'Are you working tomorrow?' I ask, as she removes her clothes and tosses them on the floor.

'Nah. Day off.'

'*I* am. I've got to meet Vasilis in four hours.'

'Yeah, of course, sorry . . . Go back to sleep.'

Back to sleep? I haven't been asleep at all yet. If every night is like this, there's going to be trouble . . .

Somehow, I manage to drift off shortly after Millie gets into bed. I set my alarm for seven-fifteen and drag myself up. After a quick shower, I choose my most sensible clothes to wear – a pair of loose linen trousers and a plain T-shirt – and make my way through the dead, silent streets to the car park. Vasilis is waiting for me. We exchange *kalimera*s, and he drives me straight to the club.

You can do this, I tell myself, as we pull up outside. *Just stay calm and act professional.*

Christakis is already there, looking freshly showered and shaved. 'Come, let's have breakfast,' he says. We sit at a table outside on the terrace. The air is cool, and the sun is behind us. He disappears inside, then returns, carrying a tablet. 'Phaedra will bring it out to us in a few moments.'

He stands the tablet between us and opens a calendar. 'Our next wedding is on Sunday the thirteenth of July. That's ten days away, so you have plenty of time for preparing. Everything is already organised, so don't worry. Despina will be there to help you.'

I study the schedule on the screen, breathing in sharply as I see how many dates are blocked off for weddings in August. Hopefully by then, I'll have worked out what I'm supposed to be doing.

'Despina has been covering well, but she'll be very pleased to hand over to you,' Christakis adds.

'Was somebody else doing the job before me, then?' I ask, trying to sound innocent. Ever since Millie told me about Lana, I've been wondering why she was sacked.

A shadow crosses Christakis's face. 'Yes,' he replies. 'She left a month ago.'

'Why?'

'She lied to us and betrayed our family.' His expression hardens.

'Oh! That sounds serious. What exactly did she—'

He cuts in immediately. 'The situation was dealt with, that's all you need to know. Please don't mention it to my father. He was very upset and finds it hard to forgive.'

'Of course. Sorry, I didn't mean—'

'Let's move on, yes? There's a lot to get through.' He forces a smile, but I can tell that he's irritated.

'Yes, of course,' I say hurriedly.

'Destination weddings are a very important part of the Greek tourist industry these days. Last year over four hundred took place on the island. Club Inios Sunset is in a wonderful spot – we have the views, the beach, the private jetty, the amphitheatre – but we can't offer accommodation. Wedding parties have to stay overnight elsewhere, which is not so good. Luckily, we have a solution.'

'You're building a hotel nearby?'

'No, better. We're developing a brand-new resort in the south of the island, able to take up to five hundred guests.' Christakis's eyes start to shine. 'The land has belonged to our family for a long time. It was my grandfather's dream, but he died some years ago. Now my father is making it a reality.'

'Sounds like a huge project.'

He nods. 'Klimeni will bring new business to the island and create many more jobs.'

An older lady carries a tray to our table and lays it down. 'Excuse me,' she says quietly.

'Thanks, Phaedra,' says Christakis. 'This is Juno, our new wedding coordinator.'

'Pleased to meet you,' she mumbles as she lays my

breakfast in front of me – a jug of coffee, a plate of pastries, a bowl of yogurt topped with walnuts and a swirl of honey, little pots of jam, hard-boiled eggs, slices of ham and salami, fresh figs, and a glass of orange juice.

'Thank you, thank you, it looks delicious.'

'You are welcome,' she replies, scurrying away like a mouse.

'Despina will be here shortly,' Christakis continues, pouring the coffee. 'She'll explain the job to you in detail. If you have any questions, please just ask.'

I have hundreds of questions, but Estelle's warnings echo in my head.

They must NOT find out who you are.

'No, all good so far,' I say instead.

Despina seems miffed that she wasn't involved in interviewing me. She is welcoming enough, but I sense that she's not going to be as easy to please as Christakis. I discover that we're going to be sharing an office too, so I'll have to be on my guard at all times.

She wastes no time with the handover. Unlike Christakis, who does everything on his tablet, she works on paper. There's a different lever-arch file for every element – from menus and flowers to insurance and legal requirements . . .

We've been wading through them in meticulous detail for three hours and my brain is starting to fry. Despina moves from one to the other without a break. She talks quickly in astoundingly good English, keen to offload the information and be done with the whole business.

After Millie's description of Despina as a 'miserable old

bag', I was expecting to meet a dowdy, sullen woman with no dress sense, but my cousin isn't like that at all. She's smart and well groomed, wearing a straight, sleeveless navy shift with an embroidered hem, and white sandals with silver buckles on her feet. Her finger- and toenails are painted pale pink. She's neither slim nor overweight. Her medium-length dark hair is parted to one side and swept behind her ears, revealing a strong jawline. She has brown eyes and a straight nose. Only her mouth shows signs of discontentment: thin lips set in a straight line.

'If the couple insists on having their legal ceremony here, it's possible, you don't have to be a resident,' Despina explains. 'Civil weddings take place in the town hall, and they can also marry in church. Everything is conducted in Greek, so they'll need an interpreter. There's also a lot of paperwork to complete in advance – documents have to be translated and verified legally. We can help with this, but it makes a lot more work for me because you don't speak or write Greek.'

'No, sorry. Perhaps I could learn—'

Despina sweeps that idea aside with her hand. 'Over ninety per cent of our clients are foreigners, sixty per cent are from the UK. Try to persuade them to marry legally in their own country first, then have their ceremony here with friends and family. It's much easier, and more personal.'

'And is that what most couples do – marry at home?'

'Yes. They start off wanting to do the whole thing here, like they're in *Mamma Mia!*, then they give up.'

I laugh. 'How come you speak such fantastic English?'

'I've been speaking it since I was a child,' Despina replies with a shrug. 'If you want to succeed in the tourist industry, you have to be able to speak good English.'

'Did you study it at university?'

She stiffens. 'No. I would have liked to, but it wasn't possible.'

'Oh. Why not?'

'It was not allowed. I was needed here.' She shuts the legal file with a bang, drawing that line of conversation to a close. 'I think that's enough for now. I have a lot of other work to do. When you want to eat, just go to the restaurant and tell them you're staff. I suggest you spend the afternoon going through the files again. Tomorrow some potential clients are visiting, so you need to be "up to speed", as you say.'

I spend the afternoon doing as she suggested and setting up a database of contacts, rather than a paper record. Then I go through every detail of the next wedding, making a long list of things to query or check. It's far more complicated than I'd realised – there's so much that can go wrong. Bluffing my way through the job interview was easy, but now I've actually got to deliver the goods. I can't let the bridal couple down. My marriage may have ended in failure, but I still want to give them the happiest day of their lives.

The time flies by and before I know it, it's five o'clock. My head is spinning, and I've had enough of being stuck inside all day, especially when the weather is so glorious and most people are on the beach. I put the files back on the shelf and shut down the computer. Presumably it's okay to go now, I don't need to ask permission or tell anyone . . . I guess I just ask for a lift back to Chora.

Luckily, I bump into Christakis on the way out. 'Have you had a good day?' he asks.

'Yes, thanks,' I reply. 'There's a lot to take in, but I'm getting there.'

'Great! I expect you'd like to go back to your apartment now, yes? I'll get Vasilis to take you.'

'Thanks.'

'Do you have any plans for this evening?'

'Not really. I haven't explored Chora yet, so I'll probably do that.'

'Don't let Millie take you clubbing,' he says with a slight chuckle.

'It's not really my scene,' I reply.

'Just one more thing. Please stay away from the expat bars. The locals support the new project, but some of the foreign residents have fought against it and tried to have it stopped.' He huffs. 'Anyway, we won the battle. We have all the permissions now and are ready to start the groundworks, but they could still cause problems for us.'

'Don't worry, I'm not interested in local politics,' I say. 'I'm just here to do the job.'

Christakis gives me a very serious look. 'We expect total loyalty from all our staff. You are one of us now.'

Yes. More than he realises.

Chapter Eight: July 1984

ESTELLE

It only took a few days for Estelle to slot into the established Inios routine. She went to bed at around 4 a.m. and slept in until eleven, when she woke with a raging thirst and a headache. After rousing Angela, the two of them would walk back up to Chora, where there were several cafes serving the necessary caffeine, vitamin C and carbohydrates. After breakfast, they strolled down to the beach where they stayed for the rest of the day, sunbathing, swimming and hanging out at the Outta Sight, where the food was cheap, the booze cheaper and where they played the Smiths, Talking Heads, R.E.M, the B52s ... Later in life, she wouldn't hear that music without remembering the intense retsina drinking competitions – known locally as slammers. Estelle did her best to compete but was staggered by some people's capacity for alcohol.

By late afternoon, she and Angela had usually had enough of the unrelenting heat. Rolling up their beach mats, they would make the long, weary climb back up the path to their room. They'd stand in the yard and throw buckets of water over each other to rinse off the sand and salt – but only when their hosts weren't looking, as there was a severe shortage of water on the island. Then they'd put on fresh clothes and walk into Chora, gathering in the lower square to drink yet more retsina before heading off to Sunset Bar.

It claimed to be the best place to watch the sunset in the whole of Inios and was 'the thing to do' at the end of the day. Like the Outta Sight, the bar was basic and self-service. If you couldn't squeeze around the plastic tables, you could sit on the rocks or the beanbags that were strewn about. As the sun went down, the owner – known affectionately as Babá Yannis – played classical music through tinny speakers, and it was the custom to stop talking and watch the horizon. The quiet didn't last long. Once it was dark, the music returned to rock classics and most people drifted back to the village for something to eat, to continue with their bar crawl or to head for one of the discos. But a few stayed behind.

Usually, Estelle and Angela followed the crowd back to Chora, but tonight Estelle felt like staying put for a change, to see what the rest of the evening here might offer.

'But why?' asked Angela when she suggested it.

'I'm a bit tired,' Estelle confessed. 'All that walking up and down . . .'

Angela shrugged. 'That's how it is here. No pain, no gain, as Jane Fonda would say.'

'I've come for a holiday, not a workout.'

'But we promised the Barking boys we'd see them at All Right Now. And remember those gorgeous Dutch lads we met at the Outta Sight earlier? They made a point of asking us if we were going to be at Paradise later.' Angela knew the names of all the bars, how to get to them, the price of the drinks, the type of music, which ones were favoured by which nationalities. Although, to be fair, everyone mixed very happily. Earlier, Estelle had described Inios (rather wittily, she thought) as Parties Without Frontiers, with a nod to the Peter Gabriel song, and everyone had nodded slowly, as if she'd just said something really deep. The only rivalry you saw was in football matches on the beach – England versus Germany being the hardest fought.

'Please. Let's stay for a bit,' she said. 'I just want to see what it's like.'

Angela pouted. 'Hmm . . . I kind of want to go now.' She glanced around. 'It's pretty obvious nothing much is happening here.'

It was the first time Estelle had felt any tension between them. They'd been living in each other's pockets for over a week, and it had been working well – basically, because Estelle had been happy to go along with her friend's wishes. After all, this was Angela's third summer on Inios, so she knew the place inside-out. She had bags of confidence and wasn't afraid to introduce herself to anyone who looked interesting. They'd already met loads of new people, something Estelle would have found hard to do if she'd been on her own. But she couldn't follow in Angela's shadow all summer. And she was supposed to be island-*hopping*, not staying in the first place she came to.

Angela played restlessly with her empty wine tumbler. Either they needed to move on or get another bottle.

'Tell you what,' said Estelle after an awkward pause. 'Why don't you go on ahead? I'll stay here and meet you somewhere later.'

Angela looked surprised, but she didn't dismiss the idea. 'You sure you'll be alright?' she asked. Instantly, Estelle wondered whether she'd been looking for an opportunity for them to have some time apart.

'Yeah, of course.' She flashed a smile. 'I just want to relax for a bit, catch my breath.'

'Okay.' Angela stood up. 'You know where I'll be. All Right Now then Paradise. Probably. If I'm not in either, try the Irish bar.'

'Will do.'

Angela gave her a final wave, then hurried off into the darkness.

Estelle went up to the counter and ordered an ouzo. She wasn't yet sure whether she liked the stuff – the aniseed was a very particular taste. The waiter poured a shot into a tumbler, then pointed at a jug of water on the side. She diluted the ouzo and watched the water turn cloudy. When she got back to her table, she discovered it had already been taken by a group of four – another disadvantage of being on her own. Feeling flustered, she turned around, looking for somewhere else to sit. A beanbag was lying against the wall. She nabbed it for herself and sat down, tucking her legs beneath her bum.

The beanbag was slightly damp. It was dark here, beyond the scope of the lights that were strung across the terrace. She sipped her ouzo, wincing at the strange taste.

Estelle started to feel disconnected from the scene. Plenty of people were still gathered around the tables which were crowded with empty bottles. Mostly, they were chatting and laughing, smoking Greek cigarettes or skinny roll-ups. A few lads were getting a bit lairy and it looked like a Metaxa drinking competition was going on. At the far end, a group of hippies sat on the rocks, listening to somebody playing Bob Dylan on a guitar. A smell of weed wafted towards Estelle, and she tried to breathe it in, hoping it might relax her. She felt tense. Nobody had made any attempt to come and talk to her, and she didn't feel brave enough to break into one of the groups.

The alcohol was making her maudlin. She began to think about Simon and how much he'd hurt her. She would never go back to him even if he begged, but right now she missed him. There were a lot of single-sex groups here. Most people gave the impression of wanting to play the field, but she wouldn't be surprised if some of them were secretly looking for love. What was *she* looking for?

She swigged back the rest of the ouzo – deciding she definitely didn't like it – and got to her feet. This wasn't working out. She needed to blot out such troubling thoughts, go back to Chora and find Angela. Wherever Angela was, you could guarantee she was having a good time.

Just as she was about to leave, the rock anthems stopped and the music changed again, this time to Greek syrtaki music. Sharp metallic sounds of bouzouki sliced into the night, as insistent as a call to arms. Babá Yannis, a stout man in his fifties who loved mixing with the kids, walked into the centre of the terrace, and stood with arms outstretched, plucking the air with his fingers, stepping from side to side. Once he'd commanded everyone's attention, he began to dance – slowly and hypnotically, lifting his legs and kicking forward, swaying back with a hop, bending his knee then rising just before he hit the ground. A couple of waiters joined in, and as the music increased in speed, the audience clapped to the beat.

People called it Zorba's dance, after the sixties film *Zorba the Greek*. It was an amalgam of various traditional dances and had become popular with tourists. Estelle had 'learned' it a few nights ago when they were at another bar in Chora.

After dancing in a row for a while, the men broke free. They gathered willing participants from the tables and formed a circle with hands on each other's shoulders. It rotated jerkily as people tried to copy the simple dance steps without letting go of each other. Estelle stayed in the shadows, observing, half wanting to be part of it, half wanting to hide.

'Hello, miss.' A young Greek man was standing in front of her, holding out his hand. He was very handsome with large brown eyes, wearing a white shirt, black trousers and, incongruously, a leather Stetson on his head. It looked silly, like fancy dress. She'd been people-watching for about twenty minutes – how had she missed him?

'Please, you like to dance?'

She smiled at him, gratefully. 'Why not?'

He took her by the hand and led her across the terrace, tapping on somebody's shoulder until they broke the circle, then squeezing the two of them in.

It was hot and sweaty facing inward. Everyone was dancing so close they could taste each other's breath. On one side of her was a young woman who kept stumbling over the steps, kicking her in the ankles and bringing the circle close to collapse. Estelle's partner was gripping her shoulder firmly. He kept turning his head to smile at her. Their eyes connected and something inside her started to melt.

As the music sped up, so did the dancers. The Greeks

called out, '*Ela! Ela!* . . . *Opa! Opa!*' and the circle expanded yet again. Now everyone seemed to be dancing, including the hippies. They hurtled around the terrace like an out-of-control Catherine wheel, bumping into tables, tripping over each other's feet, and laughing. The song reached its dizzy climax, then stopped abruptly. Momentum took the circle forward, then it crashed into a wall and broke up. Estelle lost her balance and started to fall, but her partner pulled her up and set her back on her feet.

'You okay?' he asked.

'Yes, fine. That was wild,' she replied breathlessly, looking up at the sky. The stars revolved around her, she felt as if she were still moving.

'It's the same every night.'

'Do you work here?'

He nodded. 'Yes. This is my father's bar. You are English, I think, yes?'

'Yes.'

'What is your name?'

'Estelle.'

'I am Nikolaos. My friends call me Niko.'

She laughed flirtatiously. 'Does that include me?'

'Of course. If you want.'

Later, she would tell people that it was love at first sight.

Chapter Nine: Now

JUNO

Millie is still asleep, one leg sticking out from beneath her sheet. 'Hey, time to get up.' I shake her gently by the shoulders.

After a few seconds, she opens one eye and groans. 'What time is it?'

'Six-thirty.'

'Shut up.' She turns over, burying her head beneath the pillow.

'We've got to be in the car park for seven. It's an eleven-o'clock ceremony, remember? The bride and bridesmaids are arriving at eight for their hair and makeup.' Millie lets out a muffled cry of despair.

'Not fair.'

'What time did you get in – three? Four?' I remember her pulling me from my dreams in the early hours as she stumbled into the room, throwing her clothes onto the floor, and knocking a glass of water off the bedside table. 'Come on. Don't make me late.'

After twenty minutes of nagging, I finally manage to drag her out of the apartment. We hurtle through the cool, empty streets, passing through the lower square just as the church bells chime the hour. The minibus is waiting for us in the car park. We climb in, mumbling a greeting to Vasilis.

Millie immediately leans against the window and closes her eyes, determined to extract a few more minutes of sleep from the journey. In contrast, I sit up straight, running through my mental to-do list for the wedding. It's my first one. Apart from my own, and that's not something I want to think about right now. I've been anxious about it all week, feeling like a fraud and wondering whether I'll be able to pull it off. I've got to act as if I could do the job in my sleep. Fake it till you make it, as they say.

As soon as we arrive, I go to the kitchen. Chef Michalis, Phaedra and two sous-chefs are already busily prepping for the reception. I ask if everything's okay – am told in no uncertain terms that it is – then leave them to it, picking up a pastry on the way out. Making a cup of strong coffee, I take it outside and try to refocus my attention on the day ahead.

The early-morning air is cool, and the patio is in total shade. Everything has already been cleared and cleaned, the paving hosed down, the planters watered. Two waiters are laying the long tables under the pergola at the far end of the terrace, the area usually reserved for private parties. I go over to check that they are using the correct table linen – the bridal couple specifically asked for cream, not white – then go back inside to my office.

The coffee gives me a hit. I lean over the desk and bite into my pastry, careful not to drop greasy flakes onto my shirt. I brush the crumbs and all my troubling thoughts aside. This is two people's special day, something they're going to remember for the rest of their lives. I can't let them down.

*

Despite my fears, the wedding seems to be going really well. I've already received lots of positive comments from the bride's parents, who are footing the bill in traditional style. *Lucky couple*, I think. Millie has worked wonders on the bride, who looks gorgeous in her floaty white dress. The flowers arrived on time and looking fresh, which is no mean feat in the blazing heat, and the photographer has been charming and incredibly patient.

I'm doing my best to appear calm and controlled, but like a swan: I'm frantically paddling under the surface. My deodorant is having to work overtime.

The party has just gone down to the jetty, where a boat, decorated with pink flowers, waits to take them on a short cruise up and down the coast. It's mainly a photo opportunity. I help the bride climb aboard then wave them off.

As I watch the boat disappear around the point, my thoughts drift to my own special day, some seven years ago. A destination wedding it was not. The furthest Luke and I managed was the local registry office, followed by a modest reception in a hotel on the outskirts of town. My dress was a sample from a bridal shop that had recently closed down, and Luke's mother made the cake. We spent a fraction of what today's wedding has cost, but we still had a wonderful time, celebrating until the early hours. A vision of Luke swoops into my head – sweaty face, shirt pulled out, singing along to Ed Sheeran's 'Perfect' as we kissed on the dance floor.

For all the pain we've gone through, I haven't stopped loving him.

My phone buzzes in my pocket. I immediately take it

out, hoping for a second that he's on the other end of the line, magically conjured by my thoughts. But the message isn't from Luke, it's from Estelle.

Are you back in the UK? she writes.

No, I reply. *Still in Inios.*

What??!! I told you to leave.

I'm still looking for Niko. Do you know where he is?

She ignores my question.

Come home. Now. It's important.

No. Not until you explain why.

I can't. You have to trust me.

I tut irritably. Why should I trust her when she's lied to me for most of my life?

I need to do this. Don't worry about me. I'm quite safe.

You're not.

I let her have the last word and put my phone away. I can't allow myself to become distracted by Estelle – or Luke, for that matter. There's too much to do.

I climb back up the steps to the club. The boat will be back soon. I want to make sure the tables are cleared in time for their return, when there will be cake, local speciality cheeses, coffee and liqueurs. The bridal party is moving on for the evening. Despina tried to convince them to stay and party here, but they've booked out one of the nightclubs in Chora instead. It's another reason why Andreas wants to build the resort at Klimeni. Everything else is so far away, guests will have to stay on-site.

Christakis is on the terrace, seated at a table, in deep conversation with an older man.

'Ah! Here she is,' cries Christakis, beckoning me over. 'Juno. Come and meet Andreas, my father.'

I walk towards him, my heart banging in my chest. This is my uncle. I want to throw my arm around him and plant a big fat kiss on his cheek, embrace him tightly as if I'm never going to let him go. But I can't.

Don't tell anyone that you're Niko's daughter. Even if I don't trust Estelle, I can't ignore a warning like that.

For a man in his sixties, Andreas is very handsome – slim with an upright posture. His hair is steely grey, and he has a well-groomed beard. Like Christakis, he's dressed like a businessman in smart trousers and a white shirt – too formal for this heat.

He rises and shakes my hand. I wish it weren't so clammy. I smile weakly as my knees soften beneath me. When I say hello, my voice squeaks. Hopefully, he just thinks I'm a bit nervous of meeting the big boss.

'Welcome to Club Inios Sunset,' he says, smiling back. 'I'm so happy that you've joined us. Christakis tells me that today has gone very well. Congratulations.'

'Thanks, it's been a team effort.'

'You are quite right.' He gestures at an empty chair. 'Please.'

'Um, I'd love to, but there's a few things I need to check—'

'Just a few moments of your time.'

'Okay.' I sit down.

'What made you leave the UK and come to Inios?' he asks.

I can't stop myself blushing. 'Er, no particular reason . . . I just fancied a bit of a change. It's beautiful here, I love it. As soon as I arrived, I felt at home.'

He seems pleased with my reply. 'She looks a little Greek, don't you think, Christakis?'

'Yes, I suppose she does. I hadn't thought of it before.'

'Definitely. I can see it in her face.' He turns to me. 'Do you have Greek blood?'

Suddenly, I feel totally exposed. It's as if Andreas can read my thoughts. I don't know how to respond, not wanting to lie but unable to tell the truth. 'Who knows? Maybe. Way back.' I laugh awkwardly.

'I'm certain of it!' His deep brown eyes – so like my own – radiate warmth and acceptance. 'We are lucky to find you. Despina and Christakis tell me you are doing an excellent job.'

'Thanks.'

He leans forward and dips his voice, even though there is nobody else nearby. 'Now. There's something I have to talk to you about.'

'Oh?' I scan his face nervously for clues.

'We are having a celebration here in August, a few weeks

away. Most elements are already organised, but we'd like you to be the coordinator.'

'Er, yes, of course,' I reply quickly. 'What are you celebrating – somebody's birthday?'

'No, but that's a good cover story. I think we should use it.' Andreas nods at his son.

'It's to mark the start of construction of our new resort,' explains Christakis. 'We're inviting the press, media influencers and a few celebrities, our investors, the mayor, and of course our friends.'

'It's been a big struggle, but we've made it,' adds Andreas. 'I want to celebrate our success and tell the world.'

'Okay. If you give me all the details, I'll get started on it,' I say, already stressed about the thought of managing another event when I have no experience.

'Wonderful.' Andreas beams. 'Despina said you would be enthusiastic to help.'

'There's something important you must know.' Christakis gives me a studied look. 'We need to keep the party a close secret. There mustn't be any protests, or any other trouble. It would be very bad PR and could even put off our investors. In particular, nobody from Stop Klimeni must find out about it.'

I frown. 'Stop Klimeni? What's that?'

'Expats led by that troublemaker Kevin Casey,' Andreas says. 'Most of them don't even live here all year round. They say they are saving Inios. Huh! *We* are saving Inios, not them!' He bangs his fist on the table. 'They're living in the past. But we are giving the island a future!'

Christakis says something quietly in Greek to his father,

then turns back to me. 'It's a campaign group,' he explains. 'They've been trying to stop the development for years.'

'Why?'

'They claim we're destroying the natural environment, but it's not true.'

Andreas wipes his face with a linen handkerchief. 'I'm sorry. My son tells me I get too angry. But you see, these people don't understand. Inios is *our* island, our ancestors have been here for hundreds of years. The life is very hard. There is no farming or fishing anymore, tourism is all we have. Others have run away, but I've stayed here. I've worked all my life to support my family and bring prosperity to the island. I love Inios far more than any of these – *pff!* – crazy eco-activists.'

'Yes, she understands,' says Christakis gently. 'She's on our side.' He looks at me. 'We're putting all our trust in you, Juno. This party is very important. Nothing, and I mean nothing, must go wrong.'

Chapter Ten: August 1984

ESTELLE

Dear Mum and Dad,

I hope my letters and postcards are reaching you. I'm sorry I haven't managed to call yet. There's only one phone on the whole island that visitors can use. It's in the post office. You have to queue for ages. Some people sleep on the pavement so they can be the first in line when it opens in the morning! I managed to get to the front a few days ago but when I rang, I couldn't get through. The line was down for some reason. This happens a lot!

I was supposed to be island-hopping, but now I have decided to stay on Inios for the whole summer. Mainly because I've met a gorgeous Greek chap called Niko. He's a waiter at Sunset Bar, one of the most popular places on the island. His dad is the owner, everyone calls him Babá (which means 'Daddy' in Greek) Yannis. He has a brother called Andreas who works there too. Niko speaks very good English and I now know a few words of Greek. You'll be pleased to hear that he's way more romantic than Simon ever was. I feel like he really cares about me.

My friend Angela has also got a Greek boyfriend! His name is Stamatius, and his family owns a taverna down at the port. He and Niko both work very long hours, so we don't get to spend much time with them.

The island is extremely beautiful, although I haven't seen much of it yet. There are no proper roads like in the UK. Most locals walk or go by donkey, like in the old days. A bus takes people to the port, Kalapos beach and Chora, but it's always packed and never on time, so Angela and I usually don't bother with it. We are getting to know the locals. There's an Irish bloke called Kev, who runs a bar called All Right Now – he's a little older than me and the only expat who lives here all year round. He is quite a character and loves mixing with the backpackers. We end up in his bar most evenings and always have a laugh. Kev has an old army truck – one of only a few vehicles on the whole island. Nobody knows how he got it here!

I'm very tanned now. Feeling a lot happier than I was and I'm staying put, so please don't worry if I don't manage to call or if the post takes ages to arrive. I'm fine! Very happy. Hope you both are well, etc., etc. See you in September!

Lots of love, Estelle xx

Chapter Eleven: Now

JUNO

'*Kalinychta*, Vasilis!' Millie closes the door of the minibus with an enthusiastic slam. It sweeps around in a circle and drives away. 'Phew, glad that's over,' she says to me.

'Me too.'

'I don't know why you were so nervous. Everything went like a dream.'

'Thanks. The bride and groom seemed pleased anyway. And Despina only told me off a couple of times, so I think I did okay.'

'You were brilliant. We need to get smashed,' she says, grabbing my arm. 'Celebrate your triumph.'

'It's a bit late, isn't it? We've both got work in the morning.'

'Who cares? You've been here nearly two weeks, and you haven't gone out drinking once! What's the point of coming to Inios if you're never going to party? Come on, one drink won't hurt you.'

'Honestly, I think I should just go back to the apartment.'

She stops and stares at me. 'Are you alright, Juno? Is something wrong? Issues with your ex?'

'He's not my ex,' I protest. 'We've not split up – we're just taking some time out.' She frowns like she doesn't believe me. 'I'm tired, that's all. I *will* come out with you, promise. When it's my day off.'

'Okay. Whatever,' she says, clearly a little offended.

'It's not that I don't want to go out with you . . . It's just . . . My head is in a bit of a whirl right now. I need to calm down.'

'Fine. I'll go find some other friends. See ya later.' She walks off without me.

'Sorry!' I call after her, but she doesn't turn round.

I wait until she disappears from sight, then make my way back to the apartment. I don't want to be a party pooper, but I am genuinely tired. I've also got a lot to process. Meeting Andreas today was overwhelming. He knew instantly that I had some Greek in me. There was an immediate connection between us. It was almost as if he recognised me as part of the family. I wanted to tell him the truth there and then, but Estelle's warning held me back. If I tell Andreas I'm his niece, he might react badly and send me packing. Then I'll have no chance of finding Niko. I've started the deception and I have to continue with it – at least until I've more information. And I've an idea where I might find it.

I go to the dresser and open my drawer, taking out the envelope of correspondence. The main reason I didn't want to go drinking with Millie tonight was because there's something I want to check. I empty the envelope onto the bed, searching for a particular airmail that Estelle wrote to her parents the first summer she was here.

Here it is. I open it up, careful not to tear the thin paper, which is already ragged at the edges.

71

There's an Irish bloke called Kev, who runs a bar called
All Right Now.

Could this be Kevin Casey, the guy from Stop Klimeni,
whom Andreas got so angry about?

I've been told to stay away from him, which makes things
difficult. I don't want to get in trouble with Andreas, but on
the other hand, if this *is* the same guy, I need to talk to him.
He's bound to remember my father. He may know if he's
still alive, and where he's living now.

I put the letters back in the envelope and re-hide them
under my underwear. I don't want Millie to see them. As
much as I like her and could probably trust her, I think it's
better to keep it this way.

It has just gone midnight. I'm tempted to go out and
search the expat bars looking for Kevin Casey, but it would
take a bit of explaining if I bumped into Millie. Also, I
haven't a clue what he looks like. Google might help, I suppose. I whip out my phone and type in his name plus 'Stop
Klimeni Greece'.

The campaign website appears at the top of the results.
It's published in both Greek and English and seems entirely
dedicated to stopping the Klimeni development. There are
bold claims that Andreas Zimiris has lied about the sustainability credentials of the new resort to secure investment
and government funding. The campaigners have under-
taken studies of the flora and fauna in the area and engaged
experts to give their opinions about the threats to its survival. If what they're saying is true, Klimeni is going to do a
lot of damage to the environment, which is worrying.

I move to the 'About Us' section and discover that the Stop Klimeni committee is made up of four older men. Only one is Greek, but he's not an islander. The others are a Norwegian, a Brit and Casey, who's the chair. He's the only one who lives permanently on the island, having run various businesses here over the years, including the All Right Now bar. That clinches it. It's him.

I study Kevin's photo, committing his wild grey hair, piercing eyes and worn features to memory. I need to find out where he drinks. But not tonight. I'm tired and have to get some sleep.

'Ugh! Can't face breakfast,' groans Millie the next morning when we arrive at the club. Her face is pallid, despite her tan, and there are bags under her eyes, which even her makeup can't hide. She goes straight to her Wellbeing Cabana, and I wouldn't be surprised if she has a nap on the treatment table before any clients turn up.

I take my usual cheese pastry from the kitchen, make myself a coffee, then go into the office. Christakis, Despina and I are due to meet with Andreas at ten to talk about the party, giving me a couple of hours to tidy up the paperwork from yesterday's wedding. I also need to start preparing the next one, which takes place in five days' time.

Despina arrives half an hour after me. 'Well done for yesterday,' she says. 'We were all very impressed, especially Andreas. He really likes you. So much, he's convinced you must be Greek!'

I laugh uneasily. 'Yes, he said that to me.'

'You're not, are you?'

'No, I'm half Italian,' I lie.

'Ah, that explains it,' she says. 'I also hear that you've been asked to coordinate the launch party. It's a relief – I thought I was going to have to do everything. As usual.' She sounds resentful. I get the impression that she's continually put upon by the rest of the family. It seems strange that she's not the manager, given that she's older than Christakis, and particularly when she's so capable.

'I'm sure you'd be much better at it, but I'm happy to help.' I pause, trying to think of a way to turn the conversation in a new direction. 'It sounds exciting. Will the rest of the family be there? Aunts and uncles – cousins, perhaps?'

She leaves a beat before answering. 'No. It's a business event. Anyway, there is no other family. Just us.'

'Oh. Really?'

'Yes, really. Why are you so surprised?' She looks at me curiously.

'Well, I suppose I kind of assumed, being Greek, there would be, er, you know, lots of relations . . .' I tail off, suddenly feeling hot.

'That is a stereotype,' she replies briskly. 'We are a small family. Andreas has nobody.'

'Do you mean nobody that's still alive?' I hold my breath, waiting to hear the news that I've been dreading all along: that Niko died years ago.

She fixes me with a stare. 'Why do you ask, Juno?' she says finally.

'No reason,' I bluster. 'Just trying to get my head around the event – how much family, how much business, you know.'

74

'If you must know, Andreas is a lonely child – sorry, *only* child.' My breath catches at the lie. 'We'll go through the guest list at the meeting.' She stands. 'Excuse me, I need some breakfast.'

As soon as she leaves the room, I let out an anxious sigh. That was really uncomfortable. It was as if I'd crossed some invisible line or broken a taboo. I can accept Niko not being invited to the launch event, but why did Despina pretend that he'd never existed? There has to be a reason. I guess Niko fell out with the family a long time ago and they cut ties with each other. Perhaps it had something to do with his relationship with my mother, or the fact that she became pregnant with me. Was that really such a shameful act that it warranted being banished? Is that why Estelle doesn't want me to tell anyone who I am – because she knows they'll reject me? I long to hear the full story, but I don't dare ask Despina any more questions. She already seemed a little suspicious. If she guesses the connection, she might chuck me out.

I sigh. If the Zimirises won't acknowledge Niko's existence, they're not going to acknowledge mine either. Even if they know where he's living now, they're unlikely to want to help me find him. I need to keep my mouth shut. Be patient. Observe and listen. Try to pick up clues.

Despina returns to the office. 'Andreas has postponed our meeting,' she tells me. 'There's an issue with the Klimeni architects and he has to sort it out.'

We spend the rest of the morning in virtual silence. I am nervous to chat, not wanting to raise her suspicions, and she doesn't seem at all interested in chatting. But every so often when I look up from the screen, I see her staring at me.

I take my lunch break outside. The club is busy today. People are lounging on the giant sunbeds, sitting at the pool bar, or eating in the restaurant. Electronic dance music plays through the sound system, but it's not too loud or fast and the atmosphere is relaxed. The clientele is mostly thirty-something couples without kids, people like me and Luke – not that we were ever attracted to adult-only spaces. My thoughts wander to the family holidays we used to dream about – building sandcastles, making up beach games, teaching our children to swim. We would have made such great parents. But I guess some things are not meant to be . . .

Shaking off the sadness, I go to find Millie who is sitting outside the Wellbeing Cabana, flicking through a magazine. She looks bored.

'Nobody wants treatments today,' she says, sighing. 'It's too hot. I told Christakis I might as well go home but he said I had to stay until at least three.' She discards the magazine. 'How about you? Busy?'

'Not massively. I'm trying to get ahead with the weddings because I've got this secret party to arrange now.'

'Oh yeah, I expect I'll get roped into that too.'

'We've got to make sure the Stop Klimeni guys don't wreck it.'

'Andreas hates their guts,' says Millie. 'Apparently, he and Kevin Casey have been enemies for decades.'

'Do you know why?'

'No . . . Competition for the tourist trade? Expats v. Locals? Clash of cultures? I don't know. All Right Now used to have a reputation for drugs . . . Still has, if I'm honest.'

'Where do the Stop Klimeni lot hang out?'

'In the expat bars, mainly. I think they have meetings in the Wild Duck. It's a pub behind the port. Why do you want to know?'

'To make sure I avoid it, that's all.'

'You wouldn't want to go to the Wild Duck, anyway. It's full of old guys drinking lager and talking about the good old days.'

'Sounds grim,' I lie. People talking about the good old days is exactly what I'm looking for.

After a delicious salad, courtesy of Phaedra, I go back to the office and wait impatiently for the day to end. As soon as Despina leaves, I pack up and go to rescue Millie, but she's already left early which suits me. I hitch a lift on the minibus taking day guests back to Chora.

Vasilis pulls up in the car park and everyone gets out. I make as if to walk into the village, but as soon as the minibus disappears round the bend, I turn around and take the old donkey track going down to the port.

It's a beautiful evening. The sun is still in the sky, but its light is softer now. When I reach the harbour, it's as lively as ever. At least one ferry must be due, because the bars are packed with travellers in their going-home clothes, luggage at their sides.

The Wild Duck isn't one of the tavernas in the main square. I walk around the back and eventually find it on a side street next to the ferry coach park. It has a courtyard in the front, where tables and chairs are laid out under a red-and-white-striped awning.

It's obviously an expat haunt. The furniture looks as if

it's come straight out of a British pub and all the signs are in English. A TV screen on the wall by the bar is showing motorsports with the volume turned down, while an old Rod Stewart song blares through the speakers. There's a dartboard too. But crowded it is not. There's a group of white men on the wrong side of middle age drinking Mythos beer, and two couples enjoying happy-hour half-price cocktails, but the rest of the tables are free.

An older guy with straggly hair sits on a bench in the corner, reading a novel and sipping red wine. He's wearing a washed-out black T-shirt that says STOP KLIMENI over a logo of a seabird.

I walk up to the table. 'Excuse me,' I say, clearing my throat nervously. 'Are you Kevin Casey?'

'Indeed. I am the very man,' he replies with mock seriousness. 'And who, may I ask, are you?'

Chapter Twelve: August 1984

ESTELLE

She folded the airmail, licked the gummed seal, and pressed it down. Hopefully, she would remember to put it in the post box this evening when she was in Chora.

It was mid-afternoon and the sun was at its height. The sand was so hot it burned the soles of your feet, and the sea was like a lukewarm bath. She and Angela had escaped the beach, where there was no shade, and were relaxing with the Barking boys under the thatched canopy of the Outta Sight cafeteria. The lads had been there since breakfast and showed no signs of wanting – or being able – to move.

The place was packed with backpackers of all nationalities – drinking, smoking, flirting, playing stupid games . . . It was like being at fifty different parties at once. Every table overflowed with detritus: empty bottles of beer and retsina, dirty plates and cutlery, greasy remains of moussaka, plastic baskets of bread that had dried in the sun . . .

Music blared out through the makeshift sound system, but there were still people strumming guitars or listening to their own stuff on boomboxes. Luckily, the concrete terrace was large and open enough to cope with the cacophony. Estelle didn't mind. It simply added to the anarchic feel-good atmosphere.

'So, you girls are both spoken for,' said Paul. 'The Greeks are hoovering up all the talent. Us Brits have got no chance.'

'Let's be honest, there's no comparison,' replied Angela cheekily. She stretched her legs out and rested her sandy feet on the edge of the table. 'Stamatius is utterly gorgeous.'

'So is Niko,' chimed Estelle.

Paul swigged his umpteenth bottle of lager. 'The Greek girls are gorgeous too, but they keep them behind closed doors.'

'Yeah. Did you hear what happened to Rob here?' said Tony.

Estelle turned to their hippy friend. 'No. What? Come on, spill the beans!'

Rob gave them a sheepish grin. 'Okay ... so ... where we're staying, it's like a farm. We're in an outbuilding, and the family live in the house. The daughter is completely stunning. About our age, maybe a bit younger. Oh my God, you should see her. Those eyes. And her figure ... wow ... Not too curvy, not too skinny ...'

Angela lit a cigarette. 'Okay, we get the picture. Go on.'

'So, I'm in the yard, right?' Rob continued. 'Kostas – that's the farmer – has rigged up a hose and there's a tablecloth hung over the washing line we're supposed to use as a screen. We're only allowed to shower for thirty seconds. If we go over time, Kostas comes running out of the house and tells us to turn the water off.'

'Fair enough,' chipped in Angela. 'Water is short. They have to bring some of it in by boat, you know.'

'Yeah, well, yesterday they went out, so we thought, *Now's our chance to get properly clean.* I haven't actually washed my hair with shampoo in weeks.' The others made a mocking sound. 'Seriously! You have to look after long hair.'

'No shit,' said Angela, flicking her wavy locks. 'Carry on.'

'There I was, stark bollock naked, when the daughter comes charging out of the farmhouse, shouting at me in Greek. I'm still covered in shampoo, so I take no notice. Then she comes round the side of the tablecloth and, of course, gets a shock. I cover my manhood and apologise, in English, obviously. Tony brings me a towel and turns the tap off. Anyway, the girl eventually sees the funny side of it and calms down. We start chatting.'

'In sign language,' interjected Paul.

'Still only wearing a little towel,' added Tony.

'They're getting on well, know what I mean, so we leave them to it and go into Chora.' Paul winked.

'There was nothing dirty about it,' Rob insisted. 'There was this instant connection between us. Hard to explain. How you can feel something even when you can't understand a bloody word each other is saying.'

'I know what you mean,' said Estelle. She'd felt it too with Niko, from the moment she'd set eyes on him.

'Anyway, we're having a nice time, just sitting under a tree, when her folks come back with their shopping. They take one look at us, and all hell breaks loose. They start shouting. I stand up and my towel comes off.'

'Unbelievable!' cried Paul. The three lads convulsed in laughter.

'She's packed off to the house, crying her eyes out. And I run back to the shed.'

'It gets worse!' said Tony. 'Tell 'em, Rob.'

'I'm getting dressed as fast as I can, when a few minutes later, Kostas comes barging into the room and makes it very clear that I have to come with him. He takes me back to the house. Makes me sit down. Then he gets his shotgun out and puts it on the table, right in front of me. Tells me to stay away from his daughter or . . .'

Estelle gasped. 'He'll shoot you?'

'He didn't actually say it but that was the gist.'

'Jesus! That was a bit extreme.'

'I swear he meant it. I was shitting myself.'

Tony nudged his mate in the ribs. 'Trouble is, now Rob's fallen *in lurve*, haven't you, dickhead?'

'Well . . . kind of,' Rob agreed. 'It's stupid, but I can't stop thinking about her. There was a spark between us, I know she felt it too.'

'Nah, forget her mate,' said Paul. 'Unless you want to get your head blown off.'

Later that evening, when Estelle saw Niko at Sunset Bar, she told him about the incident. He didn't seem to think it was at all strange that Rob had been threatened.

'Fathers must protect their daughters,' he said.

'That's archaic,' she replied. 'And sexist.'

Niko shrugged. 'Maybe. But it's our tradition. That girl was wrong to talk to a stranger. A man. And a foreigner, too.'

'That's all it was – talking!'

'If she is ruined, nobody will marry her.'

She turned to Niko. 'So . . . am *I* ruined then?' she asked, teasingly. 'Will nobody want to marry *me*?' She pinned him with her gaze, eyes glittering.

The heat between them was tangible. They'd already had sex several times in the past week – on the beach at night and in her room when Angela was elsewhere with Stamatius. The Greek men were quite open about their affairs with female tourists; the locals didn't seem to disapprove. If anything, it was encouraged, seen as being good for business and a way for young single men to let off steam. Although Estelle knew there was more to her relationship with Niko than that.

'English girls are not the same as Greek girls,' Niko said, stroking her cheek with his finger. 'It's their job to marry and have babies. They cook, clean the house, look after their husbands and children. Always busy – all day, every day, never stop.'

'Sounds horrendous.'

'If you marry a Greek man this is your life.'

She couldn't imagine it. 'Do people ever marry for love?' she asked.

'Of course. If they are both from a good family, then everybody is happy. The bride's family have to pay – you understand? Money, or a business – a shop or a bar, perhaps – or land, so they can build a house. This is very important. Without this, the father won't allow his son to marry.'

She rolled her eyes. Did people still give dowries these days? It all seemed hopelessly old-fashioned.

'I would never put up with that. It makes the woman a commodity, something to trade with.' He couldn't understand what she was saying, choosing to answer – or silence her– with a gentle kiss on the lips.

'You are so beautiful,' he whispered. 'Soon, I finish work.

We go for a walk, yes? There's a special place I want to show you.' She knew what that meant.

He was called away by his father who reprimanded him, no doubt for lingering too long with her. He rushed from table to table, picking up bottles and hurling them into the large bins next to the bar. He cleaned the surfaces with a cursory wipe of his cloth, glancing up at her every so often to make sure she was still there. Every time their eyes met, another part of her succumbed to his charms.

For the rest of the evening, she sat there on her own, drinking too much, feeling lonely and impatient. She was crazy about him, but she was missing out on those bar crawls in Chora, dancing and drinking until the early hours. Angela was at Stamatius's taverna doing the same thing – waiting for a man. Right at this moment, it didn't feel very empowering.

There was no point getting upset about it. They came from different cultures. She didn't want to think about the women he'd had before her or the ones that would inevitably come after, once she went home. It was a delicious holiday romance and she wanted to enjoy every minute of it, for as long as it lasted.

Chapter Thirteen: Now

JUNO

'I'm Juno,' I say. 'Hope you don't mind, only I recognised you from the Stop Klimeni website and—'

'Fame at last,' Kevin quips. 'Pleased to meet you. Sit yourself down.' He drags a chair over and nods at me to take it. 'So, have you come to join our campaign? I can sell you a Stop Klimeni T-shirt if you like. I always carry a supply with me. Three colours, all sizes.' He pats a large leather bag at his feet.

'I'd love one,' I reply, sitting down. 'Only it wouldn't be a very good idea, seeing as how I work at Club Inios Sunset.'

Kevin tweaks his shaggy eyebrows. 'Oh. I see. Interesting ... Are you by any chance the new lady in charge of "destination weddings"?'

'That's right. How did you guess?'

'I had the privilege of knowing your predecessor. Lana. Lovely girl. A committed activist and a fine journalist.'

'She was a *journalist*?'

'Yes, and an undercover one at that. Didn't you know?' I shake my head. 'Oh yes. She found out about our campaign and got in touch, said she wanted to get involved. We told her there was a job going at the club and she wangled herself into it. Genius!'

'Oh, I see. I knew she was sacked, but not why.'

'Well, they wouldn't tell *you*, would they? Sadly, that Christakis fella cottoned on to her after a few weeks and gave her the boot.' He sighs. 'I don't suppose you know where she is now, do you?' I shake my head. 'Only nobody's heard anything from her since she left Inios. The day before, she sent me a message, saying she'd discovered that Andreas had falsified figures in order to get some government grant. She was going to bring me the proof, but she never turned up to our meeting. Next thing I hear, she's been sent packing. I've tried calling, emailing, texting, the lot, but she doesn't answer. She hasn't posted any blogs online either. It's like she's vanished.'

'That is strange,' I admit.

'Maybe she's been threatened . . . or she's too scared . . . I don't know . . . I'm just worried that something might have happened to her.'

'Like what?'

He shrugs. 'I don't trust the Zimirises. Andreas is ruthless.' He offers to buy me a drink and I ask for a glass of white wine.

'My roommate Millie was friends with Lana. I'll ask her if she's been in touch.'

'Would you? I'd appreciate that. She's a good kid. I'd just like to know that she's safe. Her departure left a bit of a hole in our operations,' he continues, altering his tone. 'But now *you're* here! Things are looking up.'

'Oh, no. I'm sorry if I've given you the wrong idea,' I say quickly. 'I mean, I agree with your campaign, and I'd love to help, but I can't. It wouldn't be . . . appropriate. For all kinds of reasons, you understand?'

'Huh. You shouldn't be working for them at all – not if you have any kind of moral compass.' Kevin launches into what sounds like a well-rehearsed speech. 'Andreas Zimiris and his clan are a bunch of hypocrites, pretending to love their precious Inios, when in truth, all they want to do is cash in. The development at Klimeni will be a disaster. The island's infrastructure can't support it. Species of flora and fauna are at risk. The family own the land behind the beach, but not the beach itself – that's public. It will be illegally cut off. Only the rich will be able to access it. Inios is being ruined and the state and our corrupt mayor support it!' He thumps the table, making it wobble. 'It has to be stopped!'

'You're really passionate about it, aren't you?'

'Yes, I am. Not that it does my blood pressure any good. I know I shouldn't get so worked up. It just makes me fucking angry.' He puffs out. 'Sorry for the profanity. I can't help myself.'

'That's alright.'

Our wine arrives and I try not to drink mine in one go.

'So . . .' says Kevin, calming down. 'You don't want a T-shirt and you don't want to spy for us. What *do* you want, Juno?'

I take a deep breath while I think of the best place to start. 'It's a long story.'

'I've nothing else planned for the evening.'

'Okay . . . Am I right in thinking you've lived here a long time?'

He nods. 'Inios has been my home for nearly fifty years. I owned the first expat bar on the island – All Right Now, named after the Free song. You're too young to remember, but it was a big hit back in the seventies.'

'I think I've heard it.'

'I gave the bar up in the nineties – it was too much hassle. The police were always raiding us for drugs. All they wanted was a bung, you know?' He tuts loudly. 'It's been through several owners since then, but they all kept the name – the place is legendary. It's still going, too. Very different to how it was when I ran the joint. Music's crap for a start. It's all shots and Jägerbombs now. And they employ bouncers. I mean, what's that about?' He pauses to drink his second glass of wine. 'Anyway . . . why do you want to know about the good old, bad old days?'

'My mother came here in the eighties,' I begin. 'Her name's Estelle.'

I watch him think, then he shakes his head. 'Estelle. No, sorry. Doesn't ring a bell.'

'Are you sure? She definitely knew you.'

'No . . . Sorry. I wish I could help you, but you're going back a long way. I spent most of the eighties either pissed or stoned, often both. My memory's not what it was.'

'She had a friend called Angela. She stayed on and married a Greek guy.'

His face brightens. 'Oh, yeah, I remember Angela. She got together with Stamatius Papadakis – his family ran Atlantis taverna right next to the ferry terminal. Still do, in fact.'

'I know the place.'

'He died of cancer about ten years ago.'

'Sorry to hear that . . . And what about Angela?' I press hopefully. 'Is she still around?'

'Oh, no, she left decades ago. She tried to fit in, bless her, but the family didn't make it easy. Angie decided she'd rather live in the cold and rain than be bossed about by her mother-in-law and I don't blame her. We kept in touch for a bit. The last I heard she'd remarried and moved to Devon.'

Another dead end, I think. 'My mother's boyfriend was called Niko,' I carry on. 'Niko Zimiris. Do you remember him?'

A dark cloud briefly passes over his face. I sense him weighing his words before he speaks. 'Yes,' he says finally. 'I remember Niko. Andreas's older brother . . . Always wore this stupid leather Stetson like he was some kind of Greek cowboy . . . Why are you asking?'

'Um . . . I'd rather not say,' I mumble.

He pauses to study my Mediterranean looks. 'Oh. I get it. He's your da, isn't he?' I don't reply, but my silence is all the confirmation he needs. 'Wow. That's a turn up for the books. And you're working for the family, too. Does Andreas know who you are?'

I shake my head. 'No, none of them do. I want my father to be the first to find out. Only I can't track him down. I've tried asking a few questions, but the family are behaving as if he doesn't exist. Despina told me Andreas was an only child. Why did she lie about it? I don't understand. My mother lied to me too. I only recently found out my father's identity and that was by accident.'

'By accident? How?'

'I found some letters Estelle wrote to her parents during

that time. They don't tell the whole story, just snippets. I'm trying to join the dots. She mentions you in them – that's why I'm here.'

'Mentions me, does she?' He looks thoughtful.

'Do you know where Niko is now? Does he live on the island?'

Kevin takes another drink, his leathery forehead creasing into a frown. 'No, no . . . I don't know where he is. We weren't friends, didn't mix, you know? He was younger than me. A bit of a rebel, that I do remember. He didn't want to work for the family business, was always off with the girls. Niko Zimiris was one of the *kamakia*. They swaggered around looking for prey, wearing T-shirts with slogans like SO MANY WOMEN – SO LITTLE TIME.'

It's absolutely not the image of my father I've been holding in my mind. '*Kamakia* – what does that mean?'

'Literally, a *kamaki* is a harpoon. That's what they called the young guys who targeted foreign girls to' – he makes inverted commas with his fingers – ' "fall in love with" . . . They'd give her the full romantic treatment, then at the end of her holiday they'd kiss her goodbye, put her on the ferry, and pick the next one off the same boat. It was a conveyor belt of lust.'

'I'm sure there was more to my parents' relationship than that,' I retort. 'It lasted over two summers, at least.'

'Maybe . . . I wouldn't know. Some girls like Angela stayed on after the season ended, but it rarely worked out. Most went home eventually. As for the fellas . . . well, the AIDS epidemic put a stop to their shenanigans. Everyone was too scared to carry on like they used to. They grew up, married local Greek women, had families, became respectable members of their community. The past was swept under the carpet. Forgotten. Never happened.'

'I see . . . And was Andreas a *kamaki* too?'

Kevin laughs. 'Andreas? No. He was the good guy, the apple of his father's eye. All he was interested in was making money. And that hasn't changed.'

'Do you remember when Niko left Inios – or why?'

'Oh, a long time ago. Must be getting on for forty years. I guess he went in search of a better life – must have found it too, because as far as I know, he never came back.'

I feel crushed. 'Somehow, I thought he'd just be here, waiting for me. That it would be easy.'

'Sorry . . . Do you mind my asking if your mother knows you're here?'

'Yes, and she's not at all happy about it. I haven't told her I'm working for the family – she'd go nuts. She told me to come home straightaway.'

'Did she now? Well, I'd listen to her. Sometimes, it's better not to stir things up.' Kevin runs his finger over the rim of his wine glass. 'I'm sorry to be harsh, but the family won't want some bastard kid crawling out of the woodwork. It's embarrassing. They won't accept you. Your mother's probably trying to spare you the rejection.'

'I thought that at first, but now I'm wondering if it's more complicated than that. Something bad happened all those years ago. I need to get to the bottom of it. It's my only chance of tracking Niko down.'

He raises his hand to interrupt. 'Can I give you a piece of advice, Juno? Give up your search. Keep your mouth' – he mimes it – 'zipped. Quit working for those disgusting, cor-rupt people – sorry, but that's the truth of it. And do as your mother says.'

I feel a resistance mounting. 'But I've only just arrived. I've got a job here. Even if I can't find my father, this is still *my* island. I want to explore. I want to get to know my Greek family—'

'No, you don't,' he butts in again. 'I promise you, you really, really don't.' His voice hardens. 'I'm being serious here, Juno. Do not tell Andreas or any of the others who you are. Don't tell *anyone*. Pack in the job and get off this island as soon as you can.' He throws down a few euros for the drinks. 'It's not safe.'

'That's exactly what my mother said.'

'Well, she's right.'

Chapter Fourteen: August 1984

ESTELLE

She squeezed her parents' address onto the right-hand side of the postcard before tucking it into her beach bag. She would send it later, when she was back in Chora. They'd worried about her so much recently, especially after the break-up with Simon, and she wanted them to know she was happy.

This was a proper, grown-up relationship. She was in love with Niko in a way that made her wonder if she'd ever truly loved Simon. He seemed like a pale version of a man in comparison with her Greek lover, who was strong and certain of himself – kind and protective of her too. She loved him for that, although she was aware it didn't sound very feminist. Her university friends would be shocked that she was thinking that way.

She and Niko longed to have some proper time together, but he wasn't allowed a day off from the Sunset Bar. He'd asked but his request had been firmly rejected by his dad. They'd had a row over it, apparently, and Niko had stormed out. He'd come to find her early this morning, banging on the door of her room, much to the annoyance of Angela, who hadn't long come to bed, and the owners, who were working in the yard. Some cross words were exchanged in

Greek. Niko told her to get up and pack a small bag. He was taking her on a trip, he said. Estelle had booked a windsurfing lesson for the afternoon, but she couldn't pass up the opportunity to spend the day with Niko.

They'd set off, walking for hours in the searing heat. There were no roads, only dirt tracks which suddenly disappeared or went off in the wrong direction, forcing them to clamber over dry stone walls and make new paths through scrubland.

Niko had known the way without needing a map, using a few landmarks to guide him. As they'd trudged up and down hill, he'd explained that they were heading for a beautiful beach, near some land where his family had once kept goats. They had a hut there, which had originally been used for sheltering in the winter. It didn't have running water or electricity, but over the years had acquired a few home comforts. Estelle suspected that he was in the habit of taking girls there. Foreign girls, of course, not local ones. But she wasn't going to think about that.

The hut was almost circular, built from thousands of flat stones laid on top of each other. It was small and windowless with a wooden door. In the corner was a raised stone hearth. The only furniture was an upright chair and a single iron bedstead with a thin mattress. It would give them privacy, she thought, but they'd probably be more comfortable sleeping on the beach.

'It's our love shack!' he declared, sitting on the bed. God knows where he'd got that name from. 'Come to me, Estelle.' He held out his arms.

'Later,' she said. 'I'm too hot. Let's swim.'

They left the hut and walked back to the beach.

'What's that?' she asked, pointing to what looked like foundations for a long, thin building.

'My father is building a cafe here,' he replied. 'He'll clear the land behind for a campsite. He wants everyone to come here instead of the Outta Sight.'

'But will they? It's so hard to get to. And the Outta Sight is much closer to Chora, and the port.'

He shrugged. 'I doubt it, but my father won't listen to anyone. I don't care. It's up to him if he wants to waste his money.'

They took off all their clothes and ran into the sea. Estelle floated, but Niko showed off, slicing effortlessly through the water, diving under the surface, then bursting forth like a flying fish. His black hair gleamed in the sunlight, and his skin sparkled with tiny droplets. She couldn't ignore the manliness of him – the broad shoulders and the sprinkling of chest hair.

He swam back to her, lifting her into his arms. Their wet, naked bodies slid against each other. His lips were soft, and his mouth tasted salty. They sank down, making an octopus of their limbs, kissing, and giggling and feeling intensely aroused. It had never been like this with Simon, she thought, as a memory of him briefly flashed into her head. They had only ever made love indoors, in the bedroom of his house-share, with paper-thin walls that had kept her silent and made her put her hand over his mouth every time he climaxed.

Out here, she and Niko could scream and shout as much as they wanted. They could make love in broad daylight – under the cover of water or brazenly on the sand. She'd never felt so free before, so at ease with her body. Without knowing it, this was what she'd been longing for.

'I want to stay here forever,' she said later when they returned to the hut. 'Let's not go back, Niko.'

'*You* can stay,' he replied, 'but I have to go back to work tomorrow. My father will be very angry with me for—What did you call it?'

'Bunking off.'

'Yes. Bunking off.' He smiled at sound of the word. 'This is my first free day for two months.'

She made patterns with her finger on his chest. 'Nobody can keep going like that.'

'My father thinks I can.'

'But you shouldn't have to. You'll burn out.' He looked at her curiously. 'You know, get so exhausted you can't do it anymore.'

He lit a cigarette and lay on his back, puffing smoke at the ceiling, which was made from dry rushes. Estelle snuggled into him to stop her back scraping against the sharp edges of the wall.

'I don't want to do another summer,' he said finally. 'I don't care about the business. My brother can have it.'

'You don't mean that.'

'I do. The Zimirises are goatherders, not businessmen. We've always lived off our animals, and the land. We made cheese, and honey from our beehives. Grew fruit and vegetables, went fishing in our boat. Life wasn't easy, we had very little, but I was a happy child, you know?'

'I can imagine,' she replied. 'The simple life is very appealing. I've often thought about it.'

'Then the foreigners came, and everything changed. It was like an invasion – but a good one! The first summer my father sold watermelons on the beach. He made a bit of cash, and it helped us through the winter. The next year, he bought another donkey and sold bottles of beer, then cheese pies made by my mother. They worked day and night. We took guests into our house. By year three, Babá had saved enough to build Sunset Bar.' He sighed. 'We started working for him when we were eight –just helping out. Andreas loved it, but not me.'

'What did you want to do instead?'

'I don't know. I like plants and animals, but my father never let me study. "What's that got to do with our business?" he'd say. All he cares about is being rich. My brother is the same – he has big, big dreams. Sunset Bar is only the beginning. This winter my father wants to build another bar on the other side of Chora. One day, a hotel . . .' He pulled hard on his cigarette. 'It's too much. I've had enough of Inios. I want to go to UK.'

She laughed at the thought. 'Have you ever been?'

'No. But I know a lot about it. I read books, watch films. I speak to the tourists, ask them questions. My father made me and Andreas learn English – for the business. I hated it, but now I'm glad. I mean it, Estelle. I really want to move to your country.'

Her heart sank. 'No, you don't. It's grey and rainy and people hate their jobs there too. Life's tough if you don't have money. But at least you have the sunshine here, and the beauty.'

'Yes, it is a beautiful place,' he admitted, 'but there's no freedom. No choice.'

She rolled over him, onto the outer edge of the bed. 'What do you mean?'

'I am the oldest. When my father dies, I will take over the bar and be the boss of the family. That's how it works.' He paused to stub out his cigarette, sitting up and clasping his knees with his hands. 'But I don't want to do it. The summer is nothing but work, work, work, every day, never stopping, never sleeping. The winters are boring, they make me crazy. All we do is build and clean and paint. The houses, the bars, hotels, churches, even the streets – everything has to be white. It's the law. Then Easter comes, we open up and start again.' He sighed, drawing her closer. 'I want a different life – do you understand? One day, I'll leave Inios and never come back.'

'Surely you don't want to cut yourself off from your family.'

'I don't care. I need to be free. And now this is possible because I have you.' He turned to her. 'I love you, Estelle.'

She swallowed hard. 'I love you too, honestly I do, but . . . it would be so difficult. I'm only a student, I've still got two years of my course to go. I don't have any money or a place of my own. My parents aren't rich – I'm on a grant. And you couldn't stay indefinitely, you'd need a work visa—'

'We could marry,' he said. 'Then I could stay forever.'

'Marry?' She looked aghast. The thought of marrying Niko, or anyone for that matter, hadn't crossed her mind.

She and her friends agreed that you didn't need a piece of paper to spend your life with someone. Weddings were a waste of money, and so naff – fake virgins in silly white dresses, couples pretending to be religious just so they could marry in a pretty church, and worst of all, the bride promising to obey to the groom.

'I'm not sure that would work,' she said carefully.

'Why not? He turned to face her. 'Don't you love me?'

'Yes, yes, you know I do. I'm crazy about you, silly.' She punched him playfully. 'But we've only known each other a few weeks and—'

'So? This doesn't matter. I know already that you're the woman for me. I want to be with you forever.'

'I want to be with you too, but . . .' *not in England*, she thought, realising in that moment that she was as much in love with the island as she was with Niko. The two things were intertwined and could not be separated. She was smitten with Greece – the friendly people, the sunshine, the warm sea, the incredible beaches, the delicious fruit, the fresh calamari, the ouzo and retsina, even though they tasted rough, and she'd never choose to drink them anywhere else . . .

'But what?' he pressed.

'I don't know . . .' She felt flustered. 'It's a big thing, marriage. And I'm only nineteen. In England, we don't get usually get married that young. Some people don't bother at all anymore. It's no big deal.'

'But if we are married, I can stay in your country.' He gazed at her with eyes full of longing. For what, she wondered – herself or a British passport?

'That's true,' she said, 'but it shouldn't be the reason—'

'The only reason is love, Estelle. We need to be together.'

'Yes,' she replied weakly. 'Maybe I could stay here, and you could tell your father—'

'No. Impossible. I have to escape. We have to go to UK.'

She didn't reply, her mind too busy racing through the consequences of his coming to England. What work would he do, for a start? Be a waiter, work on a building site? The wages would be very low. His spoken English was excellent, but he might struggle to write it. She would probably have to give up her degree to support them both. She'd been thinking about chucking it in at the start of her holiday, but this would be for a different reason. Her parents would be up in arms. It would be too dismal and difficult. Niko would hate the weather. She imagined them shivering under a blanket in some crappy rented flat or waiting ages for the bus in the rain. The romance would dwindle, she knew it. For both of them.

'Maybe we try it, yes?' he said, breaking the silence. 'First, I get a job. Then marry.'

'Maybe,' she replied. 'I'm here until September. There's plenty of time to decide.' She started kissing him, coaxing his mind away from thoughts of the future, and back to the present. Everything she wanted was right here, right now.

Chapter Fifteen: Now

JUNO

After my meeting with Kevin Casey, I leave the port and take a taxi up to Chora. I feel dizzy as I walk back to the apartment, my brain sparking in different directions. I've not even been here for two weeks, but so much has happened it feels likes months. I try to make sense of what I've just heard. Although Kevin didn't remember Estelle, he knew a lot about Niko. He painted quite a negative portrait of him, which I find hard to reconcile with the lovable character I've created in my head. I suppose it was inevitable that my father wouldn't match my expectations, but I'd rather meet the man himself and make up my own mind.

However, it seems increasingly unlikely that I'm going to find him here. Inios is a very small island. Everyone knows everyone else. If Kevin Casey says Niko doesn't live here, he probably doesn't. Unless he's lying to me too . . . But why would he?

I feel more confused than ever. Kevin used the same phrase as Estelle – *It's not safe*. Not safe for whom? Me? I don't pose a threat to anyone. I'm the product of a holiday romance, that's all. I get that my existence might be embarrassing for the family, but that's not going to put me in danger. If they don't accept me, then I'll have to take it on the chin. My mother never wanted me, so I already know what it feels like to be rejected. *That's* when I might call it a day and go home, but not now.

To my surprise, Millie is at the apartment, sitting on the roof terrace drinking beer and vaping.

'What are you doing home so early?' I ask, joining her. 'It's not even midnight.'

She shrugs. 'I was bored. And I needed to do my nails.' She waggles her fingers at me – they are painted glittery blue with white flicks that I guess are meant to look like waves.

She puffs into the night sky. 'Where have you been?'

I hesitate, unsure how much to tell her. 'I went to the port. Just to look around. I went to that expat bar, the Wild Duck, and met a guy called Kevin Casey.' Millie arches her eyebrows. 'Do you know him?'

'Not exactly,' she replies, cautiously. 'I know *of* him. He's the leader of Stop Klimeni, Andreas's mortal enemy. We're not supposed to have anything to do with him.'

'I know, Christakis said.' I sit down on the opposite sofa. 'Kevin told me some interesting things about the Klimeni development . . . Including about Lana. Why didn't you tell me she was an activist?'

She pulls a face. 'Because Andreas told me I'd lose my job if I did. He was really angry about having been set up. Went completely ballistic.'

'How did he find out?'

'Lana got caught photocopying documents in the office.'

'They must have been the documents she was planning to take to Kevin,' I say. 'Proof that Andreas had obtained a government grant by false means.'

Millie shrugs. 'She didn't share the details with me.'

'Did you know she was working undercover?'

'No! She fooled everyone. I didn't have a clue until the day she got fired.'

'Kevin hasn't heard from her since.'

'Nor have I.'

'Have you tried getting in touch?'

'Loads of times, but she doesn't pick up my calls or respond to my messages.'

'Kevin said the same thing. Do you think she's okay?'

'I don't know . . .' She chews her bottom lip. 'They gave her a rough time. It was all very sudden. Christakis told Lana to get out of the apartment, like immediately. I came back from work and all her stuff had gone. She didn't say goodbye properly, just disappeared. For God's sake, don't tell Andreas I told you any of this.'

'Of course, I won't.'

'Steer well clear of Kevin Casey,' she adds. 'He'll try and use you to get at Andreas.'

'Yeah, I will . . .' I nod, now wishing I hadn't admitted I was Niko's daughter. It's given him some power over me. If he finds out that I'm organising this launch party, he could put pressure on me to give him information. I'm going to have to be more careful in future.

'Thank God we've got a day off tomorrow,' says Millie, interrupting my thoughts.

'Gosh, yes, I'd almost forgotten.'

'Any plans?'

'Well, I thought I'd hire a car and explore the island. Want to come?'

Her face lights up. 'Love to!'

'Great. There's a bay I want to check out – apparently it's really gorgeous. We could take a picnic, sunbathe, swim . . .'

'Sounds good to me. I don't care where we go, as long as we don't have to get up at the crack of dawn.'

I manage to drag Millie out of bed by ten the next morning. While she's having a shower, I pack a day bag with swimming stuff, sunscreen, water, snacks and some fruit. I add the envelope of letters and postcards too, secreting them in an inside pocket. I want to compare the old postcard pictures with contemporary views and read accounts of time Estelle spent in certain places while I'm sitting in the very same spot.

We leave the apartment and walk through the quiet, hung-over village, picking up the donkey path at the far end. The walk is downhill, but Millie still moans that we should have taken a taxi to collect the hire car.

I've booked the cheapest vehicle available, an open-topped Suzuki jeep that only comfortably accommodates two passengers. The receptionist gives us a map of the island, hands over the keys, and points us in the direction of the car.

We fling the bags onto the narrow back seat, and climb in. 'So, where to first?' asks Millie, unfolding the map. We study the slim network of roads, mainly concentrated in the north, where the tourist industry is more developed. Only one road goes south, with a few dirt tracks veering off in the direction of monasteries, archaeological sites or famous beaches. At least it will be difficult to get lost.

'I want to go here.' I point to where the road runs out at the island's most southerly tip.

Millie frowns. 'That's where they're building the new resort.'

'I know.'

'I think we should keep well away. If Christakis finds out—'

'It's okay, we won't be doing anything illegal. I just want to see what the place looks like. Before construction starts.'

'Okay,' she replies with a sigh. 'I thought we were going to find somewhere remote and gorgeous to skinny dip.'

'Yeah, we are. In fact, let's do that first. This looks like a good spot.' I point to a bay on the eastern coast.

We leave the port, driving back up towards Chora, taking the road leading east. The sun is nearly at its highest, beating down on us as I navigate the twists and turns of the mountain range that runs like a crooked spine down the island. There are very few other cars about so it's a relatively relaxing drive.

The spot I'm looking for lies only a few kilometres further on, yet it seems to take ages to zig-zag down to it. The tarmacked road comes to an abrupt halt, but I continue along a stony track which eventually opens out to a stunning beach.

'Wow!' says Millie, grabbing her bag and leaping out of the car. 'This is incredible. There's hardly anyone here.'

It's true. There are only two other cars and a quad bike parked under the trees. A couple is sunbathing to the right and there's a group of young people who've set up camp at the far end, where the bay curves round. We drop our stuff under the nearest tree and strip down to our bikinis. Millie immediately runs towards the sea, screaming joyfully as she splashes into the water.

I lay out my towel and sit down. Seeing that Millie is happily swimming, I take out the pack of airmails and post-cards, resting them on my thighs. I take out a letter Estelle sent home, describing a visit to a beach on the east side of the island. She and Niko stayed in a goatherd's hut belong-ing to his family. I don't know if this is the place, but it feels right.

I turn to survey the landscape behind me. There are a few whitewashed buildings scattered about but none of them look like a goatherd's hut. Of course, over forty years have passed. The place has probably been demolished or converted into a luxury Airbnb. I read Estelle's description again. Standing up, I try to work out where the hut might have been, when a sudden gust of wind rips the airmail letter from my fingers.

'No, no!' I cry out in a panic. I start chasing it along the sand, stupidly abandoning the other letters which take flight too. I dance about, catching one or two, but the others con-tinue to evade me. I can't lose the letters – I can't!

Millie, who has just come out of the water, walks up the beach. 'Hey! You okay?' She laughs as I frantically gather the pieces of paper. Bending down, she picks one up with wet fingers. 'What's this?' she asks.

'Please! Help me first!' I shout. 'Then I'll explain.'

Between us, we manage to collect all the letters and cards. While I'm catching my breath, she sits on the sand and sifts through them, mainly looking at the postcards.

'These photos are cool! Kalapos beach looks so different

now . . . so does the port.' She starts reading the messages on the back, 'Who's Estelle?'

'My mother,' I say. 'She came here in the eighties and fell in love with a Greek waiter called Niko.'

She laughs. 'There was a lot of that going on.'

'This was a serious relationship . . . Estelle came back the following year . . . Niko is my father.'

'No way!'

'I've never met him. In fact, I only found out about him from the letters.'

She grins. 'And now you've come to Inios to find him! I get it.'

'Yes. But it turns out he left the island a long time ago.'

'Oh no! What a shame!'

I pause, uncertain whether to tell her the whole story. Can I trust her?

'Millie. If I tell you something, will you promise to keep it a secret?'

'Of course. What is it?'

'Niko's last name is Zimiris.'

Her mouth falls open. 'You're kidding me!'

'No. It's true.'

'Well, you kept that quiet. Amazing!'

'Actually, Niko is Andreas's older brother.'

'What?! That is insane.'

I grab her arm. 'Please don't tell Andreas. Or Christakis or Despina. It's really important.'

'Okay. But why not?'

'Because I haven't told them myself. I might never tell them.'

Her eyebrows shoot up. 'But Andreas is your uncle. Christakis and Despina are your cousins. That's close family. You've *got* to tell them. They might be a bit shocked at first, but they'll be thrilled.'

'Not necessarily. Apparently, the local men aren't too keen on meeting the lovechildren from their wild youth.'

'No? Well, they should be,' she replies indignantly. 'You've got to tell Andreas. He might know where Niko is now.'

'I don't think he does. I tried probing Despina about her aunts and uncles, but she insisted she didn't have any. It's like he never existed.'

'Sounds like there was some big falling-out,' says Millie. 'Maybe it was because he'd got your mother pregnant.'

'It's a possibility. I've tried asking Estelle what happened, but she refuses to tell me. All she says is I should leave the island and come home.'

'Sounds very mysterious,' Millie says, handing the letters back. 'Don't worry, my lips are sealed.'

'Thanks.' I put the correspondence carefully in my bag and fasten the clasp. 'Shall we move on to Klimeni?'

She groans. 'Do we *have* to? It's so lovely here.'

'Please. I want to see the place.'

After a few more protests, Millie agrees to get back into the jeep. We head back west, then turn south and drive for about ten kilometres. The Suzuki bumps along with Millie holding on to the sidebar of the windshield to stop being thrown out. I keep going, praying we won't get a flat tyre. The state of the road has deteriorated, the place is deserted, and there's unlikely to be a phone signal out here.

After a scary couple of kilometres, swerving to avoid pot-holes and large cracks, we arrive at a barrier across the road. The terrain on either side is steep and rocky – it's impossible to drive around it. I stop the car and we get out. We climb over the boulders, carefully picking our way between the clumps of prickly scrubland. To our right is a large area of hilly land surrounded by wire mesh fencing. There's a corrugated-iron container by the fence, daubed with graffiti, including the Stop Klimeni logo. We squeeze through a gap in the fence.

The beach lies ahead of us, a perfect crescent of golden sand. The sea shimmers turquoise at the shore, its colour deepening further out. There are no trees, barely any green at all. The simplicity of it is unbearably beautiful.

The sand is too hot to walk on with bare feet, so we keep our sandals on until we reach the sea.

'It shouldn't be allowed.' I whisper, finally dipping my toes in the cool water. 'I can't bear to think about the damage the resort will cause. However did they manage to get permission?'

'That's easy,' replies Millie. 'Club Inios Sunset hosted the mayor's daughter's wedding about two months ago. It was an incredibly extravagant affair, champagne all the way. Lana was pretty sure Andreas funded the whole thing. The following week, the committee passed the plans. Job done.'

I stare out to sea, feeling emotional. Half of me belongs to this place – I can feel it tugging at me, begging me to save it from destruction. But I understand the need to provide work opportunities and bring more prosperity to the island; everyone knows the Greeks have had it tough these past years. But this area is so beautiful and so unspoilt; turning it into an exclusive resort for the rich ought to be a crime.

I wonder where Lana is now. It's concerning that she's vanished from social media and won't answer calls or emails. Maybe she's lying low, waiting to strike again. Or maybe my family have silenced her.

Chapter Sixteen: August 1984

ESTELLE

Dearest Mum and Dad,

How are you? I hope you're both okay. I'm really sorry I still haven't managed to call. Everything's going well, so there's no need to worry about me at all. In fact, I've never been happier.

Niko and I have just got back from a romantic break on the east side of the island. We were staying in an old goatherd's hut owned by Niko's family not far from the beach. It was very primitive! Niko's grandfather, who was an actual goatherd, used to shelter here during the winter months. It took hours to walk there but it was worth it! There was nobody else there and we had the huge beach to ourselves. It was like paradise.

Niko is so lovely, I'm sure you'd both get on with him. He speaks amazing English too, so there wouldn't be any language barriers. He'd love to visit the UK some-time, although I don't think he'd like the weather much. It's incredibly hot here, you wouldn't believe it. I'm used to it now, but I could do without the mosqui-toes! They bite me to death.

Anyway, got to go now. We're off to All Right Now this evening. Kev – the bar owner – is having a birthday party, so it should be fun. Angela's pestering me to get ready. It's my turn for the garden hose! Hot showers are the only thing I miss. And you two, of course!

Love as always, E xxx

Chapter Seventeen: Now

JUNO

My second wedding takes place today. I've been in the job for two and a half weeks, and I work hard, but I still feel nervous. Despina is supposed to be letting me take the lead, but I know she's going to be watching me like a hawk, poised to swoop down the second there's a problem. And sure enough . . .

'Juno! I need to talk to you,' she says as I step through the door on Saturday morning. 'The florists are already here. They say you told them to set up the floral arch in the amphitheatre. When I last spoke to the clients, they said they wanted to have the ceremony on the beach.'

'Yes, but they changed their minds,' I reply evenly. 'It's because of all the steps. The groom's mum is in a wheelchair, you see. They hadn't realised there was no disabled access.'

'Okay,' Despina tuts. 'But you didn't write it down anywhere.'

'Didn't I? I thought I put it on the schedule.' I call it up on my screen. 'Yes. See, here?' I point at the myriad colour squares.

She makes a hissing sound. 'How was I to know? I printed out my copy last week.'

'The good thing about Google Docs is that we can make

last-minute adjustments,' I say, trying not to sound like I'm telling her off. She glowers at me. 'But . . . er, yes . . . of course, I'll send a separate note around in future.'

'Yes, please,' she says, bristling. 'The florist is waiting, Juno. Please talk to her.'

I apologise again, then rush out to the amphitheatre to reassure everyone that they're in the right place. There's a packed day ahead. According to the schedule, the bride and bridesmaids are arriving at noon for hair and makeup, with the rest of the party assembling at three for drinks and canapes followed by a four o'clock ceremony, then cocktails and photos and a sit-down meal at six. They're also staying on for the evening, with a DJ and dancing around the pool until midnight.

I hardly slept last night – the partying in the streets was the loudest I've heard since I've been here, and there was so much going round in my head I couldn't relax. I stifle another yawn and head for the coffee machine.

I'm so busy that the morning whizzes by and it's twelve o'clock before I've caught my breath. Millie and I stand in the car park, waiting to greet the bride and her bridesmaids. Annoyingly, they're fifteen minutes late.

'Has Christakis spoken to you yet?' Millie asks, keeping her voice low.

'Only about the seating arrangements for this afternoon. Why?'

'He came into the Wellbeing Cabana first thing and asked how we'd enjoyed our day off.'

'Sounds like he was just making conversation.'

'No, he was testing me. He asked me what we did.'

'What did you say?'

'That you'd hired a car so we could explore the island.'

'Nothing wrong with that.'

'Except he already knew. Because later on, he commented on how there wasn't much room in the back of those Suzuki jeeps.' She pauses dramatically. 'I never said it was a Suzuki.'

'It's the cheapest car available, so maybe he just assumed . . .'

'I don't think so, because he also knew we'd gone down to the development. God knows how. I said we went looking for some quiet beaches, and he asked what we thought of the Klimeni site . . . It was like he wanted me to know that he'd been spying on us.'

'Maybe they've got CCTV down there,' I reply, feeling uncomfortable. 'But we weren't trespassing. There was a barrier across the road, but the site was still accessible – just about. And you can get to the beach by boat anyway. They'll never be able to stop that.'

Millie continues. 'Christakis asked me why we'd gone. I said we wanted to see where the new resort was going to be. He asked why we were so interested. Obviously, I didn't mention you'd spoken to Kevin Casey or anything. I just freestyled a bit about it being an amazing spot and how exciting it was for the family and the island. I don't think he bought it. It was really awkward. He told me to stay away unless it was an official site visit. Said it was dangerous.'

'Dangerous?' I echo. 'What did he mean?'

'Because it's a building site, I suppose.'

'It's up to us where we go. It's a public beach, you know.

The family only own the land behind it. I read all about it on the Stop Klimeni website.'

'He's warning us not to get involved,' says Millie. 'I guess he's nervous after being tricked by Lana.'

'Shit ... I thought Despina was a bit off with me this morning. That's probably why. I'm going to have to be careful if I want to speak to Kevin Casey again.'

'Don't risk it.'

'I promised I'd tell him if there was any news about Lana.'

Millie shrugs. 'Well, there isn't, so don't bother.'

'I also want to ask him more about ... ' – I pause, as if there's hidden sound-recording equipment – '*you know who.*' She mouths, *Your dad?* and I nod. 'I'm sure Kevin knows more than he's telling.'

One of the Club Inios Sunset minibuses sweeps into the car park. Vasilis jumps out and slides open the door. Several young women emerge all at once, chatting and giggling, followed by the bride's mother, who looks very flustered.

'Here we go,' says Millie. 'Have a good one. See you on the other side.'

We introduce ourselves then lead the party to the bridal room, where Millie will work her magic and everyone can get changed. I organise some prosecco and snacks, then retire to my office.

Thankfully, Despina has gone to lunch and I'm alone. I sit at my desk, still fuming about what Christakis said to Millie. I haven't stopped thinking about Klimeni since our visit. It had a huge impact on me. I felt as if I knew the place intimately and had been going there my whole life, as if it belonged to me in some way. It sickens me to think of bulldozers digging into the majestic sandstone cliffs, ripping up the land, contaminating the beach. The Zimirises' PR material makes extravagant claims about sustainability and working in harmony with the environment, but all I can imagine is wanton destruction. And now I know my uncle paid for the mayor's daughter's wedding to secure planning permission, I feel increasingly uneasy about his way of doing business.

I check my inbox and see that more guests have RSVPed to the launch party. Nearly all positively. I wish I weren't involved, but Andreas has got it into his head that I'm some kind of event expert.

The party has been planned for months and no expense is being spared. Local dignitaries and potential suppliers have been invited, and a Greek pop singer, who topped the charts a couple of decades ago, will be performing in the amphitheatre as the sun goes down. But the most important guests are coming from Athens and beyond, including the UK and Australia – luxury tour operators, destination-wedding companies, travel, lifestyle and environmental journalists, and the all-important influencers. The investors will be here too, but I'm not allowed to have contact with them.

The party is not just about celebrating the start of construction; it's about telling the Klimeni story in the way the family want it to be told. And more importantly, it's about gathering supporters for the future and winning the social media war. The right posts by the right people could make Klimeni the top wedding destination in Greece, if not Europe. Kevin Casey would love to be able to reach the guest list and give them an alternative version of the truth.

If Andreas was to be exposed as a green-washer, prepared to sacrifice his island to make huge profits for himself, the resort could fail before it's even been built. The environmental tragedy *could* be stopped . . .

Perhaps I should join forces with Stop Klimeni, picking up the baton dropped by Lana? I know details about the event that would be incredibly useful to anyone wanting to mount a protest. It's kind of tempting, and yet . . .

I would be betraying my own family.

I was so keen to be a Zimiris, but now I'm not so sure. Maybe I should keep out of current matters. I need to keep reminding myself that I came here to find my father. That's still my priority. I can't lose sight of it.

The wedding goes on until late and it's gone midnight before we collapse into the minibus to take us home. I want to doze, but Millie chatters on in her usual way, recounting the highs and lows of the day, complaining about the bride who was unhappy with her hair and demanded that Millie redo it twice.

'It was her fault for being late. And she didn't have enough length for the style she wanted,' she explains indignantly. I listen, nodding and making appropriate noises when necessary.

As soon as Vasilis drops us off, Millie continues on the same theme. 'The bride complained to Christakis, you know. It's so unfair. He's already on my case about not persuading enough day guests to have treatments. You can't force people to have a massage!'

We walk back to the apartment, squeezing past the

sweaty partygoers who throng the lower and upper squares, not to mention all the alleyways that connect them. The clubs are open now, their competing music blasting into the atmosphere. We step over a few drunken lads sprawled on the steps of a bakery, and Millie almost gets swept away by a group of hens.

'Don't do it!' she calls out after the girl with a net curtain pinned to her head. 'It costs a fortune, and you'll only get divorced!' She turns to me. 'Sorry. That was really insensitive. Me and my big mouth.'

'It's fine,' I tell her. 'I'm not getting divorced . . . Not yet anyway.'

'Right . . .' She looks at me sceptically. 'So, what *is* going on between you and your husband? You're here, he's there. You're not planning to go home any time soon. He's not coming here. You've hardly mentioned him. I don't even know his name.'

'It's Luke,' I reply. 'And to be honest, Millie, I don't know what's going on. He's really upset, keeps sending me messages, trying to phone. I'm ignoring him, which I feel bad about but . . .' I sigh. 'I'm confused . . . I need this time apart. It's a huge relief to be on my own, not trying to make babies all the time, or wondering whether I'm pregnant—'

'Oh,' she says. 'I'm so sorry.'

'We've been trying for over two years. It's been incredibly stressful, really damaged our relationship. Luke wants to keep going – he doesn't understand what it's doing to me. I reached my limit and had to get away. But now I'm here, I miss him. I still love him, but I'm not sure I can go back if . . .' The rest of my sentence disintegrates in tears.

119

'Oh, Juno.' She gives me a spontaneous hug, crushing my ribcage. 'I'm so sorry. It must be awful. If there's anything I can do . . .'

'I'm okay,' I say, struggling to breathe. 'Just need to sort myself out.'

We walk on, arm-in-arm. It feels like our friendship has taken a leap forward. A problem shared is a problem halved, as they say. I'm not sure that's true, but being more open with Millie has already made me feel a lot less alone.

She unlocks the door and lets us in to the apartment. The place is tiny, and I still hate sharing a bedroom, but it feels more and more like home. We grab a bottle of wine from the fridge and some snacks. I'm exhausted but my brain is wired. I need to calm down first to have any chance of falling asleep.

We climb the three flights of steps to the roof terrace, using our phones as torches. Once at the top, I switch on the string of fairy lights and throw my bag onto one of the sofas. It's only as my eyes adjust to the darkness that I notice there's a small bouquet of wildflowers wrapped in newspaper lying on the coffee table.

'Is that yours?' I ask. Millie shakes her head. 'How did it get here?'

'I don't know.'

'Someone must have got into the apartment.'

'Not necessarily. There's a fire escape across the way. They could have used that and climbed over next door's wall.' She picks up the bouquet, removing a small envelope that's tucked inside the wrapping. 'It's for you,' she says, handing it over. 'Look, it's got your name on it.'

I tear open the envelope, squinting as I try to read the typed message on the card inside.

'Read it out.'

I clear my throat.

'Juno, my dear.

I know you are here and why you have come. I would like to meet but they are watching you all the time. I will try to find a chance. Don't tell anyone who you are. Please. For all our sakes.

Give my regards to your mother.

With love.'

Chapter Eighteen: August 1984

ESTELLE

Bored with the relentless partying at the Outta Sight, Estelle and Angela went to the beach near the port for a change. The sand wasn't so good, but it was quieter. Estelle had finally managed to have her windsurfing lesson. It hadn't been a great success – her upper body wasn't strong enough to haul up the sail and she'd found it hard to balance on the board. The Meltemi wind was too fierce for beginners. She also regretted having her lesson topless. The Norwegian instructor hadn't been able to stop his eyes straying. She was glad Niko hadn't been there, or it might have come to blows.

She hadn't seen him since they'd returned from the love shack. Predictably, he'd had a big falling-out with his father over his skiving off. As punishment, Niko had been given the worst jobs and had been forbidden from socialising after work. He said it would only last for a few days, but in the meantime it would be better if she avoided Sunset Bar. She found it strange that he'd submitted to being grounded so willingly. He was twenty-three, a grown man. Maybe all that talk about leaving his family and coming to the UK had been just that: airing his frustrations, nothing more. If so, she was relieved. She was in love with Niko, but their relationship belonged here, not in damp, dreary England.

She and Angela were drinking in All Right Now. After some serious sampling of other bars, they'd decided this was the best. Kev the owner was very friendly and often slipped them free beers.

'There they are – about bloody time!' cried Angela. Tony and Paul, the Barking boys, were making their way through the throng of drinkers. Angela stood up and waved at them madly. They'd managed to save some stools by hiding them under the table. Estelle pulled them out and they sat down.

'Where's Rob?' she asked.

'Good fucking question,' Tony answered. 'He's gone AWOL. Disappeared. Didn't say goodbye or anything.'

'*And* he owed me five thousand drachmas,' said Paul. 'Bastard . . . What do you girls want?'

'Just a lager,' said Angela. Estelle nodded in agreement, adding a 'thank you'. Paul went off to tackle the crush at the bar.

'So how come he left?' Estelle asked Tony. 'Did you fall out or something?'

'Nah, not at all. He was sound. Seemed a bit lonely, you know, but he cheered up after me and Paul adopted him. I liked the bloke. Bit posh, compared to us—'

'Anyone's posh compared to you,' quipped Angela.

'Hah! You can talk.'

Paul came back with the drinks. 'So, what happened?' pressed Angela.

'Well . . . I think it might have had something to do with the Greek girl,' Paul answered, squeezing onto his stool. 'Remember? Her father threatened him with a shotgun. The stupid idiot has been seeing her on the quiet. Meeting her for secret midnight walks, know what I mean? Me and Tony think they might have been caught because the other night, we heard shouting and screaming coming from the house, like there was some almighty row going on.'

'And now Rob's scarpered,' Tony added. 'We thought maybe he'd got lucky with someone else, but it's been a couple of days now. Nobody's seen him.'

Estelle thought back, trying to remember if she'd seen Rob anywhere, but drew a blank. 'What about his stuff?' she asked.

'Gone. Well . . . most of it.' Tony took out a packet of cigarettes and offered them around. 'He left his sleeping bag and toothbrush, and a couple of T-shirts he'd hung on the washing line.'

'That's odd,' said Angela lighting up. She blew smoke at the low ceiling. The bar was in a cave, long, thin and with no natural lighting. By the end of the evening, the atmosphere was suffocating, and you could hardly see.

'Didn't he leave a note or anything?' Estelle asked.

Tony shook his head. 'We spent most of yesterday searching for him. Not a sign. He's probably on some other island now. I hope he steers clear of the Greek girls in future. Some of them are gorgeous, but . . . it's not worth it.'

They moved to another subject, but Estelle couldn't stop thinking about Rob and wondering whether he was okay. When she'd told Niko that he'd been threatened by the girl's father, he'd seemed to think that it was perfectly reasonable to pull a shotgun on somebody just for chatting to your daughter. But it sounded as if Rob hadn't paid any attention and the relationship had gone further. If that was the case, he *had* been stupid.

Estelle was still worrying about Rob the following morning when she woke up. She needed to know what had happened to him.

Angela was still asleep, her mouth lolling open, ready to catch flies, of which there were plenty. Estelle got up and after rinsing her face and armpits with the hose outside, put on a pair of shorts and the least smelly top she could find. Washing her clothes in cold water with a bar of soap didn't do much. She needed to find a launderette – if such things existed here.

For the first time on the trip, she started to feel homesick. In general, it'd been fantastic mixing with the locals. They were so friendly and welcoming, inviting strangers into their homes, sharing what little they had to eat, going out of their way to help when people fell ill or things went wrong. But get on the wrong side of them and there was clearly hell to pay.

It was hardly surprising, considering the huge differences between British and Greek culture. The Greeks seemed to be a few decades behind in terms of their attitudes to women. A few elderly men walked around wearing traditional dress – collarless shirts and voluminous trousers, small caps on their heads. They wore sandals made from old car tyres because the rough terrain wore out leather soles. And you hardly ever saw a young woman in the street. They were kept at home, out of sight.

Estelle took her towel and bikini off the washing line,

where they'd been drying overnight, and rolled them up. She put them in her tote bag, along with her suntan lotion which was running out. Suddenly, she didn't feel like going to the beach.

She dropped the bag onto the bed. Perhaps she should try to phone home. She'd been putting it off, worried about the questions her parents might ask. Was she eating properly? Was she 'being careful'?, which was code for using contraception. Letters and postcards were much easier, as there was no immediate reply.

Leaving Angela to sleep off her hangover, Estelle trudged up to Chora. There was, predictably, a long queue outside the post office of people waiting to use the public phone. No way was she going to hang around in this heat. She stopped in the lower square for an orange juice and a cheese-and-spinach pie and thought about how she could find Rob.

She decided to try and find the farm where he'd been staying with Tony and Paul. Last night, when they'd parted, almost at this very spot, the lads had gone around the left side of the church, where there was a long path that ran alongside a high drystone wall. She had no idea what lay beyond.

To begin with, Estelle was able to stay in the shade of the wall, but soon found herself in open land, exposed to the sun with no trees or buildings to protect her. The village quickly fizzled out. She carried on walking, uncertain of which direction to take, then saw a dusty track ahead. It curved around the base of the hill and overlooked the plain, which was the most fertile part of the island and the only area where crops would grow. The farm *had* to be nearby.

The path wound round, becoming increasingly stony and narrow in parts. After a couple of hundred yards, it merged with a grove of olive trees. She threaded her way through, looking for signs of life, a building, anything. The earth was dry and rusty, her every step kicked up clouds of dust. How did the lads ever manage to find their way back to the farm in the dark, she wondered, especially when they were drunk?

She stopped to catch her breath and heard the sound of tinkling bells. They played a discordant tune, out of time with each other. Must be goats, she thought, pressing forward, following the noise. Just then, her eyes were distracted by a patch of colour – something was caught in the trees. A piece of clothing. No, it was a bag. Its drawstrings were hanging over a branch and it swayed ominously in the breeze. As it turned, she saw that one side was stained with blood.

Her heart leapt to her throat. She unhooked the bag and opened the strings, thrusting her hand inside to see what it contained. There was a crumpled vest top stained with beer, a small bottle of water, a leather purse stuffed with drachma notes and a few coins, a packet of cigarettes, two lighters and a tatty paperback – *The Name of the Rose* by Umberto Eco – which nearly everyone seemed to be reading this summer. Digging further, her fingers felt a slim hard object, a notebook perhaps? She pulled it out, gasping as she realised it was a British passport.

Her fingers shook as she flicked over the pages. She stared

at the photo of Robert Charles Turner. It was a younger version of the Rob she knew, with short hair and a solemn face. Thoughts raced through her head.

How had the bag ended up here, swinging from a tree? Where had the bloodstains come from? If Rob had needed to escape, why hadn't he taken his passport? It didn't make sense.

Maybe her friend hadn't left the island after all.

Chapter Nineteen: Now

JUNO

'Is the note signed?' asks Millie, standing there open-mouthed, bottle of wine in hand.

'No. They're obviously worried about revealing their identity.'

'The flowers are lovely.' She pauses, unsure whether to carry on. 'They've got to be from your dad, don't you think?'

'I don't know,' I whisper, still in shock.

Could it be Niko? It was the first thought that occurred to me, but I didn't dare utter it aloud. I read the note again. The tone is affectionate. *Juno, my dear.* And the reference to my mother is particularly touching. Slightly old-fashioned too, suggesting the writer is an older person. The English is perfect, but that doesn't mean much these days – there are plenty of good translation apps they could have used. But if this *is* from my father, how come he knows I'm here? Somebody must have told him.

'I need that drink,' I say, collapsing onto the sofa. Millie pours me a glass and hands it over, then sits next to me and picks up the card.

'It's great that he wants to meet you,' she says.

'*If* it's him.'

'It's *got* to be him.'

'What does it mean, "They are watching you all the time"?'

'He must be talking about the family. Vasilis spied on Lana, you know. It wouldn't surprise me one bit if he's following you.'

'But why would he do that?'

'I dunno. In case you're another activist?'

'They don't suspect me of anything like that. Andreas likes me.'

'Doesn't mean he trusts you.'

'I guess not . . .'

'It's not just you. They don't trust *anyone*.'

I look down at the note. 'Whoever sent me this is the third person who's told me not to tell anyone who I am. I don't understand. Why are they so ashamed of me?'

'It's not that,' she says, refilling my glass. 'There's some other reason. To do with the past.'

'I didn't come here looking for trouble,' I insist. 'When I found the letters, it was like everything fell into place. Suddenly, I knew where I came from, where I belonged. All I wanted to do was come here, find my father, get to know him. *And* the rest of my Greek family.'

'And instead, you get all this shit to deal with,' she sympathises.

'Everyone is keeping stuff from me, treating me like a kid – I'm sick of it. I need to know the truth.'

Millie ponders this for a moment. 'Maybe they can't tell you.'

'Someone *has* to. I'm not leaving Inios until they do.'

*

The next couple of weeks go by in a whirlwind of weddings – five, one after the other. I barely have time to think about the note, and yet it's always there in the back of my mind. It must have been from my father – no other possibility makes sense. I feel that he's here. When I walk through Chora on my way to and from work, my eyes dart around looking for him, as if I might see him lurking in a doorway or sitting outside one of the tavernas. Every time I see a Greek man in his sixties, my heart leaps and it's as much as I can do to stop myself accosting him. Then I remember that he's not able to show himself in the street. He'll be hiding somewhere, in another part of the island, away from the rest of the family.

Or maybe all that's a fantasy and the note was from someone else. But I can't think of anyone who would want to play a mean trick on me like that. The only people on Inios who know about my search for Niko are Millie and Kevin, and they would never do such a thing – would they?

Meanwhile, I have a job to do. My world is a blur of white dresses, waistcoats and rose petals. I hear the clink of champagne glasses and the laughter of strangers in my sleep. On top of this, I have to do lots of work for the launch party.

Keeping the event a secret is proving to be very difficult. Signs are up to say that the club will be closed for three days next week, which apparently is unheard of. Everything is being deep-cleaned and the gardens are undergoing a make-over. We've hired projection screens and display panels for the presentations. I've booked helicopter transfers from Santorini for the VIPs, who are going to be whisked in and out of Inios with no chance of bumping into any locals. Site tours will take place during the afternoon, followed by an early evening reception at the club, with presentations by the architects and a speech from Andreas. A state-of-the art sound system has been hired for the pop singer's live performance, and a pyrotechnic company is mounting a firework display to round off the event. It really is extraordinary. There's more fuss being made than for any of the weddings I've seen here so far.

The family have plenty of local allies who are cheerfully pretending that it's a birthday party for Andreas, but I wouldn't be surprised if the news has leaked to Kevin and his campaigners. I need to talk to him again, but the family are hyper-sensitive at the moment, so I can't risk being spotted. It'll have to wait until after the party.

On Friday afternoon, Christakis walks into the office, looking very excited. 'Ah, Juno,' he says. 'The architect's model has arrived.' He calls out to a couple of delivery men who push some large wheeled silver cases into the room. 'We have to store it somewhere out of sight. Don't let anyone open the cases. If anyone asks what's inside, make up a story.'

'Nobody ever comes in here,' I tell him.

'I know, but Vasilis tells me there are rumours flying around in the village. You're sure you haven't told anyone?'

'Of course not.'

'Sorry. My father is so worried about the protestors, it's making us all nervous. The groundworks started yesterday. Babá put the first spade in the ground. Not that they're using spades to dig!' he laughs. 'It was symbolic. I must show you the photos. The whole family went down to see it.'

Not the whole *family,* I say to myself. *What about my father? What about me?*

Christakis sweeps out on some new mission. I stay at my desk, my thoughts drawn back to my visit to Klimeni, walking along that pristine beach with its golden sand, the sea sparkling turquoise in the shallows. I remember the rugged cliffs that towered above the bay, providing a safe haven for seabirds, who no doubt will have already been scared away by the noise of the machinery. Soon there will be 'luxury suites' set into the rockface, with plunge pools and mini terraces, linked by winding steps. They're going to plant hundreds of palm trees, even though they don't grow naturally on Inios, and may negatively affect local species. I wish there was something I could do, but I can't. Besides, I have my own issues to deal with.

At the end of the day, I go to collect Millie from the Wellbeing Cabana. As I arrive, a young woman emerges looking rather dazed, her bikini slightly askew, skin shiny with oil.

'Alright if I come in?' I ask. Millie opens the door and I enter the hut, which is lit by numerous scented candles. The air is thick with aromatic oils – sandalwood, lavender, bergamot, ylang-ylang.

'Hi. Everything okay?' Millie asks, removing a long strip of paper from the massage table and screwing it into a ball.

'Just about. Are you done?'

'Yes, thank God,' she replies, instantly removing her plastic apron. 'I've hardly been outside today.'

Vasilis drives us back to Chora. 'Don't get drunk tonight,' he says as we jump out of the minibus. 'No talking to expats.

Stay away from the Wild Duck, yes?' I slide the door shut with a slam, pretending not to have heard.

'Fucking cheek,' mutters Millie as we walk away.

'That confirms it,' I say. 'Vasilis *has* been watching me. He must know I talked to Kevin Casey.'

'They don't trust any of us since the fuss with Lana.'

'It's so frustrating. There's no way Niko's going to show his face with Vasilis sneaking around.'

We carry on through the lower square, making our way through the coloured chairs and tables and taking the small alleyway on our right. When I first arrived, I kept getting lost, but the route is so familiar to me now I could do it blindfolded. We climb the hill, passing the gift shops and restaurants with their twinkling lights. The tourists seem be out in force tonight. When we reach the main square, which is about halfway up, the place is packed, standing room only.

'Juno!'

My heart jolts. I swing round in search of the man who's just called out my name. Who is it? Could it even be . . . ?

But no, it's not my father. It's Kevin. He leans against a wall, wearing his Stop Klimeni T-shirt and brandishing a bottle of Mythos.

'Haven't seen you around for ages,' he shouts drunkenly. 'Thought you might have taken my advice and got the hell out of Dodge.'

'No, I'm still here,' I say, quietly.

He waves his bottle at Millie. 'I know you – Lana's old roommate. Any news from her? It's been radio silence here.'

'No, nothing,' she mumbles.

134

'Hmm . . . Very strange, don't you think? She's vanished off the face of the earth.'

'I expect she just went back to the UK.' She shoots me an anxious look. 'We need to go,' she whispers.

Kevin changes tack. 'So . . . what's going on at the club?'

I wince inside. 'Nothing. Just the usual.'

'Come on, you can't keep anything quiet in this place,' he laughs. 'Some mysterious boxes came off the ferry this morning. A mate of mine told me you were hiring his sound system. They're closing the place for three days next week. It's got to be something important.'

'Andreas is having a party. For his birthday,' I say.

'Yeah, yeah, I know the story! What's the *truth*? The digging started yesterday, so I'm thinking maybe it's connected. What is it, some PR stunt?'

'No, just a birthday,' replies Millie firmly. 'Sorry, got to go. We're meeting some guys, aren't we Juno?'

I nod. 'You go on. I'll catch you up.' She gives me a warning look. 'It's okay . . . I won't be long.'

Millie carries on up the hill, none too pleased. Kevin tilts his head on one side, curious.

'Got some juicy information for me?'

'No. I can't get involved I already told you that . . .' I leave a beat. 'Somebody sent me some flowers.'

'Don't look at me. You're an attractive woman, but I'm old enough to be your da.'

'There was a note with them. I think it was from Niko.'

He stops. 'Niko? Are you sure?'

'No, but . . . it seems the most likely explanation. Did you tell him I was here?'

He frowns at me. 'Me? How would I do that, now? I don't know where the hell he is.'

'Have you told anyone about me? Other expats, or locals? Andreas even?'

'No. Definitely not.'

'Nobody at Stop Klimeni?'

'I swear to you, Juno, if there's been a leak it hasn't come from yours truly.' He takes a swig of his beer.

'Then how the hell did Niko know?'

'Search me.'

Do I believe him?

'I have to go,' I say.

'Good luck with the party!' he calls after me as I walk off.

I go back to the apartment. Millie is in our bedroom, getting ready to go out.

'We shouldn't have stopped to talk to him,' she complains. 'Vasilis has spies, I'm sure of it. If it gets back to Andreas, we'll be in deep trouble.'

'I'm sorry, but I had to ask him about Niko.'

'And?'

'He swore he has no idea where he lives or anything . . . It's got to be my father that sent me that note. There's no one else it could be.' I sit on the side of the bed, suddenly feeling weary. 'I can't deal with this. It's too much.'

'Come and have a drink with me,' Millie says. 'I'm meeting the windsurfers tonight.'

'No, thanks. I'm not in the mood.'

I feel so powerless. It's as if I've been set a riddle that's impossible to solve. I have to work out why Niko left the island. I need to go through the letters and postcards again and read them with fresh eyes. Maybe there are clues hidden there . . .

The thought revives me. I pull open the top drawer of the dresser and feel around for the hard edge of the envelope beneath all the silky fabric. Not finding it, I grab handfuls of bras, pants and bikinis and toss them all onto the floor. The drawer is empty. The letters and postcards have gone.

Chapter Twenty: August 1984

ESTELLE

Estelle crouched beneath the olive tree, clutching Rob's bag to her chest as she tried to piece a narrative together. He could have staggered back from Chora in a drunken stupor, tripped, and fallen down the hillside. The ground here was firm, but there were other places where it was more slippery, and there were no barriers to save you from the drop. Maybe he'd lost his bag along the way; somebody had found it and hung it on the tree. But that didn't explain why it was stained with blood.

She stood up, slinging the bag over her shoulder, and started to retrace her steps to the village. She had to take it to the police. They needed to mount a proper search. Tony and Paul had spent yesterday looking for Rob in all the obvious places, but the locals would know better where Rob might have fallen. He could be lying in agony, weak and thirsty, unable to cry for help. He could even be . . .

No, she would not let her thoughts stray that far.

Maybe the answer was simpler than that. Rob had been chased off the island by the girl's father and hadn't been given time to collect his things. When he reached Athens, he would have to go to the consulate and explain that he'd lost his passport. They would issue him with a temporary one and he'd be able to borrow money to get home. It would be a hassle, but he'd survive. That sort of thing probably happened all the time.

Yet she still felt uneasy. Rob had been threatened with a shotgun and had taken no notice. Maybe the Greeks carried out their threats . . .

The police station was situated on the other side of the village, away from the shops and bars, and next to the town hall. Neither were grand buildings. The town hall looked as if it might have been somebody's house a while back, and the police station reminded her of a public toilet.

She pushed open the door and went inside. One of the island's two policemen – a young man wearing a beige uniform with military overtones – was sitting with his feet resting on the desk, doodling idly on a pad. Despite his casual pose, he was wearing a gun holster. Estelle went up to the counter and coughed for attention. He looked round, lowered his feet slowly to the floor, and made a great effort to stand.

'Do you speak English?' she asked. He nodded. 'Good. I found this.' She put Rob's bag on the counter. 'It contains a passport.'

'Okay,' he replied wearily, pulling it towards him. Estelle could tell that he was sick of being lost property monitor for the island.

'It belongs to a friend of mine. Rob Turner . . . He's disappeared. Nobody's seen him for two days.'

The policeman looked unimpressed. 'He's gone to another island. Left his passport . . . Happens every week.'

Estelle stood her ground. 'This is different. Rob got into

a bit of trouble with the farmer who owns the rooms he's staying in.'

'He didn't pay?'

'No, nothing like that.' Estelle swallowed, uncertain whether to continue. She didn't want to raise a false alarm, but she had to make this police officer take the matter seriously. 'He was seeing the farmer's daughter,' she carried on. 'You know, secret dates. Her father found out, and then Rob disappeared.' She paused. 'The farmer had a gun.'

'Every farmer has a gun.'

'I'm worried Rob might be hurt. There are bloodstains on the bag – look!'

The officer shrugged. 'Maybe blood. Maybe something else.' He emptied the bag onto the counter and picked up the passport. 'Okay. You can go now.'

'Aren't you even going to ask me who the farmer is?' she replied, her voice rising.

'I keep the passport safe. Your friend can have it when he comes back.'

Estelle leaned over the counter. 'Didn't you understand what I just said? He's gone missing!'

'You don't know this.'

'Not for sure, but the evidence suggests—'

He cut her off, nodding towards the door. 'Good morning, miss.'

Estelle left the police station fuming. The officer had waved her away like an annoying fly. There was no chance that he was going to set up an investigation into her friend's disappearance. Worst of all, she no longer had the bag or

Rob's passport. She wished she'd held on to them; they would have been safer in her hands.

It was late morning, yet Chora was only just coming to life. Holidaymakers were emerging from their rooms in search of hangover cures – greasy breakfasts and thick grainy coffee. She checked out the cafes that the Brits tended to favour just in case Rob was there. He wasn't. She asked around, but nobody seemed to know whom she was talking about. Tony and Paul were not to be found either. She suspected they'd gone down to the beach. Angela would be up by now and may have joined them at the Outta Sight. Estelle imagined them gathered around one of the concrete tables, cracking open bottles of beer, debating how they were going to while away yet another day. There had been talk of hiring a boat and visiting some of the more remote beaches in the south of the island, idyllic coves that you could only reach by sea. She'd been well up for that until Rob had gone missing. Now she didn't feel like doing anything fun.

Perhaps Niko could help. He might have heard some gossip among the locals. If he could find out whether Rob had made it onto a ferry, that would put her mind at rest. She didn't want to spend the rest of her holiday worrying about what had happened to him.

Niko had told her not to go to Sunset Bar, but to wait to hear from him. It had been four days now, and a small part of her feared that she would never see him again. Perhaps his father had forbade him from having anything more to do with her. Did he have that kind of power? She suspected he did.

Although it was open all day, people didn't tend to gather at Sunset Bar until mid-afternoon at the earliest, so Estelle was surprised to hear music playing as she approached. She saw several people – more than twenty – who were gathered around tables that had been pushed together on the upper terrace. Niko's father and mother were among the party, which was made up entirely of Greeks – well-off Greeks by the look of them. The women were well dressed, with puffed up hair and lots of jewellery, while the men wore suit trousers and polo shirts. They looked like businesspeople rather than islanders.

The table had been properly laid with a linen cloth, napkins and stemmed wine glasses, something she'd never seen on the island before. Rush baskets – not plastic ones – overflowed with fresh bread. It looked as if lunch was about to be served, and not just pizza or spaghetti, which was the normal bill of fare at Sunset Bar. Clearly, this was a special occasion.

Not great timing on her part.

Babá Yannis stood up and made a toast. Niko and Andreas emerged with huge platters of roast lamb and potatoes, followed by bowls of Greek salad. There was applause for the food, then Niko went back to the kitchen and Andreas took up his position behind the bar.

Estelle waited until everyone was busy eating and chatting, then emerged from her hiding place.

'What are *you* doing here?' asked Andreas scornfully. He was about her age, a few years younger than his brother, and very cocky. 'My brother can't see you. He's very busy. Go away.'

'So you know who I am,' she said, secretly pleased.

'No. But I've seen you hanging around. Like all the other girls.'

'I just need a few minutes with him. Please. Can you get him for me?'

'Nikolaos is working. We have a special event. Private.'

'Yes, I can see.'

At that moment, Niko came out of the kitchen. 'Estelle!' he cried. 'I told you not to come. If my father finds out . . .' He looked anxiously towards the long table.

'Something's happened,' she said. 'It's important.'

'Okay, I give you five minutes. Go round the back, I'll meet you there.'

Throwing a triumphant glance at Andreas, Estelle crept around the side of the building. There was a small court-yard there, littered with crates of beer and wine and large drums of olive oil. Niko came through the back door and lit a cigarette.

'What's the problem?'

She launched in. 'Remember that friend I told you about? Rob. He got into trouble for talking to a local girl: her father pulled a shotgun on him.'

His face twitched. 'What about him?'

'Apparently, he carried on seeing her. The father found out and now Rob's vanished. We all assumed he'd fled the island, but today I found his bag, including his passport. And there was blood on it! I took it to the police, but they couldn't care less. I'm really worried. Do you know what happened? I thought maybe there'd been some gossip.'

Niko inhaled. 'He was taught a lesson,' he said slowly.

She clutched at him. 'You mean he was beaten up? Oh, God . . . Do you know how bad he is? Where is he now? Does he need a doctor?'

'He was put on the early ferry. I think he woke up in Athens with a sore head, no documents, no money.'

'Poor Rob!' Her eyes filled with tears.

'Don't cry for him. Think of the girl he ruined.'

'*Ruined?* It's so unfair,' she protested. 'For both of them. How come it's alright for us to be together, but not them?'

'You know why. I'm a man and she's a woman. That's how it works here.' He dropped his cigarette, stubbing it out with his foot. 'I'm not saying it's fair, but . . . you can't change it.' When he lifted his hand to sweep his fringe off his face, she saw that his knuckles were swollen and bruised.

'How did that happen?' she asked, pointing. He didn't respond. 'Niko! Please don't tell me you were part of it.'

He hid his hand behind his back. 'I didn't want to. Her brother is my friend. It was my duty.'

'Your *duty*?' she repeated. 'You could have talked to him, told him to leave the island. You didn't have to beat him up!'

'I know . . . I'm sorry . . . It was wrong . . . I feel very bad.'

'I should think so!'

'This is why I need to go to UK. To be free to do what I want, not what other people tell me.'

She huffed. 'You're a grown man, Niko. You have to take responsibility. If you don't want to do something, don't do it.'

'Here, it's not so easy. You don't understand.'

'You're right, I don't,' she replied hotly. 'I can't believe you'd be so violent.'

'I'm sorry. Forgive me. Your friend is okay. He has gone home. Please forget about him.' He went to kiss her, but she stepped back.

'Seriously, Niko – you can't just brush it off. We need to talk about this.'

'Not now, not here. I have to work.'

'But this is important!'

A shadow passed across his face, as if he understood. 'Okay, okay. I see you later. Please don't come here again. Wait until I come to you.' He gave her a tentative smile, then turned and went back to the kitchen.

Estelle ran all the way to the beach without stopping. She was shocked by what Niko had done; furious with him for being so weak and going along with the crowd. No wonder the police hadn't been interested in Rob's disappearance. They'd probably known about the attack and approved of it. There seemed to be one rule for the locals and another for everyone else.

Whatever Niko said, she would not forget about Rob. Not until she knew he was okay.

Chapter Twenty-One: Now

JUNO

'Are you sure you didn't put the letters somewhere else?' Millie asks for the tenth time.

'Yes, absolutely. I only have one drawer, for God's sake,' I snap. 'This place is so tiny, there's nowhere else to keep anything.'

'What about your suitcases?'

'They're not in there. They were in the drawer!'

'You should still look . . . You never know . . . The memory plays tricks. The worst way to look for something is when you're convinced you know where it is.'

She's only trying to be helpful, but her attitude grates. I drag the suitcases out – just to please her – and of course, the envelope isn't there. Millie looks through her drawers too. I turn out my beach bag. I crawl under the bed, and pull out the furniture, coughing at the dust as I peer behind it. I go downstairs and check the kitchen cabinets, the broom cupboard, even the fridge.

'Perhaps you left them at work,' Millie suggests when I come back to the bedroom. She has changed into an acid-green mini-dress with lots of straps criss-crossing at strange angles over her back and chest. It makes her look as if she's been tied up.

'I've never taken them to work. I wouldn't dare.'

'What about the hire car? You definitely had them on our trip.'

'Yes, and I definitely brought them back.'

She speaks to me through the mirror while she repairs her makeup. 'Are you absolutely sure about that? Have you looked at them since?'

A flicker of doubt enters my mind. 'No, but . . . I wouldn't have left them in the car. They're precious. I'm always extremely careful with them.'

'Still worth checking,' Millie replies, eyes wide as she checks her false eyelashes.

'They were stolen from here. We keep the apartment locked. There's no sign of a break-in, so the thief must have had a key . . . Which means it must be one of the family. Except they don't know the letters exist. So why . . . ?' I tail off, as an ungenerous thought flies into my head. I search Millie's reflection for signs of guilt, but her expression is clear.

'I didn't tell anyone if that's what you're getting at. Why would I do that? We're friends.' She turns around to face me. 'At least, I thought we were.'

'Of course we are. I'm sorry, I'm not accusing you. Just trying to make sense of it.'

'Did you tell Kevin?'

'I can't remember . . . Yeah, I might have done. But why would he steal them? And how would he have got in, anyway?'

'Picked the lock? This place is hardly Fort Knox.'

I shake my head. 'No, I don't think it was him. He's not interested in me, only in stopping Klimeni.'

'Then it's got to be somebody in the family,' Millie concludes. 'Of course, they might have found them accidentally.'

'What do you mean?'

'I think Andreas suspects you're an activist like Lana. We know Vasilis followed you to the Wild Duck. He could have been sent to search the apartment. Vasilis was looking for evidence linking you to Stop Klimeni, but he found the letters instead.'

'Which means they know who I am.' I sigh. 'This is so not how I wanted them to find out . . .'

Millie pauses to put on her heels. '*Or* . . . nobody stole them, you just left them somewhere. Like in the hire car,' she says. 'The simplest explanation is usually the most likely. Sorry, I'm running late. We're meeting at the pizza place at nine. Are you sure you don't want to come?'

'No, thanks. I've got stuff to do.' I survey the mess. 'Tidying up for a start.'

'Okay. See you later . . .' She picks up her phone. 'And no more talking to Kevin Casey. You'll get us both into trouble.'

She leaves in a swirl of fluorescent green, a bit OTT for a pizzeria perhaps, but the evening won't end there. Millie may have a job, but she acts like she's on a permanent holiday. God knows what time she'll get home tonight. I don't know how she does it.

I put everything back where it was, then cobble together a salad from various leftovers in the fridge and go up to the roof terrace. As I eat, I make a mental inventory of all the letters, visualising the blue biro writing, the thin paper, the well-worn creases, the small rips. I picture the postcard photos – Chora at night, the windmills, the blue-domed churches, the deserted beaches that are now full of bars and souvenir shops. I see Estelle's cramped scrawl, the smudged postmarks, the edges of the foreign stamps peeling off. I smell their musty odour from sitting in my grandmother's bottom drawer for decades.

I'm like a psychic trying to locate a dead body. If I concentrate on the letters hard enough, I think, perhaps their current location will magically pop into my head. But the only image I have is of an unknown hand sifting through the pages, an anonymous pair of eyes reading my mother's words . . .

The following morning, I call the car hire company before I start work, on the off chance that I did leave the letters in the jeep. The agent tells me they're not in lost property but might have been regarded as rubbish and thrown away. Neither possibility makes me feel better. Either they're lost forever, or Andreas has them. If the family know who I am, it's going to make it even more difficult for Niko to make contact.

I've got to be super aware of how they behave towards me now. I haven't detected any change in anyone's attitude towards me recently, but then I don't know exactly when the letters went missing. They could have been taken at any time during the last couple of weeks since I went to Klimeni. If there's a game of chess going on, I need to be at least one move ahead. Best to adopt a mask of innocence and act like nothing's wrong, although that's easier said than done when my mind is in such a whirl.

Fortunately, everybody is focussed on preparations for

the launch party, which takes place this Thursday. The club is closed to visitors and there are no weddings or private functions. I stay out of the way as much as possible, glued to my computer, liaising with guests over the final arrangements, putting people into groups for the helicopter tours of the island. Andreas, Christakis and Despina rush in and out, talking on their phones, pausing only to bark orders at the staff.

Over the next few days, the bar and restaurant are transformed into a grand reception area, with swathes of purple satin, urns for extravagant floral arrangements, and display panels showing digital mock-ups of the new resort. A giant screen is set up to show the promotional film, which will be posted on social media at the end of the party. The architect's model is removed from its boxes and placed on a large table in the centre of the room, covered with a large grey cloth. Nobody is allowed to peek beneath it, and we've been strictly forbidden from taking photos. Andreas is paranoid about images being leaked to the press.

Millie is fed up because she's been asked to waitress at the party. 'It's not on,' she moans to me over lunch on Wednesday. 'I've got a level 2 in Beauty Therapy, you know.'

'It's just for one night,' I tell her. 'I bet I'll be handing out canapés too.'

'But you're a Zimiris!'

'For God's sake, keep your voice down!'

'You should be hobnobbing with the VIPs.'

'Huh. I'll be organising the transport and making sure there's enough toilet paper in the ladies'.'

At the end of the day, Christakis calls all the staff to the bar for a final pep talk. There's some discussion about the precise location of the projection screen, and Chef Michalis complains about the last-minute changes to the buffet menu (one of the influencers has a severe nut allergy), then Andreas steps forward to make a speech, flitting effortlessly between Greek and English.

'Thank you, everyone, for all your hard work,' he says. 'This is an exciting moment for our family. It is the realisation of a dream. We must keep the secret from our enemies for one more day, then we can tell the whole world.'

'Everyone already knows,' whispers Millie as we walk into the car park to get our lift back to Chora.

'Not the precise details though,' I whisper back.

'It wouldn't surprise me if Kevin Casey glues himself to the helipad tomorrow. We shouldn't have spoken to him in the square last week. If I lose my job—'

'You won't. It'll be fine. But if anything does happen, I'll make it clear it had nothing to do with you, okay?'

I wake up even earlier than usual, after dreaming about Niko and the launch party all night. At one point he even turned up as a guest. I lie in bed looking at the ceiling, waiting for dawn to break, a feeling of dread hanging over me. I can't stop worrying about the missing letters. Whoever took them knows who I am. Maybe the whole family know. But if so, why haven't they confronted me?

I pull back my sheet and get up, squeezing through the narrow gap between the beds. Millie stirs but doesn't wake.

I dress quickly, pulling on jeans and a sleeveless top. There will be a lot of running around today so I don't want to put on my party dress until the last minute. I'm going to take it with me and change at the club. Millie has offered to do my hair and makeup specially.

My mobile rings and Christakis's name flashes onto the screen. Why is he calling so early?

'Hi,' I say, my voice still croaky with sleep.

'We need you both to come now,' he says. His voice sounds thin and strange. 'Vasilis will be waiting for you in the usual place.'

'Is everything okay?'

'I can't talk now. Just get here as soon as you can. And tell nobody.' He ends the call.

'Tell nobody *what*?' I say to my phone, as if it could answer.

Millie wakes, yawning and rubbing her eyes. 'What's up?'

'I don't know, sounds like there's a problem. I hope to God it's not my fault.'

We hurriedly get ready and run down to the car park.

'Is something wrong?' I ask Vasilis as we climb into the minibus.

'Yes. Big trouble,' he says, starting the engine.

I lean forward. 'What sort of trouble?' He doesn't reply. Either he doesn't know any more than we do, or he's been told not to say.

When we arrive, we find the main entrance to the club locked, so we walk around the side to the pool area. Andreas and Christakis are standing there, talking quietly to each other. Phaedra sits on the edge of a sunbed, head bowed, hands twisting nervously. Despina has her arms around her shoulders and whispers to her quietly. Chef Michalis is looking out to sea, smoking a cigarette. The atmosphere is so sombre, it feels like somebody's died.

'What's happened?' I ask.

Chapter Twenty-Two: August 1984

ESTELLE

Dearest folks!

Hope you are doing okay. Things here are as boiling hot as ever. I am covered in mosquito bites. I have nearly run out of drachmas, but I should make it until the end of the holiday. Just! Good job I already have my plane ticket back.

There have been a few dramas going on. Not involving me directly, you'll be relieved to know! It's been a bit difficult. The Greeks are super lovely people, and most of the time, they are extremely tolerant of foreigners, but their way of life is very traditional and completely different to how it is in the UK. Sometimes there are clashes, which is a shame because it's the differences that make the place so magical.

I've had an incredible time and I'm going to miss Niko like crazy, but in other ways, it'll be good to come home. Back to normality! Missing you

Lots of love, E x

Chapter Twenty-Three: Now

JUNO

'We've been attacked,' Andreas says, turning to me and Millie. 'They forced entry through the kitchen door. Didn't steal anything, just wrecked the place. The models have been smashed and covered in red paint. They're ruined. So are the displays and the screen we hired. The paint's everywhere – over the walls, the floor, the furniture . . . The decorations have been torn down. It's like a bomb exploded.'

'I'm so sorry,' I say. 'This is terrible. Has anyone claimed responsibility? Did they leave a message or anything?'

'No, but we all know who it was,' interjects Christakis. 'Kevin Casey and his friends.'

I sense Millie stiffening, but I try not to look at her. 'When did it happen?' I ask.

'Phaedra came back late last night to do some extra food prep,' Andreas replies. 'She heard noises and went to investigate. Somebody came up from behind, pushed her into the cold store and locked the door. She was stuck in there all night. The cleaners heard her this morning, banging and crying for help.'

I turn to Phaedra. 'Oh my God, you poor thing.'

'Was it definitely a man?' asks Millie, crouching down

155

in front of her. 'Did you see his face?' She shakes her head. 'Young or old? Greek or foreign-looking?'

'She doesn't know,' interjects Despina. 'She's in shock, can't talk right now.'

Millie sighs. 'Pity you don't have CCTV.'

'Normally, we don't need it,' says Andreas. 'There is very little crime in Inios, only from tourists.'

'And expats,' adds Christakis, bringing us back to Kevin.

I decide not to comment. The last thing I want is for anyone to think I'm defending Kevin Casey, especially if he turns out to be guilty. Although I'm struggling to work out why he would commit criminal damage and assault Phaedra when he's such an obvious suspect.

'Have you called the police?' I ask.

The family exchange glances. 'Not yet,' says Christakis.

'Why not?'

Andreas steps in. 'Once the police know, the whole island will know, and our guests will know. That's what our enemies want. But we won't give it to them. We're going to keep this quiet for as long as we can – certainly until after the party, when everyone's left the island.'

I frown. 'Sorry, but how can we have the party if the place is covered in red paint?'

'Obviously, we can't hold it here,' says Christakis. 'We have to find somewhere else. The model is ruined, so are the photo displays, but we can get hold of another screen, new decorations. It won't be easy, but it's possible.'

Possible? It sounds like we need a miracle. 'Any ideas on an alternative venue?' I ask, trying to sound calm.

'Not at the moment,' says Despina, standing up.

I cast about for large buildings on the island but can only think of one. 'What about the town hall?'

'Too political,' says Andreas. 'The mayor is on our side. He's coming tonight, in fact, but he won't want to make his support too official.'

'Okay . . . Do you own any other bars or restaurants on the island?'

'A few, but they're in Chora. It's too visible. We need privacy.'

I look at Andreas. 'Sorry if this is overstepping the mark, but what about your own house?'

He shakes his head. 'It's not suitable.'

Christakis says something in Greek to his father, who seems to think he's just had a good idea. Despina protests but is shouted down by the others. I sneak a glance at Millie – we have no idea what's going on.

'We own a villa,' says Andreas finally. 'It's a luxury rental, just off the main road, not far from here. There's a pool and lovely gardens. It has security gates, and it's very private.'

'And it also has guests this week,' says Despina shirtily. 'They've paid a lot of money to stay there. We can't push them out.'

'But we'd only need the place for today,' I venture. 'They wouldn't need to move out completely, just make themselves scarce for a few hours.'

'I'm sure we could do a deal,' says Christakis. Andreas nods.

'Wealthy people are not interested in deals,' Despina retorts.

'Invite them to the party,' pipes up Millie. 'Make them feel special. People love that.'

'Is there another option?' I say. Christakis and Andreas shake their heads.

'We need to discuss it,' Despina says. 'Just the family.'

'Of course,' I reply. 'But you need to decide quickly, or we'll never organise it in time.'

We're sent away. Michalis goes to the kitchen, clearly upset about the prospects for the catering. Millie and I walk over to the amphitheatre, where nobody can hear us talking. We sit down on the stone steps.

'I didn't think Kevin would go this far,' I say, worriedly. 'Assaulting Phaedra. That's awful.'

Millie slaps her forehead. 'And we talked to him. In the main square of all places. I knew it was a mistake.'

'It was packed. Nobody would have noticed.'

'You can't be too sure. Vasilis has spies everywhere.'

'Do you think it could have been Lana? She could have been lying low for weeks, planning it.'

'No way. Lana wouldn't hurt Phaedra. It's got to be Kevin,' maintains Millie. 'Walking around with placards and spraying his logo everywhere is fair enough, but he's gone too far this time.'

We go back to the main building to await orders. The restaurant area, where most of the damage was done, has been blocked off. The red paint is everywhere. I doubt that they'll be able to clean it off. The entire place will have to be redecorated.

Millie begs some breakfast from the kitchen, and we make ourselves a coffee. I keep checking the time, wondering when the family are going to make up their mind about what to do. Eventually, Andreas walks up the steps towards us.

'It's sorted. We can use the villa,' he says. 'It's not ideal. The kitchen will be too small for Michalis, but there's a large patio, and the views are wonderful, almost as good as from here. We can make it work.'

'Sure,' I reply. 'Tell me what you want me to do and I'll do it.'

'Thank you, Juno.' Andreas turns to Millie. 'I need you to help Michalis, please. Phaedra's not well, she needs to go home.'

'Okay,' she replies glumly. 'But Michalis won't like it. I'm hopeless at cooking.'

He shrugs, as if to say he couldn't care less. 'We'll transport the food by minibus at the last moment.'

'Remember we're using the minibuses to ferry the guests from the helipad and the port,' I say, 'so there may be a timing issue. I don't suppose you want to use taxis, but you might have to.'

'Good point,' says Andreas. 'Thanks. What would we do without you?' He smiles at me, gratefully. 'My dear Juno, I'm so glad you're here.'

Does he know I'm his niece? I wonder. It's impossible to tell.

It's one o'clock in the morning, and the party's drawing to a close. The minibuses have already collected the first swathe of guests and taken them back to their hotels. Soon they will return for the remaining dregs – the travel reps and influencers, who are all wasted. I found traces of cocaine in one of the upstairs bathrooms. A young woman ended up in the pool earlier and had to be rescued by Vasilis.

I stifle a yawn, and shift from one foot to another, trying to give my aching soles some relief. I'm frazzled, having run around all day rearranging everything. It's gone very well, although I doubt that we managed to keep it a secret, what with private helicopters whirring in the skies all afternoon, and the live music blaring out of the speakers this evening. The performance by the Greek popstar, whose name I've already forgotten, went down very well, especially with the local dignitaries and the investor from Athens.

He's still here – a man of about Andreas's age accompanied by a younger version of himself, presumably his son. They are both handsome, tall and broad-shouldered, wearing expensive suits with a white shirt and no tie. The older one is calm and authoritative, but the younger one is too keen to impress. They were working the room earlier, switching between English and Greek with graceful ease, but now they're huddled in a corner with Andreas and Christakis, talking seriously in hushed tones. Two fathers and two sons.

I note with disapproval that Despina is not involved in the discussion. She is a good ten years older than her youngest brother and has far more experience. Despite all the advances for women, the patriarchal nature of Greek society seems to endure in the Zimiris family. Her main job tonight has been to keep the local dignitaries happy, making sure their glasses are always filled to the brim and that they get a selfie with the aged popstar. She doesn't seem to have enjoyed it much. It's as if she resents being here at all.

I walk to the edge of the garden and look out at the great

expanse of dark sea. This is a beautiful villa, luxurious and modern. Christakis told me his grandfather bought the place for the family many years ago, adapting it over the years from a traditional farmhouse to the high-spec holiday home it is today. Despite the glossy surfaces, it hasn't lost its homely atmosphere. As soon as I stepped inside earlier today, it felt inexplicably familiar – almost as if I'd been here before, which is impossible. I'm trying to remember whether Estelle mentioned the farmhouse in her letters when I hear footsteps behind me.

'*There* you are,' says a voice in a slightly accusing tone. I turn around to see Millie standing there in her black waitress dress. She looks worn out. 'We've got to clear up before we leave. Despina sent me to get you. It's all hands on deck.'

'Sorry. Just catching my breath. I haven't stopped all day.'

'Nor have I. I'm knackered.'

'We pulled it off, though. There was no more red paint, no invasions, no protests.'

'Did you hear Andreas's speech? All that bollocks about preserving and *enhancing* the island's biodiversity. Yeah, right. He was just saying what they wanted to hear.' She puts on his Greek accent, 'Inios is no longer the party island, but Paradise Island!'

'Paradise? I'm not sure about that,' I mutter. The place is toxic, full of feuds and rivalries. Maybe Kevin Casey vandalised the club and assaulted Phaedra, maybe it was Lana . . . Or someone else we don't know about. Once the VIP guests have departed, the police investigation will start. All I know is I need to stay out of it.

We go back to join the others, who are busily clearing up.

The villa residents – two families who've rented the place for a fortnight – have been very accommodating and seem to have enjoyed being part of such a glitzy occasion, but understandably they want their holiday rental back now. Everything must be cleared and cleaned before we leave tonight. That's the deal.

By the time we get back to our apartment, it's gone 3 a.m., and Millie and I are completely shattered. We undress, quickly clean our teeth, then get into bed. At first, I was very unhappy about rooming with a stranger, but I'm used to her company now. I even quite like it. After so many years sharing a bed with Luke, it feels natural to listen to someone breathing next to me.

Suddenly, I feel the need to talk to him – not just about what's going on here, but about us. I've been avoiding it, but I think maybe I'm finally ready to have the conversation. But it's one in the morning in the UK. I know he wants me to call, but I can't wake him now. It wouldn't be fair. Promising myself that I'll get in touch tomorrow, I settle down. The sound of gentle snoring lulls me into a deep, exhausted sleep.

Chapter Twenty-Four: August 1984

ESTELLE

Estelle's mind was in turmoil. She was devastated that Niko had taken part in the attack on Rob and found it impossible to reconcile such violence with the gorgeous, gentle man she'd fallen in love with. He claimed he disliked the macho culture here as much as she did, and she believed him, but he'd been weak. He should have stood up for his principles and refused to get involved. They needed to discuss it properly, but he'd told her not to go to Sunset Bar and he hadn't come to find her like he'd promised. She was furious with him, and yet terrified at the thought their relationship might be over.

Fortunately, Angela and the Barking Boys were there to keep her occupied and stop her from driving herself crazy. During the day, they hung out at the main beach in front of the Outta Sight. There was always stuff going on there: football and cricket matches, dive-bombing off the rocks, hair-cutting and ear-piercing, hippies selling homemade jewellery . . . Old men wandered up and down with donkeys laden with watermelons and bunches of grapes, crying out in broken English and flirting with the young women.

Estelle had grown fond of Angela, Tony and Paul. People assumed they were two couples, but there was no sexual chemistry between them. They felt like close friends, although they didn't have deep chats, or even make much attempt to find out about each other. All that mattered was the here and now.

Their only serious conversation was about Rob. They each had different theories about what had happened to him and where he was now. Angela, who was very much in love with Stamatius, didn't want to hear anything bad about the Greeks. She maintained that Rob had simply decided to move on and had forgotten his passport, refusing to believe the rumours that he'd been beaten up by some of the locals, including 'the one with the cowboy hat'. Estelle kept quiet.

Tony went further. He didn't believe that Rob had made it onto the ferry and feared he might be dead. 'It'd be easy to get rid of his body,' he claimed. 'Just take out a boat and dump him at sea.'

'That's a terrible thing to say,' said Angela. 'The Greeks are lovely, kind people—'

'They can't *all* be,' Tony countered.

'Who are you accusing of murder, then?' snapped Angela. 'My Stamatius?'

'Hey, calm down!' interrupted Paul. 'Nobody's accusing anyone of anything. We don't know what happened, so it's daft to fall out over it. I expect Rob's fine. Back in the UK, or on some other island. He's probably already shacked up with some other girl.'

Estelle hoped Paul was right. If only they could know for sure.

With no sign of Niko, Estelle accompanied Angela to the port in the evenings. They sat outside Atlantis bar, waiting for Stamatius to finish work, which was never until after midnight. The bar was family-run. His mother worked in the kitchen, producing endless plates of moussaka and spaghetti to feed the hungry backpackers who were either about to leave the island or had just arrived. His father was in charge, but he let his three sons do most of the work and was usually found sitting at one of the tables, smoking and drinking coffee with his friends. Unlike Niko, Stamatius was committed to his family's business. He worked long hours seven days a week throughout the summer. He was definitely not a *kamaki* always hunting after foreign girls. In fact, Angela had pursued *him*.

'He asked me what I wanted to drink, and I just knew in that moment,' she said. 'I knew he was the one for me.'

Angela and Stamatius only saw each other for a couple of hours each day, and their knowledge of each other's language was limited. But somehow, they'd managed to fall in love. It was a calmer, gentler relationship than Niko and Estelle's, which was largely based on sexual attraction.

Stamatius had asked Angela to stay on after the season ended. His family owned a small flat in Chora, which they rented out in the summer, but he'd said that she could live there for free. Stamatius promised he would stay over frequently, but they wouldn't be able to live together openly. She felt uneasy about the arrangement, not wanting to be seen as his 'bit on the side'.

Nevertheless, Angela probably would stay. There was little waiting for her in England. She wasn't in the middle of a university course or training for a career. She lived with her parents and worked in a record shop, saving money so that she could spend the summers travelling. It was a simple life, but she had no 'prospects', as Estelle's father would say. She wasn't building anything for the future. Maybe it didn't matter. Maybe her future was with Stamatius, on Inios.

Niko hadn't asked Estelle to remain with him. He was still focussed on coming to the UK, and not just because he wanted to be with her. Unlike Stamatius, he wanted to free himself from his family and get as far away from Inios as possible. Whether he would ever have the courage to leave was another question.

The island represented opposite things for them. For Niko, it was oppression. For Estelle, liberation. In these last couple of months, she'd come to realise that there was more to life than studying a subject she didn't care about, or doing a boring job fifty weeks of the year just so that she could afford a two-week summer break. She wanted to rethink everything. Investigate other lifestyles and cultures. Seek out like-minded people. Travel. Explore. Live freely, unburdened by the need to pay a mortgage or bills. All that would have to wait until she'd graduated – her parents would have a fit if she dropped out now. In the meantime, she would have Inios to return to next summer. And Niko. Assuming, of course, that they were still together.

Niko finally came to find her on Kalapos beach, a few days later. She was hanging out with Angela and the Barking boys, sunbathing and listening to music on Paul's boombox.

'Estelle?' he said. She opened her eyes and squinted up at him. He was wearing the leather Stetson, a white t-shirt and jeans. He looked like an advert for Marlboro cigarettes. Her heart jolted.

'Niko!'

'Hi,' he said. 'Will you go with me for a drink?'

'Yes . . . of course.' She sat up and reached for her bikini top, her fingers fumbling as she fastened it behind her back. The others exchanged a sly glance. She knew what they were thinking. Only yesterday, she'd sworn to her friends that she was sick of Niko ignoring her and didn't want to see him again, but now he was here, she was jumping to attention.

She left the others and followed Niko back up the sand. 'I don't want to go to the Outta Sight,' he said. 'It's dirty.' *And owned by a rival family*, she thought.

Instead, they set off towards a small taverna on the jetty on the far side of the bay. There was a whole other subculture that gathered there, mainly older hippy types who'd been coming to Inios since the sixties. They camped in the caves and sunbathed nude on the rocks. In the evenings, some of them ventured as far as Sunset Bar, where they played music and sang folk songs, but they eschewed the discos and the rowdier places in Chora.

'You managed to escape then,' she said wryly as they walked along the sand.

'I'm not a prisoner,' he replied. 'I am busy. Always lots of jobs to do.'

'Why didn't you come to see me before?'

'I wanted to, but I couldn't get away, I'm sorry. I came as soon as I could.'

'You promised we'd talk. I've been waiting and waiting—'

'Shh . . . don't be angry with me. I'm here now.' He took her hand and gripped it tightly.

They reached the taverna. It was empty now, but in an hour's time the atmosphere would be buzzing. Tables covered with gingham cloths were lined up on the terrace facing the sea. When the wind blew, water slopped over the edge of the retaining wall, making puddles and spraying the customers.

An old woman sat on a stool gutting fish and tossing them into a large plastic crate packed with crushed ice. Freshly caught calamari had been hung on a line to dry.

Niko ordered coffee and a glass of water for himself and a Sprite for her. He was acting as if everything was normal, stroking her arm, picking up her hand and pressing it against his cheek, and yet she knew something had changed between them. Or maybe it was just her feelings that had changed . . .

'There are horrible rumours going round about Rob,' she began. 'Some people think he was murdered, and his body dumped at sea.'

He shook his head vehemently. 'What? No! That's not true. Who says it? Kevin Casey? Don't listen to him. He's a liar. He sells drugs.'

'Not Kev, other people. Friends of mine. Somehow, they found out you were involved in the beating.'

He looked at her askance. 'It wasn't just me. I tried to stop it—'

'I know. I didn't say anything, honest . . . but I'm really worried. What if—'

He cut in. 'Estelle! Stop! It's not true. When we left your friend, he was okay. A few cuts and bruises, that's all. We put him on the ferry. Stop worrying about him.'

'Do you promise you're telling the truth?'

'Yes!' he replied impatiently. 'Now can we forget about it?'

'Yes . . . yes . . . I'm sorry. I just had to ask.' She looked away.

'I missed you,' he said after a few moments of painful silence.

Her gaze returned to him. 'I missed you too . . . I've only got ten days left, then I have to go.'

'Back to UK?'

She nodded. 'Back to reality. Term's starting soon, and I haven't got anywhere to live yet.'

'Maybe I'll come with you,' he said, after some thought.

'Really?' She tried to sound excited rather than alarmed. 'What, next week?'

'No, next year. I have to save some money first.' He leaned across the table and kissed her. 'You wait for me, yes?'

'Of course.'

'No English boyfriends?' He teased with a grin.

'Of course not.'

'You'll write to me. Send me photos.'

'If you like.'

'Yes. I like.' He kissed her again. 'Sorry, I have to go.' He put some drachmas on the table and stood up. 'I'll come to your room tonight, after we close. We'll talk. Make everything right. Can you get rid of Angela?'

'I don't know. I'll try my best.'

'We spend the whole night together, yes?' She nodded. 'It will be beautiful. I love you. You love me?'

'You know I do.'

'See you later, my love.'

He walked away, leaving her to finish her drink alone, still strangely troubled, staring at the octopus tentacles waving in the breeze.

Chapter Twenty-Five: Now

JUNO

The following day, Vasilis picks us up at the normal time of 8 a.m. and takes us to the club, which is still closed due to the vandalism. The police – two young guys – arrive and take lots of photos of the damage. Despina offers them 'her' office to work in and they interview the staff, one by one. For some reason, they start with me.

'Do you know Kevin Casey?' is the first question. They come straight out with it, no messing about.

'I know who he is,' I reply carefully. 'I've seen him in Chora. Everyone knows him. But he's not my friend. And before you ask, I'm not a member of Stop Klimeni either. I know nothing about the attack.'

'What is your opinion about the new resort?' is the next question.

'I don't have one. I'm here to do a job. Honestly, I have no idea who did this.' I'm not sure that either of the officers believe me.

After my grilling, I find a table in the shade by the pool and access my emails via my phone. There are various messages, mostly from couples making enquiries about availability for next summer. I dash off a few easy replies. My main concern is the next wedding, which is booked for Tuesday.

I go to find Andreas. He's pacing up and down the upper terraces, talking agitatedly into his phone. I wait for him to finish, then raise my hand, like a child in a classroom.

'Sorry to interrupt,' I say. 'Can I have a quick word?'

He puts his phone away. 'Of course. How are you, Juno? Recovered from yesterday?'

'Just about.'

'Thank you so much for all your hard work,' he says. 'You kept us calm. We couldn't have done it without you.'

'It was a team effort,' I reply. 'I've been looking at the schedule. The next wedding is in four days' time. Do you think we'll be back in business by then?'

Andreas sucks his teeth. 'To be honest, I doubt it. I've booked a specialist cleaning company, but they're based in Athens and can't get here until Monday. We'll probably have to buy new dining chairs and some tables. We can find temporary furniture, but it won't look as good.' He strokes his beard thoughtfully. 'Maybe we should cancel it.'

I frown. 'Really? Cancelling at such short notice would be terrible for the couple. They'd murder us on social media, and quite rightly.'

'We can't have that,' he says. 'Not with everything else going on.'

'We just need to keep them out of the building as much as possible. We could put banqueting tables down by the amphitheatre and set up a temporary bar. We'll have to hire in some gazebos for shade and we could throw in some more floral decoration – if you don't mind the extra expense,' I add hastily. 'Personally, I think it'd be worth it. Then they'd only need to go inside to use the toilets.'

'Sounds good. Go ahead. Do what you have to. Tell Despina I okayed it.'

'Great. Leave it with me.' I give him a small smile. 'I'm sure you've other things to worry about.'

'Once Casey is behind bars, everything will be fine,' he says, setting his jaw.

'Oh. They know it was definitely him, do they?'

'Of course it was him. There's no doubt. That man has been a thorn in my side for years, even when my father was alive. The way he used to drive that military truck around, trespassing on everyone's land, behaving like he owned the island, selling drink and drugs to kids . . . Well, he won't get away with it this time.' He fingers the collar of his shirt, pulling it away from his neck. 'Stay away from Mr Casey, Juno. He's a liar. He doesn't care about Inios – only about himself. He pretends to be everybody's friend, but you can't trust him.'

'He's not my friend,' I say evenly.

'No? That's not what Vasilis tells me. He saw you talking to him.'

I bristle. 'Has he been spying on me?'

'No, not at all. But Inios is a small place . . .'

'Kevin came to find me,' I lie. 'He thought I might be a replacement for Lana.'

'Oh. So, you know about her.'

'Only that she was some kind of activist. Kevin told me. He asked me to work for him, but I refused . . . I would never do something like that.'

'I see . . . That's good. I'm pleased to hear it.' He smiles at me. 'You're very important to us, Juno.'

'Thank you . . . You're important to me too,' I add.

He gives me the slightest of nods, then walks away, leaving me breathless. There was a strange undercurrent to that exchange. It was as if he was trying to tell me that he knows who I am. And, most importantly, that he accepts me. But if that's the case, why doesn't he just come straight out with it?

Andreas is probably right – I can't trust Kevin Casey. But I can't trust *anyone* around here. Only my father perhaps, but he hasn't made contact again and I haven't a clue where he is. He may have already left the island . . . if he was ever here at all.

Kevin is taken in for questioning that afternoon but is released the following day. It turns out that he has a rock-solid alibi for the time of the attack – several in fact. A group of guys from the old days happened to be staying on Inios this week for their annual get-together. The evening before the party, instead of hanging out in their usual haunt, the Wild Duck, they gathered in the main square, where Kevin was seen – and heard – drunkenly regaling the crowd with tales of his former exploits. There are photos to prove it. Later on, they all bowled down to the karaoke bar, run by another expat. Some serious drinking was done. Raucous renditions of seventies hits rang out across the village until they were finally chucked out onto the streets at 4 a.m.

I'm secretly relieved that it wasn't Kevin, but Andreas and the rest of the family are furious. Christakis still insists that he was responsible, organising other people to act on his behalf. But the other members of Stop Klimeni also have alibis and there are no alternative suspects. I still think Lana could have been involved, but Millie won't hear of it.

'Lana liked Phaedra,' she says, as we sit in the lower square on Saturday evening, making the most of happy hour. 'There's no way she would have locked her in the cold store. She's not violent, she's all peace and love.'

Over the next couple of days, posts start appearing on social media, denouncing the eco credentials of the new resort. Pictures of the vandalism appear in the Greek press and generate thousands of shares. Despina tells me that one of the glossy features due to run in one of the travel magazines has been put on hold, and that some of the influencers who came to the party have now decided not to support the project. I express outrage and sympathy as required, but inside I feel conflicted. I don't agree with what's going on at Klimeni and wish it could be stopped. My only real sympathy is with Phaedra, who is still in a state of shock and has gone off sick.

I do my best to steer clear of Kevin, but it's hard when the only way to get to our apartment is via the main square. He seems to be there constantly at the moment, lecturing anyone that will listen about Klimeni and how the island is being destroyed by greed. His mates are still around too – flanking him like bodyguards, although their M&S checked shirts and shorts don't make them look very threatening, and they're holding pints instead of weapons.

On Tuesday morning, the club re-opens for the wedding. The bar has been redecorated but the restaurant remains closed, cordoned off with temporary screens. The specialist cleaners haven't finished blasting off the red paint yet, which is a nuisance because I'm worried that the noise will be disturbing. The luxurious, laidback vibe has vanished and been replaced by a tense, uncomfortable atmosphere. It feels as if the place is under siege.

Millie walks into the office, closing the door behind her. 'I'm afraid we've got a bridezilla on our hands,' she says.

'Oh no,' I groan.

Despina looks up from her work. 'We don't talk about our clients in this way,' she says reprovingly.

'But she's been driving me mad all morning,' Millie protests. 'Didn't like the shade of foundation I picked, said she wanted to look "more tanned". So, I gave her what she asked for, and then her mum came in and said she looked like a satsuma. She burst into tears and smudged everything, so I've got to start over, but now she wants a break because she's so upset. I want to kill her.'

'Millie!' Despina growls.

'I just came to warn you, she's on the warpath. Doesn't like the flowers, says they're too pink. Thinks the amphitheatre is too windy and is going to ruin her hair. Oh, *and* she's seen what's going on in the restaurant and says it looks like a bloodbath.'

'A bloodbath?' I echo.

'Yes. The cleaners keep going in and out with buckets of red water. To be fair, it does look like they're clearing up a murder.' Millie laughs grimly. 'Anyway, she's worried about it getting on her dress.'

I tut. 'She won't get anywhere near it.'

'I'm just telling you.'

'When she arrived, she seemed perfectly happy with the new arrangements.'

'Well, she's not now.'

'I'll go and talk to her,' says Despina, standing up.

She must have offered a generous discount because things calm down considerably after that. Millie takes the bride, her two bridesmaids and her mum to the Wellbeing Cabana and gives them complimentary foot massages. The rest of the party including the groom arrive and I whisk them immediately down to the amphitheatre. The banqueting tables have been beautifully dressed, and the extra floral arrangements tie everything together, giving the scene a magical fairy-tale feel. Within seconds, the guests are snapping everything in sight and taking group selfies against the sparkling sea backdrop.

I take a breath. Everything's going to be okay.

After the ceremony and reception, the party moves on to a nightclub for the evening celebrations. Normally, Despina and Christakis would be annoyed that they weren't staying on, but today they're relieved. The bride and groom leave first in a smart open-top Mercedes, with everyone else following in minibuses. Millie and I have to wait until Vasilis returns before we can get our lift back to Chora.

'Let's eat out,' I say, once we've been dropped off. 'I've run out of food and can't be bothered to shop tonight.'

'I can't be bothered *any* night,' she replies, taking me by the arm. 'You're always so good about cooking for yourself. It's time you had a proper treat.'

She takes me to a restaurant on the other side of the village, which has apparently been going since the early days and is popular with expats. It's packed, and we have to wait for a table. I stand by the bar with a cocktail, feeling on edge.

I can't stop thinking I'm being watched, although there are only tourists here, no locals.

Millie starts chatting to somebody she knows. I wander over to a wall of photos, which form one huge haphazard collage. Judging by the clothes and hairstyles they were taken in the eighties and nineties. They mostly comprise groups of very drunk young people hugging each other and pulling faces at the camera. Their skin is shiny with sweat and their eyes flash red with the camera's glare.

I'm peering into the photos, trying to find Estelle – and possibly even Niko – when someone behind me says, 'That's me there, with the red T-shirt on. I was twenty-two.'

I turn around to see a guy in his sixties pointing at one of the photos. Immediately, I recognise him as one of Kevin's bodyguards, although he appears to be off duty tonight.

'Really?' I say, unable to keep the surprise out of my voice.

'Yeah, I was dead slim back then. And I had hair.' He sighs nostalgically. 'That picture was taken at the Outta Sight, summer of 'eighty-four.'

'My mother was here in 1984,' I reply, my pulse quickening. 'Her name was Estelle. Don't suppose you remember her, do you?'

'If it's the same person I'm thinking of, yeah, of course I remember her.' He looks me up and down. 'You're her daughter?' I nod, and a smile spreads across his face. 'Wow, that's amazing!' He holds out his hand and we shake warmly. 'The name's Paul,' he says. 'I'm one of the Barking boys.'

Chapter Twenty-Six: August 1984

ESTELLE

The last day had finally dawned. Estelle could hardly believe it. She'd arrived on the island exactly six weeks ago, but she felt as if she'd been living here for a year. So much had happened. She'd made some great new friends, drunk a lot, eaten a mountain of cheese-and-spinach pastries, danced until sunrise, skinny-dipped in the Aegean, acquired an extremely impressive tan. Fallen in love. However, there had also been some terrible times – particularly the attack on Rob, which still played heavily on her mind.

Niko had apologised for taking part a hundred times. She'd tried her best to forgive him, and for the most part, their last week together had been heavenly. Angela had made herself scarce most nights, which meant they'd been able to make the most of every minute. But now it was time to pack and make her way to the port. The ferry left at midday, and she wouldn't reach Athens until after midnight. It would be a long, lonely journey without her mates.

Tony and Paul had departed a few days ago on the night ferry. They'd had a farewell party at All Right Now. Kev had given them several bottles of Mythos on the house, and they'd all got horribly drunk and over-affectionate. They'd exchanged addresses and phone numbers and there had even been talk of meeting up at Christmas. Estelle knew it probably wouldn't happen, but it was a nice idea. A pact was made to return next summer, same time, same place.

Estelle rolled up her sleeping bag and tied it to her rucksack. She checked to make sure she hadn't forgotten anything, gave the room a last fond glance, and left. Then she shut the door, crossed the courtyard to the farmhouse and said goodbye to her hosts, Yiorgos and Sofia, thanking them for their generosity and kindness.

She trudged down the donkey path on her own, her rucksack banging against her bottom with each step. Tears were already in her eyes with the thought of leaving – so much so that she could hardly see where she was going. She tried to concentrate her mind on the advantages of getting home. Seeing her parents. Hot baths. Eggs and bacon. A cup of tea with cow's milk. No mosquitoes. Her own comfy bed.

But she would miss Niko so much. He'd promised to come down to the port and see her off. Angela too, who'd already moved into Stamatius's holiday flat. There had been some disapproval from his family and Estelle wondered whether Angela would still be there next year. If Niko had his way, he would be coming to England with her. But a year was a long time. It was impossible to know how things would turn out.

Niko was waiting for her outside the travel bureau. 'Got your ticket?' he asked.

'Yes. I picked it up yesterday.'

The ferry was on time for a change. Angela ran out of the taverna, and they hugged. Estelle wished her luck. Then

Niko took her in his arms and gave her a long passionate kiss, until she ran out of breath and had to pull away. They said 'I love you' over and over and promised to write every week. But Estelle had a feeling she would be the one doing all the writing.

She was the last passenger to get into the little boat which rowed her to the ferry. Taking a last look back, she climbed up the rope ladder and stepped inside. If she wanted to wave goodbye to Niko and Angela, she would have to run up to the top deck.

They were standing on the quayside side-by-side, looking out for her. Estelle felt a pang of jealousy. She suddenly wanted to jump off the ferry and swim back to shore. But she didn't. It was too late. The klaxon had sounded, and the boat was turning round. She leaned against the handrail, shouting and waving. Niko spotted her and waved back. Then Angela joined in, jumping up and down, her screams lost in the wind.

As soon as the ferry rounded the point and hit the open sea, she felt bereft. Niko was gone and she had no idea when she would see him again. No cup of tea or hot bath seemed worth going home for. She wanted to go back to Inios and be with her lover. Angela had followed her heart and done the brave thing, but she was a coward. Furious with herself, she cried all the way back to Athens.

Estelle arrived back in Manchester just before the start of term, leaving herself only a few days to find somewhere to live. Luckily, some friends had found a terraced house not too far from the university campus and needed someone to take the box room. It was very cramped, with a narrow single bed, but she didn't mind too much as she wasn't planning to invite anyone to stay. Also, she was happy to pay less rent than her housemates because it would help her to save for her next trip to Greece.

She sent her photos away to be developed, and when they came back, she stuck the best ones on the wall with Blu Tack, making a sort of shrine. The snaps mainly featured Niko in various poses, beaming straight at the camera or gazing at her from beneath the rim of his Stetson. Sadly, she only had a few shots of the two of them together.

She became obsessed with all things Greek – the food, the wine, the music – and joined Greek Soc, which turned out to consist largely of homesick postgrads from Athens university. When she attended her first social event and mentioned that she had a Greek boyfriend whom she'd met on holiday, they looked at each other, amused. She was sure she heard them gossiping about her because she heard the word *kamaki* several times. A couple of them tried to chat her up, believing, presumably, that she must fancy all Greek men and that her so-called boyfriend had long forgotten her existence.

They were wrong of course. Niko wasn't a *kamaki* – they were genuinely in love. But nobody believed her. Even her closest friends encouraged her to date other men, and her parents seemed to be praying that the romance wouldn't survive the year.

As the weeks went by, she missed Niko even more. They had agreed to write to each other, although she'd suspected he wouldn't be confident about writing in English. She sent him several dull postcards of Manchester, addressed to the post restante, where all the islanders' mail went. During the autumn term she received two postcards back – both of the main beach and saying the same thing.

Estelle mine, I love you. I think about you all the time.

Anxious for more news of Inios, Estelle also wrote to Angela; lengthy airmails in which she poured out her heart about her dismal surroundings, her boring course, and how much she wished she'd stayed on the island. Angela's replies were less effusive.

I'm not allowed out to mix with any of the other expats. I have to stay in the house and wait for Stamatius to come to me. Sometimes, I'm so lonely I just cry my eyes out. But I really do love him, and I love the island too. I suppose I'll get used to it eventually. It's just a different way of life.

Angela had hoped that she and Stamatius would be able to relax once the tourists had left, but life during the winter had turned out to be just as exhausting. Although most bars and restaurants closed, the islanders were still busy cleaning, repairing and redecorating. Those who could afford it would embark on new projects: converting animal sheds into rooms, turning barren land into campsites, building small hotels and new bars.

Atlantis taverna was open all year due to the port trade, which meant that Stamatius was still working long hours.

He often stayed the night, but simply collapsed into bed next to her and then got up before she woke.

Then another letter arrived.

Big news. I'm pregnant. I ran out of Pills so I knew it would happen sooner or later. We've got to get married now, there's no choice. Stamatius's mum is relieved because I will no longer bring shame on the family, but his dad is pissed off because I don't have a dowry – no money, no land, not even any goats!! It's like medieval times here. Wish me luck.

Love Angela xx

Then, as a PS she wrote,

Sorry to say this, but best if you forget about Niko. It was a great holiday romance – leave it at that. Of course I'd love to see you again but better if you don't come back next summer. Please trust me.

Estelle was shocked. Just a few weeks ago, Angela had seemed so unhappy. What kind of life was she going to have as a traditional Greek housewife? She liked to party – she wasn't ready to be a mother.

But it was her friend's advice about Niko that shocked her more. Why should she forget about him? Had something happened? Estelle wrote and asked for an explanation, but none came.

She wrote to Niko as well, telling him how much she

loved and missed him, gently rebuking him for not having been in touch. She tried not to sound too needy, or too upset, reminding him of her Manchester address in case he'd lost it.

She waited for his reply. Patiently at first, blaming postal delays or Niko being too busy to visit the poste restante. It didn't mean there was a problem, she told herself. The weeks passed. As the end of the autumn term approached, she became increasingly anxious. She was expected home for Christmas; if Niko sent a reply, she wouldn't be able to read it until after the holidays.

Nothing arrived. She hated herself for being so dependent, for making excuses for him and rationalising why he hadn't written. Despite all the evidence to the contrary, and Angela's last letter, she didn't want to believe that their relationship was over.

Christmas was a disaster. She couldn't summon up any enthusiasm for presents, catching up with relatives, or the food her mother had cooked specially. When her parents asked her about Niko, she snapped at them and ran up to her room crying. They seemed quite pleased that the affair was over, and she hated them for it.

'It's for the best,' her mother said. 'Long-distance relationships never work . . .'

Estelle went back to Manchester early on New Year's Eve. The coach roared up the M6, rain spattering against the windows. Estelle fought back the tears as she contemplated the coming year. She'd had it all planned out – working the Easter vacation and the month of July to get some funds together, then interrailing her way back to Athens and spending two months on Inios with her beloved Niko. Now 1985 was a miserable prospect. She didn't care about her degree or her student life; she didn't feel at home in Manchester, and she hated the English weather. In fact, she wanted to give it all up right now and leave the country. Go travelling. See the rest of the world.

The coach arrived in the city centre. Estelle caught the bus down the Oxford Road, dreading entering her student house, which would be empty and freezing cold. There were no radiators, just small bar heaters in the bedrooms that took ages to warm up and sent the meter spinning. She would have to borrow everyone else's blankets tonight, she thought, as she turned her key in the lock.

There it was. A postcard lying on the mat – the picture showing a giant orange sun suspended over the Aegean. The photo could easily have been taken from Sunset Bar. Her hands trembled as she picked it up, her breath hitching as she turned it over to read the message.

I love you. I will always love you. But I cannot come to England. I must stay here forever. I am very sorry. Please do not write to me again. Do not come back to Inios. We must try to forget each other. Niko x

Chapter Twenty-Seven: Now

JUNO

'You're Paul?' I say excitedly. 'No way! That's amazing. My mother talked about you in her letters home.'

He looks alarmed. 'Really?'

'Don't worry, they're just edited highlights.'

'Bloody well hope so!' He chuckles. 'Lovely to meet you, er . . . ?'

'It's Juno,' I reply. 'Lovely to meet you too.'

Paul and his friends have already eaten. They want to move on, but he agrees to stay and talk to me about the past.

'Are you sure this is a good idea?' hisses Millie as we take our cocktails to their table. 'He's mates with you-know-who.'

'I don't care,' I say. 'I have to talk to him.'

Paul orders himself another beer while we study the menu. 'Any recommendations?' I ask, the options dancing before me. I'm too excited to eat. I want Paul to take me back in time. I want to plunder the contents of his brain and siphon off his memories.

'I always go for the stuffed courgette flowers,' he says. 'The meatballs are good too.'

He suggests a few more dishes and we follow his advice. Millie adds a portion of chips to the order, and we ask for a carafe of local wine.

'So how is Estelle?' Paul asks. 'What's she up to these days?'

I huff. 'Not much. She's an old hippy, lives in the mountains of Portugal. She doesn't have a regular job, lives off-grid, grows her own food, that kind of thing . . .'

'That doesn't sound like the Estelle I knew,' he says. 'She wasn't a hippy back then. More of a party animal.'

'Well, she's a hippy now. Fully committed . . . We're not close. My grandparents brought me up.'

'Oh. Why was that?'

I hesitate before replying. 'Long, complicated story. Anyway, enough about me.' The drinks arrive and I raise my glass in a toast. 'To the old days! Tell me everything.'

Paul clears his throat. 'Well, I first came here in 1984 with my mate Tony. We spent most of the holiday pissed out of our brains, but we loved it. The island means a lot to me. There's a group of us oldies, we call ourselves the Returners. We come back every year, with our dodgy knees and hips, beer guts and bald heads. Nearly all of us are on statins!' He laughs to himself. 'We can't keep up with the pace of the youngsters, but we give it a bloody good go.'

'Does Tony come back every year too?' Millie asks.

He shakes his head. 'Not as far as I know. He's not on any of the Facebook groups. We lost touch years ago.' He pauses to drink his beer. 'Nineteen eighty-four . . . Yeah . . . In a way, it was the best year, although they get blurred over time, you know? Same beaches, same bars, same people . . . But I do remember your mum vividly from that summer. She was quite a calm person, nice to be around. She knew how to party – beat me in a retsina slammer once at the Outta

Sight – but she was . . .' He searches for the word. '. . . kind. She really cared about other people, wanted to make sure they were okay.'

'Really?'

I'm surprised by this description. I've never thought of Estelle as a caring person – at least, she never seemed to care about me much.

'Estelle was lovely,' Paul continues. 'I fancied her, if truth be told, but she wasn't interested in me. She hooked up with some Greek guy. So did her friend, Angela. They hung out with us during the day, and most of the evening actually, then met up with their blokes later. The girls did a lot of waiting around, you know? The Greeks had them on the end of a string.' He takes a packet of cigarettes out of his top shirt pocket and gazes at it longingly.

'What do you remember about Estelle's boyfriend?'

He looks up. 'Nothing much. Can't even remember his name. Sorry.'

'It's okay, Juno already knows it,' pipes up Millie. 'Niko.'

'Niko. Yeah, that sounds right.'

Our food starts to arrive. A pungent combination of garlic and herbs, fish, smoked aubergine, stuffed courgettes, warm bread and spicy meat reaches our nostrils. Paul orders a second pint, and we help ourselves to the food.

I look around to make sure nobody is listening. 'Niko Zimiris is my father,' I say quietly.

'Oh!' Paul raises his eyebrows. 'I see.'

'I came here to find him, but the family behave like he doesn't exist. Kevin told me he left Inios a long time ago, but

I think he might be back. If there's anything you know I'd love to hear it – *anything*.'

He looks into his beer. 'Estelle was very stuck on him. She kept telling everyone how in love they were, but I think it was quite a rocky relationship. I remember they had a row towards the end of the summer . . .'

'What about?'

Paul pauses, and I sense him weighing up his next sentence, wondering whether he should speak it out loud.

'There was this hippy called Rob,' he says eventually. 'He was travelling alone. Nice bloke, bit naive though. Not streetwise. Sort of latched on to me and Tony.'

'Yes, there's stuff in Estelle's letters about Rob,' I interrupt.

'The three of us shared a room at this farmhouse. Rob had a bit of a fling with the farmer's daughter, which didn't go down too well, as you can imagine. One day, Rob disappeared, without saying goodbye or anything.' He picks at Millie's chips. 'We all thought he'd left the island but then Estelle found his bag. He'd left his passport and wallet behind. And the bag had blood on it.'

'Blood?!' repeats Millie, shuddering theatrically.

'Yeah. Estelle went to the police and reported Rob missing, but they didn't want to know.'

'What do you think really happened?' I ask, my brain already jumping to some unpleasant conclusions.

'Hard to say. Rumour had it, he was beaten up by some local lads and put on the ferry to Athens. Niko was one of them. Estelle didn't say, but she was angry with him about *something*, that's for sure.'

I lean forward. 'And did you ever see Rob again?'

Paul shakes his head. 'No. He just vanished.'

'Oh my God!' gasps Millie. 'That's sent shivers right down my spine.'

'It doesn't mean that much,' Paul continues. 'I expect he found his way back to England somehow, vowing never to return!' He laughs briefly. 'Who knows? We didn't have ways of contacting each other in them days. It was all very casual. I don't think I even knew Rob's last name.'

'But all that took place in 1984, right?' I say. 'Estelle returned to Inios the following year. Do you remember anything unusual happening then?' I look into Paul's blue eyes, ignoring the laughter wrinkles, searching for the twenty-two-year-old he once was.

'I didn't go back, not that year. We made a pact with the girls that we'd return, same time, same place, but we never made it. Tony moved on to another job. I met my wife. She wasn't into partying, so we went elsewhere for our holidays.' He pauses to drink his beer. 'We got divorced. I started coming back to Inios in the nineties. A lot had changed by then – there were proper hotels and they'd built the roads – but the spirit of the island was the same. Kev was still running All Right Now, this place was still going . . .' He looks around affectionately. 'Kev's the person you should ask about the old days. He's bound to remember Estelle.'

'I already have, and he doesn't.'

'Really? I'm surprised. Still, he's been through a lot over the years. He knows more about the island than anyone, loves the place with all his heart. He'd do anything to preserve it.'

'Including locking an old lady in a cold store for hours on end?' Millie says, her voice sharp with accusation.

Paul shakes his head. 'No, he'd never do something like that. Anyway, I know it wasn't him 'cos he was with me the whole time that evening.'

'We don't want to get involved,' I say. 'I'm not interested in the politics – I just want to know what happened to Niko.'

'Sorry. I wish I could help.' Paul finishes his drink, smacking his lips as the last of the lager goes down. Right. Better get back to the boys.' He checks his phone. 'They're in the sports bar.' He stands up and feels in his shorts pocket for some cash.

'The beers are on me,' I say. 'It's the least I can do. Thanks for your time.'

He smiles. 'I always like talking about the old days. Makes me feel young again . . .' He takes out a cigarette, twirling it between his fingers. I can sense his eagerness to go outside for a smoke. 'Good to meet you, Juno. When you next speak to your mum, give her my love.'

We pay the bill. Millie announces that she's going to meet up with some friends and leaves me to go back to the apartment alone. The evening is still warm, and the partying is in full swing. There's no way I'll be able to sleep, not with the conversation with Paul replaying in my head. Needing to wind down, I go straight up to the roof terrace and switch on the fairy lights.

I sit down and take off my shoes, resting my feet on the sofa. Taking out my phone, I consider trying to call Estelle again. We've reached an impasse. She won't tell me what happened all those years ago until I leave the island, and I won't leave the island until she tells me what happened. Maybe I should take a different tack. I could tell her about bumping into Paul and pass on his love. It might prompt her into talking about Rob's disappearance and whether Niko was indeed involved. Little by little, I might get her to reveal the truth.

I take a few moments to compose myself, then call. I study her profile photo as it rings. The nose stud and pink-streaked hair make her look younger than her years, but there's sadness in her eyes. She doesn't pick up.

There's somebody else I should speak to, of course. My husband. I've been putting it off, telling myself I wasn't ready, or too busy, or too distracted by everything else that's been going on. But now is as good a time as any. I take a deep breath and call him.

As soon as his face appears on my screen, my heart wrenches. He looks tired and stressed and his hair, which is sticking up at strange angles, needs a wash.

'Hi,' he says, surprised. 'God . . . it's actually you. Do you realise it's been six weeks since we've spoken? I'd given up.'

'Sorry . . . It's been really difficult.'

'Tell me about it.'

'Do you want to talk?'

'Depends what you want to say.'

'I don't know . . . I just thought, I owed you a conversation.'

'Too right you do.'

We pause to contemplate each other in our different spaces. He's at home, sitting in our living room on the navy velvet sofa we chose together. On the wall behind him is a huge blown-up photo taken on our wedding day, surrounded by friends and family. We look so naive, so full of confidence for the future. That we would be able to have children was a given back then, as sure as our love for each other.

'How are you?' he asks.

'Up and down. How are you?'

'How do you think?' He looks towards the ceiling in exasperation. 'My life's a shitshow. I'm on my own, I don't know what the hell's happening, if we're still together or it's over, whether you're ever coming back. I don't know what to do, what to say to anyone. I'm falling apart here and you're in Greece having the time of your life.'

'No, I'm not,' I say. 'I've got myself into a tricky situation and I'm not sure how to get out of it.'

'Easy. Come home.'

'I can't. Not yet . . .' I hesitate. 'I think I've found Niko. Or rather, he's found me. Only we can't meet.'

'Why not?'

'He doesn't want his family to know he's in Inios. I think there was some huge falling-out years ago, maybe something to do with Estelle.'

'She got into a right panic when I told her you'd gone there.'

'I wish you hadn't. She sent me a message telling me I wasn't safe and had to leave straightaway.'

He sighs. 'Which meant you did the opposite.'

'Only because she refused to explain, Luke! I can't just abandon my search for no reason, I've come too far. I've tried to talk her about it but it's as if she's scared. Now she's avoiding me.'

'Well, I know what *that* feels like,' he replies sharply. 'You're more alike than you realise.'

'I'm nothing like Estelle,' I say vehemently.

There's a long pause.

'I'm sorry,' Luke concedes. 'I only contacted her because I was worried sick and I thought she might help find your dad. Obviously, it's something you need to do, and I respect that. But I want you back, Juno! I'm in limbo here. We can't sort our marriage out on a videocall.'

'I know . . .'

He stretches his limbs wearily. 'Look, we've had a tough time these past couple of years, but we can do this. There's no medical reason why we can't conceive. We're good candidates for IVF—'

'I don't want to do IVF.'

'Don't reject it out of hand – we need to look into it. I know it's expensive, but—'

'Maybe it's not meant to be.'

'You don't mean that.'

'I'm sorry, but I do.'

His face crumples. 'Are you saying you don't want a baby, or you don't want a baby with *me*?'

'I don't know . . . I still love you and I think you still love me.'

'Of course, I do.'

'But loving each other isn't enough, is it? All the trying and failing, it's chipped away at our relationship, bit by bit. We're no longer a couple leading a normal life, having sex because we're really attracted to each other – we've turned into a malfunctioning baby-making machine. And the problem is right here,' I point at my head. 'It's not your fault, it's mine. Something's blocking me.'

'Nobody's at fault. These things take time, that's all.'

'We don't have time, Luke. I'm thirty-nine.' I look away from him, focusing on the view, hundreds of lights twinkling on the hillside. 'I can't keep going on like this. I'm sorry. But if you really, really want kids more than anything, then maybe . . . maybe you should—'

He shakes his head violently. 'Uh-uh, you won't get rid of me that easily. I *do* want kids, but not if it means losing you. We can work through this – I know we can. We'll get there somehow. But we have to be physically together – and not just for the obvious reason.' He offers a smile. 'Running away isn't going to solve it.'

'I'm not running away,' I protest, but I know he's right.

I hear footsteps running up the steps. Millie lands on the terrace, panting for breath, her eyes wild.

'Juno!' she gasps. 'Juno – I need—'

'Sorry, Luke, got to go. We'll talk again soon, okay?' We sign off and I turn to Millie. 'What is it? What's up?'

'They've found a body,' she says.

Chapter Twenty-Eight: Now

JUNO

'A body?' I echo. 'What do you mean? Like, a *dead* body?'

'Of course it's a dead body!' Millie virtually screams. 'Oh my God, I think I'm having a panic attack.' She paces about the tiny roof terrace, hyperventilating.

'Sit down, take some deep breaths. Tell me. Where was it found?'

She drops to the sofa, clasping her chest. 'At Klimeni. In an old well. The construction guys found it. This afternoon. Called the police. Nobody's supposed to know. But everyone's talking about it.'

'I bet they are.'

'I need a drink.'

'Are you sure? You're really stressed—'

'I *need* a drink.'

'Okay. I think there's some wine in the fridge.'

'Perfect.'

'Do the police know whose body it is?'

'Don't know. The wine? Please.'

I go downstairs to the kitchen, coming straight back with a half-drunk bottle and two glasses.

'I'm scared, Juno,' Millie says as I pour the wine. 'As soon as I heard, I just knew.'

'Knew what?'

She takes a gulp, wincing as the ice-cold liquid goes down. 'Knew who it was.'

'Who?'

'Lana,' she whispers.

I gasp. 'Lana?'

'There hasn't been a peep out of her since she "left the island". She never said goodbye, I didn't see her get on the ferry, she hasn't responded to any of my messages or posted online. Nobody's heard anything from her.'

'It doesn't mean—'

'I *knew* it was strange, her just going off like that,' she carries on, not listening to me. 'I should have reported her as a missing person, or tried to contact her parents . . . She's been lying there for weeks. Ugh . . . I feel so bad . . .'

'You're jumping to conclusions. We don't know if the body's male or female, how long it's been there . . .'

'Andreas had her killed,' she whispers. 'I feel it in my bones. Maybe he got Vasilis to do it—'

'Stop it!' I put my hand on her arm. 'For a start, the family would never have buried her on land they knew was about to be excavated. It makes no sense.'

She shakes her head. 'It makes perfect sense. They thought it would be easier to hide, they just didn't realise the well would be dug up. Do you think she was already dead when they—' She breaks off, unable to speak the rest of the sentence. 'Oh God, I can't believe we're talking like this!' Tears choke in her throat.

'Please calm down,' I say.

'How can I? Lana was my friend!'

'Hey, come here.' I sit down next to her and take her in my arms. 'You mustn't get ahead of yourself. We don't have any details yet. The body could have been lying there for a hundred years.'

'You said yourself that she was working for Kevin. What was it she found?' Millie asks, freeing herself and reaching for her glass again.

'Um . . . proof that Andreas had falsified figures to get some government grant. For sustainability, I think. It was serious stuff. I imagine Andreas could face a prison sentence if he was caught—'

'There you go!' she cuts in. 'Andreas found out and told Vasilis to get rid of her.'

'Vasilis is a minibus driver, not an assassin. They'd never go that far.'

'Huh! I should have known you'd stick up for them. You're part of the family. People close ranks.'

I stiffen up and go back to the other sofa. 'I'm not closing ranks.'

'Yes, you are. Why do you want to be one of them anyway? They're evil.'

'They're not evil, they're just . . .' I scout around for the right word. 'Businesspeople.'

'Businesspeople? Murderers, more like.'

'Look,' I continue quietly, 'I don't agree with the new resort, but it's their land, they've a legal right to do it. They're keen to protect their interests, but that doesn't make them murderers.'

'Lana had some serious dirt on them. Now she's dead. Go figure.'

'You're getting way ahead of yourself. Let's just wait for more information to come out, eh? There'll be a full investigation, an autopsy. DNA tests, everything. The police will do their best to identify the body and—'

'But they won't know about Lana unless somebody tells them,' Millie says. 'Andreas won't mention it, for sure. I think I should report it – like, now. It could save a lot of time. Her family must be worried about her. She might already be registered as a missing person.'

I raise my eyebrows. 'You feel that strongly that it could be her?'

Millie nods. 'They were vile to her, Juno. I'm not exaggerating. I feel like they'd stop at nothing.'

'I don't know . . .' I suck in my cheeks. 'It's risky . . . You'd be accusing your employer of murder. If you're wrong, and it turns out to be the body of an old goatherd who accidentally fell down the well fifty years ago . . .' I pause for her to consider the consequences. 'Leave it until we know some basic details, eh? If it turns out the body's female and it's only been there a few weeks, then absolutely, go to the police. But don't go to them now. Promise me?'

'Okay . . . I promise . . . I still know I'm right,' she mutters into her glass.

There's a thoughtful silence between us. I go back over our conversation. Some of what Millie is saying makes logical sense, but the implications are enormous. I'm very reluctant to accuse the family of being involved in such a serious crime. I can't believe it. I don't want to believe it.

Maybe I *am* closing ranks, behaving as if I'm part of the family, when I'm not really. At least, not in any meaningful way. It's only DNA that links us and that's not enough to command my automatic loyalty.

Millie drains the bottle. 'Is there any more?'

'Yes, but we've got work tomorrow.'

'I don't think I can face it,' she says. 'Not after this.'

'Honestly, Millie, you've got to calm down.'

'I might quit,' she says. 'Move to Santorini for the rest of the season.'

'Please don't.'

'You should leave too. If it's not Lana's body at the bottom of the well, it's somebody else's,' she says. 'This place isn't safe.'

The next morning, Millie refuses to get out of bed. 'Tell them I've got a tummy bug,' she says. I walk down to the car park alone and meet Vasilis as usual. If he *is* the murderer, he's remarkably relaxed about the discovery of the body. I decide not to mention it.

As we drive in silence to the club, I think back to the encounter with Paul. I'd never been to that restaurant before, so it was sheer luck that we bumped into each other. It feels like it was meant to be. Several bars and restaurants in Chora have walls lined with pictures from the past, and yet there's not a single photo at Club Inios Sunset. I know it targets a wealthier market, but that doesn't mean that no old photos exist . . .

Despina hasn't arrived yet, so I have the office to myself. I switch on the doddery old computer, eating my pastry and drinking coffee while it thinks about waking up.

I may have to accept that I'll never meet my father in the

flesh, or hear his voice, or hear stories about what he was like as a boy, but at the very least I'd like to know what he looks like. What characteristics have I inherited from him, other than olive skin and dark eyes? I can see a slight similarity between me and my uncle and cousins – I have the same-shaped nose as Andreas, and my hair is black and wavy like Christakis's, but that's not enough. I want to see my father's face.

I rise and close the door, then go to Despina's desk. It's an old-fashioned piece of furniture, dark and solid, with several drawers on either side and a long one running across the front. I pull gently on the centre drawer's handle, and it resists. In fact, all the drawers bar two are locked.

The first drawer is full of stationery. The second contains personal items – a hairbrush, lipstick, a box of painkillers, a bottle of perfume. Also, a small carved wooden box. I take it out and ease off the lid. There are several tiny keys nestling inside.

I go to the third drawer and try the keys at random until one of them turns in the lock. It's full of documents in coloured folders. Contracts, I think. I shut the drawer and begin my attempts to unlock the one below. It opens with the next key I try.

The drawer is full of photos. Lots of them muddled together in a pile, all different shapes and sizes, some in colour, some black-and-white. There's bound to be some shots of Niko among all these. But it'll take time to sort through them, which I haven't got.

I hear Christakis's voice – it sounds as if he's just outside the office door. I gather as many photos as I can and run over to my desk. Opening my bag, I drop the photos into it, and am on my way back to lock everything up, when Christakis walks in.

I freeze, my eyes darting over to the drawers hanging out of Despina's desk.

'Where's Despina?' he barks, not even bothering to say hello.

'I, er, don't know. She hasn't come in yet.'

He swears in Greek. 'I need to see her now. My father has called an emergency meeting . . . Not for staff. Family only.'

I move forward, trying to obscure his view of the desk, although he's so distracted, he doesn't seem at all aware of his surroundings.

'I heard the news about the dead body they found in the well,' I say.

'Huh. You can't keep a thing quiet around here.'

'Must have been a shock.'

'A great shock.'

'I suppose they've had to stop digging.'

'Yes. The police have made the whole site a crime scene. My father is going to go crazy. If you see Despina, tell her I'm looking for her.' He makes to go.

'Any idea who the victim is?'

He swings around. 'Who's saying it's a victim?'

'Sorry, I mean . . . the dead person.'

'It's some stupid tourist who didn't look where he was going. They'll probably never find out who it is. It'll take months, years. Worst of all is what this will do to Klimeni's reputation. People will say we've got the evil eye on us. Nobody will want to come and stay.'

'Yes, they will. It could even be good for business,' I suggest. 'People like true crime stuff.'

Christakis snorts derisively. 'There is no crime! Please, do not say that to my father. Don't speak to him about it at all. He's very, very upset.'

He leaves the office. I quickly lock the drawers of Despina's desk and return the keys to where I found them. The photos are in my bag. I want to sort through them now, but I don't dare risk it.

Instead, I go to the kitchen and try to engage Chef Michalis in a discussion about the catering for the next wedding. He's in a particularly bad mood this morning, shouting at his sous-chefs. I think he's secretly missing Phaedra, who hasn't yet returned to work after the trauma in the cold store.

'Did you hear about the body they found at Klimeni?' he says. 'See? This is what happens when you make enemies of the Zimirises!' He lets out a nasty laugh.

Andreas turns up half an hour later. He's unshaven and wearing joggers and a T-shirt instead of his usual suit. For the first time, I see him as an old man – nervous and vulnerable, declining in his powers. He sits at a table in the corner of the terrace with Christakis and Despina, who has just arrived, their heads bowed in conversation.

I run back to the office and close the door, heading straight for my bag. My heart racing, I empty the pictures onto the desk. One by one, I turn them right side up. My eyes flicker across the grainy images – people standing in a row with their arms around each other, sitting at tables listening to a guy playing guitar, snuggling together on beanbags. I peer

203

into faces, trying to separate locals from tourists, waiters from customers, friends from lovers.

One picture grabs my attention. It's of Andreas, aged about twenty, with his father – Babá Yannis. They have their arms around each other and are grinning confidently at the camera. There are other people around, but the pair hog the shot, as if they are the only ones that matter. The Andreas I'm familiar with looks more like his dad than his younger self – they have the same strong nose, grey beard and craggy lines around their eyes. They've merged into one person. Andreas has become his father, the head of the family.

A young man stands in the background, looking across at father and son, his dark eyes narrowed, his mouth a grim line. He's wearing a pale T-shirt and jeans and has a leather Stetson on his head. My brain jolts as I make the connection. Kevin Casey made a disparaging remark about Niko always wearing a cowboy hat, suggesting that it was a stupid affectation.

'Hello, Dad,' I whisper, picking the photo up and holding it to my chest, pressing our hearts together. 'I've found you at last.'

Chapter Twenty-Nine: August 1985

ESTELLE

Estelle felt a fool. She'd boasted to everyone at university about her Greek boyfriend and how madly in love they were with each other. Her bedroom was festooned with his photos and Inios memorabilia. She'd bought a teach yourself Greek book with a cassette tape, all in preparation for her return visit. But those were just superficial wounds; embarrassing but quick to heal. It was Niko's rejection of her that hurt so deeply.

Her feelings for him hadn't changed over the last months. If anything, they'd grown stronger. He'd told her he still loved her, and had asked her to wait for him, so why was he pushing her away? Both Angela's letter and the message on Niko's postcard were enigmatic, more worrying because of what they didn't say than what they did. Estelle suspected Niko's family had got wind of his plans to come to the UK and instructed him to cut ties with her. He was a grown man. Why didn't he stand up for himself, tell them to stuff it?

What hurt almost as much was this feeling of being cast adrift, cut off from the place she'd grown to love. She longed to be in Greece, unable to imagine it being anything other than warm and sunny, even though it was February, and all the hotels and bars would be closed. Manchester was cold and colourless. It always seemed to be raining. The sky was permanently grey, the buildings dirty with soot and pollution. Factories were closing down, there were high rates of unemployment. When Morrissey sang 'Heaven Knows I'm Miserable Now' it sounded like a personal anthem.

She didn't want to be in this dreary city, puzzling over Old Norse poetry or contemporary linguistics. She wanted to lie on the beach, or to watch the sun sink into the Aegean from the terrace of Sunset Bar. Most of all, she wanted to be with Niko. She would not – *could* not – accept that he didn't want to be with her.

Estelle limped on through the following months, skipping lectures, drifting away from her friends, spending most of her time in the tiny bedroom of her student house, feeling alienated and lost. There were exams in June. She performed badly, but she didn't care. At the end of the summer term, she took down the photos and postcards and packed up her belongings. She told her parents she needed to store everything at home, as she didn't know where she'd be living for her final year, but in truth, she'd already decided not to return. They came to collect her, packing all her belongings into the back of their Volvo estate. She left Manchester without a backward glance, her thoughts fixed only on the future.

Living at home had its advantages. Her mother picked up her dirty laundry and returned it to her the following day, washed and ironed, in a neat pile on her bed. She had all her meals cooked and could come and go as she pleased. But it was like living in a waiting room. Her grant was spent, her bank account empty. She needed to earn some money before she could go to Greece.

She went to a temping agency, and they found her a job as a copy typist for a shipping company in the City of London. She'd learned to type at school – it had been an extra-curricular activity only available to the girls. She spent six long weeks typing ships' letters, which had to be absolutely perfect – no rubbings-out or Tippex allowed. It was brain-numbingly boring but again, she didn't care.

Over on Inios, the summer season had already started and it irked Estelle that she would be arriving late. Niko had no idea that she was coming over. He'd told her to stay away, but she hoped that once he saw her, he would realise what an idiot he'd been, and run into her arms.

Angela didn't know she was coming either. They hadn't corresponded for months. Angela had never replied to Estelle's request for an explanation. She would be married by now, seven or eight months pregnant. It would be good to be there when the baby was born. Estelle knew nothing about looking after babies but hoped she might be some help to her.

By mid-August, Estelle had grown tired of her temp job and had managed to save enough money for a flight to Athens and the ferry to Inios, leaving her with a couple of hundred pounds that would have to cover her expenses. She didn't know how long it would last. Maybe Niko would find her a place to stay, just as Stamatius had done for Angela. She would work something out. The important thing was to get there.

Estelle disembarked from the ferry along with dozens of other island-hoppers. Not knowing where Angela was living, she went straight to Atlantis taverna in the port, where her husband worked. As expected, Stamatius was waiting on tables. She sat down and signalled for him to come over.

'Hello. What would you like? Eat? Drink?' His pencil hovered over the pad.

'Hi, Stamatius,' she said. 'It's Estelle.' He looked at her blankly. 'Angela's friend. I was here last summer.'

'Yes, yes,' he nodded, but she could tell he didn't remember her.

'How is Angela? Has she had the baby yet?'

'No, four more weeks.'

'How is she doing? She must be incredibly uncomfortable in this heat.'

'My wife is well, thank you.' His tone was stiff. She felt she'd said the wrong thing.

'I'd really love to see her.'

'My mother is looking after her,' he replied carefully.

'Okay. But . . . surely Angela can have visitors. I mean, it's not like she's ill.'

He narrowed his eyes. 'She has to rest.'

'I just want to chat. I'm sure she'd love to see somebody from home.'

'I'll ask my mother.'

Estelle sensed a barrier rising. It hadn't occurred to her that Angela wouldn't be allowed to see friends. She wanted to talk to her before she went looking for Niko. Angela might know something. Then again, if she was being kept in the house all the time, she might not.

It was very hot, and the port was heaving with people.

Estelle needed to find somewhere to stay. A hostel would do, although it would be better to have her own room so that she could spend some time alone with Niko. There was the goatherd's hut, but she didn't want to be stuck out in the sticks on her own, waiting for him to roll up.

The queue for the bus stretched all the way down the street. Estelle decided to take the donkey path up to Chora instead. She would stop off on the way to see whether her hosts from last year were still letting out their outhouse.

Sofia was delighted to see her, immediately bringing out a jug of lemonade and homemade honey cake. They sat outside in the shady courtyard, skinny cats curling around their legs, waiting for crumbs. It evoked such powerful memories of last year that Estelle started crying. It was as if she'd lost something precious that could never be found again. Or maybe it was the anxiety of seeing Niko after nearly a year of being apart.

Unfortunately, there was a Swedish couple already staying in the outhouse. They'd booked it for three weeks. 'So many people!' Sofia cried, holding up her hands. 'I'm very sorry.'

Estelle said goodbye, promising to visit again, then continued on the path up to Chora. She knocked on doors, asked in shops, but there was not a free room to be found.

She passed by All Right Now. It was closed but the door was open, so she slipped inside. The cave that the bar was inside was cut deep into the side of the hill, and was blissfully cool during the day, but choked with cigarette smoke in the evening. Kevin was there, stocking up for the night ahead. He was wearing army shorts and a faded Rolling Stones lips vest. Fortunately, he recognised her immediately.

'Estelle! What the fuck are you doing here?' he said, which was his way of saying 'Welcome back.'

'Couldn't stay away,' she replied, smiling. 'Don't suppose you know of anywhere I can stay, do you? The place is bunged. I don't want to sleep on the beach if I can help it.'

Kevin put his hands on the bar. 'A mate of mine is minding a new hotel that's just been built behind the Outta Sight,' he said. 'The owners ran out of money and the construction company pulled out. It's not officially open yet but the beds are in, the showers are working – it's brand fucking new. You go and talk nicely to Cliff, say I sent you, and he'll give you a room. No charge. On the quiet. obviously. We don't want the owners to find out, know what I mean? They're not local, so it should be okay.'

'Thanks. It sounds perfect,' she said.

They had a beer together and exchanged news. Kevin said he hadn't seen Angela for months, not since the wedding, to which he hadn't been invited. She no longer drank at All Right Now, or at any bar for that matter.

'She's a proper Greek now,' he said.

'Do you know where she and Stamatius live?' Estelle asked.

'Angela was staying in one of their holiday flats but now they have to live with his parents,' Kevin replied. 'They have a house on the other side of the port, not far from the beach. You should be able to visit her, but she won't be allowed out. Not in her condition. And they won't want her to be seen with another English girl either.'

Estelle shook her head with disbelief. 'Angela used to be such a party animal. How does she stand it?'

He shrugged. 'It's how it is if you marry a Greek. You stay at home and help your mother-in-law run the house. Look after the men. And the kids, of course.' He drew her a map of the house's location on a serviette. 'I'm sure she'll be chuffed to see you. She'll be going out of her mind with boredom.'

But first, Estelle went to the hotel and found Cliff, who told her to pick a room for herself. Some of them were already occupied – sleeping bags laid out on the beds, dirty clothes, food packaging and spent mosquito coils littering the floor. Angela chose a room away from the others, which had a balcony overlooking the sea. There was no bedding, no hangers in the wardrobe, and no loo roll in the toilet. None of the doors had keys either, although you could lock them from the inside. When she took a shower, the water was cold, and the tray leaked. There were clearly a lot of snagging issues, but it was paradise compared to where she'd stayed last year. She couldn't believe her luck.

The day had almost gone; soon it would be sunset. She was hungry and needed to buy some more water. Estelle unpacked as much as she could and put on fresh clothes – a pair of denim shorts and a white peasant top with a deep ruff, worn off the shoulders. Niko had admired it last year, said it made her look innocent and sexy at the same time.

She had to see Niko tonight.

Chapter Thirty: Now

JUNO

At last, I have a day off. I decide to start it with a lie-in – not that I can sleep with Millie banging around the bedroom as she gets ready for work. I've hardly seen her these past few days; she's been out all the time, returning to the apartment in the early hours. Unfortunately for her, Christakis found out that instead of lying in bed with a stomach bug, she's been hanging round the expat bars, trying to find out more about the grisly discovery at Klimeni. He called her last night to say she had to show up this morning or face the sack. And he wouldn't pay her for the month either.

Millie drags her hair back into a ponytail with a scrunchie. 'Do you want the shutters open?'

'Might as well. I'm awake now.' She pulls them apart and bright morning sunlight floods the tiny bedroom. I sit up, yawning and stretching my arms. 'Hey, do you want to see a picture of my dad?'

She nods. 'Sure! But how come—'

'I stole it from Despina's drawer.'

'Wow . . . When?'

'A few days ago. I've been wanting to show you, but you've not been around.'

I take it out of my bedside cupboard and hand it to her. 'He's the guy in the background,' I say, pointing.

'He's fit! . . . But how do you know it's him?' She flips the photo over, looking for his name.

'I don't, not for sure, but he was famous for always wearing a cowboy hat.'

'You look a lot like him.'

'Really? Do you think so?'

'Yeah, totally. Anyone can see it.' She hands the photo back. 'At least you know what he looks like now. That's something.'

'I'd still rather see him in the flesh. It's so frustrating that we can't meet up.'

'Do you still think it was him that sent you the note?' she asks, searching for the sandals she kicked off last night.

'I don't know what to think anymore,' I sigh.

'Weird shit is happening, that's for sure.' She bangs the soles together, scattering sand across the floor. 'By the way, I was talking to some people at All Right Now last night about the dead body. I told the story about Lana, and everyone said I should report it to the police. Apparently, activists go missing all the time, all over the world. They make powerful enemies, people who are rich enough to get away with murder—'

'Andreas isn't *that* rich . . .'

'Maybe not, but his investors are. They could easily be in on it.' Millie looks defiant, caught up in the drama of it all. 'Anyway, if I don't say something, the police won't know she even existed. I have to do it. For Lana's sake. And her family.'

'Hmm, I don't think you should rush to make accusations,' I say. 'Wait until there's more information.'

'I don't need it. I've been searching for her on social media. She hasn't posted since she supposedly left Greece.'

'That doesn't mean she's dead. She could be on another undercover investigation.'

Millie considers this for one second, then declares, 'No. It's her. I can just feel it.'

'Please, hang fire for a little longer.'

'We'll see.' She checks the time on her phone. 'Shit. I'm late.'

After she leaves, I try to doze off again, but it's impossible. My brain is fired up and ready to go. The same questions keep popping up in my head. Where are Estelle's letters? Who stole them? If it was Andreas, why hasn't he confronted me? Who left me the flowers with the warning message? If it was Niko – and I can't think that it's anyone else – why is he so scared of our being seen together?

And now, there's another worry. I keep thinking back to my conversation with Paul and the story about the hippy guy who was beaten up and forced off Inios, never to be seen again. What if the beating went too far? Could it be *his* body they found at the bottom of the well? If Niko was involved, as Paul suspects, could it be connected to his leaving the island?

I draw my knees up to my chest, hugging myself as I consider the awful possibility that Rob was murdered. I hope I'm wrong and that he survived the beating and made his way back to the UK. If so, he must be in his sixties now. I hope he's living a happy life – recently retired from a decent job, in a nice house with the mortgage paid off, with a loving wife and grown-up kids, his escapade on Inios no more than an amusing anecdote from his wild youth. But if he didn't, and it *is* his body they found, it would be good for his family to find out what happened to him, even after all these years. The not knowing must be the worst thing of all.

Over the decades, there must have been dozens of back-packers who never returned from their travels because they'd been murdered or suffered fatal accidents or had committed suicide or simply decided to start a new life else-where. The old days were so different. It was very hard to track people's whereabouts. There were no mobile phones or emails, no WhatsApp groups, no trail of photos or loca-tion pins on people's social media posts. Everyone was free to go where they pleased without other people following their every move. But it also meant that if they disappeared, it was very hard to find them.

I need to talk to Kevin again. He was here during that time. Paul was surprised that he didn't remember Estelle. I have a feeling Mr Casey has been lying to me. He knows more about what happened than he's letting on.

I pull on a top and a pair of shorts, then leave the apart-ment. It's just after 9 a.m., and only the bakeries, supermarket and a few cafes are open. The streets are quiet and peaceful. I walk down to the main square, hoping Kevin might already be installed at his favourite table.

But he isn't. It's too early for him. He was probably up all night drinking with the s Returners and now he's sleeping it off. Or maybe he's gone back to hanging out at the Wild Duck . . .

I sit down anyway, and order breakfast – fresh orange juice, coffee, a croissant with honey. It's a relief not to be at the club today. I'm exhausted. The constant pressure of pretending to be someone I'm not is taking its toll. Considering that I've never organised anyone else's wedding before coming here, I seem to be doing quite a good job of it. It's my secrets that weigh me down the most. I don't even know if they *are* secrets anymore, which makes it worse. The family could be fully aware that I'm Niko's daughter. They could be playing me like a flute.

Breakfast arrives and I tuck in, glad of the distraction. All this worrying is doing my head in. Croissant finished, I wipe my hands with a paper serviette, screw it into a ball and put it on my plate. A gust of wind blows it off the table, and it skips across the pavement to the next cafe, where a waiter scoops it up. I smile at him apologetically, then take out my phone.

Estelle and I can't go on like this. We need to have this out, once and for all. I check the time. It's early, but she should be awake. I take a deep breath and make the call. I must have caught her off-guard because she answers almost immediately.

'Juno?'

'Hi.'

'It's good to hear your voice. Are you alright? How are things with Luke? Please tell me you're back together.'

'We haven't split up. We're on a break.'

'Oh. Okay, whatever that means ... Where are you living? Are you at home? Has Luke moved out?'

'I'm still in Inios,' I say, carefully.

She gasps. 'What? But I thought you'd left weeks ago! I made it clear that it wasn't safe for you to be there.'

'Yes, but you wouldn't explain why.'

'Not *wouldn't*,' she snaps. 'Couldn't.'

There's a long, awkward silence.

'Are you okay?' she asks eventually.

'I'm fine. But there's a lot going on here . . .'

'What do you mean?'

'Did you tell Niko that I'd come to look for him?'

'Niko?'

'He's been in touch.'

'Niko?' She repeats, incredulous.

'Yes. He sent me some flowers and a note. He wants to meet but he says the family are watching me so he can't.'

'There's no way Niko would go back to Inios,' she says slowly. 'Are you sure it was him? Not somebody else, trying to trick you?'

'Obviously, I don't know for certain, but . . .' I hesitate. 'It *has* to be him. It was a sweet note. He said to pass on his love to you.'

She gasps.

'Are you alright?'

'Yes . . . just taken aback,' she says. 'How did he know? I told you not to tell anyone who you were.'

'Okay, I'm going to come clean,' I say. 'But that means you have to too.'

'Clean about what?'

'You know what I mean. I'm talking about the past.'

'Okay . . .' she replies, her voice unsteady. 'I'll do my best, tell you what I can.'

'First, I've managed to get at job at Club Inios Sunset . . . It used to be Sunset Bar, but it's completely different, really exclusive. Still run by the Zimiris family. They own quite a lot of places on the island – bars, restaurants, a luxury villa. The chance came up to be their wedding coordinator, so I went for it.'

'Juno! This is crazy,' she says.

'I know . . . It seemed like a good idea at the time. Now I'm not so sure.'

'Babá Yannis must be dead. Who's running the place now?'

'Andreas.'

She exhales loudly. 'Of course. The slimy toerag . . . That's all he ever wanted – to be the big boss. I suppose he's married. With grown-up kids?'

'Yes. His wife died a few years ago, apparently. There are four children – Despina, she's about my age, two brothers who live in Athens, and the youngest, Christakis.' I wait for her to respond, but there's only silence on the other end of the line. 'You still there?'

'Yes. Sorry. I'm just trying to take it all in.'

'Christakis and Despina run the club on a day-to-day basis. Andreas deals with bigger projects.'

'What about my friend Angela?'

'She left decades ago, apparently.'

'That doesn't surprise me.'

'Kevin Casey is still here.'

There's a beat. 'Kevin Casey – who's that?'

'Kev. He used to run All Right Now. You mentioned him in the letters several times.'

'Did I? I forget.'

'It's okay, he doesn't remember you either.'

'Well, it was a long time ago . . .' She sighs.

I pause, wondering how best to break the news. 'Now something awful has happened,' I say. 'A dead body was found yesterday.'

Her breath catches. 'What?'

'It was in a disused well, at a spot called Klimeni, in the far south of the island.'

'Oh my God!'

'My roommate thinks it's the previous wedding coordinator, Lana. She went missing some weeks ago.'

'The body's recent then?' I detect a tinge of relief in her voice.

'We don't know. The police haven't released any details yet.'

'I see.' There's a long pause.

'I bumped into Paul, one of the Barking boys.'

'Really? He's still coming to Inios, after all these years?'

'Yes. He told me about a hippy guy called Rob who got into trouble with the locals and disappeared.' She doesn't react. 'You must remember . . . I was wondering . . . could it be him?'

There's a long pause. I can almost hear her working out how to reply. 'Okay, Juno, listen to me,' she says at last. 'You've had your fun. Now it's time to go.'

'I can't. I'm on contract until the end of September.'

'It doesn't matter. Just pack a bag and go. Tonight.'

'Tonight? Why?'

'Just do it.'

I bristle. 'I need a reason.'

'Sorry, I can't give it to you. It's safer you don't know.'

'You said you'd tell me the truth!'

'No, I didn't. I said I would tell you what I could.' She sighs. 'I made a promise a long time ago never to talk about any of this to anyone. I have to keep it.'

'But why? A promise to whom?' Beat. 'My father?' Another beat. 'What did you promise him?'

'I can't say.'

'What did he do?'

'Please . . .'

'What did *you* do?'

'Catch the first ferry you can,' she says, ignoring my questions. 'Don't tell anyone you're going, just slip away.'

'You know who the dead person is, don't you?' I wait, my fingers gripping the edge of the silence. 'Come on, I know you do. It's Rob, isn't it? . . . How did he die? Was my dad involved? . . . Estelle? . . . Are you still there? Talk to me!'

'Please, just get out of there as soon as you can,' she says finally. 'You're in danger. *I'm* in danger.'

'You're in Portugal,' I retort sharply. 'And I'm not leaving until you tell me the truth.'

She releases an exasperated groan. 'I *can't*! For once in your life, Juno, do as you're fucking well told!'

Chapter Thirty-One: August 1985

ESTELLE

Sunset Bar was heaving with customers. Estelle hung back at first, her eyes weaving a path through the throng as she looked for Niko. Andreas was serving behind the bar, a shorter, squatter version of the man she loved. Babá Yannis was visible too, holding court at one of the tables, gesticulating with his cigarette like he was playing with a sparkler.

Why wasn't Niko here, working the all-important sundown shift? She remembered how he used to sneak off to catch a few minutes with her on the other side of the rocks, pretending he'd gone to replenish the stock. Perhaps that was where he was right now, his tongue down the throat of this week's girlfriend. The thought felt painful, as if she'd caught her heart in a door. She withdrew to the shadows of the terrace, afraid to ask anyone where he was, wondering whether to stay or go.

Stirring classical music by some Germanic composer was blaring through the speakers, accompanying the sun on its stately descent. The sight still took her breath away. People were lying on beanbags, huddled around the tables, or sitting on the retaining wall, their legs dangling over the edge, drinking, smoking, laughing . . . She didn't recognise anyone from last year, which didn't help her confidence. It was odd that she'd happily travelled alone the previous summer and had had no trouble making friends, yet this time felt awkward about starting conversations with strangers.

Her heartrate accelerated as she saw a familiar silhouette walking up the steps towards her.

'Niko!' she shouted, a smile of relief spreading across her face. Her eyes blinked at the fierce evening sun. She opened her arms, expecting him to hug her but he held back, staring at her, still taking in the shock of seeing her again.

'Estelle?' His tone was questioning. A variety of emotions flickered across his face – joy, concern, anger. 'Why are you here?'

She laughed self-consciously. 'Why do you think? To see you, of course.'

He looked confused. 'Did you get my postcard?'

'Yes. That's why I came.'

'I don't understand,' he said after a beat. 'I told you to forget me.'

'I know, but you also told me you loved me . . .' She reached out, longing for him to embrace her, to feel the touch of his skin, but he stepped back, shaking his head.

'Not here,' he said. 'I can't be seen with you.'

'What do you mean?' She glanced over at Babá Yannis. 'Has your father forbidden it?'

'We can't talk now,' he replied. 'You need to go. You are making problems for me.'

His words stung; she couldn't hide it. 'I wanted to see you, that's all. I've missed you so much.' She looked at the ground, lowering her voice to an anxious whisper. 'I love you . . . I thought you loved me too. I wanted to come out earlier, but I didn't have the money.'

'Where are you staying?' he asked.

She explained that she was at the new hotel behind the Outta Sight. 'Hotel Aphrodite. Room 307, third floor.'

'But it's not open yet.'

'There's a few of us camping out there.'

'Okay. Good. I'll come later.'

Her throat constricted. 'Roughly what time?'

'I don't know. When we close. Around two?'

'*Two?*' That was six hours away. What was she supposed to do with herself until then?

'I'll try to come earlier. Now go, please. Before anyone sees you. I mean it.' He turned away from her and went back to the bar, picking up empties on the way until he looked as if he had bottles for fingers.

She swallowed her tears and slunk back up the hill, reaching the rough track that passed for a main road. She paused at the top. Chora was to her left, twinkling invitingly in the distance, while Hotel Aphrodite was somewhere in the unlit abyss to her right. Both destinations were about half an hour's walk from here. She had hours to kill before Niko arrived. There was easily enough time to walk up to the village, grab something to eat, then walk back down to the beach. She could hang out in All Right Now with Kev and his mates, most of whom were Brits. Some people from last year might be there. The idea was appealing, but she didn't fancy walking back later. She was concerned about finding the path to the hotel in such intense darkness. The sign wasn't illuminated and there was no lighting around the front entrance.

In the end, she compromised with a visit to the Outta Sight cafeteria on the beach. She ordered a plate of spaghetti with tomato sauce, sitting on the concrete steps to eat as there were no free tables. The busyness of the place surprised her. Last year, most people had left the beach by this time, the majority heading into Chora, with some stopping off at Sunset Bar. She watched them for a while. It seemed like a different kind of crowd. They were more raucous and fashion-conscious, the men with bleached hair, strutting around like peacocks, the girls eyeing up their competition on the next table. There were very few backpackers or hippies with guitars hung over their backs.

Estelle didn't belong to either camp. She felt alienated, although that probably had more to do with Niko's cold response than anything else. He'd been so negative. Hadn't even given her a peck on the cheek. He'd behaved as if he was embarrassed by her presence.

She finished her beer and spaghetti and bought a bottle of water for the night, then walked around the side of the campsite, picking her way through the brush, until she found a makeshift wooden sign for Hotel Aphrodite. The ground was sandy, tufted with coarse grass. It would have all been beach, she thought, thousands of years ago. She took off her sandals and walked the rest of way in bare feet, enjoying the soft, cool sand beneath her soles.

Back in the room, she tidied up as best she could and unzipped her sleeping bag so that it lay flat and open on the bed. She had no idea whether Niko was coming for a chat or to stay the night and she tried not to think about it too much in advance, just to wait and see how things turned out.

She'd bought a few postcards in Athens while waiting for the ferry. Now was a good time to write them. Her parents had not been happy about her returning to Inios – *nobody* was, it seemed – which put an extra pressure on her to prove them wrong. She composed a brief, airy message, betraying none of the anxiety she was currently experiencing. She decided not to mention the difficulties with Niko.

It had been a very long day, and she was exhausted. She went onto the little balcony to see if the breeze would wake her up a bit. There was no sound, or other light source – Cliff and the other 'guests' were partying elsewhere. The atmosphere was eerie. She went back inside and sat on the bed. She tried to read but the light wasn't good enough and ended up lying down, staring up at the ceiling, wondering when – *if* – Niko was going to turn up.

She must have dozed off, because the next thing she knew there was somebody knocking on the door, shouting her name.

'Estelle? Are you there?'

She sat up, dizzy with the sudden movement. 'Yes! Coming! Just a sec.' She slid off the bed and stood up – fluffing her hair, and pinching colour into her cheeks before opening the door.

'I've been calling you for ages,' he complained, walking in. He took his Stetson off and put it on the dressing table. She peeked at her watch and saw that it was nearly 3 a.m.

'I tried to stay up, but I fell asleep.'

'We were very busy. I couldn't get away.' He stepped

onto the balcony and looked down at the empty swimming pool. 'Do you have permission to be here?' he asked suspiciously.

'Yes, it's fine. There's a man called Cliff who's finishing things off. We're helping.' He looked unconvinced. 'There's only a few of us anyway, all friends of Kevin Casey.'

His lip curled with disapproval. '*Reh malákas . . .*' It was one of the few Greek phrases she knew.

'He's not an arsehole, he's a nice bloke,' she responded. 'And I didn't have anywhere else to stay.' Of course Niko would be on the side of the hotel owners, not the freeloading foreigners.

'It's better than last year's place,' he admitted, sitting on the bed and bouncing up and down a few times.

'That little camp bed was super uncomfortable,' she agreed, sensing him warming.

'I am sorry I was rude to you earlier. It was a shock to see you again. I was at work. It was difficult. I didn't know what to do.'

'It was my fault. I should have sent a message. I just wanted to see you as soon as possible. I'm sorry.'

He waved her apology away. 'It's okay. We are here now. Look at you. You are even more beautiful than before. Come to me, Estelle *mou*.' He beckoned her to join him, kissing her as he slowly pushed her back onto the mattress.

She lifted her head to allow him to pull her top off, raised her hips so that he could remove her skirt and pants. The room was warm, despite the door to the balcony being open, and the air was thick with a fragrance she couldn't identify. Jasmine perhaps.

'I'm happy you came back,' he murmured.

'So am I,' she replied, stroking his hair as he buried his face in her breasts. Her body tingled. She felt like an animal waking up after a winter of hibernation. He took off his clothes and they lay naked on top of the sleeping bag, kissing and writhing, sparks of static pricking the air.

She was no longer on the Pill – there hadn't been any point – so they would need to use condoms. She'd brought some with her, but they were in the toiletry bag which she hadn't yet unpacked. Niko hated wearing condoms – he'd mentioned it several times last year and had been pleased when she'd said there was no need. Telling him to put one on now would break the spell and it had been hard enough to conjure it in the first place. She decided to say nothing and hope for the best.

'I've missed you so much,' he murmured, as he entered her. 'I've thought about you every day . . . Ah, my love, this is good. So good . . .'

They held on to each other tightly, rocking together as one. All the longing that had been trapped inside her was suddenly released. He let rip too, telling her he loved her over and over again, in English and in Greek. She declared she loved him more – that she would always love him, no matter what.

The night was hot and suffocating. She could taste the fresh sweat on his skin. He was clearly at boiling point, but he held himself back, waiting for her to reach her climax. They orgasmed simultaneously, groaning with pleasure. The months of absence suddenly meant nothing. It was as if they'd never been apart.

'That was beautiful,' he said, sighing contentedly as he fell back onto the bed.

'Mm, yes . . . incredible.' She reached for his hand and kissed it. 'Aren't you glad now that I ignored your postcard?'

'Yes, I am very glad,' he replied, smiling.

'I tried to forget you, but I couldn't do it.'

'No. Nor could I.'

'Why did you send it?'

He sighed again. 'I thought it was for the best.'

'In what way? I don't understand, Niko.'

'Shh, my love. It doesn't matter now. Everything is good.'

They lay together in silence for a while. Estelle rested her head on his chest, listening to the beat of his heart. He stroked her hair. All the sadness and worry and doubts of the past year evaporated. He still loved her, that was all she needed to know. This was where she belonged. She had come home.

A little later, she was slowly drifting off to sleep when she sensed Niko shifting beneath her, unwinding his limbs from their tangled embrace.

'Hey, Estelle,' he whispered. 'Wake up, please.' Her eyes blinked open. 'I'm sorry, but I have to go.'

She stared at him, astonished. 'What – now? But you can't!'

'I'm sorry,' he repeated. 'I want so much to stay, but it's not possible. I must go home. My father will know if I don't come back tonight.'

'So what?'

'Babá is the boss. I must do as he says.'

'Why?' She sat up. 'You're not a kid anymore, you're twenty-four!'

He looked away, avoiding her gaze. 'I made a mistake and now I am . . .' He paused to search for the words. 'In a trap. My father uses it against me.'

'What mistake?' The question hung in the night air. 'What mistake, Niko? What do you mean? What did you do that was so wrong?'

He reached for his clothes. 'Nothing. Sorry – I have to go now.'

'No, no, you can't leave it like this.' She leapt off the bed. 'You have to tell me. Why are you in your father's power?'

He put his trousers and shirt back on and picked up his hat. 'I'll come tomorrow night. If I can. Or on Tuesday.'

'Niko—'

'Shh . . . It's okay . . . *agapemou*, my love. Everything will be good, I promise.' He kissed her. 'I will find a way.'

Chapter Thirty-Two: Now

JUNO

The phone call with Estelle leaves me reeling. She told me little but implied a great deal, her pauses and hesitations being most full of meaning. Now I understand – I think – why she didn't want me to come here. She wasn't worried that I'd be rejected by my Greek family. She was trying to protect herself. And Niko too. I'm sure that they did something bad all those years ago – so bad that I don't want to say it, not even in the privacy of my own head. I also suspect that it's connected to Rob's disappearance. That's why they left Inios; why they could never return.

I close my eyes for a few moments. An image of a skeleton flashes into my mind, lying awkwardly at the bottom of an old dried-up well. Because if Rob has been lying there since the eighties, he will definitely be a skeleton by now. Was he ever registered as a missing person? Not in Greece perhaps, but possibly in the UK. Of course, his disappearance happened before DNA was discovered, but if members of his family were to be tracked down . . . If a match could be made . . . Once the police know who it is, when and how they died, it'll just be a question of who did it.

But maybe it's not Rob. Perhaps my parents – that's an unfamiliar word – were responsible for some other, unconnected crime. Maybe Millie is right, and the body is Lana's after all.

Either way, I have to decide whether to do as my mother said and leave Inios or stick it out to see how the investigation progresses. I could tell the police my suspicions, but that's all they are: suspicions. It's not as if Estelle confessed to anything this morning. She was careful. Too careful to sound innocent. That's what worries me the most.

But if I leave Greece now, where am I going to go? Back home, I suppose – to Luke. To hours of couples' counselling and long nights of tearful conversation. I wish we'd never started trying to conceive, although we couldn't possibly have known how difficult it would be. Do I love him enough to keep trying? Does he love *me* enough to give up? Maybe it's not fixable either way and we have to face the sad truth that we've reached the end of our relationship. I don't know the answers to any of those questions, and probably neither does Luke.

I accept that I can't hide from him forever. We have to sort it out, one way or the other, face-to-face. But I can't leave the island yet. I have unfinished business here and I don't want to give up the chance of finally meeting my father. I'm sure the flowers and the note were from him. I have this strong feeling that he's nearby, waiting for the right moment to show himself. Estelle won't tell me the truth about what happened all those years ago, but maybe he will.

It doesn't matter how dangerous it is, I have to stay.

I return to work after my day off, anxious for news of the investigation. Despina is already at her desk, tapping away on the computer with her pink pointy nails. I open up the files and start working, checking the arrangements for the next weddings, which are in a few days' time.

'What's happening at Klimeni?' I ask when she stops for a break. 'Has the autopsy been done yet? Do they know how long the body was in the well?'

'I've no idea. Nobody in this family tells me anything.' She fixes me with a look. 'Why do you ask?'

'Oh, no particular reason,' I bluster. 'Just that there are rumours going around ... Like, some people think it's a recent thing, others that it happened years ago. Maybe it was a walking accident. A lone traveller. It's so hot, easy to get lost ...'

'Absolutely. Tourists can be very stupid,' she remarks.

'Yes ... well ... hopefully, it's nothing more sinister.'

'Indeed ... Please don't get involved, Juno. It'll be weeks before we hear any news. Maybe months. Everything in this country works so slowly. It's very annoying. We need to restart the groundworks, but the police won't release the site yet. In the meantime, we're wasting time and money. Also, it's not a good image for the resort. We are in the media for all the wrong reasons.'

'Yes, you must want it resolved as soon as possible.' I hesitate before taking my last shot. 'Do you or Andreas have *any* idea who it might be?'

Her face darkens. 'I'm only interested in facts, Juno, not gossip. I don't want to talk about it anymore, okay?'

We go back to our silent work. A little while later, Christakis enters and has a short exchange with Despina. It's in Greek, so I can't understand what they're saying, but

232

it sounds like there's a problem. Christakis in particular appears very annoyed.

Despina turns to me. 'Juno. I'm sorry, but we need use of the office for a few minutes. Would you mind?'

'No, er, of course not.'

'Thank you.' She gives me a tight-lipped smile.

Intrigued, I pick up my bag and make for the door. 'I'll be on the terrace. Just let me know when I can come back.'

I bump into Millie waiting in the reception area. She's looking down at the floor like a sulky teenager.

You okay? I mouth. She shakes her head.

'Millie? You can come in now,' Christakis says from the office doorway. She slouches in, and he closes the door. I linger outside, eavesdropping.

It doesn't take long before voices are raised. I hear Lana's name mentioned several times.

'Prove it then!' Millie shouts, finally getting a word in. 'Prove that she's still alive!'

'I don't have to prove it!' he retaliates. 'Lana betrayed us. That's why we sacked her.'

'You killed her because she found out what you were really up to.'

'You cannot make this accusation!'

''You're wrecking Inios. You're evil, every one of you!'

'How dare you speak about my family like that?'

They both start speaking at once, and I lose track. After another couple of minutes, the door flies open, and Millie runs out, almost colliding with me.

'Hey, slow down,' I say. 'Are you alright?'

'No! I've just been sacked!' she cries, eyes blazing with

anger. 'Just like that. He can go fuck himself. Calling me a liar. Who does he think he is? He's the liar, not me. I quit, okay?' she shouts back into the room. 'I quit!'

'What happened? Did you go to the police?'

She nods. 'I *had* to, Juno. There was no choice. I made an official statement so now the police have to investigate. If the body *is* Lana's, they won't get away with it.' She storms off in the direction of the Wellbeing Cabana.

'I wish you hadn't jumped the gun,' I say, running after her. 'It was inevitable that the police would tell Christakis. You might have lost your job over nothing.'

'I don't give a shit about my job,' she cries. 'Even if I hadn't been sacked, I'd want to go. They're like the fucking Mafia!' she continues, racing down the steps, not caring that everyone sunbathing by the pool can hear. 'Christakis threatened me just then. He said if I didn't get off the island by the end of the day, they would make things very difficult for me. That's what they said to Lana and look what happened to her'.

'You don't know what happened to her—'

'I do. They killed her!'

We go into the hut. I watch her throw various items of makeup into a large metal case.

'I understand how upset you are,' I say, 'but remember what Paul told us about that hippy guy who disappeared in the eighties? It could be him.'

'It's not,' she snaps.

'We don't know, do we? I'm just saying, there are other possibilities.'

'Come with me, Juno,' she urges. 'Don't stay here on your own. Let's go to another island, find new jobs—'

234

'Sorry, but I'm not ready to leave yet. I can't. Not when there's a chance of meeting my father.'

'Are you sure you want to know him? He's part of the same family.'

I'm taken aback. 'So am I.'

'Not really. That's why I like you.' She picks up her makeup case. 'Look, I get it. You do what you have to do. I've *got* to go, there's no choice.' Taking out her phone, she scrolls through her contact list. 'I'm calling a taxi.'

'Okay . . . I'll come and wait with you.'

We go back to the main building and stand outside the entrance in the shade of a large tamarisk tree. Vasilis is sitting in a plastic chair with his feet resting on an empty crate, no doubt wondering why we haven't asked him for a lift in the minibus.

Ten minutes later, Millie's taxi approaches. She turns and gives me a long hug.

'Look after yourself, okay?' she says. 'Keep in touch. If you hear anything about Lana, you'll let me know?'

'Of course. Where are going to go?'

'Paros, or Mykonos – maybe Santorini. I'll take a few days off before looking for another job. If you change your mind about joining me, just give me a call.'

'Will do. Take care. And thanks,' I add.

She frowns. 'For what?'

'For being such a good roommate.'

'You snore by the way,' she says, laughing as she gets into the taxi. I wave until it disappears round the bend.

Christakis hovers in the bar area, waiting to catch me on my way back to the office.

'Sorry about that,' he says quietly. 'Millie went too far.'

I frown at him. 'She's anxious about Lana, that's all. She disappears, nobody hears from her for weeks, then a body turns up. I told her not to jump to conclusions, but she felt she had to report her missing.'

He huffs. 'There's something I need to tell you. Can we walk and talk?'

'Sure.'

'I don't want to be overheard.'

I follow him down the steps to the lower level, then through the fragrant gardens to further steps leading down to the beach. My brain is working overtime, imagining what he's going to divulge.

We step onto the sand and walk between the two rows of sunbeds, emerging at the other end, where there are some boulders to sit on.

'Lana deceived us,' Christakis says. 'For a start, she pretended she was an experienced wedding coordinator. We quickly realised she was no good, but we kept her on because it was so difficult to find staff. She hacked into all our email accounts, went through all the company files . . .' He sighs bitterly. 'When we found out she was a journalist, we fired her. But we didn't kill her or have her killed. That's nonsense.'

'The thing is . . .' I begin cautiously, 'nobody's heard from Lana since she left Inios. You can understand why people are worried.'

Christakis inhales deeply. 'This is what I want to explain. My father paid Lana to keep quiet until Klimeni was launched. She agreed never to write about our family, or the island, or the development again.'

'Really? Activists can't usually be bought off so easily. It must have been a very large sum of money,' I say.

He nods. 'It was. She said she would donate it to one of her causes.'

'I see . . . Why didn't you explain that to Millie? It would have put her mind at rest.'

'We were afraid she'd go straight to the media. They might think we were trying to cover something up, which we're not.'

'Why are you telling me then?'

His expression softens. 'Because we trust you, Juno. You're experienced and – forgive me – older than most of the holiday staff we get here. My father likes you a lot. We all do. We feel like you're one of us.'

Is that a hint that he knows who I am? Should I say something? The words rise in my mouth, gathering on my tongue. *Spit them out,* I think. *Risk it.*

But I can't.

Maybe it's too late now, anyway. I've deceived the Zimirises as much as Lana did, albeit for very different reasons. And even if they didn't steal the letters and have no idea that I'm Niko's daughter, they might turn against me anyway. I could set events in motion that I can't stop.

'Thanks, but I'm just doing my job,' I reply, staring out at the sparkling sea, trying to keep my conflicting emotions at bay. 'And to be honest, it's going to be harder without Millie.'

'I know. I'm sorry,' Christakis says. 'When's the next wedding?'

'At the weekend. A small one on Saturday and a larger

one on Sunday. I think both brides have booked hair and makeup.'

'We'll have to find somebody local. I'll ask around. There may be somebody working at one of the other venues we can persuade to move over. I'll talk to Despina. Leave it with me.'

'Okay. Thanks.'

As soon as he's gone, I call Millie, keen to tell her the reassuring news about Lana. She doesn't pick up, so I send a long rambling text instead. She replies with two words.

He's lying.

When I get back to the apartment after work, I'm shocked to see how bare it is without Millie's stuff littering every surface. I'd got used to her untidiness and her habit of spraying her perfume like a cat marking its territory. I unpack the rest of my clothes and put them away in the wardrobe. I've the whole rail at my disposal now, plus all three drawers in the dresser. There'll be no more waiting to use the shower, no more shimmying past each other to get dressed or put on our makeup.

Suddenly, it feels like too much space for one person. Loneliness creeps out of the walls and envelops me. Not only have I lost a good colleague; I've lost a friend – the only person on this island I could trust.

It's still early. Most evenings, as soon as we came home from work, Millie and I would go up to the roof terrace with a glass of wine and some snacks. She would vape and we'd chat about our day or let off steam about various annoying clients or other people at work. It reminded me of being married – the good bits about it, anyway.

I decide to carry on the tradition, even though I'll have to talk to myself. Taking an already open bottle of wine from the fridge, I climb the steps to the very top. It's windy tonight. The TV aerials perched on roofs are wobbling. Some washing has been blown off the line next door. An envelope has been propped up against the lantern on the low table. Assuming it must be a goodbye note from Millie, I eagerly rip it open.

I take out a piece of lined notepaper, a message scrawled on it in spidery blue biro – handwriting I recognise. My hand starts to shake as I read.

Dear Juno,

Now the body has been found we are in much danger. You have to leave as soon as possible. There is no more time. Meet me tomorrow at Oceanus Bar, near the port beach. 8 p.m. I will tell you everything. Make sure you are not followed – this is very important. I trust you with my life.

Chapter Thirty-Three: August 1985

ESTELLE

Estelle stood under the canopy of a ceramics shop, studying the map in her hand. She was in the square with the statue in the centre, the sea on her left. Kev had drawn an arrow through the maze of streets behind the north end, marking the house where Angela now lived with an X. Like it was treasure.

It was late morning, and the pavements sizzled with heat. It had taken her over an hour to walk here, skirting the village, then taking the donkey path down to the port. She went beyond the ferry dock to the other big beach where the windsurfing school was. It was more developed than Kalapos, with bars and shops, most of which sold urns decorated with Priapic dancing men and items made from olive wood. New buildings sprouted on every corner – iron rods sticking out of the top floors like rusty bamboo. Eventually, Kalapos beach would be spoilt like this, she thought. Once they built proper roads, there'd be no stopping the island from development.

Her heart was heavy. She was more anxious than ever to see Angela. Niko's brief visit to her last night, although wonderful, had raised more questions than it had answered, and she needed to share her worries with someone she could trust.

Niko had changed. Last year, he'd been confident and rebellious, skiving off work to spend time with her and not caring about the consequences. But last night he'd seemed cowed, like a wild horse that had been finally broken. Babá Yannis was holding the reins and wouldn't easily let go. What mistake was Niko being punished for?

Angela might know more, she thought, stepping out of the shade, and continuing her journey. She followed Kev's spidery trail of biro to the house, tucked away at the back of the cluster of streets. It was more substantial than its neighbours' – arranged on two floors with a wide veranda covered in crimson bougainvillea and decked with overflowing plant pots. An older woman was washing the floor, chucking a bucket of soapy water onto the tiles, then mopping vigorously. She looked older than she probably was – her tanned face was weathered, and she moved awkwardly, as if she had arthritis. Her hair was tucked under a headscarf tied at the back of her head in peasant fashion. She looked up as Estelle approached, a wary look in her eyes.

'*Kalimera*,' Estelle said, almost curtseying. '*Me léne Estelle. Fílos tis Angela.*' She'd taken a few phrases from her Greek book and had been practising them in her head on the long walk from the hotel to the house. The woman, who had to be Angela's notorious mother-in-law, stared at her as if a cat had just spoken. Then she rattled off a reply in Greek that went beyond Estelle's limited vocabulary.

'Sorry. Um . . .' she struggled to remember how to say 'I don't understand'. '*Den se . . . katala . . . ?*' She gave up. 'Is Angela in? I'm her friend. From the UK. I'd like to see her please.'

The woman rested her mop against the wall and went inside. Estelle waited impatiently, not in the mood to be refused.

After a few minutes, Angela came to the door. She looked tired and enormous. 'Estelle!' she cried. 'My God, you're back!'

'Yup. How are you?' Her eyes fell to the bump. 'You look ready to pop.'

'I am. Come in, come in.'

'Can't we go out and find a cafe?'

Angela threw a glance behind her. 'Hmm ... I'm not supposed to go out. The dragon will only tell Stamatius and then there'll be trouble.'

'Really? It's that bad?' Angela nodded. 'That's a shame,' Estelle continued. 'I was hoping to talk in private.'

'It's okay, she hardly knows any English. We can say what we want.'

They sat in the courtyard at the back of the house, under the shade of a large lemon tree. Angela's mother-in-law served them some sugary homemade drink and squares of baklava dripping in honey – her distrust overridden by a compulsion to be hospitable. She sat with them at first, arms folded, looking at whoever was speaking, trying to give the impression that she understood every word they said. But after about ten minutes, she gave up the pretence and went back to cleaning the veranda.

'I'm so glad to see you,' Angela said. 'I haven't had a proper chat with anyone for months. Stamatius's English is okay, but not great.'

'You must know some Greek by now.'

'Oh, yes. He's been teaching me. I understand more than I let on.' She gave a mischievous grin that reminded Estelle of the old Angela. 'Mamá is always moaning to Stamatius, right in front of me too – "The girl can't cook, she's lazy, she doesn't show me enough respect, doesn't look after you properly." One day I'll give her a mouthful back in Greek. Hah!'

'The situation sounds dreadful. How can you stand it?'

'I can't. I hate it. It's like being in prison.'

'Can't you move back to that little house in Chora?'

'No. They're renting it out for the summer. Stamatius says he's going to build us a house of our own, but I can't see that ever happening.' She sighed, stroking her belly absent-mindedly. 'It's not what I thought it would be like. Not at all.'

'Do you regret staying?'

Angela looked away, focusing her gaze on a pot of lavender. 'Sometimes,' she said finally. 'I thought once we were married, things would improve, and the family would accept me, but it hasn't worked out. I'm not allowed to mix with the other expats or go out by myself. When there's a family gathering, I have to sit in the corner and wait for people to come and talk to me. Nobody ever does. I'm an outsider, always will be. The Greeks tolerate all kinds of stuff in the holiday season, but once the tourists are gone, they go straight back to their traditional ways. Women have very low status here. Their main function is to bear children and look after the men.' She bit back the tears. 'I love Stamatius, but . . . sometimes I think I'm not sure I can do this.'

'Maybe when the baby's born things will change,' Estelle offered.

'Yes, for the worse probably.'

'Does Stamatius know you're unhappy?'

She shrugged. 'Maybe . . . I'm not unhappy *all* the time.' She leaned over to squeeze Estelle's hand, almost losing her balance in the process. 'I do love him, and I'm really looking forward to being a mum, but . . .' She left a gap for Estelle to fill. 'Just be careful. Don't make the same mistake I made.'

'You mean with Niko?' Angela nodded. 'You don't have to worry about that. There's no way his family would have me in their house. If we want to be together, he'll have to leave the island.'

Angela pouted. 'Hmm . . . His family won't want that either.'

Estelle lowered her voice and told Angela about her troubled reunion with Niko the previous night. 'Do you know what happened between him and his father?' she asked.

'You must be kidding. I've hardly left the house for months. I haven't a clue what the gossip is. It's a different world here, they play by their own rules. We'll never fit in.' She paused. 'That's why I told you to forget Niko.'

'I know, but I couldn't. I *had* to come back. I'm still in love with him, Ange. And I think he loves me too.'

'Then ask him to leave Inios,' she replied. 'See how he reacts. If he refuses, then you'll know where his loyalties really lie.' She shifted uncomfortably, bending forward to rub the small of her back. 'Just don't get pregnant or you'll be trapped here forever.'

Niko didn't come to her that evening, or the next. She had no way of contacting him, and he'd expressly forbidden her from going to Sunset Bar. During the day, she lay on the beach, hiding behind a book so that nobody would approach her, wading out to swim by herself in the deeper water. She ate all her meals from the limited menu at the Outta Sight – spaghetti, moussaka, pork chop, hamburger, bean soup, omelettes . . .

She'd given her skin a battering from the sun all day and it prickled. She rolled up her mat and put her towel in her drawstring bag, leaving them by the steps of the cafeteria while she went for an evening stroll to stretch her legs. She walked as far as the taverna where she'd had lunch with Niko last year, when they'd made up after their argument over Rob.

Calamari tentacles were drying on a washing line over the concrete jetty. Holidaymakers sat at the tables with their plastic checked tablecloths, held down by cutlery and carafes of rough wine, laughing as the Meltemi wind intermittently sprayed them with seawater. Estelle observed a couple holding hands and gazing into each other's eyes and felt jealous. She and Niko loved each other. Why did everything have to be so complicated?

The sky was rapidly darkening, the sun having set a few minutes ago. Niko would be at work, flirting with customers as he always did, running around at the whim of his father. It was strange to think of him being so close and not being able to see him.

Estelle went back to the Outta Sight. People were dancing to rock music blaring out at full blast – Eric Clapton, the Cure, Sting, Jim Kerr from Simple Minds singing, 'Don't you forget about me,' just to rub it in.

She walked past, taking the path to the hotel. Cliff was there, trying to unblock a drain. He showed her a storeroom full of booze, destined for the pool bar which hadn't yet been completed.

'Help yourself,' he said. 'Nobody will miss it.'

She took two bottles of beer to her room and dragged a chair onto the balcony, where she sat in the moonlight, waiting for her Romeo, wishing she had the mental strength to go up to Chora and get drunk. An hour passed painfully slowly. Sod it. She would not be treated like this. She would go out.

She went back into the room and was choosing what to wear when there was a knock on the door. *Finally,* she thought. *About bloody time too.* She flung open the door, angry words already on her lips, but it was Niko's brother standing there instead. Andreas looked nervous, as if he was scared that she would punish him for bringing bad news.

'Hello, Estelle. I need to talk to you,' he said.

Chapter Thirty-Four: Now

JUNO

I hold the note against my beating chest. It feels so precious I can't bear to put it down. 'Oceanus Bar, tomorrow at eight p.m.,' I whisper. 'I'll be there, Dad. And nobody will follow me, I'll make sure of that.'

I study the few sentences scrawled on the page, saying little yet packed with meaning. *Now the body has been found we are in much danger.* It must be as I thought. Niko killed Rob and threw his corpse down the well. Estelle helped cover it up. The only thing I don't understand is the timing. Rob disappeared in 1984, the first summer Estelle came to Inios. But she came back the following year – I know that from the correspondence. There's only one letter and a couple of postcards written in 1985, which suggests that she didn't stay long. I need to look at everything again – work out the timeline, read between the lines and construct the narrative. There's as much to learn from the things Estelle *didn't* tell her parents as what she did. If only I still had the letters, I could make sense of it all.

It's crazy to think that in just over twenty-four hours, I could be with my father – a moment I've waited thirty-nine years for. I hope to God it really *is* him that sent the message, but I don't know for sure. It could be a trap. Maybe the person who stole the letters and wrote the notes is one and the same. Maybe Andreas, Christakis and Despina know who I am. Maybe I'm being played. I sit on my bed, drinking the rest of my wine, staring at Niko's grainy out-of-focus face, as if he could tell me the answers . . . In the end, I have to trust my instincts, and they're telling me to go to the meeting tomorrow night.

I will tell you everything, that's what he's promised. It's all I've ever wanted. To know is to understand.

The next morning, without Millie to cajole, I arrive at the car park on time. Vasilis is waiting for me, standing outside the minibus, pulling on a cigarette. There's a smug smile on his face. He doesn't say anything about Millie not being here, but I get the feeling he's pleased that she's left.

I miss her already and she hasn't even been gone a day. We had our in-jokes and secret signs. Sometimes in staff meetings, we would exchange a quick glance and know exactly what the other was thinking. She tended to take offence over nothing much, and she put partying above everything else, but she was a loyal friend, and her heart was in the right place. Now I'm alone, with nobody to confide in and nobody to watch my back.

Christakis is around as usual, but Despina doesn't arrive at the club until mid-morning. I don't see Andreas at all. Despina tells me he's locked in urgent discussions with the Klimeni project manager. Andreas wants the resort finished in time for the start of next season, which is less than a year away.

'It was an ambitious target before, but now it's looking

impossible,' she says. 'The police won't say when they'll let us back onto the construction site.'

'Did Christakis talk to you about finding a replacement for Millie?' She shakes her head. 'We've got two weddings this weekend,' I remind her.

She looks over the top of her monitor. 'Could *you* do it?'

'Me?'

'Your hair and makeup always look good.'

I laugh. 'Are you kidding? No way. We need somebody qualified.'

'I suppose so.' She sighs. 'It won't be easy to find anyone, not this late into the season, but I'll see what I can do.'

I try to bury myself in my work, but it's impossible to concentrate with so much going round in my head. I'm on a hair trigger, constantly looking for signs that the family are on to me – a word out of place, an odd glance, a slight change in the atmosphere. Everyone seems to be behaving normally, but I can't trust that. *I'm* wearing a mask. They could be too.

I finish work as early as I dare, asking Vasilis to drop me off in Chora, in the usual spot.

'Thanks, Vasilis,' I say airily. 'Have a good evening.'

'Now your friend has gone, you are lonely, yes?' He sneers as I slide open the minibus door.

'Not really.'

'You stay at home tonight?'

Why does he want to know? I wonder. 'Yes,' I reply firmly. 'Absolutely. Not going anywhere.'

Once I'm sure that Vasilis has driven away, I walk to the end of the village and take the donkey steps down to the port. I've already found Oceanus Bar on the map. It's on the other side of the harbour, tucked away in the back streets. It'll take me about forty-five minutes to walk there. I've got plenty of time, but I want to make sure I'm not late.

The evening is warm and unusually still. The heat of the day is trapped in the paving stones and it's like walking on a hot griddle. Tiny lizards shoot across my path, while the bushes on either side buzz with insects. But all the butterflies are in my stomach. I'm so nervous, I don't think I'll be able to eat. *Better go easy on the alcohol,* I think. *I need to have my wits about me tonight.*

There's hardly anyone else using the path, especially not climbing up. It feels like I'm going back in time, as if I'm going to arrive at the port and find myself in the eighties. All the characters I've come to know so well will be there: Estelle, Angela and the Barking boys, hanging around Atlantis taverna, playing cards and knocking back the ouzo, Rob the hippy strumming a guitar. Stamatius, Angela's boyfriend, will still be working, sneaking them extra beers and bowls of olives on the house. Maybe Niko will turn up later, clicking his fingers and dragging Estelle away for a romantic walk along the beach . . .

The real-life port is as busy as ever. Atlantis, still going after all these years, is jam-packed with waiting passengers, freshly showered, wearing their travelling clothes, drinking farewell cocktails or checking the ferry tracker app on their phones. There are no grubby backpackers, and the aisles are littered with suitcases rather than rucksacks.

I wander along, still in some otherworldly dream, looking at the boats moored up on the quayside. There's a 'pirate ship' offering day trips around the island's more inaccessible bays, and some small private yachts. I go into an olivewood shop and stare at salad servers. I venture into an expensive delicatessen and feign interest in the local artisan cheeses.

Make sure you are not followed.

I think I'm okay, but the place is so busy it's impossible to know. Millie was convinced that Vasilis had a whole army of spies, but I expect she was overdramatising.

A ferry rounds the bay, blasting its klaxon. Everyone stands up and rushes towards the terminus, clattering their cases over the concrete jetty, jostling each other as they try to stay in their groups. I weave between the crowds, emerging on the other side, where the large coach park is.

I walk along the seafront, half looking at the sunset and half following Google Maps on my phone. Reaching a square with an impressive statue in the middle of it, I enter a small maze of back streets, eventually finding Oceanus Bar.

It's very much a haunt for locals, not tourists. And it's small, with only a few tables on the pavement outside, all of which are taken by men drinking coffee and having deep conversations. None of them so much as look up at me. I hesitate, wondering what to do. I'm ten minutes early. Do I wait on the street or go in?

If this is supposed to be a clandestine meeting, it makes sense to meet inside, not out here where somebody might spot us. Taking a deep breath, I enter, finding myself in a long thin room. The floor and the tabletops are made of white-flecked marble, the bistro-style chairs of dark wood. Bottles are stacked behind the bar, where an older man is clattering glasses. Large woven baskets hanging on the wall provide the only decoration. Football is showing on the television. It's plain and characterless, lacking in charm.

There is only one other customer. An older man, in his sixties or perhaps seventies, sits in the far corner drinking a beer and reading a newspaper. He doesn't appear to be aware of my presence. I hover at the counter, unable to take my eyes off him. He's definitely Greek. A local, not a holidaymaker. He's wearing a striped polo shirt that stretches over his bulging tummy, and a pair of grey trousers. He still has a good head of hair, although it's streaked with grey. In his day, I think he would have been quite handsome. I want to get a good look at his face, but I'm not at the right angle.

Could it be Niko? My heart starts to race uncontrollably.

Chapter Thirty-Five: August 1985

ESTELLE

She sat on the edge of the bed, feeling weak, the stuffing knocked out of her. Andreas remained hovering by the door, ready for a quick escape.

'Niko's *married*?' she repeated. 'But he can't be!'

He nodded. 'It's true.'

'But . . . but when?'

'October. Last year.'

'But that was only a few weeks after I left! They must have already been engaged . . .'

He shrugged. 'What is "engaged"?'

'You know . . . the wedding was organised, planned . . .' His expression was blank. 'Forget it – doesn't matter . . .' She looked up at Andreas and tried to steady her voice. 'And when was the child born?'

'A month ago.'

'I see . . . Did Niko ask you to tell me?'

'No. I saw you at the bar. After, I followed him here. I told him to leave you alone. We had an argument, so I went to our father.'

'And he sent you.'

'Yes. You must understand, Estelle. You cannot stay here. Niko should be with his family, not with you.'

'Right. It's all my fault, leading him into temptation.'

'Sorry. I don't understand.'

'Yes, you do . . . You've done what Daddy told you to do, now get out of my room.'

'My father wants you to leave the island by Friday.'

She drew in an angry breath. 'And if I refuse? What will he do? Have me beaten up and put on the ferry without my passport? Like what happened to Rob?'

'I don't know what you're talking about.'

'Oh, stop lying to me. I know what this is all about. Your father thinks he can control everyone.'

'He's the head of the family,' Andreas replied, as if that was a given.

'Well, he doesn't control me. I can make trouble too, you know.'

'Don't try, Estelle. You can't win.'

She glared at him. 'Are you threatening me?'

'No, we ask you to do the right thing, that's all. For his wife and the baby. Stay away from my brother. Leave the island by Friday.' He turned to go, placing his fingers around the door handle. 'And you shouldn't be staying here,' he added, tossing the words over his shoulder. 'The hotel is not open. It's against the law. I will tell the owners.'

'Yeah, whatever. Like I care!' she shouted after him.

Once Andreas had gone, she flung herself onto the bed and wept. She was furious with Niko, but also with herself for being so blind. Everything was clear now. That was why he'd written to her last Christmas, telling her to forget him. He'd tried to let her down gently, but she'd ignored him. Why hadn't he just been honest about it? She couldn't understand why he'd married this local girl so quickly after she'd left. Had he got her pregnant? There was more to this story, and she wanted to hear it from Niko's mouth. He owed her that at least.

Estelle was still angry when she woke the following morning. Although the fire had died down, it left smoking embers that flared when she remembered something Andreas had said. She showered and dressed – not in her usual bikini and shorts, but in a simple sleeveless dress, normally reserved for shopping or sightseeing. It was important to look dignified. Niko may not be allowed to see her, but Babá Yannis couldn't stop her from seeing *him*.

Cliff was outside, puzzling over the pool bar he was supposed to be building. He greeted her in a friendly manner and invited her to an outing Kevin was organising.

'He's taking us to this amazing beach – you can only get there by army truck,' he explained. 'It'll be just a few of us. Hand-picked crew.'

'Thanks, I'll think about it,' she replied, feeling guilty for having inadvertently betrayed Cliff's generosity. Andreas was bound to tell the owners that there were squatters in the hotel. He could be in hot water now. Kev had said that the owners weren't from Inios, but that didn't mean the Zimiris family didn't know them. They seemed to know everyone.

She climbed back up the hill to the dirt road that led to Chora. Sunset Bar was further along, down another sidetrack. It was still early, but there was a good chance Niko would already be there, getting ready to open up. She didn't know where he lived but had no intention of going to his home. This was not a conversation she wanted to have in front of his wife.

His *wife*. The word sounded strange. Niko had virtually proposed to her last summer, but she hadn't taken it seriously.

Poor woman, she felt sorry for her. And a little jealous. Although, remembering what Angela had told her about being married to a Greek man, maybe it was just as well that she hadn't stayed on last year. It wouldn't have worked. As she walked along in the hot morning sunshine, kicking up clouds of dust, she tried to console herself with such thoughts, but they had little impact.

She turned off at the sign for Sunset Bar and walked downhill for a hundred yards or so, her empty stomach roiling with nerves, her legs feeling heavier with each step.

The bar was quiet and empty. The metal chairs had been folded and stacked up against the wall to allow the terrace to be properly washed down. Three skinny white kittens chased each other around the table legs. As she approached, they gave up their game and ran into the bushes.

She stood still, her attention grabbed by the view. It wasn't often she saw it in daylight. The land was so dry and barren, with scarcely a tree to be seen. Looking down to her left, she could see the main beach and the Outta Sight. Also, the campsite behind it. Hotel Aphrodite was one of those white blobs on the plain before the cliffs rose up, and the others were houses, rooms to let, or smallholdings. The sea stole the show, sparkling with all its might.

The place seemed deserted. The shutters on the servery had been pulled down, so it was impossible to see if anyone was inside the building. She walked around the back, to the small courtyard where she'd had that row with Niko, when she'd seen the bruises on his knuckles.

He was there, shifting crates of empty bottles into the corner. Hearing her footsteps, he turned round, rising to his full height.

'Estelle,' he said, surprised to see her. His voice was gentle, and it triggered a sob in her throat. Not wanting to appear weak or needy, she covered it up with a cough. He walked straight towards her and enveloped her in his arms. 'I missed you,' he murmured, kissing her in between words. 'I wanted to be with you, but it was impossible. We've been so busy – I couldn't get away.'

'You don't need to lie,' she replied. 'I know. Andreas told me.'

He pulled away, guilt flashing across his face.

'You're married,' she said. 'You have a baby. Why didn't you tell me the truth?'

'I didn't want to hurt you . . . I love you, Estelle.'

'Why did you marry her, then?'

He sighed. 'Let's walk,' he said. 'I'll explain, but not here.'

He took her hand and led her along a path that snaked down to the beach. The earth was bone dry, covered in a thin film of dust. Her shoulders and the back of her neck burned in the intense heat – she realised she'd forgotten to put suntan lotion on before she'd left the hotel.

After a couple of hundred yards, they found some boulders in the dappled shade of an olive tree and sat down.

'My wife is a good woman,' he said. 'I know her all my

life. My father and her father are good friends. Her family owned some land in the south of the island. It's no good for growing crops, only for keeping goats, but very valuable for tourism – you understand? There's a beautiful beach there, we call it Klimeni. My father kept asking if he can buy the land from him.' He took her hands and looked into her eyes. 'Her father said he would give my father the land if I married his daughter.'

She crinkled her nose. 'I don't understand. Why?'

'To bring the families together.'

'And what did you both think of the idea?'

He dropped his gaze. 'We weren't happy, but our opinions didn't matter. We had to obey our fathers.'

'This is the eighties, not the Dark Ages,' she snorted. 'I can't believe this is still going on, treating people like they're . . . commodities.'

'It's more complicated than that,' he replied.

'I don't understand. You've always been the rebel. You told me you hated the life here, that you wanted to leave Inios, study, do something completely different—'

'That is all still true.'

She turned to look him straight in the eye. 'Do you love her?'

He shook his head. 'Not in the way I love you. She doesn't love me either, but we respect each other. She's a good person. When we married, my father gave us a house – maybe you know it – it's on the bend of the road between Sunset Bar and Chora. It's an old farm, with land. This winter, my father wants to build some rooms for tourists. Maybe a swimming pool.'

'Sounds like you've already given up your dreams,' she said bitterly.

'No, never. I dream about you, Estelle. I tried to forget about you, but then you come back, and I see you and I know I'm still in love with you. I want to be with you. Only you. This is so hard. Tell me. What do I do?'

'I can't tell you how to live your life, who you should be with, where you should go.' There was frustration in her tone, she couldn't keep it down. 'I know what *I* want – to live a different way, to travel, see the world. To be *free*.' She kicked a stone that was lying at her feet. 'I love you, Niko. I tried to forget you too, but I couldn't. That's why I came back . . .' Her voice choked. 'But things have changed. You're married – you have a child. You can't just abandon them.'

'But it wasn't my choice,' he said.

'I know, but even so . . . You have responsibilities now.'

'Don't you want me?'

'Of course I want you!' she cried. 'But it's not as simple as that. You'd be leaving your whole family, your friends, the only life you've ever known. Your father would disown you. You'd never be able to return to Inios.'

He looked away, biting his lip as he fought back the tears. 'I know . . . It is a big decision.'

'Yes, and you have to make it by yourself, Niko. I can't help you.'

'I will think about it,' he said.

'Okay . . . good . . .'

There was an aching pause. She made patterns in the dust with her feet.

'What are you going to do?' he asked eventually.

'Well ... Andreas told me I had to leave the island by Friday, so ... I think I'll do that.'

'Where will you go?'

'Not sure – depends on whether you come with me, I guess.'

'Do you *want* me to come with you?'

She looked up. 'You know I do. But I'm not going to force you. I'm not even going to ask you. It's up to you.'

'I know.'

'All I would say', she said after some thought, 'is that if you don't leave Inios now, you probably never will. You'll have more kids, build your rooms, inherit the business, grow it, make it into a success. You'll be the next Babá Yannis.'

'Andreas can have that honour,' he said, brushing the idea away. 'I'm not interested. I don't want to run hotels and bars, I don't want to spend the rest of my life with a woman I don't love – I want *you*,' he said emphatically.

Her heart skipped, but she tried to push her feelings down. She longed for him to choose her but knew it would be wrong to try to influence him. He had to decide of his own free will.

'You'd better get back to work ...' she said, standing up and brushing a leaf off her dress. 'You know where I am. If you can't come to the hotel, leave a message for me at All Right Now. There's a notice board there, all the backpackers use it. Just say "yes" or "no". If it's "yes", I'll buy us two tickets for the first ferry on Friday morning. If it's "no", I'll only buy one.'

Chapter Thirty-Six: Now

JUNO

I sit in Oceanus Bar for an hour, first nursing my water, then two gin-and-tonics. They slosh around my empty stomach along with a cocktail of negative emotions. Niko hasn't turned up. The guy I thought might be my father – right age, right kind of looks – left thirty minutes ago, throwing me a disdainful glance as he walked past my table. My heart jump-starts every time somebody new walks in, but nobody has come looking for me.

There are four men here now – chatting to each other and watching television. I can't understand a word they're saying, but I have a horrible feeling that I'm the subject of their conversation. I'm a single foreign woman in a locals' haunt where I'm not wanted and have no right to be.

Why hasn't Niko turned up? Is he playing a cruel game with me, or wasn't it safe for us to meet tonight? I don't think I was followed here. I sigh. It's pointless hanging about – he's not coming. I stand up, scraping my chair on the tiled floor so loudly that the other customers turn round and stare.

'How much?' I say to the barman. He hands me the bill. The prices are a lot cheaper than in the tourist bars in Chora. I put some cash on the counter and leave without waiting for my change.

It's properly dark now and the street isn't lit. The few shops – a hardware store, a shoe shop, a hairdresser – are closed, their metal shutters rolled down. I peer into the shadows, half hoping, half terrified that I'll see somebody lurking in a doorway, but there's nobody there.

The street looks different. I'm disorientated and can't remember which way to go. I turn left, then change my mind and go right. Maybe it's the stress or the alcohol that's confusing me, but I seem to have entered a maze. I walk into a dead-end alley full of rubbish. A cat jumps off a wall in front of me and I let out a small scream. It contemplates me for a moment, its eyes shining yellow in the dark, then scampers away. I turn around and retrace my steps. I can feel my heart racing, beads of sweat bubbling on my chest.

I've lost all sense of direction, but I don't want to stop and get out my phone. It doesn't feel safe. I turn into another deserted street, too narrow for cars. As I walk down it, I hear footsteps behind me. Soft shoes, trainers perhaps . . . I quicken my pace, not daring to look round. The street ends abruptly at a T-junction. I don't know which way to turn, but I can't delay. I opt for the left. The footsteps seem to be getting closer. Suddenly, I hear a voice.

'Juno! Please, stop! Wait for me.'

I freeze. The voice is familiar – male, Greek – and yet I don't know whose it is.

I turn round to see Vasilis walking up to me. Of course it's him. He looks agitated, annoyed even, as if I've deliberately been leading him in the wrong direction.

'Where are you going?' he asks. 'Are you lost?'

I reply with my own question. 'Why are you following me?'

'I'm not.'

'So you just happened to see me walking down the street? Way off the beaten track. Don't lie.'

He holds up his hands. 'Okay, okay. Christakis is worried that you talk to the Stop Klimeni people. You told me you were at home tonight, but then I see you at the port. I thought maybe you go to Wild Duck, but no, you come here. To Oceanus Bar. You stay there for more than one hour. Why? Who do you talk with?'

'Nobody. Not that it's any of your business. I can do what I like with my free time.'

He sighs, as if my attitude is very tedious. 'Please. Let me take you back to Chora. My car is near.'

'I'd rather walk.'

'It's a long way. There are over three hundred steps.'

'I know. I don't care.' I cross my arms. 'Just leave me alone.'

He shakes his head. 'No, I can't. This is not a good place. You are lost, going in circles. I know the way. Let me take you home.'

Reluctantly, I let him guide me back to the square, which turns out to be much closer than I thought. Relief floods through me as I see lights and souvenir shops and noisy bars full of people dressed for a night out. They've come here to escape – two weeks when they can forget about their problems at work, or their failed relationships, or how they're going to pay off their credit-card debt. God, I wish I were one of them.

263

Vasilis tries to persuade me yet again to take a lift from him, but I refuse. I don't trust him, and I'm furious because he must have scared Niko off. Was it a coincidence that he saw me wandering around the port, or has he somehow managed to track my phone? I'm certain I wasn't physically followed to the bar, so that seems the most likely explanation.

I take a taxi up to Chora, and hurry back to my apartment. I'm on edge. I raid the fridge for snacks – anything to soak up the booze. Then I go to the bedroom. It's stuffy and I need air, but I don't want to let the mosquitoes in. I sit on the bed with a packet of salted nuts, stuffing them into my mouth until I cough, washing them down with warm water from the bottle I've been carrying around all day. Then I wipe my fingers on a tissue and take out my phone.

I've been trying to do this alone, but I can't take it anymore. I need to talk to someone. Someone who cares about me. Somebody I know would listen, who wouldn't judge or blame me . . .

I press down on his profile picture. It fills the screen. There he is, smiling back at me. Luke.

Sometimes I find it hard to believe I walked out on him. I have a lingering fantasy that our old life exists somewhere on another plain; that if I wanted to, I could walk into our old flat and find him sprawled on the sofa, feet on the coffee table, skimming Netflix for our next binge watch. That we could go back to the early years when everything was so good between us and pick up the path from that point. Only this time we'd stick to it resolutely, stepping over the obstacles, avoiding the side track that led to the destruction of the beautiful thing that was us.

What am I going to say to him if he picks up? 'Hi. I've made a load of mistakes here. I feel like shit and I've nobody else to talk to'? That wouldn't be fair. I put the phone down. I don't need to talk to Luke because I already know what he'd say. 'Enough is enough. Come home, Juno . . . Just come home.'

I was awake most of the night, the events of the last six weeks churning through my head. By dawn, I'd made my decision.

It's time to go. I know it's unprofessional to leave at such short notice, but I can't stay here – living a lie, hiding my identity, not knowing who to trust with the truth. Sometimes you just have to accept defeat. I'm never going to meet my father or be welcomed into his family. There aren't going to be any joyful reunions like the ones you see in those television shows where people find their long-lost relatives. And I'm not going to discover what happened all those years ago either. The past is in the past. It's probably best to leave it there. I need to think about my future instead.

I don't feel able to face Vasilis in the morning. Instead, I take a taxi to the club, arriving half an hour later than usual. Christakis is clearly rattled when I ask for an urgent meeting with his father. I have a feeling he knows what it's about, although God knows how. I'm paranoid. I'm frightened to think my own thoughts for fear that somebody is listening.

I sit at my desk, secretly compiling a list of things Despina will need to do when I've gone. I put the few personal items I've accumulated into my bag. If Andreas doesn't come by lunchtime, I'll have to give my notice to Christakis, or failing that, Despina. There's an evening ferry, departing a little after 7 p.m. and I don't want to miss it.

Just as I'm about to give up and call a taxi, Andreas arrives, sweltering in his smart work suit.

'You wanted to see me, Juno?' he asks. 'Is something wrong?'

'Um . . . I need to talk to you. In private.'

'Of course. Shall we go down to the amphitheatre? It's quiet there.' I nod.

The club is busy today, completely back to normal after the trauma of the attack and looking even smarter than before. Guests are wandering around looking glamorous. Club sounds are booming out of the speakers, and there's a yoga session going on by the pool.

We sit down on the stone steps facing the semi-circle. 'What's the problem' he asks. 'Christakis said it was urgent.'

'I'm afraid I have to leave immediately,' I say. 'Today.'

His eyes widen in astonishment. 'But why?'

'It's a personal issue . . . An emergency back home. I'm sorry, but I can't talk about it. I know I'm supposed to give a month's notice, but . . . that won't be possible . . . Sorry.'

He waves my apology away. 'No, I'm the one who's sorry. Sorry to lose you. You've been fantastic, everybody thinks so. Even Despina, who is very hard to please.'

'I tried my best but . . .' I tail off.

'She'll have to take over the weddings again,' he says. 'It's too late in the season to hire anyone else.'

'Yes, unfortunately. But your daughter's very capable. She did a great job before—'

266

He raises his hand to stop me. 'Despina is not my daughter.'

'No?'

'She's my niece.'

'Oh, right. Sorry, I just assumed,' I say, feeling confused. 'Your niece? Is that on your wife's side?'

'No. She's my brother's child. Phaedra is her mother. Didn't you know?'

I shake my head as my mouth dries. 'I, er, don't . . . don't, er . . . think I've met your . . . er, brother,' I say, my words sticking to my gums as I try to speak.

'Nikolaos left Inios a long time ago,' he says with a sigh. 'When Despina was a baby.'

'Oh.' I look away. *Keep it together,* I tell myself. *Don't give yourself away. Listen. Let him talk.* 'How come?'

'We don't usually speak about it,' he replies. 'Phaedra is very sensitive, you understand. My brother ruined her life, she never got over it. My father was so ashamed, he took Phaedra and Despina into his home, did his best to support them. When he was dying, he made me promise to keep up the commitment. Despina and my boys grew up together. We are all one family.'

'I see . . . Why did your brother leave? If you don't mind my asking.'

Andreas huffs. 'Oh, he was in love with an English girl. He'd met her the previous summer, we thought it was over, but unfortunately, she came back and took him away from us.' He shakes his head, still disturbed by the memory. 'I remember the day so clearly. My father sent me down to the port to stop him. I ran all the way, but I was too late. Niko was already boarding the ferry. He didn't even look back, you know. Not once. He humiliated Phaedra and abandoned his own daughter, but he didn't care.'

'What happened after that?'

'He disappeared from our lives that day and we never saw or heard from him again. He broke our hearts. In Greece, family is everything.' He sighs. 'It was that English girl's fault – once she found out he was married, she should have left him alone.'

He doesn't know who I am, I think. *He doesn't know and I can't tell him.*

Andreas stands up. 'I'm sorry you're leaving us, Juno. We'll miss you.' He gives me a brief, awkward hug. 'I hope you sort your problems out. If you ever want to come back, there will always be a job for you here.'

'Thanks,' I say, my eyes filling with tears.

Chapter Thirty-Seven: August 1985

ESTELLE

Hi Mum and Dad,

Just wanted to let you know that I'm leaving Inios at the end of the week. It's all fine. Nothing to worry about. Just a change of plan. At the moment, I'm not sure if I'll come straight home or stop off on the way. I might visit some other islands, or come back slowly overland, via Yugoslavia, Italy and France, etc. I might have Niko with me too. We want to be together, but things have got a bit complicated. I'm not sure how it's going to work out. I'll tell you the full story when I get back.

Obviously, you'll be wondering about my third year. I was going to wait until I got home to tell you face-to-face but things have changed and that's not possible now. I'm afraid I've decided to quit university, so I won't be going back to Manchester in September. I just can't see the point of it anymore. I've never really fitted in, or enjoyed studying, and my grades last year were dreadful. I have no idea what I want as a career, anyway. Normal jobs don't appeal to me. To be honest, I think I'd rather live in a commune and live off the land, grow my own vegetables. Yes, I know I've never shown any interest in gardening, but I want to learn! I hate cities. I want to live somewhere remote and beautiful, in the mountains or by the sea.

I'm really sorry. I know you'll be very upset by this news, and probably furious with me. You've always been so good, giving me the full student allowance and supporting me through. I'm sorry if this disappoints you, but I have to follow my heart.

I will keep in touch about where I am in case of emergencies, but I might go somewhere off the beaten track for a while, so don't worry if you don't hear from me for a few weeks or even longer. I'll be okay!

Love as ever and always.
E xx

P.S. Please try to understand.

Chapter Thirty-Eight: Now

JUNO

Despina is my sister.

I have a sister.

As I sit in the taxi on the way back to Chora, it's the only thing I can think about. We shared the same office for weeks, sitting opposite each other, neither of us knowing that we have the same father. I always wanted a sister.

She takes me another step closer to Niko. There must be traces of him in her features, in the colour and texture of her hair, the way she walks, the tone of her voice. He's been right in front of me all this time, hiding in plain sight. I want to stare into her face and make fresh links with my own. We have the same skin tone, the same brown eyes, but there must be other similarities between us. There are so many questions I want to ask her. But I can't.

It was agony talking to Andreas earlier. As he told the story of Niko and Estelle's affair, waves of guilt washed over me. I wanted to apologise to Phaedra on their behalf, and beg forgiveness, but I had to keep my mouth shut. I pretended that I was simply listening to an interesting anecdote, when in fact my pulse was racing, and my insides were twisting into knots. Questions tumbled through my brain. Did Estelle know Niko was already married? Why did Niko leave his wife and baby? Was it because he wanted to be with Estelle, or was he running away from a crime?

Either way, it doesn't paint him in a very good light. He sounds selfish and wilful, like he didn't care about anyone but himself. Maybe he *has* returned to Inios, maybe he genuinely wants to see me . . . but do I want to see him? Strangely, I'm not sure that I do . . .

It doesn't take me long to pack. I throw my clothes into my suitcases without much thought for creases and put my passport in my day bag. I've not acquired much since I've been here – a new pair of flip-flops and a bikini I've only worn once – and I'm leaving without the letters, which doesn't feel right. All I have left is the photo of Niko that I stole from the office. I take it out and look at it again, searching for a likeness between him and Despina, but the picture is too fuzzy to compare properly. I tuck it into a novel I never got around to reading and put it in my bag.

My mobile buzzes with a text. To my surprise, it's from Despina. I've been thinking about her non-stop and yet she's the last person I expected to contact me. I expect she's annoyed with me for leaving her to pick up the wedding co-ordination job. Cautiously, I read the message.

Hi Juno. Andreas has just told me you're leaving us. Why?

I dash off a quick reply. *I've an emergency at home.*

Oh dear. What's wrong? Has somebody been taken ill?

Yes. I hesitate, then add. *My mother.*

Sorry to hear that.

I'm not sure how genuine she's being, but it still makes me feel guilty. I hate lying.

Thanks, I type lamely. *Sorry I didn't get a chance to say goodbye.*

When do you leave?

My ferry is at 7.

Let me give you a lift to the port. We can have a farewell drink while we wait.

I'd like that.

And I would. I really would. I want to see her one last time, knowing she is my sister. I'm sure it'll help me find closure, even though I can't tell her who I really am.

Excellent, she pings back immediately. *I will meet you in the car park at 5.*

Everything's packed. I make a last check of the cupboards, look under the beds, empty the fridge. I haul my heavy suitcases down the steps one at a time, then run back up to lock the door.

The afternoon is over, and the evening is just beginning. The shops are lifting their shutters, switching on fairy lights, hanging their wares on hooks outside – clothes, jewellery, hats, sunglasses . . . Church bells are clanging. Strains of traditional bouzouki music drift towards me from the lower square.

This is my island. My paternal ancestors have lived here for hundreds, maybe thousands of years, but I was exiled before I was even born. I arrived as a stranger and I'm leaving as one. But it's okay. It's better this way. I'd rather leave gracefully than be kicked out.

Tears well in my eyes, not for the first time today. I stop and rummage for a tissue in my bag. This won't do.

'Hi! Over here!' Despina waves at me from the car park. I drag the cases to her blue Opel Corsa, and she helps me load them into the back. I climb into the passenger seat, and she starts the engine.

'I'm so glad I caught you before you left,' she says.

We turn right onto the road and drive out of Chora. I look over my shoulder, eager to catch a last glimpse of the picture-postcard view of the village before it disappears behind the hill. She navigates the bends more cautiously than Vasilis, slowing to avoid the steady stream of holidaymakers walking up from the beach.

We bag a space by the car-hire agency and go to Atlantis. It's packed as usual, but Despina knows the owners and they quickly find us a table. It's happy hour so we each order an Aperol spritz. I hand over the key to the apartment.

'Thanks,' she says as she drops it into her bag.

This is my sister, I think, for the thousandth time. *I'm sitting at a table, having cocktails with my sister.*

'We need a selfie,' I say, taking out my phone.

'Really?' She frowns. 'I don't like selfies.'

'Please? Just this once?'

I get up and crouch at her side, grinning madly. She

forces herself to smile at the lens, and I take several shots, just to be sure.

'I've got something for you,' she says when I go back to my chair.

'Oh, you shouldn't—' I begin but she waves the sentiment away.

'You don't know what it is yet.'

Despina opens her bag and takes out a familiar-looking brown envelope. I gasp, involuntarily clasping my hand to my chest.

It's the letters.

'I'm sorry,' she says, pushing the envelope across the table towards me.

I stare at her in astonishment. 'It was you?'

'Yes. I had a strange feeling about you, right from the beginning,' she starts to explain. 'It was as if I already knew you, as if we'd met before. You were very interested in our family. I could tell it wasn't normal curiosity. I asked Millie if she knew about why you were here, and she gave me the letters.'

'*Millie?*' I repeat, staggered.

'Yes. She pretended to be your friend, but she was very jealous of you.'

'No, that's not true. Jealous? Of me?'

'You outshone her at work. She hated that.'

I look away, trying to process what I've just been told. In a way, it makes sense that it was Millie who stole my letters – she knew they existed, and she had easy access to them. But I still can't believe it. She didn't care enough about the job to be jealous of me and hated the family for the way they treated Lana. We were friends and allies, weren't we?

'I'm sorry, it must be upsetting to know she betrayed you,' says Despina, interrupting my thoughts.

'I can't get my head around it.'

'People aren't always as they seem,' she replies, pointedly.

'That's true,' I admit. I sit back, trying to take it all in. 'So, you've known that we're sisters – half-sisters, I should say – for a few weeks.'

She nods. 'That's right.'

'Why didn't you say anything?'

'I couldn't, not without admitting I had the letters.'

'If you'd explained, I probably would have understood.'

'Yes, maybe. I wanted to talk to you about it, but then we had the trouble with the launch party, and the body being discovered ... These last weeks have been a nightmare, as you know. It never seemed to be the right time. In the end, I decided it was better to keep it a secret. I couldn't understand why you never told us who you were, but I was grateful. For my mother's sake.'

'I wanted to tell the family,' I say. 'That was my plan all along. I assumed that Niko would still be on the island, working in the family business, but there was no sign of him. You all behaved like he'd never existed – it was obvious there'd been some big falling-out. I felt really awkward.'

She nods, understanding. 'You didn't know he was already married and had a daughter?'

'No. I only found out this morning when Andreas told me.' I take a large sip of my Aperol spritz. 'He doesn't know who I am, does he?'

'No. Nor does Christakis. I haven't told anybody . . .' She bites her lip. 'It's difficult. For me, it's a wonderful discovery. I'm an only child. My cousins are like brothers to me, but I've always wanted a sister.'

'Me too,' I murmur.

'However. My mother can't find out about you. It's unthinkable. She's fragile at the best of times, but she's not been herself since that bastard Kevin Casey threw her into the cold store. She hasn't been back to work, as you know. Her nerves are raw. She's constantly on edge, jumps every time somebody knocks on the door.'

'I'm so sorry.'

'Maybe Andreas would accept you,' she goes on, 'but it would be yet another humiliation for my mother. She's always felt second-class, an embarrassment to the family. I know it's silly – but that's how it is. The old ways live on.'

'You must have been relieved when you heard I was leaving,' I say.

'Yes and no,' Despina replies. 'Yes, it's better that they don't find out who you are, but no because I'd like to get to know you properly. Maybe one day, but right now, the timing is bad. We have a lot of problems with the business. People are saying wicked, false things about our family. My uncle is very worried, he says the project is cursed.'

'Yes. Christakis said something similar.'

'The land used to belong to my mother's family, you see. It was her dowry. When Nikolaos abandoned us, it should have been returned.' She shrugs. 'This is what my mother says, but I don't get involved. My grandparents on my father's side were always very good to me. When they died, Andreas became the head of the family and . . . ' – she inhales sharply – 'things changed. Now his sons are the most important. I am useful to the business, nothing more.'

'It must be very hard for you,' I say, genuinely feeling sorry for her.

I go back to my drink, wondering whether I should tell Despina that I think Niko has returned to Inios. If he wants to see me, surely he'd like to see his other daughter as well? The words hover at my lips, but then I remember the warning in the first note. *Don't tell anyone who you are. Please. For all our sakes.*

Despina sighs loudly. 'It's such a shame. We've only just found each other and now you're going.'

'It's for the best,' I reply.

'Yes, but do you have to leave tonight? Can't you stay a little bit longer?'

I hesitate. 'I don't know . . . I've already booked the ferry and the flight . . . If I stay it's going to look odd.'

She purses her lips. 'Is your mother really ill?'

I look down. 'No. I'm sorry. I lied. Things were getting on top of me. I needed to escape.'

'I understand,' she says. 'You've been under a lot of stress. All those secrets.'

'Yes . . . I didn't plan for it to work out that way . . . Sorry, I . . .' I tail off.

Despina brushes my apology away. 'Never mind. It's the right decision. Where are you flying from?'

'Santorini. Tomorrow afternoon, about five.'

'Okay, here's an idea.' She leans forward. 'Why not stay on the island tonight and catch another ferry tomorrow morning? You'll still have plenty of time to get to Santorini airport.'

'I don't know . . . It's risky . . . The ferries are notorious for being delayed.'

'The winds are good. You'll be fine. It would be great to spend some time together. I'm sorry if I've been – what's the word? – distant with you. But we have this evening. Don't catch the ferry, stay here. She takes the keys to the apartment out of her bag and puts them on the table. 'One more night. I'll make sure you're on the first ferry tomorrow morning.'

'Alright,' I reply, touched by her persistence.

'Good!' She beams at me. 'Now, this evening, I'm going to take you to a very special place that belongs to my family. Sorry – *our* family.'

'Sounds great . . . Can I ask where?'

'No. It's a surprise. I promise, you'll love it. We'll have to take the car,' she says, summoning the bill, 'but don't worry. It's not far. We'll have a quick look and get back before dark. Then I'll take you to my favourite restaurant for a farewell meal.' She raises her glass. 'To sisters!'

'To sisters!' I echo feebly, feeling somewhat overwhelmed.

We go back to the car and set off in the direction of Chora. I feel slightly concerned about Despina driving those twisty roads with an Aperol spritz inside her, but she seems to be coping with them easily. She points out landmarks on the way – a monastery, a museum dedicated to cheese, a church that lays claim to being the oldest on the island. I smile as I look out of the window, pretending that driving around with my sister is the most normal thing in the world.

'Nearly there,' says Despina, taking a stony side track off

the main road. We bump along for a kilometre or so, cutting a path through tinder-dry scrubland. 'In the spring, this is all covered with wildflowers,' she tells me. 'You wouldn't believe how different it looks to now. This is Zimiris land, all the way down to the beach . . .'

The track becomes narrower and steeper as we descend, coming to an abrupt halt by a sweep of glorious sand. It's smaller and even more beautiful than the bay I visited with Millie, which is further south. Despina parks. We get out and wander around. At the entrance to the beach, there's a ruined building, its roof long gone, doors and window frames rotted away. It looks as if there were originally two or three large rooms and an outside terrace. The concrete walls are scrawled with ugly graffiti. A pile of tattered rush parasols lies in one corner, and at the far end there's a rusty old cooker.

'Did this use to be a restaurant?' I ask.

Despina nods. 'It was more of a cafeteria, like the Outta Sight. My grandfather built it, way back in the eighties. He had this vision of beach huts and a campsite, but it didn't work out. The place was too remote. Still is. Hardly anyone ever comes here, not even these days. It's a hidden treasure.' I look out to sea, the evening breeze caressing my cheeks, feeling a huge surge of happiness rise from somewhere deep within me.

'Thanks for bringing me here,' I murmur. 'It's so peaceful.'

'I knew you'd love it.' Despina hooks her arm in mine. 'There's something else. In your mother's letters, she writes about Niko taking her to an old goatherd's shelter – do you remember?' I nod. 'Well, it's here. Would you like to see it?'

I turn to her, excited. 'Of course! That would be amazing. I tried to find it myself a few weeks ago, only I went to the wrong beach.'

'It's up there,' she says, gesturing towards a path that leads upwards through a grove of olive trees. 'It's well hidden, nobody would guess. Come.'

I follow her through the trees, stumbling on the rough ground, which is littered with stones, gnarled roots and dried stubs of bushes. The path opens out into a small clearing and there it is, standing alone. It's built of stones, which have been piled on top of each other in layers, reminding me of the drystone walls in the Peak District back home.

I walk around it, surprised to find that it has no windows. The roof is thatched but in need of repair, and there's a chimney sticking out of the top. The front door is solid though, bolted and padlocked. Despina looks under various pots until she finds the key.

'Ready?' she says, stepping aside to let me enter first.

My eyes blink at the gloom. An unpleasant smell fills my nostrils – a mix of animal faeces and rotting cheese, making me gag. There's a rudimentary fireplace in the corner and a stone bench along one side. The floor is just compacted earth. The only furniture is an old iron bedstead with a thin, stained mattress. A solitary wooden crucifix hangs on the wall.

'Gosh. It's not the romantic getaway I imagined,' I say. 'Are you sure this is the right place?'

There's no reply. It seems Despina has stayed outside. I can't see anything in this darkness. *Should have brought my phone*, I think, but I left my bag in the car. 'Despina? Where are you?'

As I turn, she enters the hut, holding a large chunk of wood in both hands. For a split second, her body is silhouetted against the sunlight. Then she comes towards me, a look of pure hatred darkening her face.

'Despina? What are you d—'

With a loud scream my sister lunges forward, lifting the plank up. She brings it down on me. There's a loud crack as it makes contact with my head. I bite into my tongue, staggering about, blinded by the pain, tasting blood as I fall to the ground.

Chapter Thirty-Nine: Now

JUNO

When I come round, I see only darkness. My head thuds with a deep, sickening pain. I reach up to touch my brow, flinching as I find the wound. It's tender, sticky to the touch. At least the bleeding seems to have stopped.

How long have I been out? There's no light, not even a chink coming through the holes in the thatch. It must be the middle of the night. I stare into the nothingness, impatient for my pupils to adjust. One question asks itself, over and over again.

Why did she do this?

Gradually, I start to make out shapes – the fireplace, the stone bench, the bed, the door, which is almost certainly locked. I make to crawl over, but something stops me from moving. There's rope around my ankle. It's tied to a hook in the wall. I work at the knot but it's too thick for me to untie. I give up with a frustrated groan.

Why?

I feel around, stretching as far as I can in every direction. Eventually my fingers touch plastic – a bottle, I think. Gently rolling it towards me, I pick it up and unscrew the lid. The water is warm but drinkable. I'm tempted to swallow it in one go but stop myself after a few glugs. I don't know how long I'm going to be here, or whether Despina will even come back. Did she plan this all along or was it a spur-of-the-moment thing?

I rewind on the evening. Everything seemed fine between us. More than fine. She told me how thrilled she was that we'd found each other, we raised a toast to sisterhood. It was an act. I should have realised. She's known for a while who I am. Maybe she'd been planning to kidnap me but hadn't found the right opportunity. When she heard I was leaving the island, she had to act fast.

I should be on the ferry by now, pulling into Santorini. I've booked a room at the same hotel I stayed at on the way in, but they won't worry if I don't turn up. Nobody is expecting me at home. I didn't call Luke, or Estelle, or Millie, or any of my friends to tell them I was on my way back to the UK. Andreas and Christakis believe I've already left the island. If I'm not missed, does it mean I no longer exist?

I mustn't think like this. I've got to be positive. Hopeful. When – if – Despina comes back, I'll promise that if she releases me, I'll leave Inios and never tell the rest of her family who I am. But that might not be what she wants . . .

The air is stifling, thick with dust. I can't hear anything – no birdsong, no gusts of wind, no roar of the sea, and certainly no passing traffic. The silence scares me the most. I could scream my lungs out and no one would hear.

I feel sick. It's probably concussion. Dehydration. The rope around my ankle is just about long enough for me to crawl onto the bed. I lie on the mattress, curling my knees to my chest, my hands pressed together to make a pillow for my cheek. The pain in my head radiates throughout my entire body, mixing with the alcohol in my stomach, making me heave. But I don't want to add vomit to the foul odours in the room.

As I lie here, trying to rest, practicalities start to obsess me. How long is she planning to leave me here? Will she bring me food and a bucket to pee in? The bottle of water is a good sign – it means she wanted me to stay alive. I have to hang on to that thought.

Time passes. Quickly, slowly, I've no idea. I must have fallen asleep – God knows how – because when I next open my eyes, I can see tiny dots of light above me. For a moment, I think I'm outside in the dark, looking up at a starry sky, but then I realise that the reverse is true. I'm still in the hut, and sunlight is piercing through the thatched roof. It's the new day.

I'm hurt and need medical attention. I should be in A&E right now, doctors shining torches in my eyes, taking my blood pressure, checking my pulse. My stomach is growling, every bit of my body feels tender. The rope rubs against my ankle every time I move, tearing at my skin. And the pain in my head. I don't think I can stand it much more.

My heart starts to race, my breath quickens and shallows. I feel dizzy, even though I'm lying down. *Stay calm*, I tell myself. *You mustn't have a panic attack. It won't help, it'll just make things worse. Breathe deeply. In and out. Count slowly – in-two-three-four, out-two-three-four . . .*

It takes forever for the fear to subside. I'm so exhausted, I can hardly sit up, but I manage to lift myself onto an elbow and take another swig of water from the bottle. I slowly lick my lips, savouring the simple, exquisite taste.

More time passes.

My ears prick. What was that? Did I just hear a sound? I freeze, trying to translate the noises. Somebody's outside, fumbling with the padlock. The door shakes as the clasp is released. It scrapes open, and light bursts into the space, blinding me. I shield my eyes with my hand.

Despina stands there, wearing the same clothes as yesterday – a green cotton dress with a floral pattern. She looks as if she's had about as much sleep as I have. Her handbag is hooked over her shoulder and there's a plastic carrier bag in her hand.

'Why are you doing this?' I say. '*Why*, Despina? I thought you were happy about us being sisters, I though—'

'Happy? Of course I'm not happy.' She looks at me as if I'm completely stupid. 'You tricked us, lied to us. You heard that we were rich, so you tried to worm your way into the family. All you want is our money.'

'That's absurd. I couldn't care less. If this is about punishing me for being Niko's daughter—'

'Oh, no,' she interrupts. 'It's about much more than that . . . Here. I've brought you some food.' She throws the carrier bag at me, and it skids across the floor. I look inside. There's another bottle of water in there, thank God. Also a pastry from the bakery, a tub of salad and two nectarines.

'I'm sorry . . . maybe it's because I'm in so much *pain*,' I say pointedly, 'but I have no fucking idea why you're doing this.'

'No? Really?' She sounds genuinely surprised.

'No!'

She folds her arms and looms over me. 'I want a confession,' she says.

'A confession? What am I supposed to have done wrong?'

'Not from you. From your mother.'

'I still don't understand. A confession to what?'

'Don't insult me,' she says with a flash of anger. 'Not unless you want me to hit you over the head again.'

I flinch, backing away against the fireplace. 'I'm sorry, I'm confused. You're going to have to tell me.'

She stands with her back to the door, silhouetted against the fierce sunshine. She looks like an avenging angel. 'The skeleton. That they found. In the well,' she says slowly. 'It's my father. *Our* father,' she corrects with a sneer.

'No. That's not true.'

'Haven't you ever wondered why he never came back to Inios – why he never got in touch?'

Yes, of course I've wondered about it, I say in my head. *I've wondered about lots of things.* But I don't reply.

'Niko was a decent family man,' Despina continues. 'He would never have abandoned his wife and daughter for some English whore.'

'My mother wasn't—'

'The foreign girls wanted sex and the Greek men gave it to them. It was part of the holiday experience, it meant nothing. But your stupid mother fell in love with her *kamaki*. She came back to Inios the next year, expecting to carry on with Niko where they'd left off. When she found out he was married and had a baby, and that he'd never loved her at all, she killed him in a jealous rage. Hid his body and ran away.'

'You're totally wrong. It didn't happen like that,' I insist. 'Estelle and Niko left the island together. They ran away because they loved each other. Ask your uncle, he saw them go. Only yesterday he told me how he ran down to the port to try and stop them but was too late. He saw them getting on the ferry—'

'Yes, that's the story he tells,' Despina replies, batting the idea away with her hand. 'I used to believe him, but as soon as they found that skeleton, I realised he'd been lying to us for years.'

'Why would he lie about that?'

She shrugs. 'I don't know. But it suited him to be the only son – it meant there was nobody to share the business with.'

'You've got it wrong, Despina. Niko left with my mother. I'm pretty certain that the skeleton belongs to an English guy who went missing the year before. I think Niko had something to do with his death, that's why he had to leave the island.'

It's no good, I have to tell her.

'Niko has come back to Inios,' I say. 'He made contact, he wants to see me—'

'You're lying!' she shouts over me. 'My father is dead. I knew it as soon as the body was found. I *felt* it. I'm telling you – your mother killed him.'

'No, she didn't. She loved him! Listen to me. The English guy's name was Rob. He'd been caught seeing a local girl and her father—'

'Oh, shut up! I don't care what you think. It's irrelevant, anyway. I've already been to the police and given them a sample of my DNA.'

'And?' I say, my pulse suddenly accelerating. 'What was the result?'

'It won't come for several weeks, but I couldn't let you run off, could I? I had to keep you here.'

'Why? What is it you want?'

'Isn't it obvious? The autopsy will discover how my father was murdered, but not who did it,' she says. 'There's unlikely to be any forensic evidence linking your mother to the murder. It's all circumstantial. The letters help with the motive, of course. They prove that Estelle was in love with Nikolaos and that he rejected her. They put her in Inios at the time of my father's disappearance. But it won't be enough. We need a full confession.'

'There's no way my mother will confess—'

'No? Are you sure about that?' She steps forward. 'Not even to save her child?'

Now I understand.

'It won't work,' I say, improvising. 'All it's going to do is cause more trouble for you, more shame for Phaedra when you're arrested for kidnap and assault. More embarrassment for the family. Bad PR for the Klimeni project. Andreas won't like that one bit. When the DNA results come through and it's not Niko, you're going to look extremely stupid.'

'If Estelle refuses to confess to the murder, you're going to look extremely dead,' she snaps.

She means it. My heart starts to race. 'I understand that you're upset and angry, but this is not the way to go about this,' I say, my tone suddenly desperate. 'Wait for the DNA results. *If* the body turns out to be Niko's, the police will investigate. Kidnapping me isn't going to help. Please. Let me go.'

She takes a phone out of her handbag and holds it up. I see from the familiar blue case that it's mine.

'Give me your passcode,' she demands.

I hesitate. If I tell her, she'll be able to send whatever messages she wants to whoever she wants. If I refuse and nobody hears from me, they might eventually work out that something bad has happened. But by then it could be too late.

'Your passcode,' she repeats. 'If you give me false ones and lock me out, I'll leave you to starve. Nobody will look for you here. Once you're dead, I'll collect your body and dump it out at sea. Much smarter than throwing it into a well, by the way. That was stupid.'

Despina has completely lost the plot, but it sounds as if she means what's she says. I don't want to die here, in the pitch dark, too weak to cry out for help.

'It's 1986,' I say. 'The year I was born.'

She gives me an insolent smile, tapping out the four digits and entering my digital world – all my social media, my photos, texts, emails, browsing history, everything.

'What's your plan?' I ask.

'Can't you guess? I'm going to send your mother a message, as if from you.'

'Saying what?'

'You'll find out.' I watch her scroll through my contacts list.

'Dear Mum,' she says, speaking as she types. 'Some . . . bad . . . news. Niko's body has been found at Klimeni. The past has finally . . . caught you.' She's enjoying herself, relishing the power of being me. 'I know you killed him. It's okay. I love you and . . . I forgive you . . . but I have to know the truth. If you confess, I promise I won't tell the police. Your secret will be safe with me.' She looks up. 'There!'

My heart leaps with hope. Despina has fallen at the very first hurdle. I never call Estelle 'Mum'. She'll know immediately that the message is not from me.

Chapter Forty: August 1985

ESTELLE

They said their goodbyes before they reached Sunset Bar. Niko's lips lingered on hers, as if he was committing the kiss to memory. This could be the last time they held each other, she thought. She had given him a choice – to stay or to go. It sounded simple, but they both knew it was far more complicated than that. He had two days to make up his mind. She wouldn't seek him out and try to persuade him to leave with her. It had to be his own decision. Estelle hoped and prayed he would make the right one.

It was clear that Niko needed to get away from his family, and his father in particular. Nobody had a right to force another human being into marrying somebody they didn't love – especially when they were already in love with somebody else. But Babá Yannis didn't seem to care about his son's happiness. He had the land he wanted now while poor Niko had been left with responsibilities he'd never asked for. It was so unfair.

It was the child Estelle pitied the most. She was the innocent party in all this mess, and it was sad to think of her growing up without Niko as her father. Estelle consoled herself with thoughts that maybe, in time, Niko would return to Inios, and father and daughter would be reunited. He could explain why he'd had to leave and hopefully she'd forgive him. But that might take years.

Estelle didn't like the idea of herself as a home-wrecker, but how could you wreck something that was already broken? She was Niko's first love, his free choice. Despite her concerns and all the many obstacles they were bound to face, she remained convinced that they were meant to be together. She loved him so much. Whenever she imagined the future – quitting university, travelling the world, discovering a different way of living – he was always by her side. But it would be tough for him to leave the island, his entire family, and the only life he'd ever known. If he decided to stay, she would respect his decision, but it would break her heart.

She walked back up to the dirt track. Chora and the port lay to her left, the beach and Hotel Aphrodite to her right. She didn't know which direction to take, where she wanted to go. The day stretched before her like a wide yawn, full of uncertainty and waiting.

First, she needed breakfast. She turned in the direction of the village, walking slowly in the heat, listening to the insects singing.

Niko had said that his house was on this road. There was a lot of building going on all around, although it had stopped for the summer. Half-finished hotels, villas and accommodation blocks lined the route, but there was only one old farmhouse she could think of – and it was on a bend, as he'd described. She'd passed it many times walking to and from the village, and had always thought how beautiful it was, despite the flaking paintwork and missing roof tiles.

Now she would look at it with different eyes, knowing who lived there.

She slowed down as she approached the house, which sat behind a low wall and a curtain of lemon trees. There was nobody in the dusty courtyard, but she could hear a baby's wail coming from within, a thin strangulated cry designed to make everyone come running. It stabbed her in the heart. Surely, Niko would decide to stay. Leaving a woman that he'd been forced to marry was one thing, but abandoning his own flesh and blood was something else. She wasn't sure she wanted to be a party to it. And yet she wanted to be with Niko – he was the only good thing in her life right now. It was all so difficult . . .

She needed to think. The best place to do that was back at the hotel, where she would be quiet and on her own, but her stomach was rumbling with hunger. Turning round, she walked back in the direction she'd come in, hurrying past the sign to Sunset Bar and taking the next right turn that led down to Kalapos beach.

People were only just emerging – squinting in the bright light, breath smelling of ouzo. They were heading to the Outta Sight for a hangover breakfast (orange juice, two eggs, bacon, bread and butter, marmalade, tea or coffee), so she joined them. Estelle's stomach felt too weak to eat anything that might be greasy, so she went for the continental option. She sat at a table by herself, drinking coffee and nibbling at a bread roll. Niko's baby was still crying in her head. She had half a mind to go back to Sunset Bar and tell him she wouldn't allow him to leave his child, but the other half of her mind told her to keep out of it. Let him decide.

After her late breakfast, she went for a long swim, lying on her back in a starfish shape, staring into the pink undersides of her eyelids, gently sculling with her hands to stay afloat. She tried to calm herself, but a group of Germans were playing water polo next to her, shouting at the tops of their voices, splashing her whenever the ball strayed in her direction. You couldn't move for people having fun.

Last year, she'd been one of them, blissfully inconsiderate of her neighbours. She and Angela had spent hours and hours sunbathing, reading, playing stupid beach games, hanging out with the Barking boys, having a giggle . . . Now, everything was serious, and the stakes were incredibly high. She'd grown up overnight without meaning to – without wanting to.

She got out of the water and made her way back to the hotel. Her skin felt tender, as if the sun had burned off a couple of layers, leaving the raw flesh beneath. She took a shower and changed into a cotton off-the-shoulder dress. It was too early to go out, so she helped herself to another bottle of beer from the hotel's secret stash, and sat on the balcony, drinking to give herself courage to face the night ahead. *Niko might have left a message on the noticeboard at Kev's gaff by now,* she thought.

The walk into Chora seemed to take forever. The beer had made her thirsty and there was dust in her throat. It was still hot, even though it was early evening, but the sunshine was gentler. She shrank into the shadows when she reached Niko's house, pausing to look through the trees – wanting and not wanting to see him. For a few minutes she tormented herself with imagined scenes of domestic bliss – playing with the baby, eating a quick dinner with his wife before returning to the bar for the long shift. People walked past, eyeing her curiously. Embarrassed, she hurried on.

When she arrived at All Right Now it was already heaving. She hacked her way through the forest of drinkers, apologising as she pressed against backs or stood on toes. The air was thick with smoke, the music so loud that her ribcage vibrated. She headed for the noticeboard, which was in the far recesses of the cave, next to the bar. Kev was flipping the lids off bottles of lager at great speed, shouting orders at his new potman, a red-faced boy with chubby cheeks who looked as if he might drown in his own sweat.

Her eyes darted across the dozens of messages that had been haphazardly pinned to the cork. They'd been scribbled on small scraps ripped from paper bags, serviettes, cigarette packets, the backs of restaurant bills, the odd piece of lined notepaper. Most were brief – greetings, farewells, requests for accommodation, pleas from people looking for lost passports, wallets, cameras or even friends.

Suddenly, she saw her name scrawled on a piece of folded paper. She recognised Niko's writing. Fingers trembling, she removed the pin and took the note. She was about to unfold it, when Kev shouted to her from the other end of the bar.

'Hey, Estelle!' He gestured at her to move across. 'Over here!' She edged her way along, muttering apologies. 'You coming on the road trip tomorrow? I'm taking a bunch of people down to Klimeni in the truck. We'll be leaving around two p.m., back at dawn. I told Cliff to invite you.'

'Oh, yes,' she replied distractedly. 'He did say something about it.'

'Barbecue on the beach, booze provided by yours truly. Eight hundred drachmas all in. It's going to be wild.'

'I'd love to, but I'm leaving early Friday morning. Five a.m. ferry.'

'Perfect! I'll drop you off at the port on the way back.'

'Thanks, but . . .' She wrinkled her nose. 'I don't want to miss it. I think I'd be safer staying in Chora.'

'Come on the trip, Estelle,' he said, suddenly adopting a serious tone. 'Don't let the Zimirises bully you. Have some fun. It's your last chance.'

She didn't understand what he meant. All she could think of was the note that burned in her hand. She wanted to read it, but not here, in the smoke and noise, with Kev looming over her.

'What's going on with you and Niko?' he asked.

'Nothing.'

'You can't fool me. I saw him pin the note on the board. He's never set foot in here before, so it's got to be important.'

'I'll come on the trip,' she said, not wanting to discuss it. 'It'll give me something to do.'

She pushed her way back to the entrance, gasping for air as she landed in the street. The sky was inky. Light spilled out of the souvenir shops onto the paving stones, making their whitewashed edges glow. She stood in the doorway of an art gallery selling gawdy paintings and leather hand-bags, and finally opened the piece of paper. Her heart raced as if she were running for her life.

There was just one word, written in capitals.

YES.

Chapter Forty-One: Now

JUNO

After Despina goes, the tension I've been holding inside immediately gives way and I collapse in floods of tears. They stream down my face, clogging my nose so that I can hardly breathe. I'm angry that she could do this to me. Terrified of how it might end. I won't survive like this. I need medical help, more food and water, a torch, a bucket . . . She didn't even leave me a blanket to sleep on.

Some sister, eh?

How long will it be before she returns – hours, days? Maybe I'll never see her again. My cruel, wicked, vindictive sister. No, *half*-sister, let's be accurate now. We only share 50 per cent of our DNA. She has no natural affection for me. In fact, she hates me precisely for who I am. I expect the whole family would hate me too if they knew.

I toss and turn, searching for a better position, but the rope twists around my legs, chafing my ankle as it pulls. The mattress is thin and hard, covered in bits of thatch and dead insects that have fallen from the roof. Something crawls over my face. A spider or a beetle. I shriek and brush it off.

The hours pass with a slowness I've never experienced before. My stomach gnaws with hunger, but I try to ignore it. I eat the salad while it's still fresh. Who knows how long

I'll have to make that cheese pastry and couple of nectarines last?

I sit up, resting my back against the uneven wall, massaging my stiff neck. I look up to see that some light is seeping through the thatch. It must be the afternoon. Day two of my capture. I should make a mark somewhere, to help keep grasp of the time.

Estelle must have read the text by now, asking her to confess to Niko's murder. She'll realise immediately that somebody else sent it, pretending to be me. It'll be obvious that I'm in danger. She'll call the Inios police. They could already be out searching for me. Soon I'll be found. Despina will be arrested, and I'll be safe.

Then another scenario floats into my head. Estelle read the message and was thrown into a panic. Not because she was worried for my safety, but because this is what she's been dreading might happen for decades; this is her worst nightmare come true. It's a frightening thought, but I have to consider the possibility that Despina is right – that her DNA will match the skeleton found in the well and that Estelle *did* kill Niko; that Andreas lied about seeing him leave the island; that somebody else sent me the flowers and the notes to put me off the scent.

The more I think, the more the evidence mounts against my mother. Estelle lied to me about the identity of my father, telling me he was an untraceable Italian waiter. When I was a child, she dragged me around various hippy communes in Europe, but always avoided Greece. She was very concerned when I found out the truth about Niko. She told me not to go to Inios to look for him. It didn't occur to me at the time, but maybe it was because she knew I wouldn't find him. Not alive, anyway. She didn't want me to contact his family, told me that if they discovered who I was, I would be in danger. I didn't take her warnings seriously enough. I didn't understand what she was getting at . . .

Things are starting to make a horrible kind of sense.

But it can't be true. *Can't* be. The skeleton lying on the pathologist's slab in Athens – or wherever it is now – belongs to Rob, not my father. I'm letting Despina mess with my mind. The pain, the unrelenting darkness, the hunger, the thirst, the fear that I'm never going to make it out of here alive, are conspiring against me, forcing me into an even darker place deep inside my head.

Time is warping in strange ways, stretching around the room like a piece of elastic, every so often pinging back in my face. I've no idea how long I've been here – a couple of days, maybe three?

I'm woken by noises outside. I sit up, bleary-eyed. The door opens and Despina stands in the open doorway. I blink at her, still half asleep. She's wearing jogging bottoms and a pale T-shirt, her hair tied back from her face. Her arms are full of stuff. I make out a bucket, a cushion, a bottle of water . . .

'It stinks in here,' she says, screwing up her nose as she steps over the threshold.

I scowl at her. 'What do you expect? I have to pee on the floor. I can't even do it in the corner.' I kick out my tethered leg. 'Please. Untie me. My ankle's really sore.'

'How stupid do you think I am?' she replies. She takes a

couple of cautious steps forward, making sure she remains out of reach. 'I brought you some things.'

I attempt to contain my excitement as she lays the items on the floor – a pizza box, water and lemon Fanta, a paperback novel with a battered spine, a packet of face wipes, and – oh, joy of joys – a torch.

Despina flicks it on and off. 'The batteries are new, but use it sparingly,' she advises me, like she's sending me off on a camping trip. A sarcastic response pops into my mouth, but I swallow it down. It's not a good idea to make an enemy of your captor.

She pushes the box across the floor, then rolls the bottles to me. 'Wipes first, please,' I say, holding out my hand. She throws them in my direction. I peel off the front and take out a damp, fragrant cloth, feeling an exquisite pleasure as I clean my hands and face. Then I pick up the pizza box and put it on my lap. As I open the lid, a pungent smell of cheese and pepperoni invades the space, temporarily masking the smell of urine. I tear off a slice and stuff it into my mouth. The pizza is cold, and the cheese tastes like plastic, but I'm too hungry to care.

My stomach isn't at all sure about it though. Within minutes I feel a sharp pain of protest in my gut. I put the slice down and take a gulp of water.

Despina leans against the wall, watching me, not saying anything.

'So, what's happening?' I ask. 'Has Estelle confessed?'

'Not yet.'

'Has she responded at all?'

'No.'

My heart sinks, although I'm not surprised. 'I've lost track of time,' I say. 'How long since you sent the message?'

'Over two days.'

I explain that Estelle lives in a remote location and doesn't have wi-fi. 'Often it's a couple of weeks before she replies. If at all,' I add.

'If she doesn't respond, I'll send her another message saying you've been kidnapped. If she doesn't send the confession in the next twenty-four hours you're going to be killed. That should do it.'

I leave a beat. 'And am I?' I say, trying not to betray the fear in my voice.

'Are you what?'

'Am I going to be killed?'

'Don't ask difficult questions,' she snaps. 'Eat your pizza.'

But suddenly I've no appetite. I close the lid and lay the box next to me on the bed.

'Despina,' I begin, adopting as calm a tone as I can muster, even though I think I may be about to have a panic attack. 'You don't want to kill me – I know you don't. Even if it brought you some satisfaction, it won't end well. You'll be found out. It'll ruin your life.'

'My life has already been ruined,' she huffs. 'Do you think I wanted to work in a beach club? My dream was to be a doctor. My cousins went to university, but not me. The only subject I was allowed to study was English, so that I could work for the family business. Christakis's brothers escaped – they live in Athens. One's an engineer, the other's a lawyer. I'm stuck here with my mother. I'm all she has; she needs me.'

I frown. 'But Phaedra's only in her sixties, surely. That's not old.'

'No, but she's worked hard all her life, paid her dues to the family. And she's mentally vulnerable. It's my duty to stay with her . . . You English people wouldn't understand that.'

'I'm sorry your life hasn't turned out as you hoped,' I say carefully. 'Nor has mine. But at our age, we can't keep blaming it on our parents.'

'I don't blame my mother, I blame yours. She took my father's life.'

'We don't know that. There's no proof that he's dead. Not yet. The DNA results—'

'Will prove it, yes.' She inhales deeply, as if trying to maintain her patience. 'My mother never talks to me about my father, nobody does. It's as if he never existed. When he disappeared, my grandfather forbade all mention of him, destroyed any photographs he was in.'

Not all . . . I think, but I let her carry on uninterrupted.

'I grew to hate him. In my mind, everything was his fault. If he hadn't abandoned us, my mother wouldn't constantly be on the edge of a nervous breakdown; I'd have been able to train to be a doctor; we wouldn't be third-class members of the family, grateful for any crumbs they throw at us.'

'Sounds like you hate all of them,' I say.

She shakes her head. 'No, I don't . . . I love them. We couldn't have survived without them. But it's so unfair. Niko was the older brother, you see. When my grandfather died, he would have inherited the business. It would have been Andreas and Christakis working for us, not the other way around. Things would have been so different.'

She takes another breath and I sense that she's going to confide further in me. I'm not sure it's a good sign. Maybe she thinks it doesn't matter what she says because I'm not going to be around much longer.

'My mother doesn't agree with the new resort,' she says. 'The land belonged to her family for generations. It means a great deal to her, and she doesn't want it spoilt. But she has no power to stop Andreas doing what he likes. Nobody has. If my father was still alive—'

'Look,' I say, 'I totally get that it's more comfortable to believe that Niko was murdered rather than that he abandoned you. It would mean you weren't rejected. And that I wasn't rejected either. I *do* understand.'

'It's not a "belief", I'm not imagining it. There's a skeleton,' she insists.

'Yes, but we don't know whose it is yet.'

'*I* know.'

I decide to gamble. 'Okay, let's say you're right. Estelle *did* kill Niko. It's a possibility. He never returned to Inios. The family never heard from him again. He wasn't part of my life growing up either. Let's face facts . . . You're not the only one with a damaged mother. Estelle is vulnerable too. She carries a great sadness around with her.'

'Or a great guilt,' Despina interjects.

'Yes, maybe it's guilt . . .' I edge forward to her, as far as the rope will let me. 'Holding me hostage isn't going to work. You're just making things worse for yourself . . . Please let me go. I promise I won't press charges. I'll go

304

straight back to the UK. You've got all my contact details. Estelle lives in Portugal – I can give you her address if you want. We're not going to run away. If the DNA results come back with a match, she'll be an obvious suspect. The police will investigate.'

'I need her to confess,' she says in a low voice. 'Now.'

'Maybe she will, but not until she absolutely has to, not while there's a way out. Anyway, a forced confession isn't worth anything. She'll say she only did it to save me.'

There's a long pause.

'You can't keep me here forever,' I continue. 'I won't survive . . . Take me back to the apartment in Chora. You can lock me in if you like. Tie me to the bed. I can't leave the island anyway – you've got my passport and all my stuff.'

'Forget it. You're staying here.'

'Please, Despina, this place is revolting. I'm injured, I could pick up an infection—'

'I've got to go,' she interrupts. 'We're short-staffed. Our wedding coordinator left us in the lurch.' She smiles at me sarcastically.

'None of this is my fault. We're in the same boat.' I make a final attempt. 'We're sisters!'

'I'll be back as soon as I get the confession.'

'That could take days. Weeks.' She shrugs. 'My period is due. There are some tampons in my luggage. If you could just give them to me before you go—'

'We're not in the same boat,' she tells me, not listening. 'Not at all. You've had the life I wanted. You went to university. You got to choose your career. I bet you've travelled all over the world.'

'Not really. I've been lucky in lots of ways, but my life hasn't been perfect. I've messed up my marriage . . . I can't have kids—'

'Marriage?' she echoes, disdain in her voice. 'At least you had some choice. Did you know there are just over a thousand people who live on the island all year round? I know all the men of my age, we went to the same school, played in the same playground, grew up together. One by one, they married my friends and now they work in their family businesses – hotels, bars, shops, clubs . . . Nothing changes, it's the same life being repeated over and over for generations. Very few people escape.'

'Why didn't you marry?' I ask.

'What was the point? I only would have been swapping one prison for another.'

She's so bitter and resentful, I don't know what to say to her. Is her great dissatisfaction with life all my mother's fault?

'The tampons are kind of essential,' I mutter.

'You'll have to wait.'

'I could come on at any moment. Please, don't make me beg.'

'I'll bring them next time.'

'When are you coming back?'

'When your mother owns up for what she did.'

'Despina! Please!'

She steps outside and closes the door. I hear the key turning in the padlock and I throw the pizza box at the wall.

Chapter Forty-Two: August 1985

ESTELLE

She sat in the army truck, her rucksack wedged between her knees. About twenty of them were squeezed onto the wooden benches that would have once carried troops. It was an old Kaiser Jeep, virtually indestructible. Its forty-six-inch wheels could cope with almost any terrain. It rattled as it lumbered into the mountains, its brakes squealing in protest on the way down. Estelle's hot skin rubbed against that of her neighbours as Kevin lurched around the bends, swearing at any goats that dared to stray into his path.

The middle of the flatbed was taken up with beer crates, bags of food, beach equipment and a rusty old barbecue. Some people were already tanked up, gesturing with beer bottles, passing round the ouzo and Metaxa 5 Star. Laughter and good-humoured shouting echoed across the open landscape. Estelle would have been loving every moment of it had she not been feeling so stressed.

Her deadline to leave Inios was tomorrow, and she suspected Andreas might be planning to march her down to the port and put her on the ferry himself. With that in mind, she'd moved out of the hotel and brought all her luggage with her. If Andreas came looking for her, he would find her room empty and hopefully conclude that she'd already left the island. Without Niko.

She'd already bought the ferry tickets from the Olympia Travel Bureau. The man at the counter had asked who the second ticket was for; she'd had to lie and make up a name. He'd seemed suspicious and she was worried he might have alerted Babá Yannis. Maybe she was just being paranoid, but over the last couple of days, Estelle had felt as if she was being watched, her every move noted and reported back to Niko's family. What if his father already knew about their plans? How far would he be prepared to go to scupper them? It was a frightening thought.

She felt much safer now that she was in the open countryside, in the company of friends. Her new worry was that the party might go on for too long or that they wouldn't make it back in time for the five o'clock departure tomorrow. Niko would no doubt leave it until the last minute to turn up, so as not to raise the alarm, but she wanted to be there early. Kevin had promised he wouldn't let her down, but she was still taking a risk. It was hard to control groups of people when they were tired, stoned or pissed. And Kev's trips were the stuff of folklore. Anything could happen, and it usually did.

They reached Klimeni by late afternoon, bruised, sunburnt and dehydrated. Everyone jumped off the truck, itching to cool off in the sea, but Kev hollered at them to come back and unload. Everyone took something, dumping it on the sand in a heap. Cliff took charge of logistics. While the barbecue was being set up, Estelle went off by herself to explore.

There were a few signs that people had once lived here or had at least grazed goats on the plain behind the beach. She found a stone shelter, similar to the goatherd's hut she'd stayed in last summer with Niko, but in derelict condition. Nearby, there was an old well, sunk deep into the ground. She leaned over the edge but couldn't see the bottom of it. When she threw a stone down it made no splash.

She looked across the bay at the glorious view. The sand was soft and golden, contrasting beautifully with the sea, which was unnaturally blue, the water iridescent where it met the white gravel shore.

Such a pity that after today she would probably never come here again. She took several snaps with her Kodak Instamatic. Her amateur photography was unlikely to do the landscape justice. She'd seen shots of the beach on post-cards, but most visitors never came out this far. She hoped it would stay that way – wild and unspoilt, a secret place that only locals and intrepid backpackers knew about.

Estelle returned to the others, who were gathered around a patchwork of woven throws that had been spread out on the sand. There was no shade, but nobody seemed to care about getting burned. The hippies had weeks, even months of sun exposure behind them. Their hair was bleached and wiry, their skin the colour of well-done toast. They looked as if they belonged to the same weird tribe. She was the odd one out – more holidaymaker than traveller. Her hair had been cut in a salon, rather than on the beach, and her summer clothes came from Topshop.

She wished she were more like her companions. But it wasn't a matter of putting on a costume, it was about committing to a different lifestyle – reassessing her values, rejecting materialism in favour of personal freedom, releasing herself from her parents' expectations . . . Dropping out, as they would call it. She felt ready to make that philosophical journey, but she wasn't sure it was what Niko had in mind. He might want to go straight back to the UK and look for a job. His note had contained one word – *yes*. But what was he actually agreeing to? There were so many things they hadn't discussed. She supposed they would sort it out once they were together.

A girl gave her a paper cup of ouzo, splashing water into it from a large plastic bottle. The drink was tepid and tasted vaguely medicinal, burning her throat as she swallowed. She'd never really liked the stuff. When nobody was looking, she poured the rest onto the sand.

Several people had run down to the water's edge. They'd stripped off and were frolicking in the waves. Girls jumped about, while the men showed off with handstands and human pyramids. Estelle had happily swum naked with Niko but now she felt shy. She decided she would wait until they came out before venturing in. She couldn't think of a more idyllic place to have her last swim on the island.

The barbecue was ready. Cliff was supervising, a metal slice in one hand, bottle of beer in the other. Estelle sliced open some buns, which had gone dry in the heat, then filled them with burgers. Kev found some paper plates. An older woman opened a large plastic box of Greek salad that she'd prepared earlier and passed it round. There was no cutlery, so everyone helped themselves with their fingers. By the time the box reached Estelle, there were grains of sand at the bottom and the lettuce had turned to an oily mush.

'*Yasas!*' cried Kev, raising a bottle of beer. Everyone joined in. 'Everyone say goodbye to Estelle – she's leaving us tomorrow.'

'Oh no! That's a shame! We'll miss you!' cried the woman with the salad, although they'd never met before.

After the toast, Kev took Estelle to one side. 'I think I know what you're up to,' he whispered. 'You and the Greek cowboy are running away together, right?'

She nodded. 'Please don't tell anyone!'

'Just watch yourself when you get to the port tomorrow. Be very careful of Yannis Zimiris. If he finds out, he'll stop at nothing to keep Niko here. And he won't let you get in his way, understand?'

It was late, well after midnight. They'd made a small bonfire, more to give them light than warmth. Somebody had brought a load of candles, which they'd stuck in the sand around the edge of the camp. It looked magical, like a fairy circle.

The party had calmed down considerably. Since their arrival, there'd been a constant stream of drinking games, stupid dares, water acrobatics, syrtaki dancing and even a mock sumo wrestling contest, but now they'd run out of steam. Most people were too tired, too drunk or too stoned to move and had crashed out on the cloths, which had become crumpled and clogged with sand. The only activity was coming from a couple having sex further along the beach, their grunts and moans not quite drowned out by a young man playing guitar.

Estelle sat cross-legged, listening to a philosophy graduate from Exeter. He was quite boring, and her attention was distracted by thoughts of Niko, and of Kev's dark, drunken warnings. Were the Zimirises really that bad? Was everything going according to plan? Had Niko managed to pack a bag? Would he leave a note for his wife?

Kevin was lying on the other side of the fire with his head cradled in the lap of the salad woman who was stroking his hair, as if he were a child. Estelle couldn't tell whether he was asleep or unconscious. She checked her watch – it was half-two. It would probably take about half an hour to clear up and herd everyone into the truck. The distance to the port was less than twenty kilometres, but it had taken an hour to get here and that had been in bright daylight. Kevin had been drinking non-stop since they arrived and was in no state to drive.

She crouched down beside him. 'Kevin,' she said, 'I think it's time to go.'

'Yeah, sure,' he yawned.

In the end, it turned out that most of the party were quite happy to leave the beach. They were tired and uncomfortable. A couple of women hadn't brought warm tops and were feeling cold. The drink had run out and several were complaining of thirst. Estelle cajoled them into tidying up and taking the crates of empties and the barbecue equipment back to the truck. She checked that no litter had been left behind and made a last call to any stragglers. When they were all seated, she went to get Kev, but he was still lying on the sand. Cliff poured a bucket of seawater over his head to wake him up and he was virtually carried back to the truck.

Estelle knew it was risky to make him to drive half comatose, but there was no other option. She *had* to get to the port in time for the ferry. Niko would be waiting for her, and she couldn't let him down.

Kevin managed a few hair-raising kilometres before he over-corrected on a bend and nearly sent them over the edge of a precipice. Several passengers declared they'd rather walk back than face what seemed like certain death and got out of the truck. Estelle stayed, sweaty with anxiety but knowing there was no choice.

'Keep your hair on, everybody, I know what I'm doing,' Kev insisted, crashing the gears. He carried on with just a handful of them on board, clinging to the side bars as the truck lurched from side to side. There were some very nasty moments and Estelle saw her life flash before her eyes on several occasions, but by some miracle, he got them back in one piece.

As they approached Chora, the darkness gave way to a greyish lavender light. Kevin dropped Cliff near the hotel, and the remaining passengers got off in the village. Then he drove down to the port, as promised. Estelle had never felt more relieved to complete a journey. She threw her rucksack out of the truck and jumped down.

'Thanks so much,' she said, throwing her arms around his neck. 'You're my saviour. I don't know what I would have done if I'd missed the ferry.' She cast around, looking for Niko, but there was no sign of him yet.

'I'll hang around,' said Kev. 'Make sure you get away safely.' He sloped off in search of a strong coffee.

Several tavernas were already open, eager to make the

most of the early morning trade. Estelle sat on the front row of tables outside Atlantis, where there was a good view of the hill path. Stamatius was waiting tables. She ordered a cup of English tea so that she could speak to him.

'Give my love to Angela,' she said. 'Tell her I wish her luck for the birth.'

He thanked her grudgingly. Estelle was worried about her friend. How long would that relationship last, she wondered.

There were only a few more minutes to go before the ferry arrived. Niko was cutting it fine. People were already queuing for the rowing boats which would take them out to the larger vessel. Where was he?

Chapter Forty-Three: Now

JUNO

Despina doesn't return with the tampons. It's okay because my period doesn't come. I think my mind must be keeping it at bay. I'm not sure how late I am. I used to keep a note of when I was due on my phone, but since arriving in Inios, I haven't bothered. It's been a relief not to have to think about it, but now that I want to remember, I can't. The last weeks have been a blur. So much has happened, I've barely had a moment to think about my cycle.

I've never been regular, especially not when stressed, and I've never been in a more stressful situation than this, so it's not surprising it's late. My irregularity was one of the difficulties we had with conceiving. I used to take my temperature every day, looking for the spike that indicated I was ovulating. Then it would be all systems go, trying to inject some passion into our lovemaking while following the latest 'conception hacks' I'd found on the internet – most of them ridiculous and undignified. After that, we'd have a blissful couple of weeks, full of hope and possibility. If my period was late, I'd try to play it cool, but secretly my heart would be skipping. Then the inevitable cramping at the pit of my stomach would start, and I'd know we'd failed again.

The doctors insist our problems are psychological, nothing

to do with ovulation or sperm count. Could my difficult relationship with Estelle have been the reason I haven't been able to conceive? Luke has always maintained that it's the wanting that's the problem, but maybe the opposite is true. What if I *don't* want a baby? I'm frightened of making a mess of it, of not being able to cope and having to give my child up. Like Estelle did. I don't know how to be a mother because I've never been mothered myself, but I've been too scared and ashamed to admit it. The truth has been staring me in the face for years. It's only now, here on my own in the darkness, that I'm able to see it.

I wish I was with Luke now, spooning under the duvet, his arms around me, his warm breath caressing the back of my neck. I curse myself for leaving him, for setting out on this solo journey, for believing I belonged to a bunch of strangers more than I did to him. If I ever get out of this, I'll put everything right between us.

Night falls. The specks of light coming through the roof disappear and the scene fades to black, like in a movie. My imagination plays mischievous games with me, although having the torch helps a lot. It's a lifeline, my link with sanity, but I must ration its use. The batteries will last a few hours at the most.

I use the light to make myself as comfortable as I can, putting the cushion Despina brought me under my head and lying on my side, with my knees up, back pressed against the rough wall. I'm getting used to the mattress, and the cushion makes a huge difference. It almost feels luxurious, making me realise how much I used to take comfort for granted. Not anymore.

I turn the torch off. Mustn't waste it.

I think I've been here four days now. The ceiling is my clock, with its 'stars' of daylight. I've been eking out the food Despina left me – the last nectarine is rotting in the heat – but I will have to eat it soon. I have one small bottle of water left. I swirl the water around my mouth before swallowing and lick my dry lips.

She'll come, I tell myself, either to release me or to bring fresh supplies. She's not evil, she's a good person who's lost her way. She doesn't want to kill me. I expect she's in turmoil now, wondering what to do. She's kidnapped me for nothing. Her threats to kill me have fallen on deaf ears. It's difficult to say the least. When she was last here, I promised that if she released me I wouldn't go to the police, and I meant it. But she probably doesn't believe me. She might conclude that she's in so deep, she can't go back now and has no choice but to starve me to death. It's the logical conclusion to a very bad situation.

I can only assume that Estelle hasn't sent her confession – either because she hasn't picked up the message yet, or because she didn't kill Niko, or because she *did* and she's scared of facing justice. But where does that leave me? Regardless of what happened all those years ago, Estelle needs to come good for me, her only child. Now – just once, for the first time in her life. In my head I'm hopeful, but in my heart, I fear she'll let me down. It's happened so many times before. I have little faith in her.

Luke always says I'm too hard on Estelle – he thinks her life experiences have left her mentally fragile, unable to form relationships with other people or to hold down a job.

Now I can see how that might be true, but the child in me still struggles to forgive her. Growing up, I needed her to be strong and she failed me; handed me over to my grandparents who gave me the love and care she seemed unable to offer. I never thought about *why* she rejected me or what she might have been through. I just saw her as a selfish person who should never have had kids. But if she *did* kill my father that would have been enough to damage her mental health for the rest of her life. Perhaps, every time she looked at me, she saw him in my face and was reminded of the terrible thing she'd done.

The darkness covers me like a weighted blanket, suffocating my spirit. I feel myself sinking into despair, my limbs going numb. I quickly flick on the torch and cast it around the space, bringing myself back into the light. This is no good. I can't just lie here, waiting for Despina to decide what to do with me, scared that my mother is too weak to save me. I have to put up a fight.

But I've little strength. The wound on my forehead is still tender, my head aches constantly, every part of me is sore. I'm tethered to the wall like a goat. Even if I managed to free myself, I couldn't break down the door.

I train the beam of the torch on the rope tied around my ankle. It's been firmly knotted, but maybe I could ease it with my fingers. With the light to guide me, it might be possible to loosen it enough to slip my foot through.

I prop the torch on the cushion and place my leg over my knee. My nails aren't really long enough for this job, but I do what I can, picking away at the rope, thread by thread. My fingers soon start to hurt, but I keep attacking the knot.

Now I don't *want* Despina to come – not yet anyway. If I'm not totally free, she'll tie me up again, and do a better job of it too.

I keep the torch shining on the task. I can't rest, can't sleep . . . I have to do this. For me. For my future. To find my father. To get back to Luke.

I've lost all sense of time. My fingers are bleeding, torn by the hard fibres of the rope. I ignore the pain and keep tugging. I feel it weakening, starting to give away. Nearly, nearly there. The temptation is to try to squeeze my foot through the loop, but if there's not enough room and I force it, the knot will only tighten again. I need to slow down and relax, but my heart is galloping like an excited horse.

I turn the torch off for a few seconds to blink at the thatched ceiling. There's not one chink of light poking through. Must still be night, then . . . I take another swig of water. I'm sweating with the effort.

I turn the torch back on – its glow seems weaker than before. I have to hurry up before it goes altogether. 'You've got this,' I say out loud.

I grit my teeth and apply my fraying fingers. After several minutes of gentle tugging, the rope suddenly springs out of its knot. I fall backwards with the momentum.

I enlarge the hole and pass the noose over my foot. There's a painful blister where my ankle was rubbing against the knot, but the relief is extraordinary. I throw the rope down and stand up.

I haven't been able to walk more than a step for days, and I'm as wobbly as a newborn lamb as I explore the rest of the room. I shine the torch over the walls, looking for a loose stone, but everything is fixed in place.

I go up to the door and try to lift the latch, on the off chance that Despina didn't bother to padlock it when she left, but of course it won't budge. The door itself is solid and attached to the frame by large iron hinges. There's no way I could kick it down. I feel defeated for a few moments, then pull myself together.

Despina won't be expecting me to have got free. If I hide in the shadows and leap on her as soon as she opens the door, the element of surprise should give me an advantage. I don't know what I'm going to do after that. Strangle her with my bare hands? I'll have to hope that my survival instinct kicks in and I can follow it when the time comes.

Of course, this is all predicated on the assumption that Despina is going to return. The alternative scenario is unthinkable. I will not think it.

I've hardly slept for four, maybe five nights; I'm feeling lightheaded with hunger. Delirious. Strange thoughts are running through my brain. The events of these past weeks are jumbled and out of sequence, like a pack of cards that has been thrown to the ground. Arriving on the island, meeting Paul, Millie getting sacked, the launch party, my mother's warnings, the attack on the club, Despina kidnapping me, the discovery of the skeleton . . . Everything is connected, I just don't know how.

I feel dizzy. How am I going to be able to disable Despina when I can hardly stand?

The torch flickers and dies. Cursing, I throw it to the floor. Then, thinking I could use it to strike Despina, I fall to my knees and feel around for it in the dark, finally grasping its neck. It's not the heaviest torch in the world, but if I hit her in the face with it, it might do enough damage to disable her for a bit. What am I talking about? I've never hit anybody in my entire life.

I stay crouching by the side of the door. Waiting.

My mind starts to wander off again.

Sleep beckons. I close my eyes and submit to troubled dreams.

Noises jolt me awake. She's back. I leap to my feet, slapping my face to wake myself up. This is it. No second chances. Despina is removing the padlock, rattling at the door, pulling it open with effort. Sunlight floods the space as she enters, stopping to look around, her eyes searching for me, wondering why I'm not there.

'Juno?'

I hurl myself on her from the side, digging in with my shoulder and rugby-tackling her to the floor. With a scream, she lands heavily on her back. I jump onto her, kneeling on her chest, pushing the air out of her lungs. I'm about to punch her in the face, when I realise it's not Despina staring up at me.

It's Estelle.

Chapter Forty-Four: Now

JUNO

'Juno! Juno! It's me!'

I freeze, fist in mid-air, my eyes still adjusting to the bright sunlight streaming in.

'Oh my God . . . Estelle! I don't believe it . . .' I pull back. 'Sorry . . . I didn't mean – did I hurt you?'

'It's okay . . . A bit winded, but I'm fine.'

'You're here! You found me!'

'Yes, yes!' She looks at my dishevelled state, the bloody crack on my forehead. 'Oh dear, look at you . . . You poor darling.' She sits up and we embrace. 'I was scared I'd be too late,' she whispers, her mouth close to my ear. 'He said he was going to kill you.'

I release her. '*He?*'

'Well, I assumed it was Andreas sending me those messages. No?'

I shake my head. 'No. It was Despina . . . Phaedra's daughter.'

Her eyes widen. 'Oh . . . Oh, I see . . . Despina . . .'

'I don't think anyone else in the family knows.'

A voice speaks from behind. 'We shouldn't hang around.'

I gaze up at a male figure silhouetted against the sun.

He's wearing a hat with a large brim and has a pair of bolt cutters in his hands. Could it possibly be . . . ?

'Who's that?' I croak.

'It's alright, it's only Kev,' Estelle explains.

'Wha—I don't . . .' I look from one to the other.

Kevin steps into the hut. 'Jesus, the stench!'

'Sorry.'

'Not your fault, is it? What the hell did she think she was doing? You wouldn't treat an animal like this. Disgusting.'

Estelle heaves herself up. 'Kev's right. We'd better get out of here, before Despina comes back.'

'She hasn't visited for a couple of days,' I say, also getting to my feet. 'I'm not sure when she was last here. I've lost track of time. I don't know what's going on.'

'Don't worry, it's over. You're safe now.' Estelle hugs me again. 'Come . . .'

She keeps her arms around me as we stagger along the path to Kevin's Jeep, which is parked up at the end of the track. I feel weak, and the sunlight hurts my eyes. Estelle sees me squinting and hands me her shades. The beach is virtually deserted. Two cars are parked up, and there's a small group of people swimming in the sea. It's like a normal sunny day.

Estelle helps me into the back of the Jeep and sits next to me. Kevin reverses and we drive away.

'Where are we going?' I ask.

'My place,' he replies. 'It's remote, you'll be safe. Anyway, she won't dare coming looking for you. Not now.'

'Tell me what's been happening,' I say to Estelle. 'You got the first message, meant to be from me—'

'I knew it wasn't. The "Dear Mum" thing – that's just not you.'

'I thought you'd spot that.'

'Yes, straightaway. I assumed Andreas had found out who you were and was putting you under pressure. I didn't respond. I was scared, didn't know what to do. I contacted Kev and asked him to check that you were okay. He did some digging and found out you'd quit your job and supposedly "left the island". We started to worry that you'd been kidnapped. Then new messages arrived. They became more and more threatening. They said you'd be killed unless I confessed. That's when I knew I had to come and find you.'

'Why didn't you just call the police?'

'That wasn't an option, I'm afraid.'

'I don't understand.'

'We'll explain,' says Kev. 'Just not while we're on the road.'

I turn to Estelle. 'But how did you know where to look?'

'The last message I got included a photo of a beach,' she replies. 'It said I had one last chance to confess, or your body would be dumped at sea.'

'You recognised the beach?' I ask, impressed.

'Not as such. But there was a ruined building in the corner of the photo. I remembered that Niko's father had started building a beach cafe on some land the family owned. It was very remote. They had a goatherd's hut – Niko and I stayed there once. It was tucked away, out of sight, the perfect place to hide somebody. I was sure you were being held there. Luckily, I was right.'

'I still think you should have told the police.'

'We couldn't. I'm sorry, but it's complicated,' says Estelle. 'We'll tell you the whole story, I promise, but first, you need to rest.'

An empty, sinking sensation hits my stomach. Maybe it's hunger, maybe it's panic. I've been yearning to know the truth for months, but now I'm close to hearing it, I'm not sure I'll cope. The important thing is, I'm free. I'm going to make it home.

'Nearly there now,' Estelle says, as we take a left fork in the road. 'We'll make you some food. You can borrow some clothes. They'll be a bit big for you, but better than what you're wearing.' She gestures at my filthy linen trousers and T-shirt.

'Thank you for coming for me,' I say, leaning my head on her shoulder. Estelle doesn't wince at the smell of me but pulls me in closer.

'Of course I came for you,' she replies, as if I should never have doubted it for a second.

I lose myself in her embrace. She's warm and soft, like mothers are supposed to feel. Her scent is familiar, even though we haven't been physically close for years. Forget Niko, forget the Zimirises. *She* is my family, the closest blood relative I've got.

'Despina has all my stuff,' I murmur. 'Including my passport. I can't leave without it.'

'Don't worry about that now,' says Kevin. 'We'll sort it out.'

'How?'

He doesn't reply, but draws up outside a modest single-storey house, whitewashed in the traditional style. It's on its own, surrounded by olive trees and has amazing views of the sea to the west. To one side is a small swimming pool and a covered terrace.

Estelle helps me out of the Jeep. I stumble to get my balance and have to take her arm to walk to the door.

'I built it with my own fair hands,' he says, catching me staring.

'You did a great job,' says Estelle. 'It's gorgeous.'

Kevin hands me a large beach towel and Estelle digs out a pair of baggy cotton trousers and a top from her bag. The shower is one of the best experiences I've had in a long time. I let the cool water run over me, hoping it will wash away the trauma from the past couple of days.

When I emerge, Kevin dishes up scrambled eggs, ladled onto homemade bread, with slices of fresh tomato on the side. There's also a large bowl of yoghurt topped with nuts and honey from his own beehives. Estelle makes a pot of coffee, and we take it out onto the patio. I shovel the food in without hesitation. It all tastes heavenly.

'Don't eat too quickly,' Estelle warns. 'Your stomach might not react well.'

After eating, Kevin stands up and walks over to the pool. He lights a cigarette and smokes it while he stares out across the landscape. I can tell that he's thinking about how they're going to break the news to me.

'Have you always kept in touch with Kevin?' I ask Estelle.

'Sort of . . . We've always known how to get hold of each other, let's put it that way. It was a bit of shock to see how he'd aged. I barely recognised him. We hadn't seen each other since I left the island.'

'Why did he lie to me about knowing you?'

'Because I asked him to. As soon as I found out you'd gone to Inios, I contacted him. Kev's name was all over my letters, so I guessed you'd try to find him. We agreed he'd try to put you off the scent at the same time as keeping an eye on you.'

'What do you mean, "off the scent"?' I start firing questions. 'What's going on, Estelle? Whose body was in that well? I know you know . . . What happened to my father? Is he still alive? Are you in touch with him?'

Estelle's eyes glisten with tears. She gathers herself, then calls out, 'Kev! We need to tell her. We can't put it off any longer.'

'Okay.' He stubs his cigarette out and returns to the table, sitting down next to Estelle. He squeezes her hand. 'You're sure about this?'

She nods. 'The whole truth and nothing but.'

Kevin leans forward, looking me right in the eyes. 'The thing is, Juno, once you know, it'll be up to you to decide what you want to do. We can't force you to keep quiet. We can't stop you going to the police either. So, if you'd rather *not* know, and not have to make that decision, then now's the time to say so.'

'No, I want to know,' I say, swallowing down my fear. 'If it's about my father, then I have a right.'

Estelle takes a deep breath. Kevin nods at her encouragingly. 'Well, you know some of it from the letters,' she starts. 'Although they don't tell the whole story. I couldn't tell Mum and Dad exactly what was going on; they wouldn't have approved.'

'I kind of guessed that.'

'They were from a very different generation, had different values—'

'I know. They brought me up, remember?'

'Of course.' She smiles apologetically. 'Perhaps when you hear what I have to say you'll understand why.'

'Go on.'

'Right . . .' She clears her throat nervously. 'As you know, I met Niko the first summer I came here: 1984. I had an amazing time. Inios was an incredible place back then. The sense of freedom was like nothing I'd ever experienced. I met Niko early on and we fell in love.'

'He was a *kamaki*,' interrupts Kevin.

'Yes and no,' Estelle contradicts. 'He was trapped into playing a role, just like everyone else.' She turns back to me. 'What your father and I had was real . . . It was my fault, I should have stayed on after that first summer, like my friend Angela. But I was in the middle of a degree, and I knew how Mum and Dad would react if I threw it all in. I'm pretty sure that if I'd stayed on the island and hadn't gone back to university, he wouldn't have married Phaedra.'

Kevin shrugs. 'We don't know that. He had no choice. I still think you would have been sent packing, Estelle.'

'Yes, but then I wouldn't have come back the following year,' she replies, 'and none of it would have happened.' She returns to her story. 'When I got back to Manchester, Niko wrote, telling me he loved me but to forget all about him. Of course, he was letting me down gently, but I didn't understand. I thought maybe his family were against me.'

'Which they were,' says Kevin.

'Yes, but it never once occurred to me that he'd married a local girl.'

'You came back the next summer, hoping to carry on where you'd left off,' I say, pushing Estelle on. My imagination is working overtime, sending me into some very dark places. I need to know how it ends.

'I suppose so,' she reflects. 'I was still in love with him. University wasn't working out – I was thinking of packing it in and going to live in Greece, settling down with Niko, embracing the lifestyle.' She looks down. 'I didn't warn him. I just turned up.'

'And how did he react?'

'It was strange. He was really happy to see me, but he wouldn't let me come anywhere near Sunset Bar. We had to meet in secret. I couldn't work out why. I was staying in a half-built hotel. Andreas found out. He came to see me – told me Niko was married and had a baby. I was devastated.'

There's a beat.

'Well?' I say.

Estelle looks at Kevin for reassurance and he nods gently. 'This is difficult. I made a promise all those years ago. We both did, didn't we, Kev?'

'We did,' he grunts. 'But circumstances have changed. After what Juno's been through, she deserves to know the truth.'

'Yes,' agrees Estelle. 'It's finally time.'

329

Chapter Forty-Five: August 1985

ESTELLE

The loud blast of a klaxon made her jump. She looked up to see the *Apollo Express* thundering into the bay. It was on time for once, just when she needed it to be late. Estelle leapt to her feet and heaved her rucksack onto her back. She ran into the middle of the road, eyes wide as she stared into the distance. Where was he?

The rowing boats started to load up. Even if Niko appeared now, they would be too late. The ferry wouldn't wait.

As soon as all the passengers were on board, the ship started its clumsy manoeuvre to get out of the bay. Estelle sank to the ground, heavy with despair.

'I risked twenty people's lives to get you here on time and then the bastard doesn't even turn up.' She looked up to see Kevin standing over her. He pulled her to her feet, his tone softening as he caught the expression on her face. 'Hey, what's with the tears?'

'He's not a bastard,' she said. 'Something must have gone wrong.'

'You do know he's married? And he's got a littl'un.'

She nodded. 'He was forced to marry her. He's unhappy, he wants to be with me.'

'Hmm . . . Looks to me like he changed his mind.'

'I don't believe it.'

'Or he's been stopped.'

'Then I have to rescue him!'

'I told you – you can't mess with the Zimirises.' Kev gave her a pitying look. 'Why don't you just catch the next ferry? The bureau will change your ticket if you ask them nicely.'

'No, I've got to see him first. Find out what's going on.'

'That's not a good idea.'

'I've *got* to. Even if it's only to say goodbye.' She turned to him. 'Would you give me a lift to his house, Kev? It's a long way to walk.'

'I think you should stay well away—'

'Please! If he has changed his mind, I need to hear it from his own mouth.'

They got back into the truck, and he drove up the dirt track to Chora. The house was a mile or so further on. The sky was gradually brightening, the lavender streaks giving way to gold. She could feel the heat rising.

Kevin parked up on a patch of wasteground just beyond the bend. She climbed out and slammed the door.

'I'll wait,' he told her. 'Make sure you're alright. Any trouble, you give me a shout.'

'Thanks, but I'm sure I'll be fine.'

The shutters were closed, making the house look like it was asleep. Estelle opened the gate and walked into the courtyard. Washing was hanging on a clothes horse on the veranda – nappy squares, baby clothes, a man's shirt, several pairs of ladies' knickers, a cotton dress. It was so early they must have been put out the night before. The domesticity of it made her catch her breath.

She edged closer to the front door and knocked gently. Twice. She waited, but nobody came. Nobody locked their doors here – she could probably just walk in. Taking a deep breath, she pressed the latch down and pushed it open.

Niko was sitting on a stool next to a wooden table, looking very nervous. Phaedra was sitting opposite him, a shotgun in her hands, which was pointed at his chest.

'Estelle!' he gasped, his mouth falling open. 'Stay there!'

Estelle froze. 'I-I . . . don't understand,' she stuttered.

Phaedra swung her head round and shouted at her in Greek. 'She says if you take one more step, she'll kill me,' Niko translated. 'She wants you to go.'

Estelle shook her head. 'Not unless you come with me.'

'This matter is between me and Phaedra,' he said. 'Go back to UK. Forget about me.'

'I can't. We belong together. You don't love her, and she doesn't love you – you said so yourself.'

'It's more complicated than that.'

'No, it's not.'

'I owe her.'

'What do you mean?'

Phaedra was becoming very agitated. She shouted something else at Niko and he tried to calm her.

'Please go, Estelle,' he said quietly. 'She doesn't understand what we're saying. It's making things worse.'

But she couldn't walk out on Niko, not when he was in danger of being shot. 'Only if she puts the gun down,' she said. 'I'm not going anywhere until I know you're safe. Tell her, Niko. Tell her!'

Phaedra suddenly swung the shotgun round, pointing

it directly at Estelle. Then everything happened in a flash. Niko stood up and tried to wrestle the gun off his wife. They spun around like a roulette wheel, shouting at each other, the gun pointing randomly in all directions.

Niko screamed at Estelle, 'Get out! Get out!'

But she was paralysed with fear. As the couple struggled, Niko tripped over the stool he'd been sitting on and fell onto the flagstone floor. He was panting for breath, holding his hand up to protect his face, pleading with Phaedra to put the gun down. She was in a red mist, rigid with fury. She stepped forward and trained the gun at Niko's head, then changed her mind and swerved it towards Estelle.

Niko yelled at Estelle to run but her feet seemed glued to the floor. Her heart thundered in her chest – she couldn't control it. She felt lightheaded, couldn't breathe. Phaedra's finger was on the trigger, ready to fire. Her eyes were blazing. She looked enraged and yet desperate, like a woman who had both nothing and everything to lose.

This is it, thought Estelle. *I'm going to die.*

The silence was pierced by the sound of a baby crying. Phaedra gasped and turned her head towards a door in the corner of the room. In that split second, Niko saw his chance, leaping up and hurling himself at his wife, who screamed and twisted away from him.

The gun went off. Estelle immediately fell to the floor and lay there for a few seconds, eyes closed, hands over her ears, her brain echoing with noise. An acrid smell filled the air and there was a strange silence in the room, like the calm after a storm. What had happened? Had she been shot? She couldn't feel any pain. And where was Niko?

She sat up. Her eyes landed on him, lying awkwardly on the floor like a puppet who'd had his strings cut. His head was soaking in a pool of blood, which was trickling across the sloping floor towards the fireplace. Phaedra stood over him, the shotgun hanging limply in her hands. She swayed from side to side as if in a trance. Her white cotton night-dress was covered in flecks of red.

The baby started crying again. Phaedra dropped the shotgun and walked unsteadily towards a door in the corner of the room, arms outstretched as if sleepwalking.

Estelle stopped holding her breath. Her body began to shake. Horror and pity rose from the deepest parts of her, surging through her body and bursting out of her mouth in a strange sound that was something between a groan and a roar. She started to crawl towards Niko, calling his name softly, but she already knew he couldn't answer, that she would never hear his voice again.

Just as she reached his side, the front door opened and Kev ran in, alerted by the sound of the gunshot. He took one look at the scene and swore loudly.

'She was going to shoot me,' Estelle said. 'He saved my life.'

Kev crouched down next to Niko's body and checked his pulse, although it was obvious he was dead. His eyes were glassy, and his mouth had fallen slack.

'Where's Phaedra?' he asked.

She tilted her head towards the bedroom. 'Through there. With the baby.'

'Jesus . . .' He sighed heavily. 'What happened?'

Her words stumbled out. 'She must have found out he

was going to leave her, or maybe he told her, I don't know. When I arrived, she was pointing the gun at him. Then she turned it on me. I really thought she was about to shoot me, then Niko . . . There was a fight . . .' She faded out, unable to finish.

Kevin stood up and stepped away from the rivulets of blood. 'We need to get you out of here,' he told Estelle. 'Before the police come.'

'But I'm the witness!'

'What if Phaedra tells them that *you* shot him?'

She stared at him, astonished. 'Nobody would believe her. She's covered in his blood.'

'So are you.'

'Her fingerprints must be all over the gun. I've never fired one in my life, wouldn't know how. Anyway, why would I want to kill—' Her voice broke off. She glanced down at Niko's prostrate body and her stomach roiled. 'I love him. She's the one with the motive, not me.'

'All true,' Kevin replied. 'But you're here and you're foreign. That makes you an instant suspect.'

'Surely the police will work out the truth.'

He nearly laughed. 'You don't understand. The Zimiris family have a lot of influence. They won't want a scandal. Niko was about to bring shame on his family. A lot of islanders will see Phaedra as the victim. They'll say you killed Niko out of jealousy.' He fixed her with his gaze. 'Believe me, Estelle, you do not want to spend the rest of your life in a Greek prison.'

'But if I run away, I'll look guilty.'

'Staying is more dangerous.' Kev clasped the sides of his

head in frustration. 'Fuck! This is bad, Estelle; this is really, really bad. We've got to do something. Think smart . . . There's got to be a way out of this.'

Phaedra came back into the room cuddling the baby, who was wrapped tightly in a cotton shawl, no longer crying but making snivelling noises. She was alarmed to find Kevin there. He challenged her in Greek, pointing at Niko's body and the gun. Phaedra didn't answer, just shook her head repeatedly. She tightened her grip on the baby, as if Kevin were threatening to take her away.

He spoke rapidly, grabbing Phaedra by the shoulders, shouting in her face. Estelle looked on anxiously, straining to understand. The reality of the situation was finally dawning upon Phaedra. Tears rolled down her cheeks and her bottom lip quivered.

'*Entáxei*,' she whispered. 'Okay' – it was one of the few words of Greek Estelle knew. '*Se parakaló voíthisé me.*'

'What was that?' Estelle asked.

'She thanked me.'

'What for?'

'Helping her.'

'You're going to *help* her? Are you crazy? She *killed* Niko! We should call the police.'

'No, no, no! Listen! Phaedra says she never meant to kill him. It was an accident. She was just trying to keep him in the house until you'd left. You turned up and she panicked.'

'She was about to shoot me. Niko tried to stop her, and the gun went off. It was – I don't know – manslaughter or something. Do they have that here?'

'This is how it'll go,' Kevin answered. 'Babá Yannis will

want someone to pay for the death of his son. Either it'll be you or Phaedra. The two of you have to work together – it's the only way you'll both be safe. You've got to trust me.'

Estelle looked at him, bewildered. 'Okay . . . So, what's the plan?'

Kevin reversed the Jeep into the courtyard. Between them, they carried Niko's body, which Phaedra had wrapped in a sheet, and put it in the back, wedging it between the barbecue and Estelle's rucksack, and covering it with a crate of empties. It felt horribly disrespectful, stashing his body among rubbish, but there was no other way to hide it.

Phaedra was indoors, on her knees next to a bucket of soapy water, scrubbing the flagstones with a hard brush. Fortunately, the child had gone back to sleep. She looked up as Estelle and Kevin came back in and got to her feet, wiping her wet hands on her apron.

There were just a few more details to arrange. Phaedra went into the bedroom and came back with a small cardboard case that she had filled with Niko's clothes and handed it to Kevin.

'What's going on?' asked Estelle.

'We have to make it look as if Niko packed his things and left.'

'Oh . . . Okay.'

Phaedra stepped forward and embraced Estelle. It was a strange action for two women who until a few minutes ago had been enemies, but it felt right. They held each other for several seconds, crying and apologising in their own languages, until Kevin gently told them it was time to go.

Niko's Stetson was hanging on a hook behind the door. 'You'd better take this as well,' said Estelle, handing it to Kevin. 'He never went anywhere without it.'

They drove away, retracing the route they'd taken only a few hours ago. Estelle sat in the cab this time, eyes facing forward. If anyone saw them, the story was that Estelle had left her bag at the beach, containing her passport and ferry tickets, and Kevin had very kindly taken her back to retrieve it. As it turned out, they didn't pass a single person or vehicle either on the way there or the way back.

They hardly spoke on the journey, other than to make the last arrangements for their deception. Once they'd disposed of the body (how chilling that sounded), they would return to the port, and Estelle would change the tickets for the next ferry. Kevin would dress in Niko's clothes. Both men were roughly of the same height and weight. Kev's hair was brown and straight, but with the cowboy hat on and a pair of sunglasses, he was confident he would get away with the disguise – at least, from a distance. Walking through the square and queuing up for the rowing boats would be their biggest challenge, but there would be more tourists around at that time of day, allowing them to mingle with the crowd. Estelle and 'Niko' would board the ferry as soon as possible, then Kevin would get off at the next island, ditch the Stetson, change back into his own clothes, and return on another ferry later when it was dark.

'I've told Phaedra to wait until the last minute. Then she'll run to the family and tell them Niko's leaving. She'll ask Babá Yannis to send someone to the port to try to stop him. Hopefully, we'll be on board the ferry by then and it'll be too late.'

'Surely that's too risky.'

'They need to see him leave with their own eyes,' Kev insisted. 'Or the story won't stick.'

The sun was fully risen by the time they arrived back at Klimeni beach. The ground was far too hard and rocky to dig a grave. Estelle showed Kevin the disused well she'd found yesterday, and they agreed it would be a good place to hide the body. Taking it out to sea would have been better but they didn't have a boat.

She would never forget the horror of carrying Niko to his final resting place. It made her understand the term 'dead weight'. The makeshift shroud was bloodstained and had stuck to his head. She couldn't bear to open it to look at his face – it would make it too real – so she kissed him through the sheet.

'Forgive me,' she whispered. 'It's all my fault. I should never have come back.'

Kevin heaved Niko over the edge of the well, and then let him go, headfirst, as if he were diving. He reached the bottom too quickly, landing in the darkness with a dull thump. Maybe the well wasn't as deep as they'd thought, but it was too late to change their minds. The deed was done. Now they had to live with it.

They drove back to the port in silence. Estelle looked out at the vast landscape, physically and emotionally exhausted, unable to utter her thoughts. The island had changed her. She would never be the same again.

Chapter Forty-Six: Now

JUNO

My mother is not a murderer.

The news breaks over me like a wave. For a while I go under, lost in myself, flailing about, nearly drowning. But then I come back up, gasping for air, my face wet with tears. Estelle is holding me, stroking the back of my head, telling me everything is going to be alright.

Is it? I can't tell yet. It doesn't alter the fact that my father is dead, and I'll never get to meet him. He took the bullet that was meant for Estelle. Either way, I was destined to be without one of my parents.

'Why did you help Phaedra cover it up?' I ask when I'm able to speak. 'Weren't you angry? You were in love with Niko – you were supposed to be starting a new life together.'

Estelle withdraws, sitting back in her chair. 'I know it's hard to understand, but I wasn't angry,' she says. 'Phaedra didn't set out to kill Niko; she was trying to stop him leaving, that's all. The shotgun was to hand. All the locals had them, it was normal. When I turned up, everything changed, spun out of control. I felt as guilty as if I'd pulled the trigger myself. If it hadn't been for me, Niko would have stayed with his family. He'd still be alive today.'

'That's impossible to know,' interrupts Kevin, who has been sitting quietly all this time. 'You can't keep blaming yourself, Estelle.'

'I know, but . . .' She sighs. 'It was a tragedy all round. For him most of all, but also for Phaedra and their child. If she'd been convicted and gone to prison, she would have served a very long sentence. She didn't deserve that either. She had no control over her life, you know? First, she was owned by her parents, then her husband. As an abandoned woman she'd have no status and would be dependent on the extended family – she knew that. That's why she tried to stop him leaving.' Estelle inhales the memory. 'I have many, many regrets, Juno, but strange as it may sound, helping Phaedra to cover up Niko's death is not one of them.'

'I don't regret it either,' says Kevin, lighting up another cigarette. 'Phaedra's had a tough life. She's never recovered psychologically from what she did – spent the last forty years living in fear that the truth would come out. The poor woman has punished herself enough.'

'Kev has been secret friends with her all these years,' Estelle says, patting his arm affectionately. 'She's his mole – spies for his campaign.'

I turn to Kevin. 'Did you tell Phaedra who I was?'

'Yes, straightaway. We were terrified that you were going to tell Andreas. Phaedra was very anxious about it, but I said we had to stick to our plan.'

'Your plan?' I query.

'To stop Klimeni. If the development went ahead, we knew they'd find the body eventually,' he continues. 'Also, the land used to belong to Phaedra's family. She's doesn't want to see it ruined. Not that she's had any say in the matter . . .' He pulls sharply on his cigarette.

'And the attack on the club?'

'We were in on it together. Planned it meticulously. Phaedra told the police it had happened at a time when I made sure I was in Chora with the lads. In fact, she let me into the club at four in the morning. Allowed me to lock her up too, bless her. She was actually only in the cold store for a couple of hours.' He throws his cigarette onto the ground and stubs it out with his foot, then looks up at me. 'Didn't stop the launch from going ahead, mind. I hear you were partly to thank for that.'

'I had no choice,' I reply. 'It was part of my job.'

'Yeah, well, you know the villa where you had the party? That used to be Phaedra and Niko's house. After he left, Babá Yannis brought Phaedra and Despina to live with him and turned it into a luxury rental.'

'What? You mean, that's where Niko died?'

Kevin nods. 'Yup, that's the place. Not that you'd recognise it now . . . It's ironic, isn't it? Despina thinks Estelle killed Niko, when in fact it was her own mother.'

Estelle looks serious. 'There's a lot at stake, Juno. That's why I begged you to leave Inios. I wish you'd taken notice.'

'You refused to explain, that's why I didn't leave.'

'How could I? I promised Kev never to tell another soul about what we did.'

'You should have trusted me.'

'I was scared you'd take your father's side and tell his family.'

I look away, casting my eyes upwards to the clear blue

sky. Maybe I *would* have betrayed Estelle. She lied to me for years. I'm not sure I would have felt that she deserved my loyalty. Not without a full explanation. Right here, right now, I feel very close to her, but it's an unfamiliar sensation.

'I'm so sorry, Juno. I know I was an inadequate mother. You had every right to reject me,' says Estelle, as if reading my thoughts.

'I thought you'd rejected me,' I reply evenly.

'No. Never! ... After I escaped from Inios, I drifted around the Greek islands, not knowing where I was going or what I was doing, full of grief and guilt, constantly reliving the trauma of what had happened. Then I discovered I was pregnant. I was overjoyed because it meant Niko would live on in you, but as soon as you were born, I realised I wasn't capable of looking after myself, let alone a baby. It was a struggle, but I hung on. I didn't want to lose you as well as Niko.' Her voice breaks with emotion, as the memories flood back. 'I tried so hard to get myself back on track, but I knew I was doing a really bad job of looking after you. My mental health was shot to pieces, and I couldn't ask for help because that would mean confessing. I'd promised Kev and Phaedra to keep it a secret. I couldn't let them down. We would have all gone to prison, and what would have become of you then? I was stuck.'

'I do remember those times,' I say quietly. 'They were pretty awful. I was like some feral kid . . .'

'I know, and I'm so sorry for what I put you through. In the end, your grandparents intervened, said if I didn't let them look after you, they'd contact social services. I didn't want to give you up, but I had to accept it was the best thing.

343

For you, not me. I missed you so much. But look how well you turned out. I'm so proud of you, Juno. You're a wonderful person. Not that I can take any credit . . .'

'I don't feel very wonderful, but thanks. And thanks for explaining. Finally.' I put a hand gently on her arm. 'I didn't understand before, but everything makes a lot more sense now.'

'You did the right thing all those years ago, Estelle,' says Kevin. 'But you've certainly paid the price. We've all made sacrifices to keep our secret. Was it worth it? I don't know . . .'

'The truth's going to come out now, anyway,' I say. 'We can't stop it.'

'What do you mean?' Kevin exchanges a worried glance with Estelle.

'Despina has already been to the police and told them that the skeleton belongs to Niko. She gave them a sample of her DNA. The results could come back anytime.'

Estelle gasped. 'Shit. That's it. We're lost.'

Kevin stands up. 'Andreas will realise he was tricked. Fucking hell, I can see it all unravelling.' He turns to Estelle. 'I told you it was risky, coming back here. You need to get out of the country before you're arrested.'

'You're right, but I want to see Phaedra before I go,' Estelle replies. 'We've got to come up with a believable story we can all stick to.'

'What about Despina?' I join in. 'She's lost it, she doesn't care anymore. If she finds out you're here, there's no way of knowing what she'll do . . .'

'I'll call Phaedra,' says Kevin, going back into the house

344

for his phone. When he emerges, he's already talking to her in Greek. Estelle and I stare at each other in silence, as if we're listening in to the conversation, but of course, neither of us can understand a word. From the tone of his voice, it sounds like he's trying to calm her down.

'Okay . . . things are moving fast,' he says, as soon as he finishes the call. 'Phaedra is in a bad way. Despina has disappeared. She packed her bags and left the island yesterday, didn't say where she was going or why.'

'She left me to starve to death,' I gasp. 'If you hadn't found me—'

'It doesn't bear thinking about it,' Estelle says, clutching my hand. She looks up at Kevin. 'I guess you told her what Despina did.'

He nods. 'She didn't believe me at first, then she got very upset. She wants us to go over to her place. Says there's something she needs to tell us.'

'Is that wise?' I frown. 'Can't she come here?'

'She doesn't drive and doesn't want to take a taxi. It'll be okay. There's a back route I can take, down some unmade roads. I don't think anyone will see us.'

As soon as we get out of Kevin's Jeep, Phaedra rushes forward to greet us. She looks drained and pale. Estelle runs up to her and the two women hug – holding on to each other for a few moments, rocking gently, neither wanting to let go. Once rivals, they are now conspirators, accessories to each other's acts, their lives changed forever by the decision they took that day. As I watch them, I try to imagine how differently *my* life would have turned out if Niko and Estelle had

345

run away together. Whether we would have been a happy family, or whether he would have abandoned us eventually.

'We should go inside,' says Kevin. 'We don't want to be seen.'

'Yes. Come, come!' Phaedra gestures at us to follow her. We walk across the courtyard and step into her house. The furniture and decor are surprisingly modest, given the family's wealth. I've never been to Andreas's house, but I imagine marble floors and sleek chrome fittings. It's dark and cool here, with small, shuttered windows. The living area is one long room with a kitchen at one end and a sofa in front of a wood burner at the other. There are photos of Despina everywhere.

'Oh, it's lovely – so traditional,' says Estelle, looking around. It's as if we've come on a social visit.

'I grew up on this farm,' Phaedra replies. 'My father kept goats and my mother made cheese. It was a very simple life. When my parents died, Despina and I moved back here. I didn't want to change anything.'

'You speak English now,' Estelle says.

'Despina tries to teach me, but I am very bad student.' The mention of her daughter's name brings her up short. 'Please, sit ... I must explain everything, but in Greek. Kevin, please translate for me?'

Estelle and I take the sofa. Kevin drags a chair over from the dining table and we sit down awkwardly. Phaedra speaks, her eyes constantly flicking between me and the photographs of Despina. Kevin nods, raising his eyebrows at points, then turns to me.

'Phaedra wants to apologise for the way Despina treated

you. She says it's not in her nature to harm anyone, she's a good person, but she's been unhappy for a long time. She was very upset when the body was discovered; it pushed her over the edge. She says that it's her fault for not being honest with her daughter.'

Something we both have in common, I think, but I keep quiet.

Kevin continues. 'She says she tried to warn you – sent you some flowers and a couple of notes.'

'It was you!' I gasp. Phaedra nods. 'I thought it was Niko! . . . Why didn't you say?'

She answers. 'I was scared you tell Andreas. I want to – talk – to you . . .' She turns to Kevin and continues in Greek.

'She says sorry for confusing you. And for not meeting you in Oceanus Bar – she couldn't get away without Despina knowing.'

'It's okay,' I say. 'I understand.'

Kevin continues. 'Phaedra wants to know whether you're going to press charges against Despina – for kidnap, assault, whatever. She wouldn't blame you if you did, but before you decide, she wants to tell you the truth about the past.'

'Tell her Juno already knows,' says Estelle. 'We told her this morning.'

Phaedra shakes her head. 'No,' she says. 'There is more truth.'

'What do you mean, "more truth"?' asks Estelle.

'Hear her out,' says Kevin.

Phaedra starts to speak, and Kevin translates almost simultaneously.

'In the seventies and eighties, my parents rented their

347

outhouse to backpackers. Everybody did it. There were hundreds of them and very few hotels. It brought extra money into the family too. In the summer of 1984, three guys came to stay with us. Here. One of them was very beautiful. He had long blonde hair and blue eyes. His name was Rob.'

'I remember him,' interrupts Estelle. 'He was friends with Paul and Tony, the Barking boys.'

Phaedra's eyes fill with tears as Kevin continues to translate. 'I was only seventeen, very innocent. I wasn't even allowed to mix with Greek boys. I had to stay at home, I was virtually locked up. The moment I saw Rob I fell in love with him. I wanted to talk to him, but it was forbidden. Anyway, I disobeyed my father.'

'So, *you* were the local girl Rob had a fling with,' says Estelle. 'Oh my God. I had no idea.'

'It might have been a fling to him,' says Kevin. 'But not to Phaedra, right?' She nods.

'I remember it really well,' says Estelle. 'Your father threatened Rob. We all thought it was a bit of a laugh, but it was serious. Rob got caught with you again and then your dad got your brother and some of his friends – including Niko – to beat him up.'

Phaedra hangs her head, dropping her voice. 'That's right,' says Kevin. 'Only it went too far. Rob died.'

'Niko was involved,' admits Estelle, 'He didn't want to be but he had no choice. He insisted Rob was okay . . .' Tears well in her eyes. 'He lied to me!'

'To be fair, he couldn't admit it,' says Kev. 'Not without betraying his friends.'

Estelle nods slowly as she takes it all in. 'Did the police

348

know? I reported Rob missing, but they weren't at all interested.'

'That's because they were involved in the cover-up,' Kevin continues as Phaedra explains. 'The police didn't want the hassle of an investigation, and the locals knew the murder of a foreigner would be bad for tourism.' He sighs. 'They were different times . . .'

'What did they do with Rob's body?' I ask. 'Dump it at sea?' Phaedra shakes her head and responds.

Kevin's mouth drops open in astonishment as he listens to her words, then relays them. 'No, the men buried him in the local cemetery, in the middle of the night. It's an unmarked grave, but Phaedra always visits it when she goes to pay respects to her parents.'

'Oh my God,' says Estelle under her breath. 'This is so shocking. I can't believe how much you've suffered.'

My mind is already racing ahead. 'Then what happened, Phaedra?'

She swallows slowly and inhales before speaking in her own voice. 'I know I'm pregnant. Rob is dead so he can't marry me. My parents are very angry. I think my father will kill me too. But no, I have to marry a Greek boy. Fast.'

Estelle and I gasp simultaneously.

'Please, Kevin, you talk for me,' she says.

He listens to Phaedra continue in Greek, then turns to me and Estelle. 'My father knew that Yannis Zimiris wanted the land in the south of the island, so he offered it as a dowry. It broke his heart to lose it, but he had nothing else to trade with. Niko and I were forced to marry – neither of us wanted to, but we weren't given a choice. When Despina was born,

I told everyone she was six weeks premature, but she was actually two weeks overdue.'

'And Niko believed you?' I ask sceptically.

She shakes her head. 'I think he knew the baby was Rob's, but we never spoke about it.'

'I suppose taking on Rob's child was a way of dealing with his guilt,' says Estelle. 'I just wish he'd trusted me enough to tell me the truth.'

Kevin lets out a breath. 'Fuckin' hell,' he says, 'that's some story. I had no idea, Phaedra. The hell you've been through . . .'

'It's even worse than I realised. I'm so sorry,' adds Estelle, jumping up and hugging her.

'Despina is all I have,' Phaedra says, starting to cry. 'And now she's gone too.'

'But you know what this means,' I interrupt. 'Her DNA *won't* be a match with the skeleton. Niko will be ruled out as the victim. You're all safe.'

'Possibly,' says Kevin. 'But if the police take samples from other islanders, then the link will be made eventually. Most of them are related to each other in some way.'

'We're not out of the woods yet,' agrees Estelle. 'But there's a chance. The authorities might not want to turn it into a full investigation. It would cost a fortune and they're unlikely to be able to prove anything. We need to sit tight.' Estelle takes Phaedra by the shoulders. 'You have to keep the lie going, I'm afraid. Whatever you do, don't tell Despina who her real father is.'

'I know. But maybe I never see her again,' replies Phaedra sadly.

'I hope you will,' I say. 'Call her and say I managed to escape. That I'm fine. I'm not going to press charges. I'll leave the island tonight and never come back. Nobody in the family will ever hear from me again.'

'Thank you,' she says. 'I will try. Now I think you must go. We should not be seen together.'

We say our farewells and drive back to Kevin's house. None of us are in the mood for talking, each of us following our own train of thought. He makes some food, while I rest by the side of the pool. Estelle gets on her phone and starts searching for ferries and flights.

Kevin brings out some homemade bread and salad. 'Here, eat. You need to build your strength up.'

'Mum?' I ask, the word sounding strange and yet completely right.

'Yes, Juno?' She turns to me and smiles.

'Can I borrow your phone, please? I need to call Luke.'

Chapter Forty-Seven: A year later

JUNO

We came home from the hospital yesterday, after a whirlwind stay of just twenty-four hours. The pregnancy was rough – I had terrible morning sickness, pelvic girdle pain and high blood pressure – but in the end the birth went very smoothly. After all the waiting and dreaming, I still can't quite believe that he's here, lying in my arms. My beautiful baby son. I gaze into his eyes – they are dark blue now but I'm certain they'll turn brown.

We've called him Niko, following the Greek tradition of naming the firstborn male after his grandfather. Strictly speaking, it should have been his paternal grandfather, but Luke doesn't mind.

'Hello, Niko,' I whisper, stroking his soft cheek with my forefinger. He stares up at me and blows half a bubble with his rosebud mouth. 'I'm your mummy,' I say. 'Yes. I am. I really am. No doubt about it. And guess what? Your Nana's coming this afternoon. She's flown over from Portugal specially, just to see her little grandson. That's you. Yes, that's right. You.'

'He can't understand a word you're saying,' laughs Luke, bringing me yet another cup of tea. I'm trying to stay hydrated for the breastfeeding.

'If we don't talk to him, he never will,' I point out.

Luke puts my mug on the side table, just beyond my reach. 'It's very hot. Pass him over when you want to drink it.'

We are over-vigilant, I know, but that's a good thing – better than being too laidback. I'm a little nervous about ever letting Estelle look after him by herself. As far as I remember, she wasn't too bothered about health and safety when I was a child. She was too busy being a hippy. Still is – although these days I think it's more of a fashion statement than a lifestyle choice. She's talking about coming back to the UK and wants to look at some flats close to us while she's here. I don't know how I feel about that. In many ways, my relationship with Estelle is as new as it is with baby Niko.

It took a while to recover from the ordeal in the goatherd's hut. Estelle and I went to Paros, checking in to a small hotel in the main town. We stayed there for a few weeks – went for some long walks, had some deep chats, laughed a lot, cried a lot too. We're still getting to know each other, but I understand her a lot better now. I'm glad she's back in my life.

While I was in Paros, I met up with Millie. She confirmed that she'd had nothing to do with stealing the letters. I felt bad for suspecting her, even for one minute, but after learning what I'd been through, she understood. Millie contacted Lana and told her that we'd found out she'd been paid off to stay silent. We didn't blame her, all we wanted to hear was that she was still alive. I'm happy to say she replied. She's back on the scene now, campaigning to stop the use of ancient forests for fast furniture in Romania.

Millie and I are still friends. We don't see each other much, but we're in touch on social media. She's working in Spain this summer, but she wants to come and meet little Niko as soon as she can.

When I arrived in Inios last summer, I was in a very different place to where I am now. I thought my marriage might be over. It made me so sad, but back then, I couldn't think of a way to repair it. I wanted to run away and hide, start a whole new life. But there's nothing like thinking you're going to die to make you see things differently; to realise what you really value, who you really love.

I look down at my son. His eyes are closed, and his face is at rest. Do babies dream, I wonder, and if so, what do they dream about? My love for him is overwhelming, stronger than anything I could imagine. Right now, it's impossible to contemplate sending him away to live with his grandparents at the tender age of eleven, as Estelle did to me. For years I felt rejected by her, but if the experience of Inios has taught me only one thing, it's that my mother loves me.

'I'd like to drink my tea now,' I say. Luke puts one hand under Niko's head and the other beneath his body, then we slide him into his arms.

He sits back down in the armchair and plays with Niko's teeny-tiny fingers. I still can't quite believe we managed to make him. After all those years of trying and failing, it finally happened.

As soon as I got back to the UK, I went to see Luke and delivered the speech that I'd composed during those long hours imprisoned in the darkness. It more or less came out as I wanted it to. He did a great job of listening. And it turned out that he'd been thinking along the same lines – that it was *me* he wanted, not some fantasy of an idyllic family life. With a curry takeaway and a couple of bottles of wine, we stayed up talking until the early hours, and for the first time in years, we forgot all about making babies and simply made love. I'm not certain that it happened that night, but that's how I imagine it.

A couple of weeks later, I started having this metallic taste in my mouth and I went off coffee. My breasts felt tender. I realised my period was late, I took a test and bang. There they were – those two pink lines we'd been dreaming about. Or that previously I'd been dreading without admitting it, even to myself. Luke was over the moon, but I was still apprehensive. I was still coming to terms with everything that had happened – reassessing my ideas about parenthood and family, my obsession with knowing where I came from, where I really belonged. But when I saw the baby on the scan at the hospital at twelve weeks, his profile already looking like Luke, and his little heart beating, I fell in love, and knew that I wanted him more than anything else in the world.

I never thought I'd be able to forgive Estelle for the past, but I'm getting there. At least now I understand why she lied to me about my father's identity. I never want to lie to Niko. If – or when – he asks about his namesake I want to be able to tell him the truth, although in a way, it's not my truth to tell . . .

'Don't worry about that now,' said Luke when I tried to talk it over with him.

355

I persisted. 'What will we tell him about his grandfather?'

'We'll work it out when the time comes. You've only just learned how to change his nappy. One step at a time, eh?'

Luke is right, of course.

Estelle ... Mum ... Nana ... (I still haven't settled on what to call her) has stayed in touch with Kevin, but only by letter – never phone or email. Letters are safer – they can be destroyed. He keeps us updated with the police investigation. As expected, Despina's DNA results were not a match with the skeleton. Volunteers were asked to come forward to be tested, but according to Phaedra, nobody from the Zimiris family responded. However, it soon became clear from the DNA profile that the victim was a local man. No proper identification has been made and the investigation seems to have ground to a halt. Kevin believes that Andreas has tried to use his influence to shut it down. We're not sure why. Maybe it's because he suspects it's Niko and doesn't want the scandal. Or maybe it's just bad optics for the new resort. Either way, Phaedra seems safe.

As for my half-sister who's not my half-sister . . . nobody knows where she is. Despina doesn't answer her mother's calls or messages and hasn't contacted her uncle or cousins once. Presumably, she believes I'm dead. She remains a loose end, which I still pick at from time to time, in those dark hours when I remember the trauma of being in that hut, convinced I was going to die. If she ever discovers I'm still alive, I worry that she might track me down. I don't just have myself to protect now: I have my son. I can't let her find me.

People are complicated creatures. Families are a bloody

nightmare. Not mine though. In this moment my new little family of three is perfect.

'Pass him back to me,' I say, swallowing the last of my tea and putting down the mug. Luke reluctantly hands him over. I kiss the tip of his nose and he starts in his sleep.

'Welcome, Niko,' I whisper. 'Welcome to this strange, troubled, beautiful world.'

Acknowledgements

I first went to Greece with a friend when I was twenty. We arrived in Lindos, Rhodes, with nowhere booked to stay, but were lucky enough to be taken in by an elderly Greek couple, who gave us bed and breakfast for the equivalent of £1 a night. It was a wonderful introduction to the country which I will never forget. Since then, I have been to Greece many times and have always felt extremely welcome. Everyone is so lovely, it almost felt wrong to set a thriller there!

I had just started working on the story for *The Island Escape* when I got chatting with my cousin Paul at a family party. As a young man, he lived and worked on one of the islands in the Cyclades, and still returns every year to meet up with mates from the past. He was about to visit the island and offered to show me around and introduce me to the many locals and expats he knows. My husband and I grabbed the opportunity to join him, and we spent a fantastic few days researching. Enormous thanks are therefore due to Paul Page – without his generosity and kindness the book would be a shadow of itself. The very least I could do was name one of my characters after him!

I would also like to thank Lambi and Robbie for sharing their memories of island life in the seventies and eighties. I heard some extraordinary stories – humorous, touching and even horrifying – which inspired me to come up with my own. There is no such island as Inios, but any readers familiar with the Cyclades will probably work out which island it's based on. I have tampered with the geography to suit the story and have invented the main settings and characters. This novel is a work of fiction, but it's fair to say that it could not have been written had I not made that trip.

I would also like to thank Brenda Page for her help with more general research, and for reading various drafts. Huge thanks must also go to my editors – Emily Griffin, who commissioned the story, and particularly Claire Simmonds, who picked up the baton and helped bring the book to life. Further thanks are due to my copyeditor, Alice Brett, and everyone else on the team at Penguin Random House.

As always, I want to make special mention of my literary agent, Rowan Lawton at the Soho Agency who looks after my interests so well. Also, my film/TV agent, Christine Glover at Casarotto Ramsay & Associates. They are two very special women, whom I love working with.

Thanks and much love to my husband and 'partner in crime', David.

And finally, thanks to all my readers, both new and longstanding. When I write, you are always uppermost in my mind.